BOOKS 1-3

CONDEMNED

GEMMA JAMES

CONDEMNED

Condemned: Books 1-3

Copyright © 2022 Gemma James

Cover design by Gemma James

All rights reserved.

ISBN: 9798410043205

This book is a work of fiction. Names, characters, and incidents are either products of the author's imagination or are used fictitiously. Any resemblance to actual events or persons, living or dead, is entirely coincidental.

Note To Readers

Condemned: Books 1-3 is a dark romance with kidnapping and other disturbing themes. Intended for mature readers. Not for the faint of heart. You've been warned. Book 1 in the Condemned series.

For detailed content warning information, please visit authorgemmajames.com/trigger-warnings

BOOK ONE
TORRENT

DEDICATION

To my husband James, whose support and encouragement means everything to me. Thanks for believing in me, even when I didn't believe in myself. I love you.

PROLOGUE

We'd left the gravesite two hours ago, but Mom's lifeless eyes still accused me. The memory of finding her dead in the bathtub, the water deep and murky with her blood, embedded in my brain like a tattoo I couldn't erase.

I stood in my bedroom, a space inundated with white lacy subterfuge, and sensed the uprising in my soul. Grief turned and boiled with a vengeance. I clenched my hands and crossed them over heaving breasts but couldn't stop the eruption. I'd been simmering too long, unchecked. I hated my perfect room, my perfect family, my perfect life. Appearances were deceitful bitches that lied and covered the ugly truth.

"Open the door, Lex!" Frantic fists pounded, and I covered my ears to block out my step-brother's barrage on the door. The first drop of misery fell from my eyes and despite squeezing them shut, I was incapable of stemming the mental pictures. They flickered in my head like a child's View-Master reel.

I relived Mom's horrified expression the night she heard me cry out, recalled the condemnation in her voice when she yelled at Zach to get out of my room. I still saw her wide eyes—the same green as mine—staring at me blankly a few days later, open and void as the life bled from her wrists.

"Let me in!"

"Go away!" I screamed, repulsed by the mere sound of his voice. A sob caught in my throat, and my body shook with the effort of holding back. I was trapped inside myself, a prisoner of rage and despair. Bursting with the need to tear into something, I dug my nails into my arms.

Her face wouldn't leave my mind. Her beautiful face, twisted with shock and disgust at what she'd walked in on. I'd been too ashamed to explain. Now it was too late. I'd never see her again, never again inhale the sweet scent of jasmine as she embraced me.

Zach's fault. *My* fault.

My nails dragged down pale flesh, almost of their own volition, and left behind ugly red streaks. Letting out a roar, I hefted a chair into the vanity mirror. My reflection shattered with an echo, a grotesque replica of my soul. I was unstoppable, insane with the need to destroy, to create the sound over and over again. Breaths coming in shallow gasps, I swept candles onto the floor, followed by pictures and perfumes. My entire makeup collection crashed onto the white carpet where the colors stained with flawless imperfection, but the pressure in my chest wouldn't subside.

The assault on my door grew in strength, and I thought I picked up another voice blending with Zach's. Had to be my imagination. Dad had barricaded himself in his bedroom, just like me, though he had a sedative and a bottle of Jack to keep him company.

Afternoon sunshine streamed through the lace curtains, an assault of warmth on my face, and I scowled. The skies should have opened, should have drenched the earth until it drowned. On that day, the day I'd watched my mother go into the ground, the whole fucking world should've cried until their eyes bled.

I grasped the lamp on my nightstand and hurtled it through the window, eliciting that glorious sound of splintering glass again, and I screamed until my voice went raw like the rest of me. The door broke under Zach's struggle to get inside, and I fell backward, landing hard on the bed with both hands raised.

"Leave me alone," I said with a pleading sob. He'd never gone so far as to break down my door. My room had been my only sanctuary, other than those few horrible occasions when I found him lying in wait in the darkness; those times when I wasn't quick enough to escape within my four walls and turn the lock. "Don't touch me!"

Strong hands encircled my wrists and pulled them to

the sides, but it was Rafe's beautiful green eyes staring back and not my brother's. Tension seeped from my bones, left me weightless, and I exhaled in relief when he knelt in front of me, elbows resting on my thighs. A significant moment passed, locking the two of us in that short span of time when the world magically receded.

"I've got you. Everything's gonna be okay." His arms wound around my trembling body, and I went limp in the cocoon of his embrace.

Zach stood off to the side, arms crossed and gaze shooting daggers in our direction. I stiffened under the threat of his jealousy, and not even Rafe's warmth could combat the chill that seized me. I wanted to believe him so badly, but nothing would ever be okay again.

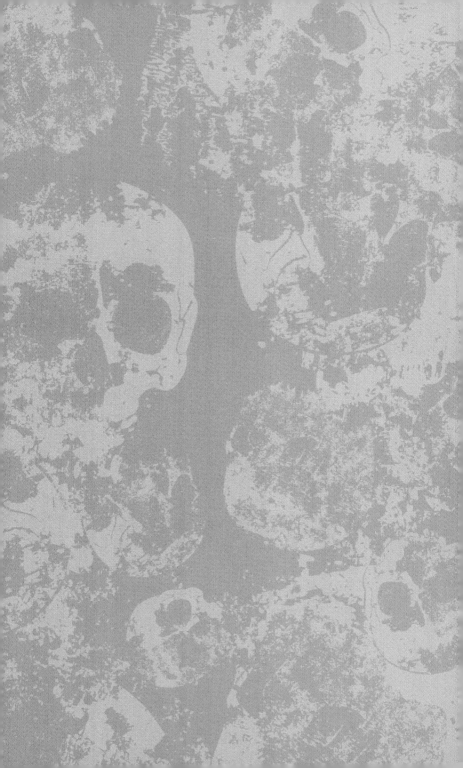

ONE

ALEX

Eight years later

When it came to karma, I wished for skepticism. Thing was, I fully believed in karma. Something had to balance the scales, otherwise the world would tip off its axis and crash into total chaos. Thanks to my belief in supernatural balance, I had no doubt I was screwed. That was never more true than when I gripped the single piece of paper on which four words were written.

I'm coming for you.

I'd found the note tacked to my door. I didn't question who left it, as only one person had reason to leave such a warning, and considering he'd been released from the state penitentiary three weeks ago, I couldn't deny the evidence. I'd been agonizing over the moment when he would confront me.

When, not if.

My knees gave out, and I sank to the bed. Rain beat against the roof in a sudden onslaught, and the panes of my favorite window seat rattled. I hadn't been home for more than a few minutes, but apparently I'd escaped inside at the most opportune time. I took the torrential tap-tap-tap and rush of wind as a sign, an omen perhaps.

He was coming for me, and I deserved it.

Someone pounded on the door, and I jumped like a frightened kitten. I stashed the note in the drawer of my nightstand and returned to the foyer, pulled the door open, and almost expected to find Rafe on the other side.

It was Zach, not Rafe, who shoved past the threshold. Immediately, the strong odor of whiskey hit my nose.

"You're not fuckin' marrying him," he said with a slur. I edged away as he stumbled into the accent table in the foyer. "I'm going crazy, Lex. Look what you've done to me." Wiping soggy brown hair from his eyes, he lurched forward and clung to my shoulder to keep from falling.

"Did you drive here?"

"Of course I didn't drive! I'm not an idiot."

"I know you're not an—"

He grabbed my chin, silencing me instantly. "You're gonna call this engagement off, do you hear me?"

The ever-present weight of dread held me in its clutches. "Dad pushed for it." I paused, one, two, three thuds of my heart pounding in my ears. "Just like he pushed for me to date Lucas. I think he knows."

"Knows what?" His fingers fell from my chin, and I stared at my feet, enclosed in trendy black heels that matched the black cocktail dress I'd worn to dinner, where Lucas Perrone had proposed.

"About us."

He faltered, mouth gaping, and it was the most unusual sight. Zach didn't normally struggle for words, threats, insults.

He blinked and the moment was gone. "I don't give a fuck what Dad knows or doesn't know. You're gonna break this engagement, and you're not seeing him again." As if the issue were settled, he staggered into the living room where he sprawled onto the sofa, one leg bent and a foot resting on the floor. I averted my gaze from the bulge behind his zipper.

I needed to get him out of my house pronto. "I'll call you a cab. We'll talk tomorrow about this, I promise."

He let out a bitter laugh. "My cab just left, and we're talkin' now." His brows narrowed over angry hazel eyes. "C'mere," he said, patting his lap.

I backed up, shaking my head.

"No? You want it extra rough? Is that it?"

I didn't want it at all, but I knew better than to voice it. I scratched my arm, digging in a little deeper than usual.

"You think marrying some mid-forties vanilla hack is

gonna 'fix' you? Make you normal? We both know you're nothing but a slut."

I clenched my teeth. His insult maimed more than his hands did, especially since he was the only man I'd ever slept with. He perceived any guy who glanced in my direction as a threat, as if I welcomed the attention, and he'd become downright vicious since Dad set me up with Lucas.

Dad had always made decisions for me, from what school I attended to which program I chose as a major. I'd earned degrees in accounting and business but harbored no desire to use them. He expected me to hop on board the family legacy in a managerial capacity, but unlike him and Zach, I had no interest in mixed martial arts or running an enterprise of venues and training centers.

I chalked it up to the fact that we didn't share DNA. Mom married Abbott De Luca when I was six, but he *was* like a dad to me, especially since he'd legally adopted me, and as such, I'd never thought of Zach as a step-brother. Not where it counted. The step part got lost in the sea of right and wrong and perversely unacceptable.

I folded my arms and put another foot of distance between us, backing toward the foyer. No one made me more uncomfortable in my own house, in my own skin, than my own brother.

He seemed pissed that I wasn't rising to his bait by responding. "You're my slut, aren't you, Lex?" He pushed off the couch, as if he only now realized I was retreating, and gripped my arms. "My little whore who loves to be fucked."

"You're hurting me," I said, barely above a whisper, but his fingers pressed harder when I tried to pull away.

"Not as much as you're hurting me!" He drove forward and slammed me into the wall, trapping both wrists on either side of my face. "You know we belong together. You'll never keep me away. *Never*."

"Let me go."

He brought his face close, lip slightly curled, and his hazel eyes stalled on the ring adorning my left hand. I unfurled my fist until the large diamond scraped the wall, hidden from his line of view. "I won't stand by and watch you marry that bastard. I'll kill myself, just like your mom."

I gasped as the familiar, crushing reminder of Mom ate away at what was left of me. I had no words for him, no protests or pleas. He tossed out the threat to hurt me, like he always did. I wondered if he'd go through with it this time. I tried to imagine him gone, but instead of despair, I found the remnants of sorrow and the promise of relief. Shame accompanied both, as I shouldn't feel sorrow after the things he'd done, and I shouldn't feel relief because he was still my brother.

"Say something!" He cried, shaking me, his face a contortion of bewilderment. "Didn't you hear me? I'm not kidding! I'll do it."

"You don't know what you're saying. You've been drinking—"

"I know exactly what I'm saying. I don't wanna live if I can't have you. Say you won't marry him."

"I won't marry him." I swallowed hard and counted the seconds. Five in, hold, five out. Repeat. All the while, I prayed he'd let the issue drop, let me go and walk out the door.

He had other things in mind. His mouth smashed against mine, tongue forcing my lips apart and plundering. I didn't fight him. I'd learned long ago it didn't do any good. He'd only get rougher, meaner, and in turn, my fucked up body would only get off easier.

I kept my eyes shut and wished to be somewhere else. Anywhere else. The distinctive slide of his zipper rang loudly in my ears, and his hands blazed where he cupped my ass and lifted.

"That's my girl," he breathed as I automatically wound my legs around him, dress bunching at my waist. He pulled my panties to the side and pushed in with a grunt. His fingers banded around my wrists, pinned them to the wall above my head, and he pounded into me, shoving me higher with each forceful thrust. I held back the vomit burning in my throat.

One more thrust, another grunt. "No more Lucas," he said.

"No more Lucas." My face tightened as his tempo increased.

"No more avoiding me."

I agreed to that too. I agreed to anything he wanted

when he fucked me. The alternative always left me battered, bruised, and torn to pieces emotionally because the more I fought him, the more he set out to hurt me beyond what I could handle, and that usually meant he brought up Rafe and what he could do to him if I didn't comply.

That threat carried more weight than ever.

Zach didn't last long, probably because it'd been a couple of weeks since he'd last cornered me alone. Lucas' presence had gone a long way in offering some form of protection, but I wasn't so naive as to think he could act as a barrier forever. Even marrying him wouldn't do that.

Zach finally loosened his grasp and allowed my feet to touch the floor. I rubbed my arms where the red impressions from his fingers marred my skin, making the faint, white scars from my nails more noticeable. He took my face in his hands, fingers gouging my jaw, and his gaze bored into me, through me.

"You didn't get off."

"I did," I said quickly, because not reaching orgasm always angered him. "I swear I—"

"You *didn't* get off. Don't try to fake it. I'll always know." Stepping back, he gestured toward my dress. "Take it off."

"C'mon, Zach, you don't have—"

"*Take* it off."

I unzipped the dress and let it fall to my feet, and my breasts jiggled in their braless state. He shoved me across the room, down to the couch, and forced my thighs open.

Sinking to his knees, he yanked me toward his mouth until my ass was half off the couch, my legs dangling on either side of his shoulders.

The instant he tore my panties from my body, my mind went blank, as the sounds of my cries were too degrading to acknowledge. I vaguely recalled him twisting my nipples in unforgiving pinches, then slapping my breasts hard. He jammed his fingers into my pussy mercilessly, and after he'd compelled an orgasm from me, he made me suck my own cum off, shoving his fingers deep into my mouth as he emphasized how *he* was the one who had made me come.

Only me, Lex. No one else.

Then he was gone, and I was in the scalding shower, eyes squeezed shut, fists crossed over tender breasts to keep from bloodying my knuckles on the tile. The only drops of water on my cheeks came from the shower head. I never cried. I didn't allow myself the luxury. My breaths came out in soft shudders, and I tried to keep myself in one piece as I recalled what he'd asked before he left.

Do you still love him?

My denial hadn't placated him, and his parting words blared through my head, more forceful than my shame. *If you go anywhere near him, I'll fuck him up for life. He's a lot easier to get to now, isn't he?*

The thought of my brother hurting Rafe terrified me, so I'd told Zach I hadn't heard from him. A lie, because I was pretty sure the note came from Rafe.

Was this always going to be my life? Lies upon lies, sprinkled with the occasional half-truth?

I could leave. I'd considered it before, had even tried once, though I only made it halfway to the California border before chickening out. Too many people close to me had suffered, like the guy I'd teamed up with my Junior year for a science project. He made the mistake of hitting on me, and Zach had given him the nastiest beat down of his life, leaving broken bones and bloody flesh in his wake. Dad's money swept that one under the rug.

There had been others, some no one knew about because Zach was intimidating enough without his reputation as a fighter to keep most quiet. They suffered his rage in silence. Fear of retaliation wasn't the only thing keeping me from fleeing though. I'd hung on to the stupid, absurd, *fanciful* hope that Rafe would someday forgive me.

Impossible. What I'd done was unforgivable.

Standing at a crossroads of sorts, I needed to find the strength to move on with my life. I glanced at the enormous engagement ring Lucas had pushed onto my finger earlier that night. No matter what Dad believed, tying myself to a man I didn't love wouldn't fix anything. Neither would continuing to allow Zach free rein of my puppet strings.

For the first time in your life, Alexandra, do the right thing.

The voice sounded like my father's. Certainly, the words were something he'd say, something he'd said again and again every time I fucked up. And I fucked up a lot. My whole life was one big fuck up.

I shut off the water, wrapped a towel around my body, and entered the bedroom, then changed into jeans and a sweatshirt before pulling a duffle from the closet. I blindly flung clothes onto the bed and stuffed some into the bag. The stash of cash I'd saved, tucked underneath the mattress, also went inside. Lastly, I tossed in my wallet. I didn't need anything else. Just myself and the courage to leave.

That was the hard part.

I took off the ring and let it drop onto the nightstand, then I closed my eyes and envisioned my escape. I'd walk down the hall, feet sinking into the plush runner one last time. I saw myself crack the door open and peek outside, saw myself hop down the stairs of the porch, my paranoid gaze buzzing around as I approached the Volvo Dad had given me for graduation.

The alluring taste of freedom, only a few feet away, tempted with promise. I just had to close the distance and take the first step. I left the bedroom and moved toward the foyer, like a teenager sneaking out past curfew. I felt like a child, excitement fluttering in my belly as my hand neared the doorknob.

Trepidation also stirred in my gut. If I disappeared, would Zach really hurt Rafe, a man he'd once called his best friend?

A knock sounded, and I jerked my fingers back. A few

tense seconds passed before the knock repeated. For someone terrified of escaping the shackles of a life unwanted, I should have given more thought to the possibilities on the other side of that door. Swinging the duffle to my back, I pulled it open, and my breath whooshed from me as I uttered his name.

"Rafe."

He was here, standing in front of me, and my knees almost buckled, weaker now than when I'd first spied his note upon returning home. A violent blast of air and rain blew in with his presence, carrying a hint of roses from the bushes off the porch. The aroma infused me with a sense of serenity despite the darkness shadowing my street.

I was the perfect prey in that moment, too stunned to keep my head. I stumbled back, a mistake on my part because he was the second man that night to shove his way into my house.

TWO

RAFE

I'd always fantasized about taking a woman, *really* taking a woman, and until Alex had destroyed me with a single lie, the fantasy had only been the depraved thoughts of a man who still had his moral compass intact. A lot could change in eight years. Fuck, I remembered her as the 15-year-old girl she'd been, so I had trouble thinking of Alex as a woman. My dick didn't have the same problem; it couldn't wait to get her alone on Mason Island.

Engaging the deadbolt, I leaned against the door and stared at her with a nonchalance I didn't feel. God help me, but I couldn't take my eyes off all those dark curls cascading over her tiny shoulders. The slender slope of her neck drew my attention, and I imagined closing my hands around her throat and squeezing the essence from her, imagined the panic in her eyes as she neared loss of consciousness.

"Miss me?" I asked.

Her eyes, already wide at the sight of me, grew even rounder. "What?"

I crossed my arms, aware of how my biceps bulged. "I didn't stutter, sweetheart. It's been a long time. Did you miss me?"

"Did I...?" She shook her head, as if I'd uttered the most ridiculous question she'd ever heard. "What do you want, Rafe?" Her words fell from her lips in a nervous whisper.

"I think you already know." You couldn't send an innocent man to prison without expecting some sort of consequences. Except Alex didn't know two fucks about me. The real Rafe Mason was about to do reprehensible things to her, like toss her deceitful naked ass into a cage.

Her gaze veered to the floor, and I barked at her to look at me.

"If I could change things, I would," she said, inching back, a fist rising to her mouth to hide her trembling lips.

"Would you now?" I tilted my head. "What would you do differently? Would you take it back, what, a week later? A month? Maybe after I'd been in there a couple of years? *Eight fucking years*, Alex. That's what you took from me."

"I don't know what you want from me." Two more steps back.

I pushed away from the door and followed, hand sliding into my coat pocket to finger the syringe. "I want to know why you lied." I'd waited so long to ask that question, and the set of her jaw told me she wasn't going to answer. "You didn't even have the guts to face me at the trial." She'd refused to make eye contact, even once. That hadn't surprised me nearly as much as Zach's cold shoulder treatment. How he believed I'd do something so vile, to Alex of all people, was beyond comprehension. She must have put on quite the performance for her family, because her testimony in court had been mechanical, as if she'd read from a script.

She'd stripped everything from me in that courtroom. My career, friends, freedom, and she'd displayed no emotion while doing it.

"I-I can't do this now," she said, a tremor stringing her words together. "I have to go." Darting past me, she made a run for the door and managed to fling it open by the time I whirled around. That's when the duffle swinging on her shoulder caught my attention, and it dawned on me she was running.

Because of the note I'd left on her door? Guess my mind-fuckery had done the trick, only I never expected her to take off. There was no way she could know what I had planned for her. Before she escaped the house, I shot an arm out and slammed the door shut, then pressed into her soft curves that fit perfectly against me.

"You're not going anywhere." Even in that heady moment, as adrenaline pumped through my veins, I hesitated. What I was about to do changed everything. I was about to become the criminal they'd accused me of being.

But no one deserved comeuppance more than Alex.

The duffle slid from her shoulder, landing with a thump on the mud mat. She flattened both palms against the door, and I covered her hands with mine, sliding cool leather over warm skin. I wondered if the gloves worried her, if she sensed the danger I posed. I wedged a leg between hers, thigh nudging her ass, and electricity spiked, a current so hot my whole body sizzled. Was she aware of it too? Did she feel my cock prodding her backside?

"You need to leave," she ground out, but even as the words left her mouth, she relaxed in submission. She turned her head and peered at me through lashes slightly lowered, disguising what I might find in her jade depths. "Please, you've gotta go."

I wanted to take her then, fuck her right against the door. "Not a chance. I've waited too long for this." I latched the deadbolt again, satisfied with the decisive click that echoed off the walls, and pulled her further into the house.

"What are you doing?" she cried, tugging against the fingers I'd clamped around her arm.

I stopped once we reached the hall. "Where's the note I left?" I couldn't leave behind any evidence. "Did you show it to Zach?"

She yanked her arm from my grasp. "No, why?"

"Doesn't matter. I want it back."

"It's in my bedroom." She opened the first door on the right. Going by the clothing piled in haphazard fashion on the bed and the floor, she'd packed in a hurry. She crossed to her nightstand and withdrew the note from the drawer.

I snatched it from her fingers, making her flinch, and pocketed the last piece of evidence. "C'mon." I dragged her into the kitchen, my pulse rocketing, and my jeans grew uncomfortably tight as I shoved her into a chair. She gazed up at me, mouth open, messy curls partially obscuring her eyes, and I was so close to bending her over the table.

Patience.

I couldn't rush this, no matter how much I wanted to. "Don't move," I warned, pressing on her shoulders to make my point. I rummaged through the room, found a pen and paper, and slammed them on the table in front of her. "Write down what I say, word for word."

"Why?"

"Quit asking so many fucking questions." I forced the pen into her fingers, and she clutched it tight, hand hovering above the paper. The fury in her eyes wavered, replaced by confusion. She wasn't scared of me yet, and I wasn't sure if that was good or bad.

"Rafe, what are you do—"

"Write 'I need some time. Don't worry or try to find me.'"

Short and to the point. The less written, the less the authorities could dissect. I expected them to look at me as a person of interest in her disappearance, but I was prepared for that inevitability. Besides, they'd need prob-able cause and a warrant to search the island, and they wouldn't have either.

Lower lip tucked between her teeth, she wrote out the words and paid careful attention to each letter, her hand trembling every so often. Once finished, she set the pen down, angled her head, and met my eyes. She didn't have to voice her alarm. Her expression was unmasked. Naively, she let me see everything.

"What happened to you?" she whispered.

She must have sensed the darkness in me, but what she failed to understand was how it had always lurked, entrapped by a code I no longer lived by. She'd blown the padlock on that cage when she'd uttered three little words that ruined me.

He raped me.

The accusation rang through my mind, as loud as the clank of the prison cell doors when they slammed shut. I grabbed the syringe from my pocket.

"What are you doing?" she cried, wide eyes locking onto the syringe. She jumped into motion and reached the foyer before I caught up to her. I wound an arm around her shoulders and pinned her against me. She bucked, kicked, and clawed, all the while letting loose a scream that made me so fucking hard I almost lost it. I uncapped the needle with my teeth and stabbed it into the side of her neck. An instant later, she went limp in my arms.

THREE

ALEX

Consciousness washed over me in dream-like phases, the first a stifling darkness that pressed from every direction. I trembled as an inescapable chill crawled over my skin like icy tendrils, licking with relish. Hard, rough concrete chafed my body. My *naked* body. Acid rose in my throat, and I thought I was about to lose my last meal, but the observation only caused more panic to set in. I couldn't recall what I'd eaten.

For a few horror-stricken moments, I couldn't recall anything at all. Then I remembered.

Rafe's face burned in my head, his older, scruffier face. His unforgiving face. The rest of my memories flooded back, and I jerked to total awareness. He'd jabbed a needle into my neck.

Now, I felt it, his presence casting over me like a shadow waiting to swallow me whole. I tried to throw my hands up, my first instinct one of protection, but something heavy and cold and menacing kept my wrists locked together, stretched behind my head and chained to...something. I whimpered as my brain tried to pound out through my eyeballs.

"Good, you're awake."

His voice shouldn't sound so sexy under the circumstances, but that gravelly timbre, barely above a whisper, registered low in my belly.

"Rafe?" I had to be hallucinating or dead. This couldn't be real.

I sensed movement, a drift of air and swoosh of clothing, and a dim light switched on. Several seconds passed as I blinked my surroundings into focus. I was sprawled on the ground of some sort of cage, my hands secured to the bars. I yanked on my bindings, and the bite of chains to metal made me shudder. My gaze shifted, taking in the space beyond my prison, which was cloaked in shadow, and I thought I spied rows of wine bottles. I returned my attention to him, mouth hanging open as I tried to comprehend that he had me bound and naked.

Rafe stood on the other side and circled the bars with white-knuckled fingers as he glared down at me. "You can try to escape if you want, but I think you're smart enough to know when you're fucked."

On some level, I'd known this day would come. The day I'd have to face him. The day he'd demand an explanation for what I'd done. I'd imagined screaming and yelling

on his part. Furious righteousness. Never this. As he withdrew a set of keys and moved to the door of the cage, any
hope of forgiveness I'd clung to vanished. I couldn't stop
shaking as he stormed inside.

"What do you want from me?" I asked, nervous about
the answer, especially when I thought of how my nudity
was on display.

"Do you really want to know what I want?" The corner
of his mouth turned up in the legendary Rafe Mason
smirk I remembered.

"Yes."

He bent and crawled over me, his knees settling at the
apex of my thighs, and palmed the concrete on either side
of my head. I licked my dry lips, acutely aware of how his
clothing tickled my skin. That mere contact, the brush of
denim on inner thigh, chased some of the chill away.

"I want to fuck you," he said, and the way those words
played off his tongue, with a riff of sinister intent, made my
heart jackhammer. His biceps flexed under the strain of
supporting his weight, and my attention closed in on the
tribal lines streaking out from underneath his sleeves.
Breathtaking ink on hard man, winding down strong forearms to the back of his hands. He lowered his face, a tilt to
his head, and commanded my gaze. "Is that what you
wanted to hear?"

I wasn't sure what I expected him to say or do, and I
couldn't begin to measure how angry he was. "I don't know
what to say, Rafe."

"You don't have to say anything. I want what's mine, what I served time for."

I gulped. "You didn't have to kidnap me."

"You're right," he said, his lips hovering, almost touching mine. "I didn't have to kidnap you, but I wanted to, and I always get what I want. The last eight fucking years notwithstanding, of course. You made sure of that."

He shifted his weight to the side and brought a key to my wrists. The lock released, and I pulled free of the bars.

"Get up," he said, rising to his feet.

The floor tilted in a dizzying whirl, but once I regained my bearings, I stood before him, face-to-face with the man I'd wronged. He was just as gorgeous as ever, though his green eyes told me things he didn't voice. They hinted at how my actions had ruined a good person, because the one before me was anything but.

My heart ached for the guy I remembered, with his deep laugh and teasing grin. The same mouth that sneered at me now used to curve into the sexiest smile when he caught me staring. I'd fallen hard, enticed by the irresistible contradiction that was Rafe Mason, a guy who displayed a quiet, gentle aura, yet used brute force on his opponents inside the cage. His only crime had been catching the eye of damaged goods.

"Why'd you do it, Alex?" He moved, blocking the opening of the prison and hindering any chance I had to escape.

I wrapped my arms around myself, feeling sick as I

recalled the day they arrested him. The media had splashed footage all over the news, and I'd never forget the way his head hung in shame as they hauled him outside my father's gym where he trained, hands cuffed at his back as if he were really guilty. Sometimes, merely being accused of something, even when innocent, could psyche a person into experiencing false guilt. Zach was an expert at that particular mental warfare.

"I asked you a question," he snapped.

The moment had arrived, the one I'd dreaded for years, but my mind drew a blank. What could I tell him? There was no excuse or explanation that would make this right. Even the truth didn't excuse sending an innocent man to prison. "I'm sorry," I said, fighting tears. "You have every right to be angry."

"Are you refusing to give me an explanation? Don't you think I deserve that much?"

I dipped my head, thick hair falling forward and shadowing the shame warming my cheeks. What he deserved was nothing less than the truth, but it caught in my throat, perpetually trapped by my need for him to never find out about Zach and me. "I can't give you one. It won't change anything."

"I see." He came closer, hands bunching at his sides, and ordered me to lower my arms.

I backed up, hating how my body throbbed with indecent anticipation. My eyes burned, but I hadn't cried in a long time, not since my mother died and Rafe had embraced me while I lost it. That seemed like a lifetime ago. I blinked several times, willing the tears to dry up, but the sight of him lowered the gates. Something fundamental in him had changed.

My fault.

My doing.

A tear slipped free. With casual ease, he scooped it up and sucked the moisture off his finger. "Hands at your sides, *now*."

I shook my head, and the gesture probably came off as defiant, but really, I just wanted to crawl into myself and die. The thought of putting my body on display for him sent me into a panic. This body betrayed me, it attracted the wrong attention and glorified in it. All it would take was one touch of his hand for him to realize how I wanted him.

"I-I don't understand."

"What do you not understand, Alex? Sounds pretty clear to me."

"Don't do this," I pleaded, retreating until I bumped into the bars with nowhere to go. I hid myself as much as possible, thighs pressed together and palms covering my breasts.

He unbuckled his belt and pulled it from his jeans.

"Please—" I couldn't breathe, couldn't budge even as adrenaline coursed through me.

"Do as you're told, or I'll make you wish you'd listened the first time."

My arms weren't part of me. Somehow, all on their own, they dropped to my sides like two sticks of dead-weight. His eyes traveled over me, starting at my feet and slowly lifting to my belly before roaming higher.

"Look at the set of tits on you."

I stood on a precipice of indecision, and taking the plunge could bring about two different outcomes. Fear, the kind that made your heart beat so fast, your mind tricked you into believing you were seconds from death. Or, I could take a free-fall into insanity. Rafe Mason was, essentially, the love of my life. I could lie to everyone else, but not to myself. Nothing he did would change that.

Even now, as his hand formed an angry fist around that belt, I came alive. Or maybe it was *because* he posed such a threat. God, I was fucked up. I knew what he was capable of. A memory of swollen and bloody flesh sprang to mind, so vividly I could describe it in Technicolor. That last cage fight before they'd arrested him, the one to trump all others, burned in my memory.

His attention lingered on my breasts, and the mere heat of his stare branded me. Here was a man furious, a man few would blame for wanting to do horrible things to the person who'd wrecked his life.

That person was me, and despite the threat in his expression, something about the way he caressed my body with a single glance reduced me to a puddle of need. It pooled between my legs until everything was tight and wet and hot.

With careful patience, he feathered the back of his hand across my nipple, and I felt his touch everywhere, especially between my legs where I ached and burned from the inside out. Until now, I'd never known what it was like to be on the receiving end of Rafe's attention. He was the only guy capable of making me feel this way.

Hot.

Alive.

Needy.

Our gazes entwined, and the feelings spearing through me were too intense to ignore. I'd lost count of the number of fantasies I'd had of this moment when he would touch me. Really touch me. Not as the kid he treated like a sister, not as the bothersome girl who mercilessly drove him to madness, but as a woman.

A woman he wanted.

His hand drifted lower, fingers skimming over quivering stomach muscles. Breath eluded me. The circumstances mattered no more. Fear evaporated into particles of mist that lingered but weren't powerful enough to douse the feelings I thought I'd buried years ago. All that mattered was his hand, lowering...lowering still. I clenched my thighs to keep from spreading them and braced my back against the bars, hands balled at my sides.

His body pressed into mine, and I closed my eyes, cataloging each sensation from the way his chest flattened my breasts to the heat of his thighs. He lifted my arms above my head and curled my fingers around the bars.

"Don't move," he growled, hands squeezing one last time before falling away. "You are such a fucking tease." His words drifted across my cheek. "I never touched you. No matter how much—" Abruptly, he sprang away as if I'd burned him. "I *never* touched you." He reached for the belt that must have fallen to the concrete. "You destroyed my life," he said, fingers playing with the buckle. "I was *this* close to making it to the UFC, and you snatched it from me." He snapped his fingers. "Just like that, you took my freedom, my reputation. You fucking took everything, Alex. I have to register as a sex offender now? Did you know that?"

"I'm sorr—"

The belt landed across my breasts hard, and I cried out as the breath stole from my lungs. My arms dropped, automatically moving to protect, but he struck again with a powerful crack. I gasped and clung to the bars as my nipples burned.

"Don't you dare tell me you're sorry! You've had eight fucking years to be sorry, but you left me there to rot." The belt slid to his feet, and he kicked my legs apart before shoving a finger inside me.

My eyes grew wide as he probed me, though his jerky thrusts were far from gentle.

"I rotted while you dated that jerk who probably doesn't know the first thing about setting you off." He added three more fingers, wrecking my concentration, his touch stretching and reaching higher. "Did he make you feel this good?"

I squeezed my eyes shut and began counting. Five in, hold, five out. Repeat.

"Answer me!"

"He didn't." Lucas' kisses and wandering hands had made me feel nothing, but Rafe...he made me feel everything. I swallowed past the self-loathing constricting my throat, tried to ignore the slippery plunder of his fingers, but a strangled moan escaped anyway.

"Do you want me to stop?"

Yes.

"No." I extended to my toes, fingers gripping the bars for support, and barely breathed as his thumb rubbed circles on my clit. "Rafe!" I pushed my pelvis against his hand even as tears leaked down my face. His mouth opened over my throat, and I inhaled sharply, my pulse throbbing an erratic beat underneath his tongue.

This wasn't happening. My body wasn't betraying me again. No, no, no, no...

"I still remember how to touch a woman," he said. "I bet my fingers are the best fuck you've had. Can you imagine my tongue on your pussy?" He licked up my throat, and I whimpered, imagining it all too well. I saw myself on my back, legs spread wide and his dark head disappearing between quaking thighs. The visual was too much, and I hurtled into deep space. I saw the celestial heavens.

"I'm coming," I sobbed.

"Yes, you are, sweetheart. Enjoy it because it won't happen again."

I clawed at his dark T-shirt, my spine bowing and knees threatening to give. The orgasm came in waves around his fingers, each one more intense than the last, and each one filled my heart with so much shame my chest was heavy with it. Riding the waves, I howled his name, my cries resembling a cat in the throes. Afterward, as my heartbeat slowed, I collapsed to the floor.

"You're at my mercy," he said, crouching to eye level. "You don't eat unless I allow it, you don't drink. You don't get clothes or a shower or even a bed to sleep in unless I say so. I control every piece of you, including your fucking pussy." I wrenched my head to the side, pained by the hardened features of his beautiful face, but he pressed his fingers into my jaw and forced me to meet his gaze. "You're going to earn every damn privilege known to man. Do you understand me?"

"Yes." The force of his fury penetrated deep, and I would have agreed to anything in that moment.

"You are nothing to me, Alex. You will never be more than a piece of ass." My heart cracked as he let go, forming a jagged chasm I feared would forever remain. I watched him walk away, tears sliding down my cheeks, one after the other in an endless stream of regret. He exited the prison without looking back and the lock clicked into place with an unsettling echo. He bent to retrieve a pile of neatly folded clothing—my clothing, by the looks of it—and then climbed a staircase. An instant later, the light shut off.

Total blackness.

I couldn't stop crying. Not because I was scared. Not because he'd just humiliated me. I muffled heaving sobs into my palms because his utter contempt sliced to my soul. And now I knew.

He was going to break me.

FOUR

RAFE

I'd just lied through my fucking teeth. She did mean something, which was why she was down in that prison. If she meant nothing, I wouldn't have wanted her in the first place. The musky scent of her sex lingered on my skin, and I sucked a finger into my mouth, unable to resist tasting her. I couldn't wait to spread those thighs, thumbs biting into soft skin, and bury my tongue in her heat.

Before she sent me away, I'd done my damnedest to do the honorable thing by keeping my distance, though there'd been times I'd slipped up. Like the time she baited me into a game of pool by implying she was unbeatable. We'd played a fiercely competitive game, all the while bantering about horror movies and alternative rock music. She loved the horror and loathed the rock. Not surprising, since she adored the piano.

I'd smoked her the first game. During the second, she conceded and asked for my help in positioning her for the end shot. That was the first time I acknowledged the familiar tingle rushing through me as I bent over her, my hand sliding along hers and guiding her to set up the shot that would win her the game.

I'd also realized, too late, how she'd used the game as a ploy to get close to me. We'd both jumped a foot apart when Zach's boots thumped down the stairs, and our faces must have given us away because he was furious. The protective thumb he held over her wasn't new. Guys couldn't go near her without him losing it, but he should have known better when it came to me. Beyond helping her with a game of pool, I would have never crossed that line. Twenty-one and fifteen didn't mix.

I didn't touch her again, until the day, a few weeks later, when she had a total meltdown after her mom's funeral. I'd needed her in my arms, needed to absorb some of her pain.

Leaning my head against the cellar door, I let my breath even out as a tremor seized my body, and the memory of our history together vanished. I fought the urge to go back down there and finish what I'd started. My dick throbbed with the need, though I held back. I was still too fucking raw, and I didn't want to make the kind of mistake that proved fatal. With the visual I had going through my mind—hands wrapped around her delicate throat as I emptied eight years of pent-up rage and desire into her—I knew I couldn't rush this. Control was imperative.

But shit, I wanted to fuck her.

I waited, listening for a while, but she didn't make a sound, and I had to give her credit. I'd left her in total darkness, naked, and no doubt, freezing. These next few days were going to be hell compared to her pampered princess life.

I'd scared the utter crap out of her, and some sick part of me rejoiced in reducing her to nothing. She didn't even have a bucket to piss in. Watching her cower had been the biggest rush of my life, and that was saying a lot, considering I used to live for pummeling bodies inside the cage.

Maybe it was because I'd fixated on her in prison. At first, nothing but hatred consumed me, but then as my incarceration started playing with my mind, I'd let my imagination run wild. I'd fucked her every way possible, and in each scenario, she'd sobbed and pleaded for me to stop. I'd envisioned sexually torturing her in ways no sane, normal man should be able put into words.

Those fantasies kept me on the brink of sanity, especially during the endless weeks I'd spent in the hole, bereft of interaction with humans and confined to a dark cell smaller than most bathrooms for twenty-three hours a day.

When I looked in the mirror these days, I didn't recognize the man staring back. The guy who'd wiped the sorrow from her face the day she buried her mother, absorbing liquid grief that dripped from her eyes in torrents of despair, was gone, replaced by a man who thrilled in eliciting her tears. Darkness turned at the core of my being, a turbulent need that had simmered for years.

No one knew of my fucked up nature better than my old cellmate Jax. As I entered the kitchen, her clothes weighing heavily in my hands, he watched me carefully from the kitchen table as I disposed of them.

"Did you fuck her yet?" That was the thing I liked most about him—he didn't beat around the bush. He put everything out there without reservation.

As I prepared dinner, I didn't answer, and he didn't speak at first. His silence wasn't uncomfortable. We'd spent hours upon hours in the same cell with nothing but silence and each other.

We'd forged an alliance after I'd beaten the shit out of his would-be killer in prison. He owed me, or so he insisted, and when they paroled him two years ago, he'd set out to repay the debt by keeping tabs on Alex. He'd also taken care of the island since the deed transferred to my name. In exchange, I gave him a place to live.

After last night, I considered the debt more than paid. He'd helped drag Alex's limp body from her car to mine, then we'd shared a minute of silence as we watched her Volvo sink into the river.

"Well, did ya?" he pressed, breaking into my recollection of how satisfying it'd been to follow through with my plan.

I gave him a single glance, and he laughed.

"Man, you're whipped. I can't believe you didn't fuck her yet."

"I didn't say a word, so how do you know if I fucked her or not?"

"I know you," he said, pushing his dark blond hair back from his forehead. "You go all quiet and shit when you don't wanna talk. Alex De Luca has been our topic of choice for years. What the fuck is the holdup, man?"

"I don't know. I can't go there yet." I dropped my head with a sigh. Going where I wanted to go would probably turn what was left of me to stone.

"'Cause you're not a rapist. I told you so. No way can you do that to her. Not after what you've been through."

"No, believe me—I *want* to go there." I returned my attention to the oven and slid the chicken onto the rack. "She wanted it too much."

"You want her to put up a fight?"

Blood rushed to my cock, confirming his theory. "I'm fucking whacked."

"No, you just want payback. Ain't nothing wrong with that."

Thanks to Alex, I knew firsthand what it was like to be helpless, though I hadn't made a single sound of defeat once in the last eight years. Not when they closed the bars on me for something I didn't do, not when other inmates jumped me, held me down, and took turns ramming into my ass. Not even when my father died and I'd been denied the chance to go to his funeral.

I hated to consider what he'd think of me now, how much shame calling me his son would bring him. I'd taken the island he'd willed to me, the one place I equated with happy summertime memories during my childhood, and had turned it into my own personal Alcatraz.

No amount of guilt or shame would change what I wanted most—to unleash the same torment I'd experienced on my single prisoner. The way she looked at me though, the way she responded, really pissed me off. I wanted a fight. I wanted her fingernails digging into me. I wanted her kicking and screaming and begging for mercy. I wanted her tears *and* her fucking pain. "Payback is one thing, but the things I want to do to her..."

Jax settled his chin in his hand, and a wide grin split his face. "Have you forgotten we used to jack off in the same cell? You also talk in your sleep. I know what you want to do to that girl. I just never thought you'd have the balls to go through with it."

"Trust me, my balls aren't the problem. And she's not a girl anymore."

"All the better. What are you waiting for? Go fuck her rough-like. Find the right buttons and push the fuck outta them. Hell, if you don't want her, I'll take her."

He only said it to goad me, and it worked. "Stay away from her," I said with a growl.

Jax held up his hands. "'Nough said. I'm a firm believer in the code."

"What code?"

"The leave-my-woman-the-fuck-alone code. You want her? She's all yours." He pushed up from the table. "I've gotta be back in town." He paused with a wicked grin. "Got plans tonight."

"Seriously?" I arched a brow, surprised because Jax had issues when it came to women. Being with a woman usually involved physical contact, and he couldn't stand to be touched.

"Plans as in a date?"

"Uh-huh."

"With a woman?"

He leveled me with a stare. "Yes, with a *woman*."

"Hey, I'm just surprised, is all. Whatever gets you out there, man."

"Goes both ways. You need to get down there and fuck her senseless. Eight years is a long time to wait."

Shit. He was good at turning a conversation on its head.

He lifted his jacket off the back of the chair. "Gotta work tomorrow, so I won't be too late."

My brother Adam had given Jax a job when no one else in the area would touch a felon. I also put in hours at Mason Vineyards, but it was mostly to uphold the illusion I was a positive contributing citizen. I didn't need to work, thanks to my inheritance. However, idleness drove me nuts, made me want to rip into something, and Alex had ruined my career as a fighter, so working off steam the way I used to wasn't an option. A punching bag didn't deliver the same gratifying release as pounding flesh. Since I'd taken her though, my presence at the winery was about to become nonexistent, at least for a while.

"Seriously, Rafe. Fuck the shit outta her."

"Is that an order?"

"Damn right. You've earned a piece of that."

I was one sick SOB because I felt he was right.

FIVE

ALEX

The first time I saw Rafe Mason, he was beating the crap out of my brother. Okay, that was an exaggeration, but watching through the inexperienced eyes of a 13-year-old, even I'd realized Zach didn't stand a chance.

Rafe was all rippling muscle, sweat dripping down his biceps as he tightened his choke hold. Let me back up here. They hadn't *really* been fighting. They'd been in the middle of an intense sparring match at one of the gyms our father owned. Fuck if I'd cared though. I couldn't take my eyes off Rafe. His dark and wild hair, plastered to his forehead from sweat, had curled slightly above squinted green eyes. I remembered Mom's stiff posture and the rigid set of her back as we stood watching. Her mouth had fallen open, as if she were *this* close to shouting "let him go!" We'd come in on the tail end of the session, and Mom should have known better. She never could stomach watching Zach get his balls handed to him.

Rafe hadn't just handed them over—he'd shoved them down his throat. That was the day he and Zach became best friends. Predictably so, that was also the day I developed the biggest crush on Rafe.

By the time I entered my freshman year of high school, I became Miss Popularity because of two reasons: one, I was a De Luca—the adopted daughter of Abbott De Luca, famous for his impressive record in the UFC; and two, I was sister to rising star Zachariah De Luca. Having a connection to Rafe Mason, who had surpassed my brother in skill, tenacity, and ruthlessness in the business sealed my fate. I became an "it" girl.

I hated "it" girls, but they didn't seem fazed by my blatant indifference, as not one of them passed up an opportunity to hang out at my house. They were in it for the testosterone, and I didn't really care, so long as they kept their hands off Rafe. He might have been six years my senior, but in my head, he was mine, though someone forgot to tell him.

However, Zach noticed me noticing his best friend, and that's when the jealousy began, the dangerous possessiveness. Their friendship had shifted to more of a competitive nature.

Ever since our parents married, Zach and I had been tight, probably closer than most blood related siblings. We often slept in the same bed, huddled under the covers when Dad's drinking got out of hand, or when my mom had another episodic break that necessitated a trip to the mental ward. Their marriage had crumbled under screams that pierced ears too young to understand the words being launched through the air like weapons of mass destruction.

Having Zach at my side calmed me, but as I grew older, I realized how off our relationship was, especially once Rafe's presence got under Zach's skin, and my brother had morphed into a stranger before my eyes.

The police arrested the wrong guy, and I let them.

In hindsight, I had no one to blame but myself for my current predicament—naked and freezing, ass chafed from the concrete, utterly humiliated. I almost pissed myself every time something scampered in the darkness. How silly to be scared of rodents when a man I once knew so well held me prisoner.

A door opened unexpectedly, and the overhead light came on. I squinted, the dim bulb too bright on eyes accustomed to nothing but suppressing blackness. Rafe stomped down the stairs and halted outside the cage.

I couldn't say how much time had passed since I'd awakened in this hellhole, but if I had to guess by the coarse hair on my legs, the smell of unbathed skin, and the tangled, greasy mess on my head, I'd say about three days. I'd lost count of his visits. The first was the most notable, as he'd tossed a bucket to the ground for me to do my business in, left a tray of food and a bottle of water next to it, and exited without a single response to my pleas. The visits that followed wielded the same results, and I stopped begging, accepting I might be down here for a while.

Crouched in the corner, I draped my arms around shaking legs. "I-I'm cold," I said through chattering teeth. "Can I have a blanket? Please?"

He unlocked the door and sauntered inside. "I spent weeks in the hole, naked just like you. Do you think I got a blanket?" He knelt and lifted my chin. "I usually got a beat down before they threw me in, and some days, they didn't even feed me." His mouth flattened into a grim line. "Lucky for you, I'm not as nasty as the guards who had it out for me."

I stared, overcome by the guilt that chiseled off another piece of my heart. I wished I could comfort him, erase the last eight years. What an impossible idea.

"What do you want with me?" I asked. "Do you want to hurt me? Fuck me?" Whatever he was going to do, I hoped he'd just do it. The waiting made me a nervous wreck.

"You took eight years of my life. I think it's only fair I take eight of yours."

I couldn't believe what I was hearing. His words turned in the pit of my stomach like acid. "You're going to keep me here for eight years?"

He tightened his hold on my chin. "Are you hungry?"

His refusal to answer didn't escape me. Something felt different about this visit. He was deviating from his routine, and I wasn't sure what it meant. The thought of eating made me nauseous, but I wasn't about to argue with him. Maybe he'd finally let me out.

"Yes. I need to use the restroom too." I prayed he wouldn't make me use the disgusting bucket again. Even from the other side of the cell, the stench of port-a-potty contaminated the air.

He stepped back and gestured toward that awful thing. "Better go then."

I climbed to my feet and stretched the deep ache from my body, then I suffered the indignity of squatting over the bucket while he watched, inked arms crossed as a corner of his mouth turned up. Once I'd relieved my bladder, I stood, unsure of where to put my hands. If I folded them over my chest, I might anger him, so I let them dangle at my sides.

"Follow me," he said, "and don't do anything stupid unless you want to end up back down here."

I scurried up the stairs after him, each step landing with uncertainty. We entered a large kitchen where a burst of sunshine streamed through the skylight. Dark clouds roiled, a sign another storm threatened on the horizon and the rays were only a temporary reprieve. I searched the area beyond the windows and found thick and sodden greenery outside. A door off the kitchen drew my attention, and I wondered what my odds were of making it outside before he grabbed me.

I was peeking into the adjacent living room, as the cabin took advantage of an open floor plan, when he said,

"You reek. Shower's that way." He indicated a bathroom straight ahead and to the left of the dining table. "Towel's on the rack. You've got five minutes before I come in after you."

I hurried inside and plopped down on the toilet, shaking too much to do anything else. I lowered my head between my knees and breathed deep. Five in, hold, five out. Repeat. By the time I stood on jittery legs, I'd lost at least two of my five minutes. Another thirty seconds passed as I puzzled over how to escape, but the bathroom was a windowless cubicle with no way out. As I switched on the shower and stepped inside the stall, I wondered where I'd go if I did manage to break free. I'd been an instant away from leaving my house, duffle packed, when he'd shown up. How stupid, considering I hadn't put together even the flimsiest of plans, and if Zach ever tracked me down...I didn't want to think of how he'd punish me for running.

A shiver went through me, and I quickly washed up before drying off with a towel. Despite spending the last few days in the nude, exiting the bathroom sans-clothing felt exceptionally violating. I finger-combed some of the tangles from my dark locks and returned to the dining area.

Rafe had his back to me, bent over with his head in the refrigerator, and I almost ran for it, except fear of what he'd do if I failed paralyzed me. But the real reason I didn't run was harder to stomach. I wasn't ready to leave. Some masochistic shred of my being didn't want to walk away from him yet, even though staying defied logic and common sense.

Reality check, Alex. He's kidnapped you, drugged you, and he's obviously not right in the head. Run for it, stupid!

But running for it meant arriving back at square one. Still, my pride wouldn't let me lay down without a fight. "My father will find me."

He pulled out a carton of orange juice and turned around. "No one's looking for you, so you might as well take a seat and get comfortable."

I folded my arms. "You should know better. You spent enough time with my dad. You know how dogged he can be." Especially when it came to his kids, Zach in particular.

Setting the juice down, he picked up a paper and shoved it across the table. Slowly, and with worsening dread gnawing my gut, I picked it up and read the headline:

Portland woman presumed dead after car is found in the Columbia River

I collapsed into a chair, thoughts buzzing in dizzying speed, and the paper fluttered to the table. Dad and I often navigated a rocky relationship, but even so, the news would devastate him, and Zach would go insane knowing I was gone.

Wait...he thought I was dead.

Seconds slipped by as the ramifications sank in, and I worked it from every angle. If he believed I'd been killed, then he'd have no reason to come after me, and no reason to go after Rafe.

But that still didn't give Rafe the right to keep me here and torture me. "You have to let me go." Surely, he didn't intend to keep me locked in this cabin, or God forbid, the horrible cellar, for eight years.

"You're not going anywhere," he said through clenched teeth, "so get that through your head."

"The guy I remember would never do this."

"The guy you remember is as gone as you are to the world." He yanked me up by my wet hair. "You can either learn that the easy way or the hard way."

"And this is the hard way?" I asked, flinching as his fingers tightened. "Kidnapping me? Stripping me? Locking me up?"

"You sent me to hell, Alex. I'm just returning the favor."

He let go, and I sank into my seat again as his words echoed through my heart. "Will you at least give my clothes back? *Please*," I begged, sliding my hands under my thighs, as the urge to cover myself nearly overpowered me.

His gaze settled on my breasts, and I felt my nipples harden. "I like the view. Eight years is a long time to go without seeing a pair of tits. You'll get clothes when I'm good and ready." He set a plate of food in front of me, and the smell of scrambled eggs, something that had always reminded me of wet dog when I cooked them, turned my stomach.

"I'm not hungry."

He sat across from me, his own plate in front of him. "It's not optional. Eat your damn food."

Rage erupted from me, refusing to be contained, and I had to act, had to do something, if only to alleviate the madness festering inside me. I knocked the plate off the table, and though I was disappointed it failed to shatter, the way the food spattered the floor gave some satisfaction.

He rubbed the stubble that shadowed his jaw, as if contemplating, and rose from his chair. He rounded the table, furious green eyes narrowed, and I grabbed my seat to keep from bolting. Oh God. I'd never been more sorry about losing my temper. He settled next to me, and I couldn't comprehend what happened next. One second I was sitting upright, and the next he'd pulled me over his lap.

His palm came down fast and hard, but I didn't make a sound, didn't even fight him. I was too shocked, too aware of him underneath me as his thighs burned into my abdomen. His hand stalled on my ass, lightly massaging, then he continued spanking me, each smack landing with more intensity than the last. He set me upright again, and only then did I register the deep sting in my bottom. He reclaimed the seat across from me, and I opened my mouth but nothing came out.

All I could do was stare. There were no words, no fits or hysterics, just pure stunned silence on my part.

"If you think a tantrum will get you out of eating, you're sorely mistaken." He pointed at my breakfast on the floor. "Get down there and eat it."

"I'm not a fucking dog."

He jumped from his chair so fast, I didn't have a chance to bolt. His fingers pressed into my jaw. "Last chance before I use *that* on you." He forced my gaze to the thick paddle hanging on the wall by the door. "And trust me, that sucker is unbearable, so unless you want to experience it first-hand, get your ass on the floor and eat your breakfast. I won't tolerate you starving yourself. Not under my roof."

Warmth flooded my face as I slid from the chair to my knees, and as I used my hands to shovel in mouthfuls of eggs, the same old shame surfaced. It was never far, always hidden beneath layers of forged normalcy. "I haven't had a problem with that in six months," I said, despising the weak quality of my voice. The eggs didn't want to go down, and I almost gagged. The potatoes weren't much better.

"Good, and we're going to keep it that way."

"How did you know?" I asked. He'd just been released from prison, so how had he found out about my problem with anorexia?

"I know everything about you."

Our eyes connected and held, and I searched for the

truth, because surely he didn't mean *everything*. Seconds ticked past, each one whittling away my thin grasp on sanity. I held my breath, horrified by the possibility that he *knew*.

He broke our stare, his expression unchanged, and I exhaled in relief. Silence ensued, interrupted by the scrape of his fork against china, but it wasn't the uncomfortable kind of disquiet that made every second feel like an eternity. My mind was numb. I hadn't processed, and I wasn't ready to do so.

"Why did you starve yourself?" he asked, jerking me to awareness.

I had no idea how to explain. I couldn't explain, not without going into things I didn't want to reveal, like how after the first inpatient treatment, I'd relapsed on purpose because being locked inside that facility had been the most peaceful three months I'd experienced in a long time. My treatment had kept Zach away. "I don't know."

"Bullshit."

I scooped up a handful of potatoes. "It started after..." I began, raising my eyes to his, "after you went away."

"Your eating disorder is my fault then?"

"No, that's not what I meant. I was dealing with a lot of stuff and—"

"Save it, Alex. I'm sure you were really struggling in your daddy's mansion, going out on the weekends with boyfriends and friends, loading up your closets with expensive clothes. Spare me the sob story, 'cause I'm not buying."

"Why'd you ask then?" With a tilt of my head, I raised my brows.

"Don't get smart with me. I thought you might actually tell the truth for once in your life." He pushed back from the table. "Clear the table and load the dishwasher." He swept a hand toward the messy floor. "And clean up this mess."

Indignation rose, but I kept my mouth shut. Rising to my feet, I grabbed my plate from the floor and his from the table before making my way to the sink. I took my time scrubbing the few dishes from breakfast, and after I'd loaded them into the dishwasher, I slammed the door, turned around, and found him watching me. He was leaning against the counter, arms crossed and biceps bulging.

"I need a broom."

He fetched one from a closet near the door leading to God knew where. Where the hell had he taken me? I saw nothing but trees, though the distinct hum of a highway gave me hope that help existed beyond all the thick foliage.

He shoved the broom into my hands, and our fingers brushed together—the kind of touch that lingered enough to make me shiver. I swallowed hard and swept up the mess, sensing him behind me the whole time. His warm palms settled on my hips, fingers curling around to my front. I swayed into his body.

"Can...can I ask you something, Rafe?"

"You can ask."

"Have you..." My voice faltered, and I had to swallow hard in order to force the question out. "Have you had sex since getting out?"

He trembled. "No," he groaned as he dipped a finger inside me, and I quaked at the thought that he hadn't been with anyone in such a long time.

"Now it's my turn to ask you something," he said. "Just how badly do you want me to fuck you?"

A whimper escaped. It was no secret my body wanted him, had always wanted him. But me, the woman he'd kidnapped, she *didn't* want him. That's what I told myself, anyway.

"You wanted it back then too." With a growl, he pushed me away. "I don't want you like this."

"What's that supposed to mean?" I turned to face him, the broom handle keeping me upright.

"It means I don't want you willing." He knocked the broom to the floor and gripped my wrists. In the rays of the sun peeking through the skylight, my scars stood out as lines of abstract art on my forearms, sketched in blood by my inability to cope with stress. He pulled out my arms and put the marred skin on display.

"What the hell happened to you?"

"Nothing," I said, trying to pull away, but he wouldn't

let me.

"Who did this?"

"No one."

He jerked me close, and his immovable hands framed my cheeks. "Who. Did. This?"

"I did."

For the first time since he'd re-entered my life, he appeared speechless. His gaze scoured my face, as if looking for answers.

"Why?"

I shook my head, unable to speak, scared he'd see too much. But I couldn't look away. I didn't want to look away. I wanted to bathe in the gentleness breaking through in that instant when I glimpsed the old Rafe.

He blinked and the moment shattered, his emotions going into lockdown. Without another word, he dragged me toward the cellar.

"Don't put me back down there," I pleaded.

He flung open the door and herded me down the stairs. I was shaking too much to fight. Back in the cage, he fastened shackles around my wrists and jerked my arms high, attaching the chain to a hook in the ceiling. "This should keep you out of trouble for a while." He held my chin, fingers bruising my jaw. "Every time you rebel, this is where you'll end up. Learn to obey me, and we'll get along fine."

And that's how he left me. Alone, cold, and in the dark, with my arms suspended above my head.

SIX

RAFE

Dante's Pass, population 893, and half of them thought I was guilty as fuck. The place still felt like home, in spite of the busybodies who wanted to see me rot in jail until I was nothing but bones for what I'd done to that "poor girl." They were the ones who sneered at my reputation as Rafe "The Choker" Mason from my fighting days. They were the ones who sensed something was off about me.

But others, mostly people who'd had connections to my family for decades, or people who'd known me in high school, they believed I was innocent. Unlike the crowd that condemned me, they saw past Alex's lie. They *knew* me, or so they believed.

Either way, it was too much drama, so I avoided town as much as possible, save for the weekly trip to the post office and my work at the vineyard. Despite the town

gossip, people mostly left me alone. I imagined it was difficult to harass a guy on an island.

As I sorted through a stack of mail, mostly bills and
advertisements, someone uttered my name. Locking the
P.O. Box, I swiveled my head in time to see a blonde whirl
around and push the door open. She grabbed the hand of
the kid at her side and ushered him outdoors, as if the
place were about to burn to the ground.

I folded my mail inside an advertisement for local businesses and glanced through the front window, catching the
woman's profile as she walked away. My heart almost
stopped. I'd recognize that stubborn jaw anywhere. I
rushed after her, the door closing with a thud upon my
exit, and spotted her a few feet down the sidewalk. She
opened the back door of a white BMW, and in hushed
tones, hurried the kid to get inside and buckle up.

"Nikki!"

She lurched upright, and her deep, brown eyes met
mine. Yeah, I remembered those eyes, especially how they
bored into mine during sex. Nikki had never been the shy
closed-eyes-during-sex kind of girl, and that had been the
biggest turn-on.

She slammed the door and rounded the hood to the
driver's side. "I heard you were back," she said. "Seeing you
caught me off guard. I shouldn't have said your name."

I stuffed the mail into my back pocket and sauntered to
her side. "Why the hell not?"

With a sigh, she paused, one hand on the door handle.

"C'mon, things didn't end well. You made it clear you never wanted to see me again."

"Nik," I said, voice suddenly wobbly as I slid a hand onto her shoulder. I had to touch her. After eight damn years, I needed to. "I didn't want you waiting around for me."

She opened the door and wedged it between us. "Well, I didn't wait around, so you have nothing to worry about." She held out her left hand, and my eyes widened at the huge rock on her finger. "I'm getting married in a few weeks."

It was disconcerting to see how much things had changed while I was away. While time had all but stopped inside that prison, the world kept turning without me. "So I see," I said, giving in to a weak instance of self-pity. I moved around the door and put one hand on the window and the other on the roof of the car. Her body stilled, but she had nowhere to go, and shit, just being this close to her brought everything back, all the summer nights we'd spent twisted in the sheets, fan blowing hot air on bodies slick with sweat.

"I didn't realize you were back in town," I said. "Figured you worked in some swanky office in downtown Portland by now. When did you come back?"

"Last year, when Lyle asked me to marry him."

I quirked a brow. "Wait, you're not talking about Lyle Lewis."

She nodded.

I tried not to grit my teeth but failed. How the fuck had that asswipe gotten tangled with my ex? He'd followed her around like a horn dog all through high school, and that was only half of it. The guy had been the cruelest bully in town, and he'd hated me down to my toes for looking out for a few of the kids he'd abused on a daily basis. He'd also despised me because of my friendship with Nikki.

"You know he's the sheriff now, right?" she asked.

Wonderful. She was marrying a fucking bully-turned-sheriff. If I didn't get Alex under control soon, he might be slapping cuffs on me in the future, and I could only imagine the thrill he'd get at arresting me.

"I guess congratulations are in order." I tilted my head, one brow raised.

"I guess so," she said, her gaze veering to the backseat of the car. "I've really gotta go. It was good to see you again, Rafe." Her voice softened, the same breathless quality I recalled from years ago. She slid into the driver's seat, and that was when the kid in the back called her "Mom" and asked what they were having for dinner.

I froze as it dawned on me. I'd been so focused on Nikki, part of me still thinking of her as the twenty-year-old girl I'd known, that I'd unconsciously written the kid off as a nephew, or perhaps a child of a friend.

But he was *hers*.

As she moved to pull the door shut, I shot out a hand

and blocked her. Peeking into the backseat, I laid eyes on the kid for the first time. Really looked at him. Fuck. He was a spitting image of my childhood photos.

"How old is he, Nikki?"

Her body slumped, and with a loud sigh, she said, "Seven, and I know what you're thinking. I was going to tell you. Swear to God I was, but now is not the time." Her eyes pleaded with me. "Can we meet for dinner? In about an hour?"

I couldn't speak at first. I could have said so many things, but the truth hit me like a sledgehammer. Unless I was reading her wrong, or misunderstanding, she was telling me I had a son.

"Rafe?"

"An hour?" I asked, giving myself a mental shake.

"Yeah, I'll meet you at Doc's Grill. You remember where that is, right?"

"I remember."

She pulled the door shut, and this time I let her. I stood frozen in that spot long after she pulled away from the curb, the kid's green eyes burning a hole in my mind. His curious eyes that reminded me so much of my own. Had he seen it too, or was he too young to pick up on the resemblance?

Someone jostled me to awareness, and from the pinch of disproval on the woman's face, she must have been in the "he should rot in prison" camp.

"Sorry," I mumbled, then shook my head because I'd just apologized to a judgmental broad for simply standing in public. Fuck these people. I wandered down the main drag of the town until I reached the highway and stepped onto the shoulder. Checking my watch, I began walking to kill time before I met up with Nikki. The idea of that meeting sent my pulse racing. I wondered what he was like. Had he asked about me?

Hell, I didn't even know his name.

Behind me, the sun dipped toward the horizon, and the shadow of the island emerged in the river up ahead. The private piece of land, situated on the Oregon side of the Columbia River, had been in my family for generations. My mother split when I was young, and my anger over her absence had slowly burned until it flared during my teens. Dad tried to stem my violent tendencies by enrolling me into martial arts classes. He'd thought if I learned to fight with respect and a code of ethics, it would curb my thirst to pound on people. It wasn't like I'd gone around beating on everyone, just the idiots who deserved it, but he'd had the right idea. Those lessons had probably saved my ass.

I wondered if my son—even thinking of him as mine set my head spinning—was angry over the gaping hole I should have filled all these years. Cars whizzed past, and for some strange reason, the hum of traffic settled my nerves. The island grew larger as the distance narrowed. I put the issue of fatherhood on the back burner and wondered how Alex was handling being locked up in the dark, her naked body shivering. I imagined her legs shaking, thought of how out-of-control she must feel, strung up on her toes and knowing she was at my mercy. My jeans grew unbearably tight.

Such helplessness shouldn't turn me on so fucking much, but it did. Always had. My dad's efforts to teach me right from wrong hadn't touched on sexual deviance.

The mountains had turned to dusky blue against an orange backdrop by the time I turned around and retraced my steps back to town. Doc's Grill, known for their unique dishes and secret sauces that couldn't be duplicated anywhere else, was boisterous with activity. The restaurant had never suffered for business. That hadn't changed in my absence, though so much about the town had, like the remodeled school, or how the post office no longer shared space with Cathy's Quik-N-Go.

I entered, nodded at the waitress, and told her I was there to meet someone. I found Nikki sitting by herself at a corner table, nursing a beer. Candles lit the wooden tables, giving an intimate feel to the place, though the peanut shells covering the floor spoke of the casual setting.

I slid into the chair across from her. "Sorry I'm late." I'd lost track of time, plus, I'd needed several minutes to convince my dick to settle down. No way was I walking in to meet Nikki with a raging hard-on.

"No problem. I was enjoying the quiet. William can be a handful, and I don't get much 'me' time."

"William?"

She dipped her head, and a curtain of blond hair obscured the left side of her face. "I named him after you."

William, my middle name. How was it possible I'd had a son all this time, one who shared my name even, yet I'd known nothing about him? Seven years of missed birthdays, milestones, laughter and tears.

Thankfully, the waitress arrived to take our orders, and as Nikki asked about the daily specials, I took a few seconds to collect myself. I was a father. A dad. I had a kid. If I told myself that enough times, maybe it would sink in.

The waitress, a young brunette on the short side, turned to me and did a double take. "I thought you looked familiar. You're Rafe Mason. My boyfriend is a huge fan. He never believed you raped that girl." She winked at me. "A lot of people around here don't."

Unfortunately, a lot of people still did.

I autographed a napkin for her and gave her my order. Once she left, thick silence fell over us.

Time to rip off the Band-Aid. "You should've told me, Nik."

"What good would it have done?" She leaned back and crossed her arms. "You were locked up, and you weren't getting out anytime soon. Besides, let's not delude ourselves. We were never serious. Getting pregnant...it just happened. I can't say it was a mistake because I wouldn't have William, but we never meant for it to happen."

I picked up a spoon and swirled the ice chips in my water glass. "I actually thought I'd marry you someday."

She laughed. "C'mon, Rafe. We were kids back then."

And now we had a kid together. Neither of us spoke the words, though they hung in the air, as potent as the spices from the restaurant's kitchen.

"We both know someday wouldn't have come," she continued. "You had your whole career in front of you before..." She lowered her head, and I despised how she didn't say the words.

"Do you think I did it?"

"I told you a long time ago I knew you wouldn't do something like that." The corner of her mouth curled. "You never needed to force yourself on anyone. You had women begging at your feet."

I tried not to squirm in my seat. Ironically, I had a naked woman, bound and locked up at that precise moment, just waiting for me to hold her down and fuck her hard. Nikki had no idea who I was. Who I'd become. She should have, though. She'd been the only woman who'd ever allowed me to get rough with her. I'd explored some of my baser urges with her, and she'd let me. She'd gotten off on it as much as I had. That's why we'd worked. Our deep friendship had kept the drama to a minimum. We truly had been friends with benefits. Until I was arrested.

And now, to find out my relationship with her had resulted in a kid...

"What did you tell him about me?"

"The truth. I've always wanted you to be part of his life. Eight years seemed like forever to you, but I knew you'd get out eventually." She brushed her bangs from her eyes —eyes suddenly bright. "I didn't want to make things worse for you in there, so I kept quiet about the pregnancy."

Ah, shit. I hated when chicks cried. Except for Alex. Her tears affected me differently. I craved them. "It's water under the bridge. I'm here now, so let's deal with this. You told him his dad went to prison?"

She shook her head. "I told him you had to go away for a few years, but you'd come back when you could. He's at that age now where vague answers aren't cutting it anymore. He wants to meet his father, Rafe."

This was unbelievable, and bad fucking timing. I'd just committed a felony—for real this time—and I was about to compound felony upon felony. I couldn't stop what I'd started, especially now. If I let Alex go, she'd run straight to the cops.

What a fucking mess. I pushed back from the table and resisted the urge to grab at my collar. "I need some time."

"I understand."

"No, I don't think you do. Nik...I've done things. Things I can't undo. I'm not the same guy I was eight years ago."

"I realize that."

"No, you don't." Sighing, I ran a hand through my hair and pulled at the strands until my scalp burned. "You should've told me. You should've fucking told me."

I tossed a few bills onto the table to cover the dinner I wouldn't eat, and then I rushed from the restaurant like the coward I was. But the question remained; if she *had* told me, would it have changed my mind about taking Alex?

SEVEN
ALEX

I wanted to die. I didn't know how long he'd left me suspended, but it was messing with my head. I'd lost all sense of time and direction. My body was numb, almost weightless, except for the burn that circled my wrists. That pain didn't go away, no matter how much I tried to block it out. At some point, I started counting...at some point I'd also given up. By the time 7,200 seconds passed, I was about to go out of my mind. The time after that was endless. My voice had gone hoarse long ago from screaming his name.

He never came, and I began to panic. Maybe the past eight years had made him snap and tormenting me this way was his only source of relief. Images popped into my mind, scenarios of him beaten in prison, or worse. The helplessness he must have experienced, just as I was now. I tried to wrap my mind around eight years, but I could hardly wrap my mind around the few hours since he'd slammed the door shut, once again leaving me in darkness. A sick feeling formed in my gut.

God, he must really hate me. My actions, born of cowardice and shame, had labeled him a rapist. In that moment, as I stood on tiptoes in a most punishing way, I hated myself more than he did. I deserved this.

The turn of a knob ricocheted, ringing through my ears, and a sliver of light beamed toward me an instant before it was extinguished. Impossibly, the blackness became even more suffocating. I heard him coming near, though he barely made a sound.

His touch landed on my shoulder, and I wondered how he found me so easily. His fingers were warm and soft, starkly different from the chill I couldn't escape. My teeth chattered as his caress fluttered across my breasts, and my moan rent the air like a sword, tearing the quiet in two.

Clothing swished, and his arm brushed mine as he moved to stand behind me. His breath hit my ear before his words did. "All those years I was in prison, did you even think of me once?"

Twisting my aching wrists, I shuffled my feet, but my limbs refused to stop quaking. "Please let me down."

"Answer the question."

"I wrote you letters," I blurted, then drew in a quick breath. In the wee hours of the morning when sleep eluded me, I'd bared my soul to him on paper. All the guilt I'd carried, how I felt about him. I'd also laid out every last detail of the secrets I kept locked away.

"I never got any letters."

"I never sent them." Why had I opened my mouth about the letters? If he ever found them...oh God.

"Then why write them?"

"Because I..."

"Spit it out, Alex."

"I missed you."

"You missed me?" He fisted my hair. "You do realize how ridiculous that sounds, right? *You* sent me away."

"I know." I grimaced as his tug on my hair increased.

"What part of me did you miss? The guy you couldn't resist gawking at, or the guy who actually gave a shit about you?"

Past tense. He didn't care about me anymore. I couldn't blame him, but the knowledge hurt something fierce, threatened to chew a hole in my heart. "I just missed you, Rafe."

"Did you write about all the dirty things you wished I'd do to you?"

"No."

"Liar," he murmured into my ear. "Tell me about your fantasies."

I tried shaking my head, mortified, but his fist in my hair immobilized me.

"If you don't start talking, you're staying down here until morning." His hand dropped, and I sensed him retreating.

"Don't go!" I cried. "I'll tell you."

"I know you will. You haven't changed. I knew eight years ago I could probably do anything I wanted, but I knew better."

"And now?" I asked, hesitance creeping into my tone.

"Now I'm black on the inside. I just don't give a fuck anymore."

"I don't believe that. I still remember who you are, even if you don't."

"Would the man you remember have strung you up on your toes?"

Definitely not.

"Didn't think so," he said, as if he'd heard my thoughts. "So talk. Tell me all of your dirty secrets."

Oh God. The way he breathed those words into my ear was enough to unravel me. "I've thought about you making love to me."

"Do I seem like a making-love kind of guy?"

"No." He seemed like a fuck-you-until-you-split-in-two kind of guy. The kind of guy who'd bring new meaning to the word passionate.

"C'mon, Alex. Last chance to spill before I walk through that door alone."

"I've thought about you going down on me."

He rimmed my earlobe with his tongue, invoking a

jittery sigh. "Did you get yourself off thinking about my tongue on your pussy?" He closed a hand around my throat, arched my neck, and darted his tongue inside my ear in an erotic demonstration of what he could do with his hot mouth on other areas of my body.

"You're an ass," I said, though the breathless quality of my voice took the sting out of the words.

"I want to fuck yours."

I couldn't help but tremble. The idea wasn't pleasant, but at the same time, the thought of Rafe sliding inside my tight, forbidden hole...there was something tantalizing about it.

His harsh laughter brought me back to the here and now. "Fuck, you're getting hot thinking about it, aren't you?"

"No." I shook my head, as if the denial alone wasn't good enough, as if he could see me anyway in the darkness.

"I'm calling bullshit. You want me to fuck your ass."

"I've never...done it before." Anal sex was the one area where I was still a virgin, untainted by Zach's brutal obsession. The thought of Rafe penetrating the last place left untouched turned me on in ways I couldn't explain, yet it also terrified me.

"I can be your first." He wedged a finger between my lips. "I bet you've dreamed of my dick in your mouth too. Do you like sucking cock?"

I closed my lips and sucked, unable to stop myself. His

finger tasted of salt and something that was undeniably *him*. The way he stroked my tongue made me ache to have something much bigger in my mouth. I'd never wanted it before, had often endured Zach's forceful intrusion while giving it my all just so he'd finish that much faster. But Rafe...putting my mouth on him would be different.

He withdrew his finger and traced a wet path down my throat. "I'm going to release you, and you're going to obey every fucking demand, do you understand me?"

"Yes," I said, biting back a moan.

He set me free from the shackles, and my arms fell to my sides, as if weighed down by cement blocks. Not allowing me a chance to stretch my protesting limbs, he pulled me though the blackness, as if a sudden charge of urgency drove him, and my heart thrummed an erratic beat as he pushed me up the stairs, fingers pressing into hips with a touch that was so *not* gentle. His hands on me, gouging with pain and power, flooded my pussy with heat and dampness. My breaths came rapidly, a wheezing sound more in tune with fear than with want, but wanted him, I did.

We entered the living room, and his hands rose to my waist as his mouth closed over my neck, sucking and nipping as he walked me forward, one step at a time. I dropped my head against his shoulder and moaned, eyelids drooping. Parting my lips, I thought I spoke his name, but if I did, it was lost to our heavy breathing.

He halted at the edge of the room and pulled down a stepladder. "Climb up," he said with a groan. His hard-on jabbed my spine, and his large hands wrapped around my sides as he guided me up the steep passage. He switched on a light, and I saw the top consisted of a loft bedroom with a slanted ceiling. Double skylights undoubtedly gave the illusion of space during the day, though the king size bed took up most of the room. It was cozy and inviting, and I wanted to sink into the mattress and find out if it was as soft as it looked, preferably while his naked body blanketed mine.

He whirled me around, and I met his gaze, plummeting into impossibly green depths shadowed by lashes longer and thicker than mine. Those eyes radiated manic obsession, devouring me with a feverous edge. He pounced without warning, muscles bunching as he hoisted me up by the neck. I kicked my feet helplessly as he strode across the room and slammed me onto the bed. This was about more than sex. He wanted to hurt me—I felt it in my bones where his hands had left their imprints.

Gasping, I propped up on elbows and watched him warily, my shaking knees falling to the sides. He stalked me slowly, shedding his clothes with each step closer, and his fierce expression said I belonged to him. I shouldn't feel excitement, shouldn't feel warmth pooling between my legs, but that was me—the fucked up girl who got off when she shouldn't.

"Turn over," he growled. "On your hands and knees."

I rolled to my stomach, pushed onto all fours, and the mattress lowered when he climbed behind me. He wrapped his large hands around my hips and dragged me backward until my bottom pressed into his lap, my thighs spread as far as they would go. A rough hand shoved my cheek to the mattress, and my strangled moan tore through the air as his erection teased the opening of my sex.

"Are you on birth control?"

The question evoked a deep ache in my heart. I'd been on some form of contraception since I was fifteen. "I just had an injection a couple of weeks ago."

"Are you clean?"

"Are you?" I countered.

"I've been in prison for eight years. What do you think?"

I didn't answer, as I didn't like to think of Rafe in prison.

"I asked you a question," he bit out in that unnerving tone I was beginning to recognize. "Are you clean?"

I'd only been with one man, and considering Zach's obsession with me, I doubted I had to worry about STDs. I *wished* Zach had turned his focus onto someone else, as horrible and selfish as that sounded. "I'm clean."

He curled his fingers into my hips and nudged me. "Do you want this?"

God yes.

I let out a pleading moan. I shouldn't want him this way. It was twisted and wrong, but just the thought that he'd do it anyway if I fought him made me even hotter. I hated my body; it had it all backwards. Sex shouldn't be about power and control.

His hands closed around my wrists and yanked them to the mattress, next to my spread thighs, and I'd never felt so helpless and exposed—not in a way that was so exhilarating.

"I won't be gentle."

My whole body shuddered. "I don't expect you to be."

"Good, 'cause I'm not stopping." Something ominous laced his words.

"You're going to hurt me, aren't you?" Another shiver went through me, and I couldn't decide if I was excited or horrified. Zach had hurt me so many times that it had become second nature, but Rafe wasn't my psychotic stepbrother. Rafe was the guy I'd obsessed over for years, and now he had me pinned down and spread, easy prey, and I worried he was about to figure out just how fucked up I was.

"No orgasms allowed."

I groaned. "You're crazy if you think I can hold back." Every atom in my body zinged with the need for him to fill me.

His fingers flexed around my wrists. "I think you're gonna find a way, unless you really want to test me. I'm not fucking you for your pleasure, sweetheart. I'm fucking you because you're my piece of ass."

That was all I'd ever be to him. A piece of ass, a *thing* he held in contempt for unforgivable sins. Lips trembling, eyes stinging with unshed tears, I tried to swallow the hurt, but this wasn't how I'd imagined our first time.

EIGHT
RAFE

I *wasn't* a monster. If I told myself that enough times, maybe I'd believe it. She swiveled her head and looked at me, dark curls tumbling over her shoulder, and her jade eyes glimmered with unspoken hurt. She still didn't understand that I hungered for her pain, her tears.

"Keep your head down." I smacked her hard on the ass then slammed into her, and her spine arched under my onslaught of savage greed.

My entire body ignited with the sensation of being joined. No latex barrier, just pure skin-to-skin contact. Shit, her pussy was ready for me. Tight, wet, hot. If I weren't so on edge, I'd bury myself in her for hours. Finally, after so many fucking years of wanting this girl, I was inside her. The sense of power intoxicated me, as did the discovery that this was more than just sex. I could deny it all I wanted, but our chemistry didn't lie. There was something irresistible about her. It was true when she was fifteen, when my values kept her safe from me. Now she was even more irresistible because she'd come of age, morphed into a woman I wanted to consume, and I was more than justified in taking her.

Swiveling my hips, I shoved deeper and thrilled at the way her body sheathed my cock like a glove. We slid together in sweat and need, and I pressed my thumbs into her wrists where her pulse galloped in tune to my thrusts. The sounds she made, so guttural they vibrated straight to my dick—fuck they sent me flying. I plunged harder, faster, and squeezed her wrists until my fingers whitened at the knuckles.

"You're hurting me," she said, her voice wafting in the air like a tattered feather.

I yanked her upright and wrapped an arm around her shoulders, one hand clamping her arm to trap her against me. The other gripped her throat, fingers on either side of her neck, forcing her head back. Her spine arched as I pumped.

"You feel that? That's my cock inside you." I drove into her violently, increasing the pace, the pain. I wanted to hurt her, wanted her tears. Each thrust was an angry, unforgiving act of punishment—a way to hide what tortured me deep down; things I'd grappled with for eight years. I craved this girl yet hated her guts, all at the same time.

"Please..." she whimpered.

"Please what? You wanted me to fuck you, and now...I... am." I bit back a grunt and flexed my fingers around her throat.

"Rafe...oh God, Rafe! I'm gonna come," she bit the words out through gritted teeth, and those blessed tears I craved slipped from her eyes.

I licked each salty drop from her cheek and let her shame linger on my tongue. "You're *not* coming," I said, clutching her throat and angling her neck to the side. I sank my teeth into tender, creamy skin and clamped down harder when a screeching cry tore from her lips. My dick celebrated that wail.

"That's right, sweetheart. Cry for me. Fight me."

"Can't...stop...it." Her voice lilted into a continuous moan that wrecked me as her pussy clenched.

She wasn't fighting, wasn't struggling or begging. She was fucking getting *off*.

Oh fuck no. She *would* struggle.

I inhaled deeply, seeking absolute control because anything less was dangerous. It'd been too long since I'd experienced the addictive rush of adrenaline flooding my system, a high I only achieved by stealing someone's breath and sanity, when I was God to them in those seconds when they straddled the line of life and death at my hands.

I couldn't screw this up because no matter what I told her, she meant too much. I wanted her struggle and her terror, but I didn't want to kill her. I tightened my fingers around her throat, adding just enough pressure to restrict the blood flow to her brain.

She writhed like a rabid animal, her fingernails digging into any part of me she could reach. Blood rushed my cock, and I'd never felt so hard, so insane and frantic as I rammed her from behind. Her body bowed backward, and I counted the seconds as I came. She relaxed in my arms as the last bit of pleasure shot from my dick. I withdrew, heart pumping too fast, and laid her limp body onto the mattress.

NINE

ALEX

Strong, muscular arms surrounded me as I gasped, and I clawed at my throat, fighting against the horrifying experience of not being able to breathe. Despite the disorientation and confusion, I sank deeper into his warmth, loving how his body folded around mine. I coughed and gasped some more, and little by little, clarity returned. Cold, harsh reality doused the warm and fuzzies.

Rafe had tried to choke me.

I struggled from his hold and made it to the edge of the bed before he trapped me in his arms again. "Where do you think you're going?"

"You fucking choked me!"

"You fucking came."

"Are you trying to kill me? Do you hate me that much?"

"I don't hate you *that much*, Alex." He moved one arm

from my waist and wound a fist in my hair. "You need to remember I'm the one in control here. Just because you have a hot pussy doesn't mean you can disobey me. When I say no orgasms, I mean no orgasms."

Intense hurt welled, unstoppable, and I let out a sob. More followed until I was bawling like a baby. He'd taken something from me—something I'd held onto for years. He'd taken my first time with him, had sullied the memory with his cruelty.

That was something I'd never get back, and it hurt so incredibly bad because he didn't seem fazed. I was just another piece of ass. Even worse, I was someone who deserved his contempt.

I did deserve his hatred, but I didn't deserve to die.

"Stop crying, or I'll put you back in the cellar."

"Why do you have to be such an asshole?"

"Why did you have to send me to prison?" he shot back, adding another painful yank on my hair.

"I didn't want to. God, Rafe...I didn't want to."

"I'm done tiptoeing around this. Either tell me why you did it, or I'll choke you again."

Another sob escaped, and I tried to speak but the words wouldn't come.

He rolled me to my back, pinned both wrists to the mattress with one hand, and circled my throat with the other. My pulse pounded out of control. But he didn't apply pressure. Instead, he stared into my eyes, as if searching for an answer.

"Please...don't. Please..." More tears seeped from my eyes and dripped down the sides of my face. He leaned down and licked them up.

"Either tell me the truth, or you go nighty-night again."

"Please!" I begged. "I didn't want to do it. Rafe...you have no idea."

"Oh, I think I do. That's the interesting thing about being locked up, Alex. I had way too much time to think. You wanted me, only I wasn't giving in, was I?" He lowered his face until we were nose to nose. "You couldn't handle the rejection."

I didn't know if I was more appalled or indignant over his assumptions.

"Admit it! You were nothing but a pampered, spoiled little brat, and you didn't think twice about throwing me away like trash when you didn't get what you wanted."

"I loved you!" I screamed into his face. "I loved you so fucking much." I turned my head and wished the mattress would split open and swallow me.

Oh God. I was ten shades of mortified.

His silence weighed more heavily than his body did. He flexed his fingers around my locked wrists. "You have a funny way of showing it," he finally said.

I had no answer to that. His hand twitched around my throat, still threatening punishment. "Please, Rafe," I whispered, my voice cracking. "Don't do this."

"Don't do this? You have no idea what *you* did," he said. "I want to squeeze every last breath from you. I want to fucking break you until you're nothing but pieces in my arms."

"Please," I gasped.

"They raped me in there, Alex."

I couldn't breathe, and not because his hands threatened to shut off my air, but for the first time, I really allowed myself to see what I'd done to him. "Kill me," I said, hot, salty drops of regret trickling into my mouth. "I deserve it."

He narrowed his eyes—eyes suddenly bright with pain—and pressed harder on my throat.

My mouth opened, and I gasped as spots floated in the air. The room narrowed, walls closing in a little more with each thump of my heart. I thought it would pound out of my chest. "Do it," I squeaked.

"*Fuck* me," he choked out. The vulnerability in his tone tore me in two. He let go of my throat, and I sucked in air until I thought my lungs would burst.

"I wish I could take it back," I said, squeezing my eyes shut. I'd caused him so much pain, had ruined his life. I'd done this to the only guy I'd ever loved. "I'm sorry. I'm sorry." I said it over and over, wishing he'd believe me, wishing I could turn back time. "If you need to talk about it—"

"Shut up." He returned me to my side and trapped me against his body. "It's late. Get some damn sleep." Instead of returning me to the cellar, he clung to me, one hand fisting my hair while the other claimed my breast. His legs tangled with mine.

I knew this conversation was far from over. He wouldn't stop until he got the truth, and I wondered how long I could hold out. How many choke holds could I handle? How many hours suspended by my wrists, alone in the cold, dank cellar? How many times could I withstand him torturing me with sex?

I brought my fists up, pressed them to trembling lips, and dug sharp fingernails into my palms. When it came to Rafe, I never knew what was coming next, and I didn't know what he was capable of, especially in light of his admission. I shuddered to think of what he'd been through. I *was* a pampered, spoiled brat. Selfish to the core. I should have stopped it. I should have spoken up and told the police the truth, but as the first hours passed, most of them spent in a state of shock, I lost what small bit of courage I might have possessed. Hours turned into days...days into months...months into years.

All the while, Rafe had been in hell.

For all the tough guy front he put up, I believed he did care about me, somewhere inside him where the guy I remembered still existed. He might have loved me, if things had turned out differently. If I hadn't wrecked him.

Life was what it was. I couldn't change the past. I could only deal with the present as it hurtled toward me.

Sometime later, his breathing evened into gentle snores, and I carefully tugged my hair from his fist and lifted his warm palm from my breast. Little by little, I extricated myself from his hold and crawled from bed. When a floorboard creaked under my foot, I froze, fear rising in my throat in the form of a lump. He didn't move. I swallowed hard and inched toward the panel that would drop the ladder onto the first floor.

God, I was quaking like a leaf. The situation reminded me of one of those scary movies I used to make Lucas watch with me—the ones where I'd yell at the heroine, lamenting her stupidity because there was no way she was getting out of there alive.

I had to. For both our sakes. I didn't hold anything against him. The horrors he'd experienced in prison were my fault. I wouldn't take that from him, wouldn't attempt to deflect blame. We all made choices, some good, some bad. When it came to bad decisions, Rafe and I were batting one for one.

So I *had* to get out of there before the situation escalated and he did something we'd both regret.

I kept his sleeping form in my periphery and released the ladder. It dropped to the floor with a ridiculous amount of racket, and my whole body stiffened. He rolled over, underneath the layers of blankets, and for a moment I wanted to crawl back into bed with him. What a ridiculous notion.

As soon as his soft snores resumed, a burst of adrenaline shot through me. I climbed down the steps and landed with a soft thud on the hardwood floor. I turned in the darkened room, thankful for the heavy rain hitting the roof in a cacophony of taps and dings. Under the cover of noise and shadow, I rushed through the house in search of my clothes. Heck, I'd settle for a jacket at this point.

If need be, I'd walk out of that house buck-naked.

I headed toward the kitchen, hoping to find a coat in the closet by the door. Turning the corner, I shook with a mixture of anticipation and dread. It was *deja vu*, and I was back in my house on the night of my engagement, preparing to take hold of freedom with both hands, to hell with the consequences.

I smashed into a body, and at first I thought it was Rafe until the deep voice registered—a voice I didn't recognize.

"What are you doing wandering around by yourself?"

"Rafe!" I screamed, turning and running toward the loft, as if my life depended on it. I screamed for him again as my feet threatened to slide across the hardwood. I was in such a frantic hurry to get up the ladder that my foot slipped on the first rung, and my chin hit the wood hard. I fell on my ass, my jaw throbbing, and palmed my breasts as a figure loomed over me.

TEN
RAFE

Her scream jerked me from sleep, and I sprang to my feet. Adrenaline flooded my system, and I couldn't recall how I got to the opening of the ladder, but I was peering into the darkness when a light switched on. Alex cowered at the bottom, her petite hands covering her tits.

Jax stood next to her. He looked up and took in my questioning glance with a shrug. "She freaked the fuck out, man."

"Just a sec. I'll be right down." I threw on a black shirt, leaving it unbuttoned, and pulled on my jeans. The belt hung over my dick, unbuckled as I descended the steps.

Alex sent me a nervous glance, eyes wide and chest heaving behind those hands that did little to conceal her tits. Part of me wanted to drag her back to bed and fuck her again. The other part wanted to see how this played out. I already tasted her humiliation, craved it even.

"Get up," I said, my face hardening into a stern expression. I turned toward Jax. "Want a look?"

He arched a brow. "She's a naked woman. What do you think?"

Alex scooted away, bare ass sliding across the hardwood. I grabbed a fist full of her hair and brought her to her feet.

"Leave me alone!" She attempted to pull away, though she still didn't move her hands, and I almost laughed at the way she was standing, like a comical version of a woman needing to pee but trying to hold it.

"Arms at your sides," I ordered. She needed to know I was willing to go to any length to control her, and that included sharing her. Of course, I'd cut off my arm before I'd share her, but she didn't know that. The threat of handing her off to Jax should go a long way toward breaking her stubborn will.

I yanked on her hair. "Hands at your sides!"

Her sob should have cut me to pieces. That would be the normal reaction, but her cries made me want to do dirty, nasty things that would turn those cries into screams. I bunched my hands as she dropped hers. Her nipples puckered, no doubt from the chill in the cabin.

"Touch her tits," I said to Jax.

He narrowed his eyes. "You sure?"

No, not at all. "Yeah, I'm sure."

Alex needed to know she had no sway with me. What better way to show her how little she meant than to let another man fondle her? He reached a hand out, paying no heed to her struggle, and brushed a fingertip across her nipple. Watching him touch her was harder than expected. She sucked in a breath and her body went lax against me, as if she knew she was outnumbered and couldn't stop this.

She was right. She had no control on this island, and it was time she figured it out.

I gritted my teeth as Jax stepped closer and settled both palms over her tits. "You're a lucky man, you sonofbitch."

I might have taken offense, but the name fit my mother perfectly.

"They're a little on the small side, but she's a looker," he said, continuing to mold her tits to his hands.

Agitation twisted her face, and she spit at him. "Get your hands off of me!"

He stepped back, out of the line of spit, and I jerked her back by the hair. "You need to learn a little respect, especially toward my roommate. Jax lives here, so you'd better get used to being naked around him." I grabbed her face, forcing her watery eyes on mine. "If I tell you to let him touch you, you fucking let him touch you. If I tell you to suck his cock, you wrap that sweet mouth around his cock. You're going to do as you're told, got it?"

"No, I don't 'got it,'" she said with a sneer. "I'm not a

plaything you can pass around to your buddies. What the hell is wrong with you?"

I raised a brow. "What the hell is wrong with me?" I shoved her to her knees and held her head between hands that shook with rage. "What's wrong with me is your attitude." Fuck, she was getting under my skin. "Jax, unzip." I took in his stunned expression. Obviously, he hadn't expected this development, and neither had I, but it was too late to back down, even if the thought of her mouth touching his cock before it touched mine set my blood boiling.

He only displayed a moment of hesitancy before unbuttoning his jeans. Alex was a tempting package, and I doubted there was a straight man alive that would pass up the chance to have that mouth fastened around his dick. Even Jax, who had issues when it came to being touched, wouldn't say no.

He lowered his zipper and whipped out his junk. She tensed, inching her head sideways as he came near her. I tightened my hold, indecision warring within me. I wanted her mouth around my cock, no one else's, but I needed to see this through.

Jax took another step and stopped just short of brushing his tip against her lips.

"Open your fucking mouth," I told her.

She jerked her head back and forth, so I pressed my fingers into her jaw until she had no choice but to open. I glanced at Jax. "Give her a taste."

Visibly swallowing, he slowly inched his tip past her lips.

"You like him on your tongue? How about if he really goes for it? Have you ever had a man deep-throat you?"

Her protest came out as a mangled reply around his dick, and her tears slid onto my hands while I forced her head still.

Jax's eyelids fell, and I caught the slight shudder in his body. The tightness of his face wasn't one of pleasure, and I realized this was going too far for him. Fuck, who was I kidding? This was going too far for me.

"You either suck his cock, or you go back into the cellar. Your choice."

She jerked her head back. "Cellar," she said, no hesitation whatsoever, and I smiled. The only cock she wanted was mine. I pulled her to her feet, and Jax stumbled back and zipped his pants.

I pushed her to the door of the cellar, and he followed, though he didn't trail us down the stairs. The door shut with a loud bang. She flung my hands off her and backed up, toward the racks of wine bottles. The tears that trickled down her face, dripping onto her tits, should have softened me, but they didn't. I wanted to lick each one from her skin, savoring the salt on my tongue. Savoring her pain.

The law saw me as nothing more than a rapist. A degenerate. I wouldn't want to disappoint them now.

"Get in the cage."

"No!" She snatched a wine bottle, stared at it for a couple of seconds in her shaking grasp, and busted it on the wall. Deep red wine splashed at her feet. Lifting an unsteady arm, she gripped the jagged neck with whitened knuckles and widened her stance, as if ready to fight me.

Shit, she probably was. Maybe I'd finally found the secret button of hers—the one that sent her into a corner cowering with the realization that a cruel sonofabitch held her life in his hands. No more notions of romance and love-making. But she wasn't exactly cowering now. She was ready to take me on, like a cornered tiger.

Fuck, it was a turn-on, especially since my claws were bigger than hers. "Put it down," I said, the words tearing from my lips in a snarl.

"You're crazy, Rafe! How could you offer me up to him?" she screamed the words, her face distorted into something I'd never seen on her delicate features. "How could you choke me?" Her entire body trembled, and I recognized the adrenaline rushing through her, the need to take control, but I didn't believe she had it in her.

Until she jumped at me with the makeshift weapon and swiped the air.

Shit. She wasn't kidding.

I put my hands up. "Calm down. At least I wouldn't try to slice you up, sweetheart."

"Stop calling me that!" Her face twisted in despair. "Please, let me go. Please...Rafe. I don't want to hurt you."

"Sweetheart," I said, just to goad her, "you're not even close to hurting me."

She only hesitated an instant before her arm shot out again and jagged glass came way too close for comfort.

Ducking, I caught her wrist and squeezed until the bottle dropped and splintered at our feet. "Come at me like that again and you'll wish the devil was down here with you." I wrenched her hands behind her back, trapped her against me, and wrapped an arm around her throat. Her breaths puffed out, each slow exhale indicating she was giving in. At least, that's what I thought. I loosened my arm, a mistake, because she sank her teeth into my inked bicep, stomped on my foot, and tore up the stairs.

ELEVEN

ALEX

Why isn't he grabbing me? That was my only thought as I ran up the stairs. Each step seemed agonizingly slow, as if I were in a dream, someone on my heels chasing me, and I couldn't get my legs to move fast enough. I pulled the door open and ran smack into a broad chest.

Jax grabbed my shoulders, and his fingers gouged my bones.

"Let me go!" I lifted a knee and aimed for his balls, and when he doubled over with a groan, I took off running. Time seemed to slow, and every footstep felt as if I were forging through mud. I reached the door, flung it open, and lurched into the cold. I didn't dare look back. They could have been a foot behind me and I wouldn't have known, and I was too scared to find out.

Breaths coming in shallow gasps, I raced over rough

ground. Rocks bit into my feet and wind whipped hair into my eyes as rain drenched my body. At this point, I didn't care that I was running naked in the middle of nowhere, exposed to the weather.

A streak of lightning lit up the sky, and I saw a break in the trees.

"Alex!"

My heart pounded in my chest, as loud as the thunder overhead as I recognized the fury in Rafe's voice. He sounded much too close. I buckled down and made for the trees, hoping to find a road on the other side, the source of the highway noise I'd noticed before from inside the kitchen.

"Stop! Alex!"

I broke through the line of Douglas firs in a full out sprint, but it wasn't a road beyond the trees. Lightning lit up the sky again, and for that mere second, I saw the water. Rain pounded the surface, causing a choppy and violent scene. I skidded, my bare feet scraping over pebbles and dirt, and tried to halt forward motion.

I was too late.

With a terrified shriek, I tipped over the edge, my body twisting around as I fell in with a splash. More lightning streaked the heavens, and I saw Rafe's horrified expression. I screamed for him, arms reaching and thrashing as I sank into the freezing depths. Water closed over my face, and the murky void pulled me under.

Pulled me away from him. Away from my only hope of

being saved. I sure as hell couldn't save myself. I couldn't even swim.

I fought, kicked, prayed to reach the surface, and blindly grasped for something to cling to. My lungs burned with the need to breathe. Oh God, it was unbearable. Body going limp, I finally gave up the battle, accepting imminent death. Maybe I deserved it. Maybe it was better this way. At least I'd get the chance to see Mom again, get a chance to explain, to beg her forgiveness.

I thought of Rafe as I opened my mouth and allowed the water to fill my lungs. A sense of peace cocooned me, and I said goodbye to him, told him I loved him. As everything faded to black, I felt hands grabbing me. My body moved swiftly upward, then...nothing.

"Fucking breathe, Alex!"

Someone pounded on my chest.

"Shit, man. I'm so sorry. I shouldn't have let her get away."

"Breathe!"

The voices were strained, as if coming from constricted throats. Cold, wet drops fell on my face, and at first I thought they were tears, but tears were hot and salty, and these drops were like icy pinpricks on my cheeks. Something loud rumbled overhead, blocking out the voices, and the ground vibrated. I felt soft, surprisingly warm lips on mine, opening my mouth and breathing life into me. I came to with a violent cough that seized my body.

"That's it, cough it up." Cold fingers turned my head to

the side, and a flood of water erupted from my mouth. I opened my eyes and found Rafe perched over me, his arms supporting his weight and his face inches from mine. "You scared the fucking shit out of me!" he screamed. Water dripped from his hair, down his nose and off his chin.

And his eyes...they narrowed to furious slits. He jumped to his feet and reached out a hand. "Get up," he said between tight lips.

I let him pull me up, and my body quaked uncontrollably. I was still trying to calm down from almost drowning, but as soon as another streak of lightning shot across the sky, the situation hit me head-on.

Too much water.

All around me.

My heart pounded in my ears, galloping at an unbearable speed as panic took over. A keening cry tore from my lips, and I doubled over, hugging my midsection as the world around me tilted. "Why?" That single word squeezed from my throat. "Why would you bring me here?"

"Why do you think?" Shaking his head, Rafe glanced at Jax, who stood off to the side observing the drama unfolding between Rafe and me. "I knew you couldn't escape, but I never thought you'd run and almost get yourself killed!"

I decided not to point out the fact that any sane person would try to run. "Where are we? What is this place?"

"Mason Island." He swept the area with a hand. "But

since you're so set on leaving, there's a boat at the dock. Feel free."

"You know I can't!"

"Don't I know it," he said with a sinister laugh. "Why do you think I brought you here?" He pushed me back enough so his eyes bored into mine. "You'll fucking do as I say because there's nowhere for you to go. We both know you won't come anywhere near this water again."

"I hate you!" I screamed, pounding on his chest.

He easily deflected the blows. "Not nearly as much as I hate you. Now move your ass." He pulled me away from the river, toward the cabin, I assumed. I stumbled along numbly, eyes on the ground, one foot in front of the other, and never quite registered anything around me. I could only think of one thing.

Water. Too much water.

He hadn't needed to lock me up. My fear held me prisoner more effectively than any conventional method he could have used. The chains, the shackles, the cage—they'd all been props to mess with my head. As I followed him back toward the cabin, something inside me finally broke. My fear of water stemmed from a near-drowning experience when I was four, and I'd never learned to swim.

Rafe had known. He'd been the one to fish me out of my family's pool when I was fourteen, after Zach "accidentally" knocked me in. My brother had been particularly mean that day, probably because Rafe had stopped by, and I hadn't been able to keep my eyes off him.

How ironic that my phobia was his most powerful weapon.

The three of us entered the cabin through the door off the kitchen, and Rafe switched on a light. Unable to stop shivering, I wrapped my arms around myself and clenched my jaw to stop my teeth from clanking together.

Rafe shrugged out of his soaked black shirt, flung it over a chair, and moved it away from the table. "Jax, take a seat over there, would ya?"

Jax gave him a funny look but followed the request.

"No, I need you to turn the chair around, so the back faces the table."

"Sure thing." Jax turned the chair and plopped onto it before removing his own wet T-shirt.

My gaze traveled between them, back and forth, and I felt as if I were missing something. I'd just tried to escape. I'd almost drowned, and they were acting nonchalant. Too nonchalant. What the hell was going on here?

Rafe's gaze fell on me, and for a few heavy moments, I didn't breathe. That look, his lips thin, eyes narrowed, made my pulse rocket. A clap of thunder sounded, and I jumped.

Rafe pulled the belt from his pants.

I backed up. "What are you doing?"

He didn't give me a chance to retreat. With a yank on my arm, he brought me closer and wound the belt around my wrists.

"Rafe...please—"

He pulled the leather tight, and I gasped as he bent me over the table with a hard shove. Drops of water landed on the wood, and my breasts flattened against the surface.

He pushed my arms across the table and tossed the other end of the belt at Jax. "Knot it around the chair."

"Rafe?" My voice came out unusually high-pitched, and I swiveled my head in time to see him take down the paddle he'd pointed out earlier that morning. "You wouldn't."

Jax snickered as he attached the belt around a slot in the chair. I pulled on it, but it wouldn't give.

"I definitely would." Rafe brought my attention back to him. His voice chilled me, sending dread and remorse through my blood. Dread for what was coming, and remorse for my actions. I should have been smarter about trying to escape. I should have taken a few days to gain his trust first. This attempt had turned into a disaster.

"My old man only used this on my brother and me a handful of times. It hurt like hell, and you can bet your ass we learned quick. You're about to learn quick too."

I stiffened as he halted behind me. Waiting for that first strike was the worst part, and when he finally did crack that paddle across my ass, I lost my breath for what seemed like forever, though it must have only been a mere instant before he did it again. I jumped from foot to foot and bit into my lip to keep from yowling. I wouldn't give him the satisfaction of voicing my pain.

And I never, ever wanted him to know how this was

turning me on. My face burned from humiliation—not from what he was doing, but rather from my own sick reaction to it.

"C'mon, sweetheart, scream for me. Beg me to stop."

"No," I ground out through gritted teeth.

He struck again, and this time I let out an involuntary yelp.

"That's better."

Crack!

"Stop!" I clenched my thighs, and my hands fisted within the restraint of the belt. Jax caught my gaze, and I noticed his fingers curling around the chair back, knuckles turning ash-white. He licked his lips, eyes glazed over with arousal.

Rafe continued to paddle my ass, and the three of us fell into an odd sort of silence. There was no talking, and I held back any sounds of pain, or God forbid, pleasure. Only the smack of thick wood to skin echoed through the room.

I drifted into a space outside myself as Rafe increased the pressure of the strikes. After about thirty, he set the paddle down on the table, his breathing coming fast and hard. I sensed him moving closer, heard a zipper lower, and I tightened my already clenched muscles.

"Spread your legs."

Hands forming fists, I let my head drop to the table as I parted my thighs. Mortification burned my cheeks again, hotter than before because he was about to fuck me in front of his friend. Even worse, they were about to learn the truth about me.

His hands fell to my hips, and he entered me with a single, forceful plunge. "Fuck, you're wet." He laughed, thrusting so hard, he pushed me higher onto the table until my feet left the floor. "I would've never guessed. You get off on this shit, don't you?"

A tear leaked out, and I squeezed my eyes shut. "I'm sorry," I said with a moan.

"Are you apologizing because you get off on pain and humiliation, or are you apologizing for something else?"

"I'm just...sorry." Sorry for being the way I was because my fucked up nature was at the root of why he'd gone to prison. I was sorry for so much.

He slowed the pace, his cock sliding in and out with gentle rhythm. I scratched my nails on the surface of the table and moaned.

Jax let out a moan too. I lifted my head as he reached for his zipper. His head fell back, hooded eyes watching me as his hand pumped in his lap.

Rafe's shallow thrusts tormented me, rubbing in just the right spot. My need dripped down my thighs, seeping from my body in a gentle pull that made me grind my teeth. I abused the air with deep, throaty cries.

"I need to come," I begged.

"No, you're not getting off. If you do, I'll choke you again."

I gasped. "I can't hold back!"

"I said no." He smacked my ass and rammed me. Hard. Painfully hard. I concentrated on anything but him moving inside me. The thunder reverberating overhead, the hard edge of the table biting into my belly, the eerie howl of a train. Even Jax's grunts as he neared orgasm. Anything but Rafe.

It wasn't enough. I was going to come again, and he was going to choke me, a thought that terrified me. I could handle a lot of things, but having my air cut off wasn't one of them. Unbidden, the image of Zach entered my mind, and I held onto it, remembered all the times he'd dragged my panties down and pinned me to the bed. My bed. The one place I was supposed to feel safest. I recalled how he'd muffled my sobs in the pillow, how he'd beaten me in places where the bruises wouldn't show. Still, my body had turned on me.

This was his fault. He'd made me the way I was, and I hated him for it.

Rafe pushed into me one last time and stilled, fisting my hair as he came. Jax came too, as if they'd timed it. His breathing gradually slowed as he traced a lazy path down my back. Gooseflesh erupted from his touch—a sensation that contrasted with the searing ache in my core. He released my hands, picked me up, and threw my soaked body over his shoulder like a sack of potatoes. Water dripped from my hair and left a trail on the floor as he carried me toward the cellar. He stopped on the way and grabbed a towel from the bathroom.

I was shivering violently when he approached the cage. "Don't leave me in there. Please." I clutched his wet jeans, but he dislodged me way too easily and set me on my feet.

"Two nights, Alex. That's what your little escape attempt earned you." He kept me at his side, one hand fisting my hair as he unlocked the cage. He shoved me inside, and the towel landed on the concrete at my feet.

I turned around and helplessly watched while he shut and secured the door. "Rafe...please..." I blinked several times, but his unwavering expression swam in my vision.

"Do I need to restrain your hands?"

"Why would you need to do that?" I gestured to my prison. "It's not like I'm going anywhere."

He laughed. "No masturbating."

The idea of touching myself was the last thing on my mind. In fact, I was pretty certain if I did, it would only make me want the real thing more. I still ached for him, so much, despite the wall of bars standing between us while he held the key to my freedom.

"I'll be back in the morning to feed you." He turned, as if I meant nothing, and once again the darkness suffocated me.

TWELVE

RAFE

Two things haunted me: I had a son I'd yet to meet, and I had a naked captive in the cellar—a tempting, kinky one I ached to fuck again. I adjusted my jeans and tried to force my mind onto other things, but the fact that two days had gone by, in which I hadn't dealt with either issue, wouldn't leave me alone.

Neither would Nikki. She'd tried calling several times —I had eight unheard messages on my cell but was too chicken-shit to listen to them, let alone return her calls. I had no clue what to say to her anyway, mainly because she had no clue I'd kidnapped a woman and was now holding said woman in my cellar. Those weren't exactly the actions of father material. The kid was probably better off never knowing me.

The cabin was too fucking quiet, too still. Alex had remained unnervingly silent, even when I'd gone down there to feed her, and Jax had gone into work. Enough was enough. She was mine—mine to play with, mine to torment. Fucking *mine*. If I wanted to fuck her again, I would. No more thoughts of how terrified she'd looked when she'd fallen into the river, or how my heart stopped as I tried to get hers working again.

My footsteps fell heavily on the stairs, and when I reached the bottom, I found her huddled in her favorite corner, her cheek to the concrete and body curled into a ball underneath the towel I'd left with her. It was cruel and inhumane, but damn, it was a sight I'd never forget. Besides, better to be hard and mean now, get her to fall into line, than return her to the cellar numerous times because I'd been too soft on her. I definitely didn't want a repeat of the river.

Something enfolded my heart and squeezed. Fuck, she'd almost died, and whether I liked it or not, part of me would have died with her. My actions had nearly gotten her killed, and regardless of what she'd done, I couldn't live with myself if anything happened to her. I wanted to punish her, but I also couldn't deny that I straight up wanted her. *Period.*

She'd become my world, my obsession, and I had no plans to let her off this island.

"If I let you out, will you behave?"

"Yes," she said, the word falling from her lips in lifeless fashion. Maybe I'd finally broken her.

"Will you try to run again?"

"You know I won't. Where would I go?"

"Things are going to change around here. No more tantrums, no more back-talking or throwing dishes." I paused long enough to unlock the cage and enter. "No more escape attempts. You'll do as you're told, when you're told, without argument, or next time you'll spend a lot more time down here. Do you understand me?"

"Y...yes," she said through chattering teeth. "I'm so cold."

Damn it. I was walking a fine line between breaking her and risking her becoming ill. "Okay." Crouching, I brushed tangled hair from her eyes. A strand caught between her lips, and I ran a finger along the seam of her mouth to remove it. Her lips were chapped, her face pale, but what bothered me most was the emptiness in her expression. I remembered how deep her fear of water ran, and I shuddered as images flashed in my mind. Her eyes wide with terror, arms reaching for me as she splashed into the murky river.

Shaking off the recollections, I pulled her to her feet, then stood back and gave her time to stretch her muscles. "C'mon," I said, reaching out a hand. "Let's get you clean and warm, then you can start that good behavior by making dinner." We made our way up to my bedroom, where I directed her into the bathroom. Her eyes grew large and round at the sight of the garden tub.

"Alex, the shower." I pointed to the huge stall tucked on

the other side of the tub. Last thing I needed was an episode of hysterics.

She folded her arms. "You don't have to stay. I can shower on my own. There's nowhere for me to—" She cut off when she turned to face me. Her gaze followed my movements as I lifted the hem of my T-shirt up my chest, and I couldn't help the smirk that flitted across my lips.

"No, sweetheart. I'm getting in with you." I gestured toward the stall, a large enclosure of walls made with blue and grey tile. A narrow opening served as the entrance. She gawked at me for a few seconds, and I was so close to shoving her inside because shit...I couldn't wait to get my hands on her body.

THIRTEEN

ALEX

M y mouth gaped at his muscular chest, and I couldn't tear my eyes from him when he lowered his jeans. The charcoal gray boxer briefs went the way of his pants. He displayed his body without shame or modesty. I took in every inch of him, especially the dark tribal lines that streaked across the left side of his chest and down both arms. I wanted to follow that map with my lips and fingertips, wanted to lick down his muscles, past his abs, only stopping long enough to tease his erection with my tongue.

"Have you seen enough yet?"

I jumped, lifting my attention to his face, and felt my own flush. Furious Rafe scared the shit out of me, and naked, lustful-looking Rafe made me just as nervous. Both versions were passionate and cold, stable one minute yet irrational the next. I lowered my gaze to his erection. Moisture collected at the tip, and some secret part of my psyche celebrated. I did that to him, without even touching him.

He couldn't hide his desire like I could mine, collecting between my closed thighs, stowed away and out of sight.

This was the first time I'd felt anything during the past two days. While locked away in the dark, I'd found a way to shut down. Maybe I'd experienced a delayed reaction to the horror of nearly drowning, but when he left me alone in that cellar, shivering more violently than ever before, my brain simply stopped functioning like normal. Somehow, I'd found a way to cope.

I'd pretended to be somewhere else. Someone else. I'd made up a new identity. In my new dream world, I called myself Amy. Amy was plain and boring and absurdly *happy*. Amy had a loving, devoted husband, two adorable kids, and a perfect, non-smelly dog named Zippo. Amy lived in the south, possibly Arizona, where it was dry and sweltering under the sun.

"Get in," Rafe said, bunching his hands, and the fantasy of another life dissolved, leaving cold, hard truth in its wake.

I resisted the urge to cover myself as I entered the shower. Next to his beautiful physique, my filthy and unkempt body with curves in all the wrong places paled in comparison.

He stepped in after me and turned on the dual shower heads. Hot spray filled every corner, hitting us from all directions. I gasped when he shoved me against the freezing tile. Without a word, he grabbed a bottle of shampoo and squirted some into a palm before rubbing both hands together.

I closed my eyes and focused on breathing as he started washing my hair, but when he added more soap and slid his hands down my shoulders and over my breasts, I almost came undone, unprepared for those hands gliding over me. As his fingers blazed along my skin, I wrestled with my demons, the ones that lived to remind me of what a dirty whore I was. I'd never experienced what was considered a normal physical reaction to sex, the ability to enjoy it without the threat of force or violence. No one had ever made me feel like this. Rafe had more power in a single touch than Zach had in his entire being.

The heat flaming between my thighs was undeniable, unbearable, and I whimpered when those strong hands drifted over my stomach and smoothed down my legs.

"I'll have to buy you a shaving kit." He caressed behind a knee. "I want to shave these legs."

A shiver traveled along my skin from head to toe, contradictory to the hot shower. He worked his way up my body and tilted my head so the water sluiced over my face and hair.

"Soap's gone. You can open your eyes now." His gaze transfixed me, capturing me in green depths from which I'd never return. "Raise your arms."

Later, I might question why I did it without hesitation. I brought my arms up and held them high. I didn't think about disobeying, especially when he dropped to his knees and licked his lips, his gaze on my pussy.

"Spread your legs."

Holy hell. Sucking in a breath, I widened my stance. He wrapped his arms around my hips, hands clutching my ass, and pulled my pelvis toward his face. But he didn't put his mouth on me. Not yet. He took his time, languid gaze roaming past belly and breasts before settling on my face.

The sight of Rafe naked and on his knees, dark hair plastered to his forehead and drops of water hanging on his lashes, was the most gorgeous view in existence. Reality was far better than the dream.

Except for the part where he'd kidnapped me.

"What do you want from me?" I whispered, confused because he was being so gentle. He'd shown me nothing but cruel detachment since he'd taken me...until I'd fallen into the river.

A violent tremor raced through me, and that night came rushing back; the freezing water closing over my head, the realization I was going to die. Something else broke through the fog that had blanketed me for the past couple of days. Him. The way he'd reacted, how he'd been furious and punishing but also fearful of losing me.

It dawned on me that my almost drowning had rattled him, and I wondered what it meant.

His gaze held mine, unblinking as water streamed down his face. "I want many things from you, but right now I want to taste you." He leaned forward, and I thought I'd pass out when his tongue slid between my folds.

"Oh God, Rafe."

His fingers dug into my ass, and he let out a long groan that vibrated straight to my core. I balled my hands, struggling to keep them raised, and let my head fall back against the tile. My body sang for him, quivered and ached with the mere brush of his lips, the teasing scrape of teeth. My breaths burst out in short gasps, and I closed my eyes and let the water wash over my forehead and cheeks as an orgasm built. I was so close. Two more strokes of his tongue, and my toes would curl. I'd slide to the floor in completion, limbs as fluid as the water beating down on us.

He jerked back and looked up at me, a hard glint in his eyes.

"Don't stop." I thrust my hips toward him, a silent plea for him to finish. He rose and held my face, mouth hovering an inch from mine as our eyes locked, and licked the water from his lips.

My jaw slackened, and I felt the spray from the shower misting on my tongue. He was going to kiss me. I was sure of it. "Rafe," I whispered, aching to taste him. Just once.

He pulled my arms down. "Wrap your hand around me."

I closed my fingers around his erection, and my palm glided over silky smooth skin. His breath shuddered out with every stroke and mingled with mine in a frenzy of want and need. The air between us grew moist and warm from the steam of the shower.

"Fuck," he groaned, his forehead falling against mine, "that feels incredible. Keep going."

Mindlessly, I rubbed him and watched in wonder as he lost himself to my touch. With each groan and sigh that erupted from his beautiful mouth, my own need bloomed out of control.

"I want you so much," I said.

He let out a growl and stilled my movement. "You're not getting off."

If he intended to drive me mad by using my desire for him as a weapon, then he'd have no problem succeeding.

Rafe had turned into a cruel son of a bitch.

"Get on your knees, sweetheart." How I hated that endearment coming from his lips. He said it with scorn, made it sound like an insult. Hands gripping my shoulders, he pushed down hard until my knees buckled.

The thought of sucking his cock shouldn't excite me so much. Shit, I was in big trouble. He was toying with me, making me hot and wet for him, and leaving me with no end in sight.

He angled my head back, his touch somehow gentle despite the iron-like hold he had on me. I opened my mouth, my heart thudding in my ears as he pushed his cock inside.

"Fuck. I haven't had a woman suck me off in eight years."

His admission filled me with a sense of power. I'd be the one to bring him pleasure after all this time. I closed my lips around his shaft and peeked up at him, needing the connection, but he avoided eye contact. He tipped forward, palms slamming against the tile, and his chest rose and fell shallowly, biceps rippling, tattoos a dark sheen underneath the water.

He grunted with each thrust, and his essence infused my tongue with the heady taste of him. I wanted him inside me so badly—a desperate need I was certain would destroy me.

You're not getting off.

Eventually, he was going to fuck me again.

And eventually, I was going to break from frustration.

FOURTEEN

RAFE

Holy shit. Her mouth was heaven. Hot, almost too damn hot, and tight around my dick. She took her time with the tip, rolling her tongue in circular motions before licking down the underside. My head dropped against the tile, and my mind shattered, thoughts lost to the roar of the water. I couldn't look at her, didn't want her to see how completely unglued I was.

This spitfire of a woman, a woman I had every reason to hate, made me question everything.

Damn, it'd been too fucking long since I'd had a woman on her knees pleasuring me. I tried convincing myself that was the only reason for the intensity in my groin, that it had nothing to do with *who* was sucking my cock, but that didn't fly. I thrust my hips forward, needing to go deeper. Faster.

She edged back and made a gagging noise, but I

shoved my hands into her wet, tangled hair and growled. No way in hell was I letting her pull away. She was going to swallow my load, every last bit of it. I expected her to fight me, but instead she did something that stunned the hell out of me; she fondled my balls in her warm palm and moaned. Fuck, Alex getting off on sucking my cock was fucking amazing.

I glanced down and found her gaze trained on me as her lips slid along my shaft. Hot damn...she was good at this. The sexiest thing about her eyes was the genuine need in them. She wasn't putting on a show or giving me a fake sultry stare like other women used to. She took me deep in her throat and gagged, but she didn't retreat.

"Alex..." I hissed in a breath between clenched teeth. "That. Keep doing *that*. Almost there."

She gagged again, and that was my undoing. Thank God for small favors. I curled my fingers in her strands, holding her immobile, and pushed deeper. I wanted as deep as possible—wanted her helpless because up until then, she'd held all the power.

My mind disconnected, floating where only liberation existed, and I ground my eyes shut, groaning as my release spurted down her throat.

She finished swallowing, and reluctantly, I let her pull those amazing lips from my shaft. Her needy expression was almost too much, and when she placed a tender kiss on the tip of my cock, something inside me wanted to crack. I almost did. She was bringing me back from the brink, bit by bit, and only the reminder of the hell she'd put me through kept me on course.

She whispered my name, a question in her tone.

"Quiet," I said, not ungently, but I seriously needed a few seconds to collect myself. Damn it, my dick was still hard. I hated that I didn't have a handle on my control, but I guessed that was to be expected after going so long without sex, and fucking her twice wasn't enough. I suspected it would never be enough with her.

I was *this* close to taking her to bed, and if I had my way, we wouldn't leave it for at least three days.

I couldn't do that. Giving her exactly what she wanted, which ironically was me, wasn't what I intended to do. Maybe someday, after she came clean with the truth, we could really work past our problems and find a fucked up version of normal.

Our normal.

I didn't see that happening for a while. Too much of me still hated her...but too much of me still wanted her. How more messed up could I get?

I shut off the water, stepped from the shower, and grabbed two towels before handing her one.

She wrapped her body in soft green terrycloth. "Can I please have my clothes back now?"

"No way." I ran my gaze up and down her body, taking in her long legs, the gentle swell of cleavage, and the curve of her waist. Even obscured by the towel, she was the definition of fuckable. "I like knowing you're naked and accessible at all times. If I tell you to bend over so I can fuck you, I don't want clothing in the way."

She wouldn't look at me as she finished drying her skin, then, with her lower lip caught between her teeth, she slowly let the towel drop. "I'm ready."

Somehow, I guessed there was a double meaning to those words. I'd bet the deed to this island she was still wet and throbbing for me, which was how I wanted her. In fact, I wanted her in a constant state of arousal. My cock twitched at the thought. Playing this game with her could be more fun than I imagined.

I quickly dressed and led her down the ladder and into the kitchen. Grabbing a beer from the fridge, I settled at the table and popped the cap. "Start dinner."

She seemed lost at first, her gaze veering in my direction every so often as she perused the kitchen. I wondered if she even knew how to cook, considering her spoiled upbringing included an on-demand chef and a housekeeper. I didn't feel obliged to give her any pointers. I rather enjoyed watching her flounder. If she wanted to stay out of trouble, she'd figure out how to make something edible. After five minutes of opening and closing the cupboard doors, followed by the fridge and freezer, she settled on baking chicken.

She bent over, her perfect ass aiming straight at me, as she slid the pan into the oven, and by the time she shut the door, I had a raging hard-on again. My body wanted her constantly, and I couldn't stop myself from grabbing her, mid-stride, and settling her on my lap. I pushed her legs apart until she straddled me, and she had to realize exactly what I needed from her. Wrapping a hand around the back of her neck, I drew her close, aching to taste her lips, but I stopped before we connected.

Kissing was intimate. Kissing usually fucked everything up by bringing feelings into the mix. But hell, she smelled amazing—a mixture of soap and something that was one hundred percent Alex.

Her stomach rumbled, reminding me that she was supposed to be finishing dinner, not sitting on my lap, tempting me to fuck her or do something as asinine as *kiss* her.

"You're driving me crazy," she said, head falling back and eyes drifting shut. A frustrated sigh escaped her lips.

She was driving *me* crazy. I grabbed her hips and pulled her snug against my cock, and the only thing keeping me from fucking her was my own damn clothing. Maybe we should both walk around naked. I rubbed against her, and the rough texture of my jeans created friction on her clit.

She moaned, her head falling to my shoulder, tits smashing against my chest as she clung to me. "I can't take much more of this."

"If you tell me why you lied, I'll make you come so fucking hard, you'll forget your own name."

With a shudder, she tangled her hands in my hair, fingers clutching in desperation. "You're evil," she groaned.

If her touch didn't feel so good, I would have trapped her hands behind her back.

"Tell me, sweetheart," I said, my lips brushing her ear. "Tell me what I want to know, and I'll put you out of your misery." I gripped her nape and scraped my teeth across her throat. "But if you keep up this bullshit, you're gonna learn what the female equivalent of blue balls is." I rubbed against her again to make my point. She trembled in my arms, and I felt the dampness from her pussy seeping through my jeans.

"You were right the other night," she said. "I was young and selfish. I couldn't handle you rejecting me."

Now that she'd said the words, they didn't ring true. I'd known she had a thing for me, but would she really sink so low as to ruin my life because I wouldn't touch jailbait? I wasn't sure why I hadn't considered it before, but something else was going on...something she was hiding. I pushed her to her feet, gave her a dark smile when she pulled that lower lip between her teeth, and reached for the button on my pants. Her gaze settled on my lap and never strayed as I inched down my zipper. I freed my cock, grabbed her hips and twirled her around, and pulled her onto my shaft.

She was so fucking wet.

Wrapping both arms around her, I brought a hand up and circled her throat. Our bodies slapped together in a crazy rhythm that tilted me closer to the edge with each thrust.

"You're lying to me."

"I'm not," she bit out with a groan, and it was such a torturous sound one would think I was beating the shit out of her instead of fucking her.

I flexed my fingers. "Tell me the truth and I'll let you come."

She remained silent, and I wasn't sure if she flat-out refused to talk, or if she was scared to. Either way, I'd find out the truth, and I wouldn't stop pushing until she told me. I nibbled her neck, eliciting a moan from deep in her throat. I increased the pressure of my hand and held her to me when she started thrashing.

I needed this, needed those few heightened seconds as she fought for survival while I spilled into her. I was doing just that, her body going limp in my arms, when Jax walked through the door. "Damn, man. You didn't tell me tonight was dinner and a show night."

FIFTEEN

ALEX

I slept in Rafe's bed, and for the first time since he'd kidnapped me a week ago, I actually slept. Really slept. Most surprising was how he liked to cuddle. I remembered the way he held on to me the night I tried to escape, but I thought he'd done it to keep me from taking off.

Now that he knew I had no intention of leaving the cabin, the way he held my body all night—one palm on my breast while the other wedged between my thighs—I realized this was how he liked to sleep. But what I found even more surprising was how I got any sleep at all, considering the placement of his hands.

So was the way in which I awoke, with his fist clamping around both wrists and his erection pushing into my mouth.

I opened my eyes and found him straddling my chest,

dark hair tumbling onto his forehead as he gazed at me. Well-defined muscles rippled underneath black lines of ink. His body was a masterpiece, God's finest art, and those green eyes...I'd never tire of losing myself in them. I hadn't outgrown him at all, not during the last eight years, not even now that he'd kidnapped me and revealed the darkness festering inside him.

Part of me craved his sinful obsidian desires.

He pulled out and plunged back in, and I rolled my tongue around the tip, tasting the musky salt that signified his need. He braced himself upright, one hand on the headboard, and pushed deeper. I loved how smooth and solid he was in my mouth. I always gagged while giving head, but I wanted to take him all the way in, deep in my throat, and I didn't give a shit if I gagged or not.

He stilled with a shudder, and his lids drooped, though his eyes never left mine, never stopped giving off their hypnotic vibe. "Do you like sucking me off?"

His husky voice doused my skin in a blissful chill, and I tingled all over, tightening my lips around the base of his cock.

"Fuck, Alex, you've got the hottest damn mouth." He started moving again, a slow, torturous pace—torturous because the longer he took, the more I wanted him filling someplace else.

"You're fucking gorgeous, curls everywhere, those lips wrapped around my dick." He tightened his hold on my wrists. "I could get used to waking you up like this."

Oh God, so could I, if he'd only let me come. I clenched my thighs together, but it did nothing to relieve the ache that had throbbed since last night, since he'd choked me into unconsciousness.

He increased the pace, and the taste of him intensified, as did the pressure on my wrists when he edged back and pinched my nose. I flailed in a panic, legs kicking, and tried to pull free of his erection, but he shoved it down my throat and smothered me.

Our gazes crashed together, and my pulse pounded in my temples, ticking away the seconds.

"Trust me, I won't kill you, but I can do this all day. Thirty more seconds, and your lungs will ignite. Blink twice if you're ready to tell me what you're hiding."

I didn't flutter an eyelash. Thing was, I did trust him. He wouldn't kill me. He wouldn't. My body was fast forgetting that though as I struggled for air, as my lungs burned for it.

He pulled out, and I sucked in a gasping breath before he pushed in again, deep down. "How long do you wanna play this game?"

I told myself not to panic and resorted to using the only weapon I had—my mouth. I added suction and swirled my tongue, flicked and darted until his hips thrust in abandon. I couldn't breathe, but I didn't care because I was about to send him over the edge, I could already tell.

"*Fuck*," he said with a growl as he came. He let go of my nose, and I almost choked as he spilled down my throat.

He yanked out, and some of his cum spurted onto my lips and chin. "You play dirty."

"Not nearly as dirty as you!" I said, still gasping for air.

His lips quirked up in a lopsided grin. "You have no idea." He curled my fingers around the bars of the headboard before sliding down my body. "Spread your legs."

"No!"

"Spread your *fucking* legs."

Something about his tone made me tremble. I opened my thighs without another word of protest, and he slid his hands underneath my ass, thumbs skimming the entrance of my sex. His mouth parted, hot breath igniting me, and I arch into his erotic kiss with a moan, fingers squeezing the shit out of the bars as his tongue burrowed into me.

My legs fell to the sides, quaking uncontrollably. I gritted my teeth as my center coiled, seconds away from coming undone when he switched to light, closed-mouthed kisses that torturously teased. I held my breath, refusing to cry out in frustration. I needed to come, so bad, and I was seconds away from begging him for it, from grabbing at his skin as if it were my lifeline.

I wanted him all over me, inside me, and wrapping me in his raw and brutal strength.

"Please, Rafe—"

He closed his lips over my clit, and I bowed over the mattress with a wail. He flicked his tongue, just light enough to drive me insane. "Rafe, please...for the love of

God, I need more." The headboard shook under the force of my grip.

"So do I," he said, words vibrating along my pussy. "I need the truth." He worked his way to my core, tongue lapping up moisture, before returning to my downfall— that little spot that was an instant away from sending me hurtling into ecstasy-like chaos. Pushing a finger into me, his tongue pressed on my clit hard.

"Oh God...oh my fucking *God*..."

He pulled away, and an anguished cry tore from my throat. He propped his head on a hand and looked at me between shamelessly spread legs, my knees bent on either side of him and feet flat on the mattress.

"How bad do you want it?"

"Stupid question."

"Wrong answer." He kissed my hip, then dragged his lips up my stomach before sucking a nipple into his mouth. He slid a palm between my legs and stoked the blaze raging inside me. I thrust my pelvis into his touch, arched my spine, and was about to shatter when he stopped again. My breath expelled in a rush. I hated and loved him all at once, and my body was on the same page.

He brought his hands to my neck and clamped down, and I knew without a doubt he was going to choke me again. I prepared my useless fists to pound against his steel body.

"Fight me, sweetheart."

I stiffened at his demand and refused to move. Part of

me wanted to rebel, wanted to gain the upper hand even as he threatened to stifle me.

With a growl, he increased the pressure until I opened my mouth under his crushing weight.

"You're gonna put up a fight, whether you want to or not."

Bastard.

The compression on my neck became unbearable, and the need to break free kicked in. I beat on his chest, shoved against his arms, and made it to my knees, a move he must have allowed because he was too strong for me. My face screamed for relief as I used all the force I had, but I still couldn't get his hands off my throat. We fell to the floor, and I landed hard on my back. He pinned me down, forced my legs apart, and settled his erection at my entrance.

"You want my cock?"

I gasped, more concerned with breathing than with fucking. "Rafe...stop..." I clawed at his fingers, desperate to get free. His gaze never left mine, and I realized this was how he got off. He craved my helplessness, perhaps because my actions had rendered him helpless for so long.

Or maybe because Rafe "The Choker" Mason got his kicks in holding the lives of others in his hands.

"You're hurting me." Tears leaked out and burned tracks down my cheeks.

He pushed into me violently. "Fuck," he groaned. "Your refusal to tell me the truth is hurting you." His hands pressed harder on my throat.

My body reacted instinctively, and I kicked and squirmed, my useless fingers gouging his. "Please," I squeaked, but the fucked up part was how I was getting wetter with each thrust, despite him choking me. The edges of the room grew dark, and I felt weightless as I drifted into nothingness.

His erratic breathing washed over me as my lids fluttered open. I gripped my throat, wheezing air into burning lungs. He was still pumping, and I was on the verge of coming, even after losing consciousness, when Jax dropped the ladder and popped his head through the opening.

"Dude. Someone just showed up."

SIXTEEN

RAFE

Too many thoughts battled in my head. The possibilities were endless and in each one, someone discovered Alex. A cop. Nikki. Even Zach. I didn't like unexpected developments. Since her declared death had hit the news, I'd grown lax.

My mistake.

I pulled out of her and wound an arm around her neck, smothering her mouth with my hand. "Who is it? Did you let them in?"

Jax shook his head. "It's a woman. I have no idea who she is or what she wants."

"Grab the duct tape from my dresser," I told him. "Top drawer."

He moved quickly and pulled out the tape, and all the while, Alex struggled, her protests coming out as muffled whines. As Jax pulled a strip from the roll, I picked her up and tossed her onto the bed. He and I worked together to get the tape over her mouth. I wound my belt around her wrists and anchored her hands to the headboard.

"Sit tight. We're not done yet." I got to my feet and threw on a pair of jeans and a T-shirt, and Jax led the way down the steps.

"A woman's here?"

"A hot blonde," he said. "I didn't let her in, and boy was she pissed."

Fuck.

Had to be Nikki. Once we touched ground, Jax folded the stepladder to the loft. I cast a glance toward the front door, dread twisting my gut for what waited on the other side.

"I tried telling her you were sleeping, but she wouldn't leave."

"I'm not surprised. If it's who I think it is, she doesn't have an agreeable bone in her body." I strode to the door, Jax on my heels, and pulled it open. She stood tapping a foot, arms crossed with a scowl on her face. "Who's the watchdog?" She jabbed a finger in Jax's direction.

"I think the real question," he said, lip curling, "is who the hell are you?"

"Who the hell am I?" She clenched her hands.

Double fuck.

"That's what I said, 'cause from where I'm standing, you're nothing but a stranger on my doorstep. A gorgeous stranger, but still."

She let out a growl of indignation, and I spoke before things escalated. "He's my roommate. What are you doing here, Nik?" And how could I get rid of her before the whole damn situation crumbled to the ground? I glanced over my shoulder and let out a small breath, as if I expected to find Alex standing behind me.

"I'm overwhelmed by the warm welcome." Nikki stepped forward, a sign she wanted to come inside. "I've been calling, or had you not noticed?"

"I noticed." Another glance behind me, another expelled breath. Thankfully, nothing but silence came from upstairs. "Can we meet somewhere in town later? Now isn't a good time."

She shook her head. "That's what I've been trying to tell you. You might want to avoid town for a while. Lyle's got it out for you, been saying all kinds of crazy things. People are starting to talk. He thinks you had something to do with that girl's death."

Jax stood straighter, his back rigid. I knew what he was thinking, but I wasn't about to let some small town gossip bring us down. I willed my face into a mask, though my pulse throbbed at my temples. "What girl?"

Her eyes widened. "You haven't heard?"

I arched a brow. "Heard what?"

"The girl who sent you to jail, her car was found in the river a few days ago. They said it was an accident, but Lyle thinks you had something to do with it." She raised her brows, and her forehead creased under honey blond wisps of bangs. "The timing's kind of convenient though. They found her car just twenty miles from here." She swept a hand between us. "And now you're here."

"You think I had something to do with it?" I dragged a hand through my unruly hair.

"No, I'm just saying I can see why some people might talk."

Jax folded his arms. "My head is spinnin' here, guys." He gave Nikki a slow once-over. "Who's Lyle, and who the hell are you?"

The first woman to catch his attention, and it would have to be the mother of my kid.

"Jax, this is Nikki."

"Well that tells me a lot."

I sighed. "We went to high school together. She's engaged to..." Fuck, he wasn't going to like this. "Lyle, the sheriff."

"*Perfect*." He gave me a pointed look, and I hoped Nikki didn't notice.

She took another step forward. "Can I come in, please? You took off so fast the other night—"

"Let's go for a walk," I interrupted as I wedged my feet into my sneakers by the door. I glanced at Jax, and he gave an imperceptible nod. We were good at communicating without words. A dip of the head, a flick of the wrist, a furtive glance. We'd learned to talk in code long ago. He'd keep an eye on the prisoner while I chased off the threat.

I closed the door behind me and followed Nikki down

the steps of the front porch. We walked in silence for a while, the hum of the highway and the roar of a freight train blending into one in the distance. "That yours?" I asked, gesturing toward the small fishing boat docked next to my larger form of transportation. It was a stupid question, but I didn't know what else to say.

"My dad's."

"How is he?"

"Not good. He's been drinking again, ever since Mom left."

Muttering the word "sorry" wouldn't cut it, so I said nothing. As we neared the dock, a few more feet down the sloped path, she slowed.

"I didn't come by because of Lyle."

"I figured as much."

"I mean, you always could handle yourself when it came to him."

I raised a brow, waiting for her to get to the point.

She twirled the engagement ring around her finger, a large princess cut diamond that looked as if it weighed down her hand. I wondered how a man on a sheriff's salary could afford such a ring. The whine of the train's engine grew louder, closer. She cleared her throat. "Thing is, Lyle doesn't know you're Will's father."

Her words stopped me cold. "Who does he think *is* his father then? Was there someone else?" The thought hurt more than it should.

She shook her head. "A few one-night stands when you

were away at competitions or busy training, but no one around the time of conception. It was just you."

"But he doesn't know that?"

"Well, he didn't. I think he suspects now, since we met up for dinner. Small town and all that. You remember how it is. Nothing goes on in this place without everyone knowing about it."

I almost snorted. I guess living on an island gave me certain advantages, like being able to kidnap a woman and hold her prisoner. No one knew about that. Talk was one thing, but knowing was something else entirely.

"So what are you saying?" I threw my hands up in the air. "I don't know what you want from me. You didn't even tell me about him until a few days ago." I folded my arms to ward off the chill wafting from the river.

"Because you were locked up!" Wind whipped her blond hair into her face, and she angrily swiped it from her eyes. "The last time I saw you, I didn't recognize you, Rafe. I'd never seen you so pissed, so...so..."

"So what? Just say it." I stepped toward her, invading her space.

"So broken."

I took a deep breath. "Let's not do this shit. What do you want from me? You want me to step aside so you can have your perfect little family with Lyle?" I rolled my eyes. Lyle and picturesque family dynamics didn't mix. Who the fuck was Nikki kidding? I might have been dead to the world for the last eight years, or *broken*, like she said, but people didn't change. Not like that. If they did change, it was usually for the worse.

She lowered her head. "I don't know why I'm here, don't know what I'm doing anymore. Lyle is just getting nasty when it comes to your name. You need to watch your back, Rafe. He has a lot of power in this town. You already went down once for something you didn't do."

I stared at the river, recalling how Alex had fallen in the other night. I tried not to display any emotion. No clues, no ticks that would give away my guilty ass. "You should go," I said, knowing I was being rude but unable to stop myself. I had no explanation for Nikki. I didn't know what to do about my son. Fuck, I didn't know what *she* wanted me to do about him. "If you want Lyle to be his dad, I'll honor your wishes. Eight fucking years is a lot of time to miss. Maybe it's too late."

Why did that abrade so much? I'd barely glimpsed the kid, but the thought of letting him go, just as I'd found out about him, chiseled a hole in my heart.

She frowned. "You're his father. He should know you."

"He's probably in what...second grade now?"

She nodded.

"Kids talk, and they're mean as fuck. Maybe it's best if we keep it under wraps for now. Last thing I want is to disrupt his life by meeting him, then do it all over again by the talk that'll follow." I grimaced. The poor kid would take a lot of shit because of my time in prison.

"Okay." She turned and headed toward the dock,

though I glimpsed the sadness in her eyes before she went. A few minutes later, after she'd started the motor and began across the river toward the boat ramp, I headed up the path to the cabin, my thoughts on Alex and whatever it was she was hiding. I didn't like it. Too much of the situation was on the verge of crumbling. I couldn't afford to be in the dark about anything, especially with a kid to think about.

Jax met me at the door, shrugging into his jacket as he stepped onto the porch. "Gotta go. I'll be back late tonight. Work is getting heavy."

"See you later." He and I needed to have a heavy talk, but first things first, Alex was going to spill, and seeing the river, remembering how absolute her fear was, would give me the perfect leverage to make her stubborn ass bend.

SEVENTEEN

ALEX

The tape was hot and sticky over my mouth, and the feeling of being smothered almost put me into panic-mode. I kept my mind focused on whoever had landed on Rafe's doorstep, relieved that it wasn't Zach. A woman, Jax had said. Whoever she was, would she find me here? The idea of freedom unsettled me. I'd never stood on my own two feet. Someone had always told me what to do, who to see, who not to see, even what to eat. That was especially true once Dad found out about the anorexia. Rafe imprisoning me on this island had sent my life into a tailspin, but it was the most free I'd felt in a long time.

If my captor had been anyone else, I'd feel differently.

The ladder dropped, and I tensed, wondering whose head would pop through the opening. Rafe climbed into the loft and pulled up the stairs, effectively shutting the door to the outside world. It was just us. No rescue person in sight.

He stomped toward me, and I tried not to flinch as he yanked the tape from my mouth. He released my hands and dragged me from the bed by my hair. "What's going on?" I gasped, thrown off by his foul mood. Rafe wasn't the happiest guy on the block, but something had him worked up. "Who was here?"

"You've been lying through your deceitful little teeth, and it's gonna stop." He let go of me long enough to pull his shirt over his head and shed his jeans. I was still trying to process that he'd stripped naked when he shoved me in front of him and propelled me toward the bathroom. He picked up his belt on the way, and I dug in my heels, shaking as images of all the things he could do with that strap of leather popped into my head.

"What are you doing?" I didn't like where this was going, especially when he slammed the door behind us and bent me over the granite counter, wrenched my arms behind me, and wound that belt around my wrists. He moved away, and the sound of rushing water filled me with horror. I ran for the door.

He jerked me back, hand fisting my hair, and turned me toward the bathtub, my back to his front. His hand clamped down on my shoulder. The tub was huge, big enough for two and deep enough for an adult to drown in.

"What are you gonna do?" I twisted my neck to look at him, but what I found in his expression sent icy terror through my veins. A resolute line took hold of his mouth. My body quaked as the tub filled, and goose flesh erupted on my skin. He didn't answer my pleas and questions, and he didn't shut off the water until it reached the rim. The sudden onset of silence brought my fear to an all-time high. I tried to pull air into my lungs but failed.

He stepped around me, and my head jerked forward as he lifted a foot into the water. "Get in," he ordered once he stood fully in the tub.

"Don't do this!" I didn't recognize my voice—it echoed off the walls in thundering panic.

He yanked on my hair, and I slammed my knee on the porcelain with a yelp. "You did this," he said, "and you can come in willingly or I can drag you in, but one way or another, you're getting in this fucking tub."

Lifting a trembling leg, I stepped over and straddled the edge, and he pulled me in the rest of the way. He folded into a sitting position, back against the opposite end of the faucet, and brought me to my knees. I began to cry, big drops of salt that disappeared into the water enclosing me up to my belly button. It sloshed over the side with the smallest of movements.

The whole time, his grasp on my hair never loosened. "Scoot closer," he said, spreading his legs. I walked on my knees and fit between his, and he pulled me lower, forcing me onto my haunches until the undersides of my breasts brushed the water's surface.

My lips parted, breaths escaping in shaky bursts as our

gazes tangled. He held me captive inside my worst nightmare, with the hold of his hand in my hair, the belt looped
around my wrists behind me, and water rippling and stirring from the way my chest heaved.

I knew what he was about to do, and a sob bubbled up,
tearing from my throat as I sensed the mere inches separating my mouth from the abyss. I didn't dare glance down,
didn't dare break free of his stare. The nightmares I'd had
as a kid came rushing back, more vivid than they had in
years, and I hyperventilated, remembering the suffocating
terror, the blackness and how I'd been helpless to save
myself. That dream had tortured me, and the only way I'd
woken up was by letting out a scream I never remembered,
though my mom had described it as the most chilling
thing she'd ever heard.

"Please don't. Oh God, please, Rafe!"

His expression was passive, tightly held in check, and
that only added to the horror, until his smooth voice
settled over me like a warm blanket. "Calm down. Deep
breaths, Alex."

I inhaled, drawing air into lungs that didn't want to
work right. He instructed me to do it again, and I repeated
the exercise for several minutes, adding the calming ritual
of counting until I no longer sounded like an asthmatic
that had run a marathon.

"That's better. Hyperventilating isn't going to help you
with this." He pulled my hair, bringing my face toward his
submerged lap. "Don't even think of biting me."

"No! No!" I screamed. "Stop!" The last word cracked, as did the final thread of my composure. I thrashed, hair pulling painfully at my scalp as he pushed my head down.

"Take a deep breath. You're gonna need it."

I did at the last second before my face broke the surface and he pushed his erection into my mouth. I couldn't think beyond closing my lips to keep water from rushing down my throat.

He flexed his fingers in my hair and bobbed my head up and down in quick yet controlled movements that kept pace to the seconds ticking in my head. My heart beat much faster, at an insane speed that made my chest hurt, and I mentally chanted two words, over and over again.

Don't panic.

His salty flavor hit my taste buds, but before he came, he pulled me up. With a huge gasp, I sucked in air, hoarded it as if I'd never breathe again. Water trickled down my face in rivulets, lost to the locks of hair clinging to my nose and lips, and I fell into the sea of his eyes.

"Tell me what you're hiding." His tone left no room for maneuvering. I was in deep water, figuratively and literally, because he wasn't going to let this drop.

When I didn't answer, he yanked on my hair again, bringing me toward the water, and I cried, "Wait!"

"I'm done waiting, sweetheart."

With a violent downward thrust, he shoved me under the water once more, and I fastened my lips around his cock. He pushed against my tongue, and water forced its way down my throat. Lungs on fire, wrists burning at my back, I fought him, my whole body tense and vying for survival. Logically, I knew he wouldn't kill me, at least, I didn't think he would, but I was smack in the middle of fight or flight and trying to do both simultaneously.

Pockets of air escaped my nose and mouth, bubbling to the surface as my dark hair floated around me. My pleas came out as muffled rumbles. I was at the end of my ability to hold my breath and experienced the same panic I had when I'd fallen into the river. I was considering biting him, and weighing the consequences, when he yanked me up.

"Tell me why you accused me!"

"It was Zach!" I sobbed, gasping for air, coughing uncontrollably, and trying not to hyperventilate all over again as my brother's name rang in my ears.

Rafe froze, his eyes going wide. "You're lying."

If I had any reason to be terrified of him, this was it—that tone which told me he'd submerge me again.

"Zach was my best friend," he said. "He wouldn't do that."

"But he did..." Another sob burst free, and I closed my eyes so he wouldn't see the truth in them. "I didn't stop him."

"Fucking look at me! Why, Alex? Why would he...why would you go along with it?" He stood, water sluicing down his body, and stepped onto the rug. He dug both hands into his hair and pulled. "Why would you guys do that to me?"

I was openly bawling, and all the emotion I'd battled with for years erupted. I was Mt. Saint Helens, shooting ash of despair on anything and anyone around me. "He... he..."

"He what?" Rafe shouted. "Spit it out!"

"He was jealous!"

"Jealous of what? That doesn't make any sense."

"Don't make me say it. Don't make me tell you this." My head drooped, chin to chest, and my shame poured from me in gut-wrenching sobs. I wished I could stop the dam from bursting, hide it all from him, but I'd never felt more exposed in my life. "He couldn't stand the way I felt about you."

"Look at me, Alex."

I peeked up, watching with dread as he studied me for the longest seconds of my life. His mouth fell open. "*He* raped you?"

Unable to face him, I lowered my head again because that was only half of it, and I couldn't bring myself to tell him the whole truth. It had started out that way, but then, at some point, I'd stopped fighting and my body had given in to Zach. My own step-brother. The step part didn't make it any easier to swallow. It was sick and disgusting, and Rafe knowing twisted in my gut like a tornado.

He pulled me from the tepid water, gathered me in his arms, and strode into the bedroom where he deposited me on the bed, sopping wet. Warm hands settled on my face, fingers pushing tangled hair back, and when I risked looking at him, I fissured in two.

"I didn't want it," I sobbed. "I didn't, I swear. I'm so fucked up, Rafe." Humiliation, swift and debilitating, washed over me, and I gagged, close to vomiting. I struggled with the belt holding my hands at my back. "Let me free! Please, I need free!"

As he worked at releasing my hands, I nestled my cheek against his chest and took deep breaths to stem another episode of hyperventilation.

"How did it happen?" He spoke in a perilous tone, and when he inched back, I wanted to recoil at the unyielding set of his jaw. "How did I get brought into it?"

"I-I had an abortion." I wiped my eyes, palms digging in as that horrible day flooded back. "Someone from the clinic leaked it. Dad found out and kept the story from spreading, but he was so furious—" My voice broke, and I stared at his bunched shoulders, my face flaming even hotter. "He flipped, demanded to know who I'd slept with. That's when Zach pointed the finger at you." I squeezed my eyes shut. "He said you raped me. Said he couldn't keep quiet about it anymore."

Rafe's silence was too disturbing, and when I opened my eyes to face his reaction, utter betrayal blanketed his expression.

"You went along with the lie." No question, no inflection in his words. Just cold, hard truth.

"I'm *sorry*," I said, a sob constricting my throat. "I didn't know what else to do."

"How about tell the fucking truth?"

I jerked back as his rage thundered over me. "I c-couldn't."

"Couldn't, or wouldn't?" He leaned over the mattress, arms supporting his weight as he dripped water all over the bed and me.

"Couldn't." Our gazes collided. "He said he'd kill you if I didn't keep quiet."

Closing his eyes, he dropped his head and let out a breath. The admission seemed to burrow beneath his rage. His body pressed into mine, and we stayed that way for a few seconds until he suddenly bolted and let out a roar I was sure reached every crevice of the cabin. He whirled around and all but flew into the wall, his fist slamming into it, again and again, until his knuckles dripped with blood.

EIGHTEEN
RAFE

She cried for me to stop, but I continued to beat my fist against solid log as memories flickered behind my eyes in red-hazed horror. Instead of me taking the abuse, it was her. Zach holding her down, violating her, smothering her cries as he rammed into her.

The images shifted, and I was back in prison, full of rage yet unable to do anything about it as they took turns fucking me while the guards let it happen. All this time, I thought she'd callously tossed me aside, but I hadn't known why. Knowing didn't resolve anything, didn't bring me closure, and it sure as fuck didn't absolve us of our sins. Knowing only made me feel worse, because she'd suffered in silence out of fear for me.

I risked a glance at her, searching her expression for signs of duplicity. I'd rather find she was lying than accept what she'd told me as truth, but the same harrowing pain

I'd seen in the mirror, day after day for the past eight years, haunted her face. I had trouble reconciling the Zach I remembered with the picture she painted. We'd been close, fiercely competitive but like brothers, and to find out such vile poison ran through his veins, that he'd hurt his own sister and threaten me...I couldn't comprehend it.

I dropped my bloodied fist, and it was a miracle my hand wasn't broken. Her whimpers tore through me as I staggered into the bathroom, heart pounding so fucking hard, I thought it would rip from my chest and tumble to the floor. Flinging the door to the medicine cabinet open, I pulled out gauze and wound it around my hand, but my head was still back in the bedroom with her, still wrapped up in the waves of shame that emanated from her being.

I couldn't get enough air into my lungs, especially when I laid eyes on the bathtub. Water still pooled around it, evidence of my torture methods. What I'd done to her in order to get the truth...now I wanted nothing more than to undo it, to go on believing she'd been a spoiled teenager, pride bruised over rejection. Just a selfish kid who'd flung out a single lie without giving thought to the destruction she'd cause.

Swallowing hard, I brought my injured hand to my throat, as if that would alleviate the need for air. I had to get out of there for a while, had to get my head on straight before I tried to straighten out hers. I almost laughed. How did one straighten out so many years of pain and betrayal?

She was huddling under the bedding when I returned

to the room. I pulled on a pair of jeans, and the weight of her stare pressed on me, burned to my bones.

"Where are you going?" she asked.

"Outside." I shrugged on a T-shirt, then escaped the room and the desolation seeping from her gaze. Her soft cries followed me down the ladder, but I was in no shape to comfort her, especially since I was no better than her brother, no better than the men who'd raped me in prison. If only I'd stopped long enough to think of all the angles, past my fury, maybe I would have considered she was a victim in this.

I'd kidnapped a girl who at age fifteen had been help-less in a situation forced upon her. I'd punished her without knowing the whole fucking picture. It wasn't even the sex that bothered me, as she'd wanted it. It was every-thing else—like being a cold and heartless ass who'd used her fear against her, debased her, and made her feel like she meant nothing to me.

I stormed outside but didn't go far, as if an invisible line anchored me to the house, to her. I clenched my jaw with the need to find Zach and dismember his dick from his body, but I couldn't leave her alone, and it dawned on me that I couldn't confront him either. He thought she was dead.

Fuck.

The whole world thought she was dead. I balled my fists. I'd taken her, and it was too late to go back. I didn't want to go back. I wanted her, all of her—her pain and sorrow, her joy and triumphs, her orgasms and her agony when I held them at bay. But letting her go would be the *right* thing to do.

I glanced toward the cabin and stilled. She stood in the doorway, eyes red-rimmed and haunted, her body wrapped in my sheet. She'd just admitted to being raped by her own brother, yet I wanted to tear that sheet from her and throw her to the ground. The memory of her mouth around my dick in the bathtub hit me, as did the fact I hadn't reached orgasm. I was royally fucked up.

I crossed the distance, climbed the steps to the porch, and shoved past her. Her footsteps pattered on my heels as I entered the living room. She walked timidly, as if scared to make a sound. Slumping to the couch, I held my head in my good hand while my injured one dangled between my knees. She sank to the floor and took my bad hand in hers. It didn't seem to matter what I'd done to her, or what I would do to her—I was starting to believe she was incapable of flushing me from her system.

She unwound the gauze and brushed her fingers over my swollen knuckles. "Does it hurt?"

"It's not bad."

"I'm sorry."

I angled my head and looked at her. "You didn't force my fist into the wall."

"I'm not just talking about your hand. I'm talking about all of it."

"Why didn't you tell me?" I asked. She inched away,

gaze downcast. I grabbed her hand and pulled her near again. "If I'd known what he did to you—"

"It's my fault you didn't."

"It doesn't matter, Alex. I took every fucking thing that happened to me in the last eight years and dumped it on you." Holes riddled my soul, each one representing something I'd never get back. My father's funeral, the first years of my son's life, having my career snatched from me—all because of Zach's jealousy. Even knowing she was a victim didn't quench my thirst for her pain, and that made me the vilest form of a bastard. "I got off on hurting you." I stared at her long and hard so she'd understand just how screwed up I was. "I still want to hurt you, so fucking much."

Her breath escaped in a shaky sigh. She wiped underneath her eyes, though she tried to hide it.

I hauled her onto my lap, unable to contain myself, and settled her knees on either side of me. The sheet draped open, and her hot pussy smothered my lap through my jeans. My cock sat between us, hard and painful, a reminder we had unfinished business.

"It's all my fault," she said, clutching my shirt.

"You were just a kid. You need to know it *wasn't* your fault." I swallowed hard as memories of my own assault broke free. I'd learned to contain them, to continue getting out of bed every morning and living life without freezing whenever something—a smell, a sound, or simple touch—triggered the flashbacks. "Zach knew better. Fuck, he was my age, and I sure as hell knew better." I ran a hand through her hair, fingers catching in the tangles, and pulled. She winced, but I didn't stop. "For fuck's sake, he was your brother."

"*Step*-brother."

"I don't give a fuck." How it was possible for us to carry on this conversation with her naked and in my lap, my erection growing by the second, was beyond me. "He had no right to touch you." Instantly, I dropped my hand from her hair as my own words came back to me like a boomerang. "I'm no better. I shouldn't have taken you." And I sure as fuck shouldn't entertain the thought of bending her over the couch and pushing into her.

"I'm glad you did."

Did she not realize what she was saying? I'd put her through hell, and my dick wasn't done with her yet, not even close. "I *wanted* to take you." My gaze veered to her neck when she swallowed hard. I settled a hand around her throat, surprised when she didn't fight me. The compulsion to squeeze the breath from her beckoned. "I have a demon inside me. That's what happens when a man has dark tendencies and no outlet for them. I used to fight them out of me in the cage."

"Rafe." My name fell from her lips with a breathy sigh. I pressed a thumb against her collarbone where her pulse fluttered as fast as a hummingbird's wings.

I didn't want to think it, let alone say it, but fuck, somewhere inside me a conscience still pulsed. I had to set her free. Except I had no end game. I'd fantasized about taking her for years, had planned out every last detail, but I hadn't foreseen the need to let her go. I didn't think she'd run to the cops, as her guilt came off her in palpable waves, but where would letting her off this island leave me, besides my life in utter disarray? I cursed my fucking conscience and its bad timing. "This has to end, Alex."

"What are you saying?"

"I'm saying I'm letting you go." The words hung between us, and now that they were out there, I wanted to snatch them back. There were so many reasons *not* to keep her here, namely that she wasn't as guilty as I initially thought in sending me to prison. She'd played a part, but how much choice had she really had? Fifteen was young, much too young to deal with rape, abortions, and blackmail.

"Why?" she whispered, as if the thought of getting her freedom back was unbearable.

I moved my hand to the back of her neck and drew her close, aching to take her mouth. "Because I still want to hurt you," I said, my attention drifting to her parted lips, "still want you in ways that isn't right. By the time I'm done with you, you'll beg to be mine, and that's a bad idea."

"I want to be yours," she said without hesitation, as if she wanted to be my everything, as if the idea of my being done with her tortured her. What we shared was pure obsession, nothing more and nothing less, and it was the sweetest madness in hell.

I shook my head, trying to convince myself as much as

her. "I can't keep doing this to you. I battled with myself enough before I knew Zach's part in this, but now..."

She averted her gaze, but not before new tears formed. Watching her emotionally withdraw pissed me off.

"What is it? What are you thinking?"

"Nothing."

I clutched her jaw and forced her to look at me. "What are you holding back?"

"Nothing," she said again, though I saw the lie in her eyes.

"You need to be straight with me, on all of it, because I'm so fucking close to hunting his ass down and killing him." The need to make him pay for what he'd done to her, for what he'd done to me, was strong and growing stronger with each second she tried to hide shit from me. And he would pay. Someway, somehow, I'd make him wish he'd never met me.

She shut her eyes to the tears slipping down her face, and I was a bastard because I wanted to taste them.

"Just tell me, sweetheart." Before I lost control and gave in to the boiling need inside me, to the demon that gnashed his teeth and almost broke free at the sight of her pain.

"He made me come."

"You got off when he raped you?" I wasn't surprised, not if the way she'd responded to me was any indication.

"Yes." She blinked several times but the flood had started and wouldn't stop. Her chest heaved with rising sobs. She didn't even try to pull away. She fucking sat in my lap, her chin trapped in my grip, and let me witness her shame. "He's been fucking me for years. I'm not as innocent as you think."

Her deviant nature pulled at me like a habit I couldn't quit. I took her mouth with greed, forcing her lips apart and thrusting my tongue inside. No build up, no closed-mouthed kisses to ease us into it. We plummeted into a full-on mouth fuck. With a deep moan, she pushed her tongue against mine, and I sucked her deeper, tasting her flavor and her tears.

Her needy fingers sifted through my hair and yanked, and I thought I'd die if I didn't taste more of her. Her perky tits with nipples partially obscured from the sheet, her belly button where I ached to dip my tongue. Her drenched pussy. I wanted to work her body until she begged, then push her further, making her scream and writhe with the need to come. I held her by the nape, placed my bloodied hand at the small of her back, and locked her in my kiss.

The issues between us didn't matter. Nothing mattered so long as she surrendered her soul to my demon and let him devour her. That single thought was powerful enough to make me pull away. I wouldn't let him finish her off. She'd been used and abused by her own brother, no one around to protect her. I'd be damned if I destroyed her too.

I pushed her from my lap. "This isn't happening." I

rose to my feet, silently cursing as she folded the sheet around herself in shame, and adjusted my pants.

"W-what are you doing?" she asked as I headed toward the loft. Her bare feet scampered after me.

"Getting you some clothes." Until Jax and I figured out what to do with her, I wasn't going to tempt myself with her naked body. I climbed the steps and marched to my dresser, where I'd stashed a couple of outfits in her size. I pulled out a T-shirt and a pair of jeans and tossed them at her.

"Rafe...please." Her voice cracked on a sob. "Don't push me away. I need you."

"I'm the last person you need." I stumbled toward the bathroom without looking at her, my heart in my throat, and prepared myself for a long, cold shower and sex with my own fucking hand.

NINETEEN

ALEX

"What'd you do to him?" Jax asked. He sat across the table from me, working on his second beer, his plate from dinner empty in front of him. Rafe had inhaled his food before returning outside to work in the yard some more. He'd found "things" to do all day, the type of mundane tasks that kept him away from me.

"Nothing," I said, my shoulders slumping.

"So you sitting here, fully clothed, I might add, while he's out there attacking the shrubbery is a normal everyday occurrence? I won't even go into how no one said a word over dinner. I know him, and I know when something's off."

My gaze fell to the sweatpants and T-shirt I'd slept in. Rafe had taken the couch, leaving his bed to me. I glanced through the window. The late afternoon sun beat down on him, and his naked torso glistened in the heat. I wiped sweat from my brow. Today had been a hot one. I followed the lines of his tattoos with my gaze, and he caught me staring. His mere glance made my panties damp. I'd brought myself to orgasm last night, surrounded by his sheets and smell, but the release had been empty and anti-climatic, only serving to make me want him more. I'd ached to have him next to me, inside me, his body indiscernible from mine. I wanted him to make me come, craved it, because as long as he withheld that gift, he withheld his forgiveness.

Jax rose with a sigh. He exited through the back door, leaving it open, and hopped down the stairs of the patio to where Rafe was indeed abusing the shrubbery. He dropped the clippers as Jax approached, and though I couldn't hear what they said, it looked as if they were arguing. Jax gestured toward me, his lips tight, and Rafe shook his head. They exchanged words for a few minutes, then Jax stomped into the kitchen with Rafe on his heels.

"This is gonna blow up in our faces and you know it," Jax said. "She'll go straight to the cops, man. Never trust a woman, especially *that* one. I thought you'd figured that out by now, or did she castrate you?"

"You think I want him to go back to jail?" I interrupted, clenching my teeth and matching his glare.

"Why not? You sent him there once, didn't you? What's to stop you from doing it again?"

"Fuck," Rafe said. "I'm just trying to do the right thing. She doesn't belong here."

I sat up straight, my mouth dropping open, and I was about to protest when Jax spoke.

"What changed? Is she a rotten lay?"

Rafe's fist shot out and caught Jax in the nose. "Watch your fucking mouth."

"What the hell, man! We're really doing this over a chick?" Jax grabbed a paper towel from the counter and staunched the blood.

"We're doing this because you're not listening! Things have changed. She's gotta go."

"I'm not going anywhere," I said, and they both stopped and stared. I stood, gathered the dishes, and moved to the sink with as much calm as I could manage. "I've got nowhere to go, Rafe." What I didn't say was how I'd rather eat glass than leave him.

Jax sighed heavily, blowing his shaggy hair from his eyes. "I'm not sticking around to argue about it. If it's gonna blow, it's gonna blow. I'm not staying around for the explosion." He pointed a finger at Rafe. "Just think about it. If you let her go, we can kiss our freedom goodbye. I don't give a shit what she says otherwise." He tossed the soiled towel into the trash, spit out a mouthful of blood, and grabbed another paper towel on his way to the door. "Besides, you're never getting her outta your system. You took her, so deal with it. She's yours."

"Jax, wait—"

The door slammed on his exit, and the echo made the silence between Rafe and me that much louder. I was frozen, afraid to turn around and look at him. A chair scraped across the hardwood, and I heard him settle into it. Not knowing what else to do, I loaded the dishwasher as questions roared in my head, feuding with each other until one finally broke free.

"Did you tell him about Zach?"

"No, but I should have. He has a right to be pissed. His ass is on the line too. If I let you go—"

I spun around. "I don't want you to let me go!"

He jumped to his feet and knocked over the chair. "Have I not made you suffer enough? Fuck, Alex..." His voice cracked, with guilt and regret. I didn't deserve either.

With a growl, I hurtled a dish through the air and jumped when glass rained to the floor in a grating symphony of fury. "We already went over this. I got off on it! While you were in prison, being *raped*"—I choked on the word—"he was fucking me." I sank to the hardwood, knees to my chest, and hid my face behind my palms. "You should hate me. I hate me."

His footsteps thundered across the hardwood, and he yanked me up by the hair. "You don't *get* it," he snarled. "I want you off this damn island, far away from me, because I *don't* hate you." His fist clenched my strands, and he lifted until I stood on my toes. "Seeing your mouth twisted in pain, watching you battle the need to fight me, it *fucking turns me on*."

My lips parted, breaths coming in soft pants. I widened my stance, wincing again when the pull of his grip became unbearable. I slid a hand beneath the waistband of my sweats and dipped into slick heat. "All you have to do is glance at me, and it makes me wet." I lifted my fingers and pressed them to the hard line of his mouth, bathing his lips with the evidence of my arousal. "But when you're rough like this"—I gasped as he jerked my head back and sucked my fingers into his mouth—"I swear I'm gonna break if you don't fuck me."

His eyes met mine, holding me prisoner as his tongue darted between middle and forefinger. He bit down, watched my reaction, and when I didn't recoil, he let my fingers slip from his mouth.

"I'm giving you one chance to walk away." He let go of my hair and retreated. "You'll never hear from me again, never see me again."

I followed his backward motion. "How can you think I want that? I want you, Rafe." To make my point, I cupped his erection through his jeans.

He clamped his fingers around my wrist. "You're pushing it."

"What are you gonna do? Strip me naked? Lock me in the cellar again? Paddle me?"

"No," he said with a scowl, "but I can choke you, or better yet, I can drag your ass into the tub and make you suck me off."

I fought against his hold and stumbled, my heart pounding an erratic tune. "You wouldn't."

He tugged me close until our chests smashed together. "You know I would. No delusions, sweetheart. It's decision time. Stay or go?"

"Stay." The alternative of never seeing him again, of never experiencing his kiss or the possessive way his body claimed mine, that was something I wasn't willing to give up. If taking the pain he needed to inflict would grant me freedom from the burden of my guilt, would grant him relief from his own pain, then I'd take whatever he dished out.

He hefted me into his arms and strode to the stepladder. I slid to my feet, shuffling them with impatience as he brought the stairs down. As soon as we reached the loft, he pulled me against him, my back to his front.

"I'm gonna make you beg for it, gonna make you cry until you can't breathe for wanting me."

"Too late."

"Do you understand why you reached orgasm with him?"

I bit my lip, nodding, my mouth trembling as the memories surfaced. "Because I'm fucked up."

"So am I, and we're gonna be fucked up together, but I want you to answer something first."

I peeked at him over my shoulder. "What is it?"

"Did you crave him the way you crave me?" He grabbed my thigh and lifted, urging my foot around his calf. "Did your body ache and throb for him"—he slid a hand inside my sweats, fingers dipping into the inferno raging inside me—"the way it does for me?

"Never," I groaned, pushing into his palm.

"Then drop the guilt and shame. He exploited the way you're wired, used it against you. I'm gonna make you fucking embrace it."

He moved around and jerked my pants down my legs. My panties went next. He fisted the collar of my tee in both hands and pulled until it split in two, right down to my navel. I stared at him in wonder, mouth hanging open.

"Rafe—"

"Don't talk. Just feel."

I felt, all right. He pushed the tattered shirt from my shoulders and slid my bra straps down my arms. He lowered the satin cups, and somehow, leaving the garment on made the act more forbidden. I felt the weight of his gaze on me, his tongue darting between lips I craved, and I would have given anything to have his tongue on my skin, but he didn't taste, didn't touch. He only looked, and looked some more until I thought I'd explode from his stare alone.

"Get on the bed."

I stumbled back, legs too shaky to do anything else, and fell onto the mattress. I reached behind me to unclasp the bra, but his growl stilled my hands.

"Don't do anything unless I tell you to, understand?"

I nodded.

"Stand on your knees, hands behind your back."

I obeyed without hesitation, barely containing the excitement bubbling in my stomach. He closed the distance slowly, a predator with prey in his sights, and peeled the clothing from his body as he went. Jeans, gone, on the floor. A step later, boxers flew into parts unknown. He climbed onto the bed behind me, and I gasped when he splayed a tattooed hand on my abdomen, fingers reaching past my navel toward the crevice of pulsing arousal. He yanked my head back, until my eyes aligned with his chin, and lowered his head. His lips opened over my collarbone, feverish and hungry, teeth scraping tender skin. My nipples hardened into two tight buds, and my skin broke out in goose bumps from head to toe. I'd never been so worked up, so ready to fly apart from touch alone.

He teased upward, across my cheek to the edge of my mouth, his stubble leaving a rough path in his wake. His fingers slid inside me. I moaned, a second away from begging for his kiss.

"You're so wet. Drenched and hot." He let go of my hair and gripped my throat, holding me prisoner against his body. His gaze fell on my mouth, and he couldn't hide it—the need to kiss me.

This man brought out so many emotions, but above all else, intense yearning. I'd rip myself apart to get to him. "I need you, Rafe," I whispered, eyes threatening to spill so much more than tears. He saw everything, laid bare before him just as my body was. I gave him my submission, opening my thighs wider to his touch, arching into his possession of my throat, my breasts jutting forward, unabashedly on display. "I need you so much."

"Tell me something," he said, his fingers sliding in and out of my pussy in slow ecstasy.

"Anything."

"Have you been with anyone else?"

"Just you." I wouldn't mention Zach. He didn't count, and from the hard glint in Rafe's eyes, I'd said the right thing.

"Good." He groaned, then his mouth was on mine, parting my lips with desperate urgency, tongue thrusting inside as his fingers fucked me. His mouth tasted of the strawberries he'd eaten earlier.

I couldn't be contained. I had to touch him, or I'd combust. I shoved my fingers into his hair and clutched him as if I'd never let go, urging his tongue deeper into my mouth. Kissing him from this upside down angle unraveled me, destroyed me, and I never wanted to be whole again. Not if coming unglued in his arms meant feeling this way for even a second longer. I was his, every frayed thread of my aching soul.

"Fuck, Alex," he said, wrenching his mouth from mine. His erection jabbed my ass.

"I need you. Please."

"I'll fuck you when I'm ready. Put your hands behind your back."

"Ahhh!" I screamed, fists tightening in his hair.

He flipped me to my back and forced my hands to the mattress. His body towered above, trapped me with his dangerous masculinity, and I was a willing prisoner. I freely turned over the key to the metaphorical chains that bound me to him.

Rafe's dark head dipped to my breasts, and I cried out, unprepared for the hard bite on my nipple. Sharp pain radiated through me, gathering strength until it coiled low in my belly. I arched my spine, muscles taut when he moved to my other breast and clamped his teeth into tender flesh.

I hissed in a breath to keep from howling, writhed beneath the punishing attention of his mouth, but he didn't stop. He wouldn't stop. Mercy was his to give, his to withhold. I'd given up my one and only chance at freedom.

His fingers became painful vises around my wrists, holding me down and rendering my struggle useless. He wedged my legs apart and settled his cock at my entrance, pushed in the tiniest bit, then withdrew.

"Please..." I was going to die. If it was possible to drop dead from being teased and tortured so excruciatingly, to be in a constant state of arousal, only heightened by the pain he kept unleashing on my body, then I was a goner. "Rafe, for God's sake, fuck me."

"You're gonna give me everything." He raised his head and looked at me. "I'm gonna choke you. Still wanna stay?"

I bit my lip to keep it from quivering. "Do I have a choice?" I only asked to test him, to see how far I could push. If he was still willing to let me go, then I'd know some part of him still battled with his former self. That guy would always give a choice, always do the right thing, even when he was being fucked in the process.

He let go of my wrists and wrapped his hands around my neck. "Your chance for freedom has passed. Hold onto the bars. If you let go, I won't let you come."

I grasped cold, hard metal and held on tight. "Why do you need this?" I asked, the question guttural because my airway felt so narrow under the weight of his hands.

"Choking your beautiful neck gets me harder than fuck." He leaned down with a barely contained groan, and our faces lingered inches from each other. "Nothing else gets me off so good." He paused for a beat, tilting his head. "But it's about trust too, about you knowing your place. Your pleasure comes with a price. I want every piece of you, every time."

He pushed his cock in slowly and trembled. "I mean it. Let go of those bars, and I'll make you suffer for a week."

I gripped them with all I had, determined to obey him, to prove I could be what he wanted, what he needed, but my heart drummed too loudly. If not for the sensual rhythm he set, shallow thrusts that teased, barely pushing into the wetness dripping onto the sheets, I would have panicked as the pressure on my throat increased.

His sensuality came as a surprise, and I surrendered to it. Through the haze, I saw his face tighten in a mixture of pain and pleasure, and I realized being face-to-face like this, with our bodies coming together in tender agony—something about it hurt him on a deep level. I saw it in the way his hooded eyes drew me in and demanded I bear some of the anguish. Mine drifted shut, because watching him watch me, specks of the past shining in his gaze, tore me to shreds.

"Don't hide from me. I want your eyes."

"It hurts to see you like this." It was easier to face what I'd done when he was angry, righteous, contemptuous. Not while he bared the part of himself he kept hidden. My heart grieved because he was loving my body while showing how I'd destroyed every facet of his being.

"Open your fucking eyes."

I lifted my lids and the connection between us was unbreakable. Neither of us looked away as he pushed to the hilt. He slid in and out, his movements still tender, yet his hands were unrelenting. They tightened further, constricting my airway as an orgasm built, as his neared the brimming point.

"Let me come," I begged.

"Not until you're screaming for it." He drove his cock in with renewed fervor, and we both cried out. "Not until you can't breathe," he said with a groan. "Fuck, I want you waking up on fire." His hands squeezed, and I resisted fighting him, holding so tightly to the bars, my knuckles cramped.

Our gazes remained locked together as he choked the air from me. The moment was surreal, his eyes sparkling like emeralds for those few seconds when I turned my life over to him. Everything around him narrowed to black, and there was only him in my vision, in my world, in my heart. I opened my mouth, needing to say his name, but it wouldn't come out.

"Don't fight it. Just a couple more seconds—"

When I came to, his name a sigh on my lips, I felt his head disappear between my legs. He flattened his tongue on my clit and pressed hard. I squirmed and bucked, limbs quaking high on his shoulders, and gasped for breath. I wanted to claw at my neck, but my fingers remained one with the headboard. I wouldn't let go, no matter what.

"Rafe!" I rasped. "I need to come. Let me come." I repeated the plea until it became a continuous prayer. I didn't know how he did it, but he was skilled at keeping me on edge. His tongue and fingers brought me higher, and my cries tore through the loft. Nothing on Earth felt as good as him between my thighs, licking and sucking, entering a finger and curling it just the right way.

Holy fuck.

He entered another finger, moved his mouth to my inner thigh, and bit down. His fingers worked me as I arched above the bed with a shriek. His teeth sank in deeper and that bite spread through me until I was out of control and lost in helplessness. He brought a hand up and twisted my nipple, eliciting a full-on scream.

Don't let go of the bars...whatever you do, don't let go.

"Please...please...give it to me."

He pulled away and sat on his haunches, and I cussed at him, out of my mind as blood pumped to my core and begged for release. My foul-mouthed rant seemed to amuse him. "You're an instrument I like to play. I can strum you for hours. I like you this way—wild, desperate, and fucking insane with lust."

"Will you ever forgive me?" I squirmed as salty frustration drenched my cheeks. "I'll do anything. Please, I need you."

"Forgiving you won't erase the last eight years. I can't just wipe that shit from my head."

I flushed with shame, acutely aware of how I was spread before him, wet between my thighs while his mind dwelled in past horrors. "I'd do anything to go back, Rafe."

His brows furrowed over contemplative eyes. "What am I to you? Some fantasy you held on to all these years? What do I mean to you?"

I groaned. "You're my beginning, my end. You're my everything."

Slowly, his face relaxing in something close to tenderness, he slid up my body and folded me in his arms. "You sure know how to twist the knife, sweetheart." With a heavy sigh, he pushed into me again. His strokes were just right. His hand on my nape, holding me in place as he nibbled at my neck, was just right. His body enveloped mine, like a cherished present he was carefully unwrapping.

He gripped my neck, sank his teeth in, and I screamed

when the tsunami began. I pulsed and clenched around him, ached long and deep, and I couldn't stem the howl erupting from my being. I clutched his hair, no longer able to hold on to metal when I could hold on to him, not with the way I was coming. And just as the tide ebbed, another wave crested. He never stopped thrusting, didn't slow or quicken his pace. He worked my body as if I were made for him.

"Do it again," he said with a gruff quality that was sexy as hell. "Howl for me. Come undone. I'll put you back together."

I screamed again, my face a mess of sweat and tears, and grasped his shoulders, my fingernails biting into hot, damp skin. "I fucking love you," I choked as the last ounce of strength fled. I was gelatinous skin and bones in his embrace.

"No, stay with me." He still moved inside me, and his lips mashed against his teeth as he neared orgasm. He dropped his head into the crook of my shoulder, smothered a deep groan, and emptied into me.

Time stilled, seconds ticking in an endless loop while we held each other, and eventually our breathing slowed. Twined together in sweat, twisted in each other and in the sheets, the charged air blanketed us. I didn't know how much time had passed, but his face took up space only inches from mine. I breathed in when he exhaled, our chests dancing together to the same beat. My skin tingled and sparked from head to toe, and I shivered because he was still nestled inside me, his erection growing by the second.

"I'm still fucking hard. I can't get enough of you." He pressed me into the mattress and pinned my arms above my head. His need to control no longer scared me. If anything, it made me feel more connected to him, more alive. By giving him this, I felt I was giving him back a small piece of himself. I'd never be able to atone for my sins, for the years of torment I'd put him through, but I could do this, could give him every broken piece of me.

"I've never felt this way before," I whispered.

"What way?"

"Like you. Like I can't get enough."

"My insatiable little slut." His lips curved against mine, taking the sting out of the insult. Unlike when Zach said it, the word held different connotations when coming from Rafe's lips. Pride, possessiveness. His fingers tightened around my wrists. "My sexy little slut. I've waited so fucking long to be inside you." His free hand circled my jaw, and his lips and tongue battled with mine endlessly. We came up for air, and he bit into my shoulder.

I drew in a breath between clenched teeth.

"Does my need to hurt you scare you?" he asked.

"No."

"This is nothing, Alex. I have some really fucked up fantasies, things I've never tried with anyone."

I should have felt at least marginally afraid by his

admission, but I could only grasp a single detail—he'd never done the things he wanted to do with me.

"Like what?"

"That's a conversation for another day."

"Rafe," I groaned.

"I'll need to make you cry. Often. I love the taste of your tears."

"My heart's already bleeding them. Do what you need. I'm yours."

"You're gonna regret being mine."

A tremor of fear speared through me. The way he said it, with unmitigated certainty, took my breath. He didn't need to use his hands to steal my lifeblood.

He pulled out of me and crawled to his hands and knees. "Turn over."

I flopped to my stomach and shivered as chills traveled over my back.

"I'm not done with you, not even close."

TWENTY

ALEX

Something was wrong. It pulled at the edges of my mind and demanded I take notice. I reached for Rafe, but my fingers grasped empty space. His side was bereft, though the sheet still radiated his body heat, so he couldn't have been gone long. I jolted upright, eyes blurry, and blinked. We must have fallen asleep after our second round of sex.

The loft was the way we'd left it, though it was cast in shadow, indicating the sun had set. Once my eyes adjusted, I noticed the ladder was closed and the bathroom door shut. Darkness seeped from underneath, so he wasn't using the toilet. Grabbing the sheet and surrounding my body with it, I tiptoed to the ladder and let it drop to the floor with a loud clank that made me jump. I was about to call out his name when another voice stopped me.

"Who's here?" Zach's question thundered up the stairs,

and I slapped a hand over my mouth to keep from crying out.

"Just some girl I hooked up with. Listen, we should talk about this when you're sober." Rafe's calm tone poured over me like warm honey, and I let out a breath until it sank in that Zach was really here, just a few feet away. And he was drunk.

I stumbled back, gouging my fingernails in my arm, and lost precious seconds as I thought of my brother discovering my presence. They exchanged more words but none of them penetrated. I was too frozen in a waking nightmare of Zach finding me in nothing but a sheet. He'd go irate and kill Rafe. Frantic, I searched for my clothes and found my sweats on the floor. The T-shirt was ruined, so I jerked a drawer open and grabbed a shirt that was sure to swallow my tiny frame. I stepped lightly across the room, gritting my teeth when the floorboards creaked, and listened, remaining out of sight.

"You're a fuckin' liar! I know she was on her way here."

"What are you talking about?" Rafe's voice held steady, but even so, I balled my hands. He could handle himself, I knew he could, but I couldn't get the memories out of my head. Zach was insane when jealous and irrational, and it was like watching a lion let loose all its ferocity onto a weaker species.

Rafe had taken him down so many times during their matches, but this was real. This wasn't a training session or a controlled fight inside a cage with screaming fans crowding around to watch. This was bad.

"The little bitch was running straight to you. I'm not stupid. Did she call you? Tell me what she said, every word. I need to know."

"Seriously, Zach. I never heard from her."

"She's always wanted you, and now she's"—his voice broke—"gone. Just like that. This is *your* fault! I swear to God, I'll tear you to pieces if you don't tell me what she told you."

"I was convicted of raping her, remember?" Rafe's tone barely concealed a lethal edge. "So why would she come here? That doesn't make any sense."

God, he was clever, and it made me love him all the more. Zach couldn't argue with him, not without incriminating himself.

"Then why'd they pull her car from the river down the fucking highway?" he yelled.

"I don't know."

"I can't go on without her," Zach choked. "I won't."

"C'mon, man..." Rafe's voice faltered, and my spine stiffened. Something had him scared. "Put the gun down."

I gasped, then slapped my hands over my mouth, but it was too late. The sound echoed in my ears like a blaring siren, and I was certain Zach heard it.

"Tell your *hookup* to get her ass down here."

"This is between you and me," Rafe said. "I barely know her. She doesn't need to be part of this."

"Get down here now!" Zach shouted.

I stumbled down the stairs, my legs shaking so badly, Rafe steadied me to keep me from sprawling on my ass. He pushed me behind him, but not before I saw Zach's eyes bulge.

"The hell?" He jabbed the gun in Rafe's direction. "Lex?"

"Go home," I told him, hating how my voice quaked. "I called the cops. Th-they'll be here any minute." It was a lie, Rafe knew it, as I didn't have access to a phone, and I was positive Zach knew it too from the way I tripped over the words.

"Un-fucking-believable." Zach's bitter laugh made me cringe. "Do you think I give a shit about the cops? Let them come."

Rafe was strung so tightly, I worried he'd strike at any second, but he reached a hand behind his back and clutched mine, as if I could anchor him. "What do you want, Zach?" he asked.

"I want you dead."

I swallowed a sob and clung to Rafe's hand. "Please, leave us alone."

Zach gestured at me with the gun. "Get over here."

"N-no."

Rafe's shoulders bunched, and his fingers squeezed mine.

"Now!" Zach staggered forward. "Get over here, or I swear to God, I'll shoot him."

A sob escaped, as I recognized the truth in his words. Even though he was wasted, a gun evened the playing field. He was much too close, and it wouldn't take a straight shot to hurt or even kill. I went to move away from Rafe, but he wouldn't let go.

"You're not touching her. You want to shoot me, do it, but you're not laying a hand on her."

"Don't test me!" Zach roared, raising the gun a few inches.

I yanked free and flung myself at Zach, clutching his shoulders, and the barrel pressed into my chest. "I'm here. Don't hurt him."

"What are you doing?" Rafe shouted.

"Stay back," Zach warned him. "Don't make me hurt her."

I couldn't see Rafe's reaction to my brother's threat, but Zach's lips thinned into a dangerous line. "Did you fuck him?"

"Zach," I pleaded, avoiding his furious gaze.

He gave me a rough shake with his free hand. "Answer the question!"

"Yes!"

He spit at me, and I resisted the urge to inch back as I wiped my cheek on my sleeve. He'd only pounce on it, see it as a display of weakness. As long as I stayed between the gun and Rafe, Zach couldn't shoot him. Somehow, I had to get the weapon away from him.

"Why, Lex? Why can't you love me like I love you?"

"If you love me, you'll calm down and think about what you're doing." My words seemed to have the desired effect. He let out a breath, and I felt the gun slide down my chest by a few degrees.

"Of course I love you, baby. I'm the only one who loves you. He's just a fucking waste of space." He tried to push me to the side, but I clung to his jacket.

"Let's go," I said. "Right now. We'll get far away from here, just you and me." I inched a hand down his chest, disguising my aim for the gun as a caress.

Rafe jerked me back before I got close to the weapon and shielded me with his body. "Fuck no. You're not stepping foot out of here with him." Holding my hand tight with one hand, he gestured toward the gun with the other. "Why don't you put that down and fight me, like we used to, or are you too washed up to take me?"

With a snarl, Zach switched on the safety and jammed the gun into his waistband. "Bring it, asshole. I can take you in my sleep."

With the gun no longer a threat, and Zach too wasted to be a real challenge, Rafe wouldn't have a problem taking him down.

"You haven't been locked up with hardened criminals," Rafe said as he moved toward my brother, his grip slipping from mine. "I'm gonna rip you a new one for what you did to me, for how you raped your own sister, you sick fuck." He rolled his shoulders, his stance wide and hands balled at his sides.

I jumped back and slapped a palm over my mouth as he charged Zach. He grabbed him and brought his knee up, one, two, three times until Zach fell to his knees. Something insidious unleashed in Rafe, and it scared the shit out of me. I'd never seen him so unhinged. He pounded on Zach with his injured hand, but it didn't slow him down.

Zach countered the next onslaught of punches and managed to get an arm around Rafe's neck. I screamed, my heart in my throat as I watched them fight for survival. This wasn't a battle for something as inconsequential as a title. This was a battle for life. Rafe's, mine, even Zach's.

Rafe tried to turn into the choke hold, but my brother was high on adrenaline and obsession and wasn't about to let go. Rafe's face blanched, eyes rolling back, and I recognized the burn for air by the grimace on his face, certain it was the same expression that crossed mine whenever he choked me. Except Zach wouldn't stop at unconsciousness. He'd kill him, and not even a bloodstream full of alcohol would hinder him.

"Stop!" I pounced on his back and reached into his waistband, desperate to get my hands on the gun. I curled my fingers around the handle and jumped back, flipped off the safety, and held it in shaking hands, aiming at Zach's head. "Let him go!" I hoped he'd hear the steel in my voice, realize how serious I was, because if I had to choose between Rafe and him, it would be Rafe. "Now!" I shouted, steadying the gun, my finger on the trigger. "You know Dad taught me to shoot. I won't miss."

Zach scowled but let Rafe's limp body drop to the floor. "You're not gonna shoot me."

I fired a shot over his shoulder, thankful for all the times our father had taken me to the range. Zach put his hands up and backed toward the door. Rafe gasped for breath as he pushed to his hands and knees. My attention wavered from Zach for an instant, just long enough for him to flee through the front door.

Rafe rose to his feet, his breaths coming fast and hard. "Give me the gun."

The aftereffects of jumping my brother hit me, and the gun wobbled in my hand. "I-I..."

"C'mon, hand it over. He's gone now."

For how long?

Rafe took the gun and curled a hand around my bicep. "I'm getting you out of here."

"W-where are we going?" Of course, I knew, but even with my brother on the run and posing a real threat, I couldn't stem the panic at the thought of leaving. "I can't do this."

"No choice. I'm getting you off this island."

I pulled against his hold, my heart pounding so hard, I thought my chest would rip open. "No! Please. Let's just call the cops." Even as the words left my mouth, I realized why he couldn't. The cops would come, and the island and cabin would become a crime scene. They'd find the prison down in the cellar and they'd start asking questions, namely why someone who was supposed to be dead was still very much alive. I struggled as he forced me from the house, down the porch, a few steps closer to the water.

"I need you safe," he said, "because I'm gonna fucking kill him."

I dug in my heels, bare feet sliding over dirt and rock. "You *can't*! You're not a murderer, Rafe!" He was too prone to guilt. I'd seen it firsthand. "It'll destroy you."

He picked me up and flung me over his shoulder, and I kicked, clawed, screamed, hit...all of it seemed to bounce off him as he strode toward the water.

"I'm doing this for you."

I screamed, coming unglued as he tossed me into a boat. The water terrified me, but as he unwound the rope anchoring me to the dock, that almost split me in two. "Come with me! Please, Rafe! Please—" I broke into unintelligible sobs, left with nothing to do but drift away from the island. From him.

"Alex!" he called as he let loose another boat—Zach's I guessed. It floated in the direction mine had. "You'll hit land a little ways upstream. Stay calm. I'll find you."

I nodded and squeezed my eyes shut. I couldn't speak.

"He won't hurt you anymore. Not when I'm through with—" A loud grunt tore through the night, and my lids popped open.

I scrambled to my knees as he battled with Zach for the gun. Holding both hands over my racing heart, I screamed Rafe's name. And I screamed and screamed some more when they fell to the ground and Zach beat him over the head with a rock. Rafe stopped struggling.

He wasn't fucking moving. The scene before my eyes crawled in slow motion as Zach pushed to his knees, then to his feet. He stepped back, body swaying, and aimed the barrel at Rafe's unmoving form.

OhmyGodohmyGodohmyGod...

I screamed at him to stop, but my voice cut out when the blast echoed off the mountains. I almost fell into the water, reaching, pleading, praying for Rafe to get up, but Zach kicked his body into the river.

My mouth opened, yet no sound came out. This wasn't happening. That shot was a car backfiring from the highway, or someone testing their illegal mortars a few weeks early of the Fourth of July. Any second now, Rafe's strong arms would pull him to safety and he'd beat the shit out of Zach.

But he didn't surface.

Zach dove into the water with a splash, and his strokes brought him straight for me with the stealth and speed of a shark. I could do nothing to save myself. Water lapped against the boat, paralyzing me. My fear trapped me, held me prisoner in my own mind, and Rafe...

He wasn't coming up, wasn't gasping for breath and diving after Zach.

My heart fractured, split wide open, and I didn't recognize the howl of agony spilling from my being. Zach pulled himself into the boat, his sodden clothing weighing him down, and shoved a hand over my mouth. I flailed as he wound an arm around my neck. I fought him with everything I had, even as my gaze fastened to the spot where Rafe had gone under. I longed to slip into the void after him, to vanish as he had. I didn't want to live if he didn't.

The headlights crawling along the highway, like pairs of lightning bugs, blinked out in my periphery, and the night narrowed to nothing, yet that empty spot in the river burned in my mind.

TWENTY-ONE

RAFE

I jerked awake in the depths of icy water, kicked weak and useless limbs, and eventually broke the surface. Gasping, I pulled myself onto land with jittery arms and spewed water from my lungs, coughing until I puked. I rolled to my back, and the throb in my head made itself known. So did the fire in my left shoulder. The sky spun like a damn acid trip. Wet and itchy grass cradled my body, and I groaned as I ran my fingers along a nasty gash in my skull. I pulled my hand away and winced at the blood covering it. Too much blood.

Shaking uncontrollably, my heart rate doubled as I tried to sit up, but I couldn't get myself off the ground. The stars seemed to distance themselves, as if they knew I'd suck the light out of them. I thought I heard someone scream, and something about that hysterical plea fisted my insides. What the fuck had happened to me? I recognized my dad's island, but why I was sprawled on it, hurt and bleeding, I didn't know. Another scream cut through the air, abruptly cut short as it carried in the night. Someone was in trouble, needed my help, yet I couldn't move... couldn't stay...awake.

Someone lifted me, followed by the unmistakable sway of a boat ride. A voice kept talking to me, telling me to hold on.

Almost there, buddy.

Almost where?

A horn blared, tires screeched, and frantic voices exchanged meaningless words because everything was meaningless. None of it made sense. Where was I?

Didn't someone need help?

A sharp pain stabbed my chest at the thought. I was unworthy, a sadistic ass who'd done horrible things...who had I done this to? And why would I do something so... what had I done? Why was trying to remember making my head throb like a fucking drum, pounded on by brutal drumsticks that inflicted the most horrid pain? I felt those strikes clear though my eyeballs to my teeth.

Hands grabbed my body and lifted, sliding me onto something cold and hard and bumpy. An engine rumbled to life. I groaned as I rolled, though an arm steadied me, as did the leg stretched out at my side.

A bright light woke me, searing my eyes and intensifying the throb at my temples, which kept time to the rhythmic beep that irritated my ears. I rubbed the blurriness from my vision and took in the small room. What the hell? Had I lost a fight, beaten so badly I'd needed hospitalization?

Why couldn't I remember?

Someone shifted on my left, and I found a guy slumped in a chair, his dark blond hair a mess on his head. His drawn face displayed signs of fatigue.

"Thought I'd lost you, man."

I blinked. Something wasn't right. He must have been in the wrong room, or confused.

I closed my eyes, but when I opened them, he was still staring at me, waiting for an answer. "Why are you here?"

"Seriously? We get into one fight and this is how you're gonna play it?" He brushed the hair from his brown eyes. "That's cold. If I hadn't come back, you would've bled to death. Lucky for you, you sonofabitch, it was a clean shot, so no permanent damage."

I blinked again, feeling as if I were missing several cards from the deck. "I don't remember. How long have I been here?"

Some of the anger left his shoulders. "You've been laid up three days. It was touch and go for a while. You lost a lot of blood, and they didn't know how long you'd gone without oxygen."

What the hell? No one choked me out. It just wasn't done. *I* choked my opponents.

"Must have been some fight."

He raised a brow. "That's a mild way of putting it. No one can piece together what happened." He gave me a heavy look, then lowered his voice. "Which is a good thing since *you-know-who* vanished, though I'd like to get my hands on whoever did this."

"What are you talking about?"

"Well, I'm guessing you let her go? There's been no sign of her since. I said I found you on the side of the highway, so the island is secure. No cops crawling it." He sighed. "So what *do* you remember? Because fuck, Rafe, I don't have a clue what happened out there."

I studied this tattooed stranger through squinted eyes, still having no idea who he was or what he was talking about, yet he acted as if he knew me. "Um, I remember seeing Nikki the other night." Hell, that girl could fuck a guy raw. My dick twitched as I remembered how she'd ridden me.

"How bad did you bump your head? Nikki showed up a few mornings ago. Close call too." He ran a hand through his hair. "I knew the risks when I signed on for this, but I gotta say it—these past few days have been a bitch."

"What?" Was he purposefully speaking in riddles? I'd fucked Nikki the night Zach and I had gone head-to-head. I was still on a high from winning that title, knowing my dream of fighting in the UFC was a real possibility now. As for the rest of what this guy at my bedside said, it made about as much sense as his presence.

I glanced around the room and tried to figure out what I was missing. Plain white walls, standard hospital machinery, and that fucking beeping that increased the throbbing in my head. Most notably, someone was absent. "Where's my dad?" I wasn't surprised my brother hadn't shown up. He was always too busy to differentiate his asshole from his mouth, and he'd never approved of my career anyway, but Dad would be the first one here.

The guy narrowed his eyes. "Something's not right..." He jumped to his feet and hit the call button.

"What are you doing?"

"Getting help, 'cause you're not acting like yourself."

"Dude," I said, "How would you know? I don't even know who the hell you are. No offense."

He collapsed back into the chair, eyes wide, and his panic penetrated my tough veneer. His reaction scared me, and I didn't know why.

"That is *not* funny," he said. "Cut the crap."

I shook my head. "Seriously, who are you?"

He pushed his hands through his hair. Three times now, he'd done that. Must be a nervous tick. "This isn't happening." His gaze bored into me. "Who's the President?"

"Of the UFC?"

"No! Of the fucking United States."

I furrowed my brows. "Bush, why?"

"Shit," he said, then dropped his head into his hands. A

few seconds later, he looked up, his face taut with stress. "What year is it?"

"2006. What the hell is going on?"

"You've lost eight years of your life, man. That's what's going on."

BOOK TWO

RAMPANT

DEDICATION

To my fellow lovers of the dark side.

ONE

ALEX

Another drop of sweat crawled down my nose like a spider. In the stifling air of the trunk, I struggled to draw each breath. Perspiration pooled at my temples, irritating, flushing my cheeks with too much heat. I wiped the dampness on my sleeve. The vehicle swayed with the road, and I curled into a ball with a groan. At some point, the hum of the highway turned to gravel, then to a bumpy ride that rocked me back and forth. I shot an arm out to steady myself, and my belly protested the smothering heat and swerving motion. Chunks of what I'd eaten for dinner erupted from my mouth, souring the air. I scooted away so my cheek wouldn't smear in it.

Bump, bump, sway. Oh God...taking in shallow breaths didn't help. The air was too thick, and the overwhelming odor of vomit made me heave again, but my stomach had nothing left to purge. A few minutes later the car jerked to a stop and the engine shut off. The heavy thump-thump-thump of feet on gravel pounded through ears trained to recognize and dread that purposeful gait. When Zach lifted the lid, the black night engulfed him, yet I sensed the fury seeping from his being.

He grabbed my hair, angled my head back, and thrust a bottle against my lips. "Drink."

My mouth resembled the consistency of sandpaper, so I didn't hesitate. I clutched it, both hands covering his, and sucked down every last bit. Spent of energy, I dropped my head to the bed of the trunk, right into the expelled contents of my stomach.

"You've reached a new low, Lex. You're lying in your own puke." As I inched away from the vomit, he retreated a step. "Fuck. I've reached a new low. It wasn't supposed to be like this! What the *fuck* am I supposed to do now? Everyone thinks you're dead. *I* thought you were dead!" Hands yanking at his mussed up brown strands, he began to pace. His clothing clung to his body, as if still damp from the river.

Rafe's face infiltrated my mind, and I blinked to hold back the hot sting of tears. Devastation pressed on my breastbone, coiling around me and tightening until I couldn't move or speak. I tried shaking his image from my brain, but it stuck like tar.

I didn't want to think or feel.

Doing either would crush me, and I couldn't afford to break down. Not yet. I knew I would eventually, when I could no longer hold off the anguish strangling my wind pipe. When I had no choice but to confront the truth poking my insides with the burn of a hot fireplace poker.

Rafe was gone.

Zach muttered something indecipherable, pulling me from the dark place in my mind, and his agitated pacing continued. A bullfrog's call joined in, croaking through the night with the finesse of a chain-smoker. Frogs meant water was nearby, right? I followed Zach's movement, my heart racing even faster at the perceived threat. How close were we? I visualized jumping out and running...and falling in, just like I had the night I tried to flee the island. My limbs stiffened, and I scooted further into the depths of the trunk.

"It's gonna be okay. Everything's fine," he said, more to himself than to me. He started to lower the lid.

"Wait!" I cried, a moment away from sobbing. "Where are you taking me?"

"Enjoy the ride." A trace of malice tainted his sonorous tone.

The lid slammed down with a clunk, and the darkness suffocated me. The helplessness. Letting out a hiccupping mewl, I counted the seconds before Zach started up the engine. And I kept counting, as it was the only thing keeping me from totally unraveling as the car continued its winding path. After a while, I drifted in and out of consciousness. Or maybe it was a fog. I couldn't say if I slept or not. Part of me latched onto the hope that this night was a bad dream. But hope was dangerous. Hope made you do stupid things, all in the name of trying for a better outcome that would never come to fruition. Accepting reality was harsher but best in the long run.

I'd been kidnapped. *Twice.* I'd survived the first time because my captor had harbored a sadistic streak *and* a conscience. My chances of getting through this were nada. Zach would never let me go. Not with the world believing I was dead. Not after he'd found me with...

Don't think of him.

I squeezed my eyes shut, willed my mind blank. I must have fallen asleep because I awoke to Zach lugging me from the trunk. I fell to the ground and winced, rocks and dirt gouging my knees. He hefted me up by the back of my shirt, flung my aching body over his shoulder, and stalked toward a small cabin. I squinted against the morning gray, and the cool air on my face came as a relief after the confines of the trunk. Rolling slopes of timber enclosed us —a mixture of Douglas fir and pine. In the distance, the snowy peak of Mt. Hood offered a point of reference. But I found the utter quiet, interrupted only by the song of birds, especially unsettling. Besides the wildlife, not a hint of existence stirred beyond those trees.

"Home sweet home," he said as he climbed the porch.

I cranked my neck as he ran a hand along the door-frame. He withdrew a key, steadied me with one hand, and used the other to shove it into the knob before kicking the door open. He stomped through the main room, dim in the dawning light barely peeking through the curtains.

"Put me down!" I kicked my feet and dug my nails into his strong back as he entered a bedroom.

"Stop it, Lex." He yanked my sweats down, baring my bottom, and smacked my ass hard. "Don't try to run," he said, letting me slide to the floor in the adjacent bathroom. "You won't get far. No one's around for miles."

As I jerked my pants up, my gaze lowered to his muddy sneakers, but he gripped my chin and forced my attention on his face. "You understand me? No one will hear your screams up here. Nobody knows we're here, and the owner's in Europe for the summer, so it's just *you* and *me*."

Five in, hold, five out. Repeat.

I'd lived by the ritual since the day he'd stolen my innocence. Only now I was stuck on hold. If I didn't breathe, then I wasn't alive. If I wasn't alive, then I couldn't feel.

His gaze lowered to my filthy tee. "Take that damn thing off."

Air whooshed from my lungs in a rebellious rush, and my chest resumed its natural rise and fall. But I wasn't breathing, and I didn't know how my arms moved without a heart that pumped life through it, how my fingers grasped the bottom of the shirt that belonged to Rafe.

His shirt. On *my* body.

If I closed my eyes and pretended, I could almost feel Rafe's arms around me, his mouth moistening my neck, his warm palms on my breasts, brushing across hardened nipples. Could almost hear the husky way he spoke to me, his tone full of command yet quiet with vulnerability. I chewed my lip to stop it from trembling, but my chest shook with the rising tide of grief.

"Now, Lex."

I jerked my gaze to my brother's hardened expression. Even after all he'd done, I couldn't think of him differently. I still remembered him as the boy I'd latched onto when I was six, when our parents made the colossal mistake of merging our families. Reality demanded I think of him as a murderer, but that only brought me back to the fact that I wasn't breathing. Still. Not. Breathing.

Rafe's not dead. Not dead. Dead, dead, dead...

The thought fired through my synapses, on constant repeat.

"You fucking reek of him!" Zach's hazel eyes spit poison, as potent as the arsenic boiling in his soul. "Take it off."

I lifted Rafe's shirt over my head and stared, transfixed as the soft gray cotton dropped to the hardwood. I wanted to yank it back and bury my nose in it, inhale Rafe's essence the way lungs hungered for air. Zach pulled me from the trance by sliding my sweats down my legs. I stepped free, holding onto his shoulder to keep from tipping over.

"Get him off of you," he said with a rough shove into the shower stall.

A zipper lowered, clothing rustled, and the familiar sounds shivered through me. He switched on the water, and for a few blessed seconds the chaos in my mind fell silent, immersed in the roar of the spray. I crossed my arms over my chest and clawed at my biceps, dug my nails in deep until all that penetrated was pain. Leaning my forehead on the cold tile, I welcomed the numbness that blanketed me. I knew what was coming, and I didn't want to be present for it.

Numb, Alex. Pay no attention to his hand slithering down your spine.

My protective cocoon threatened to dissipate as he bent me over, his naked front pressed to my back. My palms slammed against the wall, and he wound an arm around me, his fingers dipping between my thighs. I clenched my teeth to keep from crying. I wouldn't cry for Zach. There was only one man I wanted to spill tears for and he was...

I gasped a breath and held, clenching my jaw as Zach's cock pushed past my body's rigidity. Warm droplets of water coursed down my face and shoulders, but the space between my thighs remained dry as a desert. I pressed closer to the tile, wishing I could escape him, wishing I could melt into the wall and disappear forever.

"The hell, Lex? You're dry as fuck." He pulled out then shoved in so violently, I arched to my toes. My teeth tugged at my lower lip and the metallic tang of blood lingered on my tongue. "I spent years molding you," he said with a grunt, pumping a steady, harsh rhythm that punished from the inside out. "Bastard corrupted you."

A whimper escaped my tight lips. "You're hurting me."

"Isn't that how you like it? Come for me."

It wasn't going to happen. Icy fear doused my skin, battling the warmth of the water. How could I come if I wasn't breathing? Wasn't alive? I *wasn't* alive.

I'm not here. This isn't real. I'm safe in Rafe's arms right now, having the nightmare from hell. Wake up...

Zach roared his release with a final plunge, ramming to the hilt and triggering sharp pain that spread outward from my cervix. The fog in my head enveloped me, and I barely noticed him rubbing my body down with soap until he turned me in the spray to rinse it away. He shut off the water, ushered me from the stall, and hauled me to the bed, dripping wet.

"You're gonna scream my name." He shoved me to my back and grabbed my ankles, his fingers trapping like shackles, and dragged me to the edge of the mattress. Forcing my thighs apart, he dropped to his knees. My mind left me, floated to the island and the memory of the dark abyss that had claimed Rafe. I visualized him breaking the surface and pulling himself onto land, but the daydream fractured, and I let out a startled yelp.

Something pinched my clit.

Zach, on his knees with his face buried in my pussy. His teeth clamped down unbearably hard, but the pain did nothing, didn't even ignite a spark. No feeling, no forbidden rush of adrenaline storming through me. It might have been minutes. It might have been hours. I never came, never even got close, and no amount of him slapping me, pinching flesh and twisting nipples, would bring about an orgasm. Some previously dormant switch had been tripped.

Rafe had done that in the week we'd had together, when the walls had crumbled between us and I'd learned what it was like to feel cherished.

Possibly even loved.

"Snap out of it!" Zach slammed his fist into my face, and I cried out as the blow echoed along my cheekbone. He'd never hit me in such a visible place. I gaped at him as his finger curled inside me, pressing the spot that usually sent me soaring. He returned my stare, eyes narrowed dangerously, waiting. "Squirt like a fucking whore."

"Never again," I said, gritting my teeth. "Not for you."

He jerked forward, fist raised.

"Go ahead! Hit me again. *Kill* me." Please, God, let him kill me. "I'd rather die than be with you."

A combination of hurt and violence darkened his features. I flinched, certain his knuckles were two seconds from connecting with my cheekbone again.

"You don't mean that," he said, his voice incongruent

with the hard line of his jaw. "You'll love me again. Some- where inside you is the little girl who made me her world."

"That girl was your sister!"

"I've never looked at you that way, Lex, and you know it. There's no blood between us, so stop hiding behind shame. What we have is unstoppable."

"What we have is fucked up. For God's sake, Zach, we grew up together." The echo of innocence pinged through my heart, leaving me bereft. Long ago, we'd been two kids playing in the yard, building forts that stood as tall as skyscrapers to my young eyes, yet they'd barely allowed Zach to stand inside the carefully constructed walls. He'd been my big brother, someone I always counted on and looked up to.

Until the day he'd wrecked me. I recalled that life- altering moment as if it happened yesterday. Only thirteen, too unsure of the change in his touch, struggling to under- stand what it meant. I'd sprawled stiffly beside him, inca- pable of moving as his fingers slipped beneath my panties. He'd smothered my fearful cry with a sweaty palm and had spread my thighs before burrowing past my inno- cence. Zach had taken something precious from me that night, and in turn I'd taken the freedom of the only man I'd ever love.

I'd *killed* him.

The reality of what had happened at the river was too painful and a tear crept down my cheek, as if trying to sneak past Zach's watchful gaze.

"You never cry." He slowly lowered his fist. "In all the years we've fucked," he said, "you never cried. Not once. Why now? Because of *him*?" His mouth twisted into something ugly...something arrestingly terrifying. "He's your past, Lex. I'm your future, and I'll do whatever it takes to bring you back to me."

TWO
ALEX

We slept the day away, Zach's naked body trapping my own. Several times, I tried to extricate myself from his grasp, but his arms always tightened in warning. At some point, I'd fallen into a restless sleep where images of Rafe and the island tormented me.

Still haunted by the echoes of convoluted dreams, I hugged my knees from my spot on the four poster bed as Zach raided the closet. "Who's cabin is this?" I asked, glancing at the window, where bright light had filtered through the curtains before we fell asleep. Now a strip of black peeked through where the material hung open, indicating the sun had set long ago.

"A friend's. He comes up here in the fall to hunt." As Zach sifted through flannel shirts, sweatshirts, and jackets,

I wondered if the owner stored his rifles somewhere in the house. My gaze zoomed in on the closet, hoping to catch a glimpse of a gun.

"You're so transparent," Zach said. "You won't find a gun in this place. He doesn't keep them here." He removed a black wife-beater from the dresser and pulled it over his defined pecs and abs. The sweats he wore swam on his toned frame, drawstring cinched tight. My brother was all hard muscle, and obviously, the owner of this place wasn't. He grabbed a white tee and tossed it at me. "All you need to know is we won't be interrupted for a few weeks." Pointing a finger in my direction, he told me to get dressed.

I tugged the soft cotton over my head and eyed the door. The dresser and the closet were on either side, and Zach stood smack in the middle of the doorway, effectively blocking the exit. Watching me with the air of a predator, he rubbed the stubble on his chin.

I avoided the intensity in his probing stare and instead took in the room, the unfamiliar cabin walls, the smooth oak furniture. That damn window that taunted me, whispering to my desperation to slide it open and crawl through, except I knew he'd stop me before I could. The adjacent bathroom was a dead end for escape as well, with only a small vent-type window to allow air in.

"A few weeks, Zach?" Maybe logic would penetrate his thick skull. "What about your career? Won't interrupting your training like this set you back?"

"My career is gone. It went down the drain the minute I thought I'd lost you."

"Dad won't be happy about that."

"I don't give a fuck what Dad's happy about. I don't care about any of it, Lex. I'm done with MMA. You're all that matters to me."

I shook my head, feeling completely cornered. "I can't live like this. Don't make me." Clenching my hands to keep from gouging flesh, I gnawed on my lip instead. "C'mon, Zach. If you don't let me go, you'll be on the run for the rest of your life. That isn't a life."

"As far as the world knows, you're dead." He shifted his feet and poked a finger at his chest. "I don't have to run at all—I just have to make sure no one finds out you're still alive. We'll lay low here for a couple of weeks and go from there."

His twitchy gestures made me nervous, and I wondered if alcohol was the only substance he was withdrawing from.

"How'd you do it?" he asked, his sudden question derailing my train of thought.

"Do what?"

"Fake your death." He leaned against the doorjamb, folded his arms, tapped his foot. A dragon breathed fire down his right bicep. Unlike Rafe's tattoos, which were beautiful, symmetrical, and understated in their simplicity, Zach's begged for attention with detail and flaming color. "Better yet, how'd you get past your fear to do it?"

He clenched his jaw. "You must have been desperate to get to him, for you to go anywhere near the river, let alone crash your car into it." He tilted his head. "Must have been desperate to get away from me to fake your own death."

I averted my gaze. Zach read me too easily. What would he do if he found out Rafe had kidnapped me? He might read something into it that wasn't true. Just because Rafe had taken me, that didn't mean I hadn't been where I'd wanted to be in the end. But even worse he might get the same idea as Rafe and use the phobia against me. If he hadn't thought of that already.

"Answer me," he said, bringing me back to the moment with his biting tone.

"It wasn't easy." I stood, straightened my shoulders, and the muscles in my thighs tightened, readying to fight, to flee. I quelled the urge, as he had me trapped and there was no way I'd get past him and out that door. My stomach grumbled, reminding me I hadn't eaten in twenty-four hours, and it gave me the perfect excuse to try and get out of the room. "Is there anything to eat in this place?"

He signaled for me to go to him, and I couldn't help but notice the tremors in his fingers. I tried to pinpoint when he'd started drinking, but the onset of his alcoholism had been gradual, like a bad cold that begins with a sneeze and a vague ache in your glands until the next thing you know, you're laid up in bed feeling like death incarnate. His drunken fits had been sporadic at first, beginning somewhere around the time I'd graduated college and escalating after I'd started dating Lucas.

"I'm sure there's gotta be some soup or something." He clamped his hand around my upper arm and ushered me from the bedroom. On the way to the kitchen, I eyed the front door, just a few feet away, yet it seemed like yards. The promise of escape disappeared from view too soon, leaving behind the fleeting idea of freedom. He pulled out a chair at the kitchen table, wooden legs scraping across the floor unnervingly, and shot me a pointed look, but he didn't push me into the seat.

Rafe would've shoved my ass into it.

I gave myself a sound mental slap. I had to stop torturing myself with thoughts of him. It fucking maimed too much, but unbidden, his voice haunted my mind, his words gruff with sexual need.

Howl for me. Come undone. I'll put you back together.

My knees buckled, and I choked back a sob as I slid into the chair. I hadn't accepted the idea that he was gone. I didn't feel it in my heart, and like a dope addict clamoring for another fix, I clung to the frayed thread of hope that he was alive and looking for me.

Zach either didn't care about my rocky emotional state, or he didn't notice. He turned his attention to the cupboards and chose two cans of soup. As he prepared our food, he never quite turned his back on me. This was my brother, a guy I'd shared a house with for twelve years, which meant he knew me too well, knew what buttons to push, what words to use as weapons. He'd be stupid to let his guard down for a second.

I might have a sick attachment to him, but I despised him too. And I'd never felt so torn. Love for a brother, and hate for a twisted, obsessive...I didn't even know what to call him. The term *lover* came to mind, but that wasn't right either. He'd fucked me. A lot. And I'd let him.

Maybe if I'd fought harder, Rafe would still be alive.

My stomach roiled with renewed self-loathing, and when he carried two bowls of steaming soup to the table, I couldn't fathom forcing the liquid down my throat. His gaze lifted and clashed with mine. I looked away, fearful my thoughts were plastered all over my face. He rounded the table, and his fingers brushed my cheek, making me flinch.

"I'm sorry I hit you."

He was always sorry, yet it never stopped him from doing it again. I edged away from his touch. Even the feather-like caress of his fingers against my cheekbone hurt.

"Don't pull away from me." He grabbed a fist full of hair and jerked my head forward. "I'm trying to apologize, Lex, but fuck, you sure know how to piss me off."

"It's not hard." I yanked violently from his grasp. The cost of freeing myself remained in his fist—several clumps of my hair. "You go off on the smallest things. Ever hear of anger management?" Or a cell for the criminally insane.

"Ever hear of the words *shut up*?" He stomped across

the room and began rifling through drawers. As he busied himself with his frantic search for whatever he was looking for, my attention veered to the living room where the front door beckoned just beyond.

He took out a roll of duct tape, and I flew from my seat, my feet carrying me into the next room before I'd given thought to the consequences. The exit pulled at me like a net, as if dragging me from the depths of terrifying deep sea. My momentum slammed me into the door, shaking the coat rack in the corner by the closet. I hoisted it, launched it behind me, and prayed the obstacle slowed his thundering footfalls.

That's when I spotted the keys hanging on the wall. I grasped at them with one trembling hand while the other fought with the knob, panic taking root in my fingertips. Finally, I flung the door open, catapulted off the porch, and ran toward his BMW.

"I disconnected the battery, Lex."

His words halted me, and I whirled, expecting to find him on my heels, but he hadn't ventured further than a foot from the porch.

"There's nowhere to run!" he yelled, throwing his hands in the air and turning in a slow circle. I followed with my gaze, taking in the *nothingness* surrounding us. The black nothingness that came with nightfall. Above, a vast canvas of stars lit the sky, but without the moon to light the way, getting lost wasn't just a possibility, it was an inevitability.

Maybe he's lying...

I could try the car, but if he was telling the truth, I'd be trapped for sure. Tightening my grip on the keys, I pushed one out to use as a weapon and took a step away from him, toward the edge of the trees.

"We're in the middle of nowhere, baby! Where're you gonna go? You wouldn't last the night in this forest."

He underestimated what I was capable of surviving, but he had a point. The nights were notoriously chilly, even during the summer months, and I didn't know where I was. I also didn't have any shoes—another nail in the coffin of things that would slow me down.

I could make a run for it, hope to find help. Hope he didn't have a spare set of keys in his possession. Eventually, the gravel road had to lead to civilization. But knowing Zach, he *did* have a spare set, and he'd pick up my sorry ass in no time.

As if my desperate thoughts blinked on my forehead in neon glory, the curve of his mouth turned cruel. "You know I'll find you." A threat dangled in that statement. A promise. I could run, but if he caught me, I'd find out what he was truly capable of.

I took another step anyway, despite the unmistakable lump of fear clogging my throat. Despite the rocks digging into my bare feet. My gaze zigzagged in every direction, searching, hoping. So many trees, and I had no idea what waited beyond them. Hopelessness crawled down my spine, an inescapable chill that threatened to ice my blood.

He had nothing holding him back now. The facade our father created, society's watchful eye—none of it mattered out here, in this desolate place no one would think to look for me, because according to the world, I was dead.

In the twitch of an eye, I turned and fled.

THREE

ALEX

My feet skidded across rock and dirt, and I heard him pound the ground behind me. "Are we really doing this, Lex?"

I cranked my head, horrified to discover him gaining so fast, and doubled my efforts, picking up speed as I careened down the slope of the road. Sharp rocks tore into my bare feet with every frantic step. But I was an easy target, in plain sight, no matter how much distance I managed to put between us. Getting lost in the woods was my only shot at escaping.

My gaze swerved to the blackness beyond the trees, and I gulped. Get lost, or turn around and face him? Face possible years under his control. Endless years that would surely break me. Another glance over my shoulder told me I had but seconds to decide.

Pure adrenaline spurred me to jump into the foliage. I

sprinted over roots, swerved around boulders, and stumbled to the ground, still damp from the torrent of rain last week. I didn't remember getting up, though mud caked my bare knees. The ground became especially treacherous. I lost my balance and hurtled down an embankment, a victim of gravity, rolling over rocks, gouged by sticks, and grunting with each strike. I smashed into the trunk of a tree, finally coming to a stop. Stars burst in my vision, and the night narrowed until blinding light battled the dizziness.

His voice seared the air, my name a furious epithet bleeding from his lips. He sounded too close, but in the darkness, disoriented as my head throbbed from striking the tree, I couldn't tell if he was three inches or three yards away.

Clenching my teeth against the pain, I pushed to my hands and knees, key still tightly wedged between my knuckles, and peeked around the massive tree trunk. Without the luminescence of moonlight, visibility was a bitch out here, which turned out to be a blessing and a curse. If I couldn't see him, then he couldn't see me. That also meant I couldn't see my way out of there.

Who was I kidding? I *wasn't* getting out of this. Even if he wasn't waiting, hunting me like prey, I didn't have the skills to make it out. Not on foot. Not without proper clothing, food and water, a compass at the least. I closed my eyes and brought a fist to my mouth to keep from totally losing it.

Don't you dare give up. If you don't get out of here, then Rafe's dea— A sob ached in my throat, but I forced myself to finish the thought. *Then Rafe's death was for nothing.*

He died protecting me. Oh God. I was going to get sick. My pulse quickened, and my chest squeezed as every last memory of him edged into my soul. Not just the way he'd made me feel, but the gentleness that lingered inside him. The spark of compassion I'd seen in his eyes years ago, before I'd ruined his life. What I'd felt for him back then was real, was still as real as the scent of pine teasing my nostrils.

I wanted to lay down and give up, let the wilderness claim me. How could I fight knowing he was gone?

"Game's over!" Zach shouted. "Your ass is going to pay for this stunt."

I sucked in a breath, counted to five, then jumped to my feet. I'd find a way to survive. I'd do it for Rafe. I took off running again, and the forest whirled around me in a kaleidoscope of doom—every way I looked seemed the same. A huge boulder blocked my path straight ahead, and I was pretty certain going right would take me too close to the road. The easier way, for sure, but also the one that would expose me the most. I made a sharp left and bumped into another tree.

A warm tree. An angry tree with arms that reached out and folded me in a crushing and possessive embrace. "Stupid, stupid girl."

His hand gripped the back of my neck. I lashed out

with the keys, screaming, and did little more than swipe the air until his fingers banded around my wrist painfully. My grip loosened, allowing him to apprehend my makeshift weapon. He turned me around and propelled me forward, back in the direction I'd come.

"Let me go!"

"Sure thing, love." He forced me to my knees and backed away. "I find it interesting you're trying to run. Didn't you tell me we'd get far away from the island, just the two of us?" Breathing hard, I angled my head and watched as he tested the branches. He paused long enough to glower at me. "Or were you lying?"

"I-I didn't—"

"Shut your deceitful mouth, or I'll shut it for you."

I pressed my lips closed, and dread coiled in my belly, intensifying after he broke off a switch. With a cruel growl, he hefted me up by the back of my shirt. "Zach—"

"I said shut up! Not another fucking word."

I was familiar enough with that tone to know when to give in. A deep ache tore through my chest. I held my fists to my breasts, as if I could keep my heart from beating through my ribcage. We cleared the last of the trees, and I realized I hadn't run as far as I thought. I stumbled toward the cabin on trembling legs. Adrenaline seeped from my bones, leaving behind a coward who nearly sank to the ground with each step. Once we reached the porch, I fell to my filthy knees. Zach pulled me to my feet, dragged me up the stairs, and kicked the door open. He shoved me toward the bedroom and left me in the middle of the floor where I turned to a puddle of skin, bones, and a heart that beat too rapidly.

"Don't you fucking move. If I have to chase you through those woods again, I'll beat you unconscious." He dropped the stick, as if to taunt me with its promise and the reminder of how little of a threat I posed to him.

After he left the room, another surge of adrenaline fueled my veins, and I crawled to the stick. But it was flimsy, barely thick enough to pass as a branch. What was I going to do? Whip him to death with it?

"Playing with your implement of punishment?"

I pushed to my feet and wielded the switch as if I could cause real damage. "Stay away from me."

In one hand, he fisted a coil of rope. In the other, he gripped a bottle of what looked like cheap whiskey. He brought it to his lips, took a long swig as if his life depended on it, and placed the bottle precariously on the edge of the dresser. Reaching out a hand, he appeared unworried as he gestured toward me. "Hand it over and I'll go easy on you."

"You call whipping me going easy?"

He launched himself across the room, grabbed my arms, and the stick fell to the floor as he slammed me against the bedpost, facing outward.

"Zach!" I pleaded as he wrapped the rope around my wrists, tightening the knots with quick and jerky movements. He secured my hands to the post above my head, and the smile that graced his face was so cruel, I flinched from its impact alone. He withdrew a knife from his pocket and snapped open the blade.

"Zach, no!" I recoiled, but the sharp edge didn't sear my flesh. Instead, the rip of fabric slashed through my ears. He slit my tee down to the navel, parted the material, and slapped my breasts once they swung free.

"God, I love your tits." With a moan, he rubbed his rough cheek against them. Retrieving the switch from the floor, he took a step back, and we exchanged a moment of understanding, of silent communication between punisher and punished. Still, I wasn't ready.

He'd hurt me before, with his hands, his teeth, but when he swung that stick down on my breasts, the point of contact served as an epicenter, and every muscle in my body spasmed from the deep ache. I clenched my teeth to keep silent.

He lifted his arm again, a tilt to his head as he regarded me, and I yanked at the bindings, composure slipping. "Don't." I twisted my hands, but that only made the rope dig into my wrists. "Please, please, please! Oh God—" The stick cut across my nipples, and I screamed his name. For the first time ever, he made me cry. More than cry. I bawled, begged, sobbed under each brutal lash.

"Shhhh." He kneeled, bringing him eye level with my heaving chest. "Lex..." His whisper carried a strangled plea, and I wondered what the hell he had to plead for. He wasn't the one on the receiving end of that stick. "Why do you make me hurt you? I should be inside your tight cunt, exactly where I belong." He wedged my thighs apart and dipped his fingers into dry heat, then pulled back with a frown. "I want you drenched. You know how hard it gets me."

Fingers spreading the lips of my mound, he buried his face there and dragged his tongue over my clit. I groaned, repulsed by the slick heat of his mouth. He kissed up my stomach, leaving a wet path to my breasts, and I stiffened. He licked the peaks, first the left then the right, and when he moved away, crimson stained his lips. My blood.

"This hurts me as much as you." The muscles in his left arm tensed, fist tightening around the switch, readying for another swing.

Nothing on Earth prepared me for strike after strike on my breasts and stomach. "Stop!" Fire danced across my flesh, and I howled at the excruciating sting. I resisted glancing down, scared to see the blood smearing my skin, the ugly red welts he must have left behind. Instead, I focused on him, on the rapid rise and fall of his chest, the rigid set of his jaw. The regret in his eyes that made me want to gouge them out. He had no right to feel regret or pity. If either of those elusive emotions existed inside his cold heart, they were fleeting—like dust obliterated by an unstoppable storm.

The stick struck the floor an instant before he gingerly probed my pussy. His frustrated gaze clashed with mine, and I knew I was in deep shit.

"Zach," I whispered. "Please..."

"Please what? What do I need to do to make you wet? What did *he* do?"

I shook my head. No, I couldn't talk about Rafe. A sob broke free, then another. Tears slid down my cheeks, and each one amplified the grief simmering in my soul until all I felt was denial. Anger.

Rage.

"You killed him! I hate you." I lifted a knee and struck his erection. "I fucking *hate* you! Do you hear me?"

Zach stumbled back, out of striking distance. While he doubled over, wheezing between lips tightened in pain, I unraveled, my gut-wrenching sobs tearing through the air, my feet uselessly kicking as acceptance finally penetrated.

Rafe was really gone.

I wailed, aching to clutch my breasts and contain the agony pouring from me. Zach might as well cut my chest open and carve my heart out with his teeth. It wouldn't devastate any less. Nothing mattered anymore. He could beat me, cut me, kill me...I felt nothing beyond hatred and the remnants of despair.

I lifted my head, peering through tears and the messy curls clinging to my face, and caught his gaze, blasted all my hatred in that stare. He turned away, as if he couldn't stand to look at me. But was it the sight of me that bothered him, or the truth that stared him in the face?

FOUR

RAFE

"You have a condition called dissociative amnesia." Before I could ask the doctor what the heck that meant, my brother beat me to it. Typical Adam behavior. He'd just arrived, but he was already taking over.

Clearing his throat, he leaned forward, dark hair brushing his brows as he cast a glance in my direction. "What does that mean, exactly?" His get-to-the-point tone commanded Dr. Brady's attention.

"Dissociative amnesia usually occurs due to a psychological trauma, rather than a physiological one." The doctor gestured toward me. "In the case of your brother, it's unusual, as it's neither generalized nor selective. He hasn't forgotten his entire life, or bits and pieces, he's lost a large segment of it instead."

"And you're positive this isn't from physical trauma?" Adam asked.

"Going by the MRI results, no. Everything looks good."

I shifted carefully so the hole in my shoulder wouldn't throb too much. "Then why the fuck can't I remember the last eight years?" The doc's brows furrowed, and I winced. "Sorry, I'm just..." *Pissed that you guys are talking like I'm not here.* "This doesn't make any sense."

His ruddy face hardened. "This type of disorder doesn't always make sense."

"Now you're calling it a disorder? Am I crazy? Is that it?"

"No, Mr. Mason." He crossed his arms over his broad chest, and I was certain he meant to intimidate with the firm set of his mouth. He didn't approve of me, that much was obvious. Maybe he took issue with my career as an MMA fighter. Or the tats. Possibly, he detested foul language and the pricks who spewed it. "For whatever reason, your brain is burying part of your life."

"What can I do about it? Is there some sort of treatment or medication? When will I get my memory back?"

"There isn't a specific treatment for amnesia. Surrounding yourself with familiar people and places, getting back to your normal routine, those things might help your memory return. I recommend consulting with a psychologist. I believe working with a professional will help you get to the root of the cause."

So he was saying I was crazy. Fucking wonderful.

Adam stepped forward and shook Dr. Brady's hand. "Thank you."

The doctor nodded, his stony expression unchanging. "I'll be back soon with those referrals." He directed his cool blue eyes on me. "Tell the nurses if you change your mind about the pain meds."

"Sure." The psychoanalysis wasn't happening, and neither were the drugs. I couldn't stand the drowsy, looped, out-of-control state they put me in.

Dr. Brady left and shut the door upon his exit. The dead silence that engulfed the room weighed on my nerves. I didn't know how much longer I could take in this place, gunshot wound or not. I'd regained consciousness a few hours ago to find a stranger at my bedside who claimed it was 2014. Imagine my shock when I learned it was true. He'd informed me I'd been out for three days, spouted a bunch of other stuff, things that didn't make much sense, and then the doctor had come in, followed by the nurses, who all poked and prodded. Tests were ordered, more words said, and it all hazed in my mind like smoke.

"You're refusing medication for pain?" Adam frowned as he took a seat. "You've got nothing to prove. No one's going to care if the big, bad Rafe *The Choker* Mason takes a pain pill. There's no reason for you to suffer."

If I listened beyond the condescending tone, he almost sounded like he gave a shit. I met his tired green eyes, noting the pronounced wrinkles surrounding them. He'd certainly aged since the last time I remembered seeing him.

Which was eight years ago...wait, longer.

"I'm fine, Adam." At least I knew his name. Fuck, at least I knew my own. My memory had a warped sense of humor. How could eight years just disappear? It pissed me off that everyone seemed to know more about those missing years than I did, including a guy I knew nothing about. Jax wanted to talk. I felt it in my marrow, but I wasn't sure I was ready to hear what he had to say. The doctors, the nurses— they all treated me with a professional air, but underneath, I sensed an undercurrent of hostility. Disgust even.

Who had I become? And what was up with the way my brother was looking at me? Like he fucking cared. Most of all, the absence of one person ate at me like a maggot.

"Where's Dad?"

Adam perched his elbows on his knees. "Dad is...he's... busy."

I pushed myself up despite the pain, needing to be on equal ground. "Don't feed me that bullshit." Jax had been dodging the question since I'd first opened my eyes in this place. Now Adam was doing the same.

He dropped his head into his hands then dragged his fingers through his hair. When he looked up, stress etched across his features, tightening his mouth and jaw. "We're on much better terms than we used to be, so you can cut the attitude."

"Since when?"

"Since you got out—" He cursed under his breath.

"Got out of what?"

"I think Jax should be the one to tell you about that. He should be back soon."

"I don't even know the guy."

"You know him better than you think. He was your cellmate." Adam closed his eyes. "Shit."

A heavy glob of dread pressed on my chest. "Cellmate?"

He rose from the chair. "I realize this is horrible timing, but I have a meeting I need to get to. I just stopped in to check on you. I heard you were awake."

"Some things never change," I muttered. "Whatever you're keeping from me, just tell me. It couldn't get any worse than this."

"I'm not sure how much you *should* know. We don't know what caused the amnesia. Maybe you should take the doc's advice and talk to someone who specializes in this stuff."

"You mean a shrink?"

"Yes, I'm talking about a *shrink*." Sarcasm dripped from the last word. "Excuse me for worrying about my little brother." He wandered around the room, and each second of disquiet niggled at my irritation. I didn't like being left in the dark.

"The sheriff's waiting to talk to you," he said, clearly

changing the subject. "And speaking of, so is Nik. Are you up to seeing her yet?"

I shook my head. The last memory I had of Nikki involved a night of the wildest, roughest sex of my life— the kind that marred skin with bruises.

Eight. Fucking. Years. Ago.

I was scared shitless to find out what had happened since that night.

Had I made it to the UFC?

Were Nikki and I a...thing? A thing didn't encompass how I felt about her. I was far from ready to settle down, but if that day ever came, it was too easy to see her filling that role. Easier to think of her than the brunette who tested my sanity and willpower every time I saw her. I wasn't about to touch jailbait.

Except she wasn't jailbait anymore.

My head spun, though whether from the puzzle pieces of my own mind, or the constant ache in my shoulder, I didn't know.

The door suddenly opened, and Jax stepped inside. "How're you feeling?"

I glanced down at the bandage covering the area where a bullet had passed clean through. "Good as can be expected." My gaze veered to my brother. "Adam won't tell me shit."

They exchanged a look, and I gritted my teeth.

"This is getting old. Spill, or I'll find out on my own."

Adam looked at his watch, and the shuffle of his feet

told me he was itching to ditch. "I think you should fill him in, Jax. You know him best anyway."

What the hell? How could this stranger know me better than my own brother? Okay, so we weren't exactly close, but still. We were family.

"I'll call you after my meeting ends." He reached for the door.

"Adam," I said, sitting up straighter. "Where the fuck is Dad?"

"I don't think now is the time..." He swallowed hard.

"Just tell me. Is he sick? Out of state on business? What the fuck is going on?"

"Dad passed a year ago." His voice was so soft and low, it took a few seconds for those words to penetrate. Strength fled my body, and I sank into the pillows. A lump formed in my throat, preventing me from speaking. Something foreign burned behind my eyes. Tears. Grief. I never cried. Crying was a weakness. Crying was for pansies.

Adam dropped his head, one hand on the open door. "Rafe? Did you hear what I said?"

Through my blurry vision, I saw a nurse move past in the hall. "How did it happen?" I didn't recognize the thick quality of my voice.

"Cancer."

I thought back to all the years I'd seen a cigarette dangling from Dad's mouth, all the times Adam and I tried to convince him to give up the habit. "He never quit, did he?"

"He was the definition of stubborn," Adam said, shaking his head.

"Did he suffer?" I knew it was a ridiculous question, but I had to hear it.

My brother lifted his eyes, so like my own, and the weight of his sorrow crushed me. "You know Dad. He fought with everything he had."

"Did we get to say goodbye?" The thought of him passing alone was too much, and I swallowed hard before clearing my throat. "Was he at peace with it?"

Again, Adam and Jax traded a glance. My brother nodded. "Yeah."

Jax scowled. "Don't lie to him. Not about this."

"Jax," he warned.

"No. He deserves the truth, no matter how much it sucks." Settling into the chair Adam had vacated only moments ago, Jax rubbed a hand down his face. "You weren't there when your old man died. They denied your request for furlough."

As I tried to process what he'd said, what they'd *both* said, my gaze swerved between them.

Furlough.

Cellmate.

Eight years gone.

I wasn't there for Dad.

Wasn't there for Dad...

"Somebody start talking."

FIVE

ALEX

The slam of a door sent a shot of adrenaline through my veins, and my heart galloped in time to his steps coming closer in the hall. Rope pulled at my sore wrists, rubbed raw from hours of trying to get free. We'd spent the last three...maybe four days in this room, fucking, fighting, and fucking some more, barely taking time to fuel our bodies with what little canned goods Zach found in the cabin. It was like a nymphomaniac had taken over his being. Now that he had me here to himself, he couldn't stop thrusting his cock into me.

Or beating me when my body wouldn't turn to liquid for him.

The bedroom door opened and banged against the wall, and Zach set two paper bags on the dresser. He'd tied me to the bed before leaving to "get supplies." My stomach grumbled, and I hoped he bought something other than soup, chili, or SpaghettiOs.

As he stumbled toward me, a sheen of sweat broke out on my skin. I recognized that glazed-over expression, the off-kilter sway of his body as he moved. "You've been drinking and driving?" As the hours passed, I'd started to wonder if he'd ever return. "What would happen to me if you never came back?"

The mattress depressed under his weight, and the stench of whiskey drifted to my nose as he fumbled with the complex knots keeping me prisoner on the bed. "I can drive just fine." He cursed under his breath. "The reason it took me so long was because Dad's being Dad." His lips tightened as he pulled the rope from my wrists.

"What do you mean?"

"He's about to put an APB out on my ass if I don't go home. I told him I needed some time to deal with everything, but he isn't letting this go."

As soon as my wrists were free, I massaged some circulation into them. But my attention veered to Zach's hands, the pockets of his jeans, even the dresser. A sense of defeat threatened to strangle me. No phone, no keys. After my last attempt to get away, he wouldn't be so careless, even while intoxicated.

He grabbed my chin. "Are you listening to me? My fucking career means more to him than it ever did to me. He's furious that I disappeared."

"What are you gonna do?"

His mouth curved into a smirk. "Don't get any ideas. I'm not letting you go, if that's what you're hoping for. I held him off for a while longer." He planted a kiss on my mouth before backing away. "Get up."

"Dad won't stay silent forever. He'll find you," I said, sliding off the bed to stand on weak legs. I folded my arms. "When he does he'll see I'm still alive."

"Don't worry about Dad. I can handle him." The nasty smirk never left his face. "And I can handle you too." He wrapped his hands around my hips and pushed forward. I shot my arms behind me, palms pressing into the mattress to keep from sprawling onto the bed. Not an inch of space separated our bodies, and I was grateful for the T-shirt he'd allowed me before he left.

"I'm gonna make you love me again, Lex." He dipped his head, gaze zeroing in on my mouth. "We'll be together, just like we were always meant to be."

"You're delusional."

"I'm pragmatic. If pain doesn't do it for you anymore, we'll try pleasure."

"Stop." As his lips neared, my hands left the mattress and pressed against his chest. "I can barely stomach the sight of you after what you've done." I choked on the last word, the thought of Rafe trying to creep in again, and cleared my throat. "You forced me, Zach. *For years.*"

He jerked his head back and forth. "You can't fake this kind of connection." His palms slid along my cheeks, his fingers tangling in my hair as he tilted my head back. The intensity of his stare pummeled me. "You're the only one who's ever cared about me. Dad sure as hell doesn't."

"That's not true. You're his whole world."

"I'm fucking tired of being his world. I'm tired of it all. You don't know him like I do." He swallowed hard, and his eyes glistened with a lifetime of resentment. If I thought Dad had been tough on me, he'd been harder on Zach. Pushing him to be the best, to fight rougher, meaner. *Never back down, son! Don't be an embarrassment. Losing isn't an option.*

He rested his forehead against mine. "Quitting is a relief. I don't want to fight. The belts, the championships, none of it matters. I just want you. Everything is so easy with you, second nature, like breathing. Remember when we were kids and we'd hide under the covers every time they'd get into another fight? You made me feel needed. Wanted. Let's just hide here forever, Lex."

Damn him. I blinked, suppressing the burning tears in my eyes. How could one person pull me in so many directions? He repulsed me, made me furious, made me feel the most intense hatred a person could harbor...yet he still made me care. What would it take before I forgot the good times, the years when he was there for me as a brother should be? While our parents had waged war in the house, he'd been my safe place, the one who held me and told me to hang on a little longer because it would be over soon. If I'd known back then how dark he'd turn, if I'd been capable of understanding what that darkness meant, I wouldn't have gone to him for comfort. I wouldn't have looked at him as a brother, because that connection made hating him messy and complicated.

Zach was a minefield of which I was stuck in the middle. It didn't matter which way I stepped, an explosion strong enough to dismember was bound to happen.

"I have to pee," I said, needing the distraction, needing distance. I squirmed, and my bladder begged for release.

He pulled away and gestured toward the bathroom. "Come back naked. I have a surprise for you."

"I don't want your surprises. I want you to let me go."

Thick brows furrowed over intense eyes filled with determination. "That's not gonna happen."

I turned my back to him, thinking how the eyes of someone so rotten to the soul shouldn't hold so much beauty. The weight of his scrutiny followed me into the bathroom. After I took care of business, I deliberated removing my clothing, but self-preservation won the battle. The thought of igniting his wrath made the decision for me. I took my time undressing, then glanced down at my breasts with a cringe. Fading bruises and criss-crossed welts covered my skin in a grotesque mural of purple and yellow. I feathered my fingers over the marks of his rage, and my feet refused to move, as if they sensed the pain waiting for me. But stalling would only delay the inescapable. I had no way out.

I returned to him, avoiding eye contact, and folded my arms to hide my breasts. *Not* fighting him seemed wrong. I had nothing left to lose and everything to gain with my freedom.

"Bend over the bed."

I gave a swift shake of my head.

In three strides, he grabbed my arms before hauling me across the room. I dug in my heels, pulled against his strength, but in the end he shoved me against the bed. "This is happening, Lex. Bend the fuck over and hold still, or I'll beat the fight out of you."

I went limp under the threat. My breasts flamed with the memory of his strikes, as if the wounds were hours old instead of a few days. Even now, each sharp bite of his switch ghosted through me. It hadn't been a paddle to my ass, a punch to my gut or face, or a slap or bite. He'd lost his mind when he'd wailed on my body with that stick. I bent over the mattress, gripped the bedding, and waited, hoping he'd fuck me instead of beat me.

No warning. He pushed a finger in my ass, and I shrieked from the scorching burn of dry skin forcing entry into my rectum. He splayed one hand on my back, holding me in place while his finger stilled in my hole. "Don't move."

"Ow! What are you doing?"

"In a few minutes, you won't give a shit what I'm doing." He burrowed his finger in deeper, intensifying the sting. I let out a wail, terrified he was about to rape me anally.

"Please don't do this!" My voice trembled so badly, the

words came out wobbled and unrecognizable. Every spark of my being told me to flee, yet my body wouldn't jump into motion. He didn't have to threaten bodily harm—he'd already beaten the fight out of me the other night, when he'd drawn blood with his switch.

"Zach?" His name fell from my lips with uncertainty, an inquiry that sounded far off. A strange heat wave flushed my skin, and my pulse thumped at my throat. A flood of...something washed over me, making my head swim. I couldn't explain or describe it, but my surroundings held new meaning. Fear evaporated, and things that were previously hidden, like the gold strands in the pattern of the bedspread or the knots in the walls, sprouted in a burst of vibrancy. Like a rosebud unfurling its petals in slow motion. I licked my lips and tasted the air. God. Nothing had ever fired up my taste buds so good.

The pressure in my ass subsided, but I remained sprawled on the bed, held captive by the details burgeoning around me.

Zach helped me stand, and the ground wobbled, the room warping in a blur...it was the most amazing feeling in the world. I didn't care if I tipped. I was one with the floor, the hardwood incredibly smooth against the soles of my feet. He brushed me from behind, and I moaned at the velvety texture of his skin. Silk covered my eyes, so fluid it could have been milk, and cast me into a pit of sinfully dark bliss.

"Zach?" The name was wrong, and it rang through my

ears, causing a hint of fear, but mostly a question, one I couldn't formulate verbally.

What had he done to me?

"Shhh, it's okay. Just feel me. Feel how much I want you. How much you want me."

A whirl of air caressed my nakedness, and his breath feathered over my parted mouth. I inhaled his heady scent, like decadent chocolate, and darted my tongue out to lick the richness of his lips. Mmm...lips. I reached forward and thrust my tongue between them.

A groan rumbled from his throat. He commanded my tongue, sucked me in so far I fell into the cavity of his mouth. I pictured my body curled in a ball, as precious as a pearl and enclosed in slick heat, buoyed by his tongue.

"Baby, I need you." His hands fell on my shoulders, two heavy weights I welcomed. I buckled to his demand, and my knees kissed the floor. His fingers crept up my neck, slid into my hair. Every inch of my skin came alive from the follicles of my scalp to the rough pads of my heels.

I purred under his caress. "Do that again."

"This?" He repeated the motion, his fingertips dancing over my skin like a ballerina. I hummed the music that matched the steps, imagining my fingers flying over piano keys. The dance peaked at my chin and tilted me upward to greet the soft, wet mushroom seeking entrance to my mouth. My hum vibrated against the silky tip, and I envisioned the notes as colors, spirals of reds that glowed incandescent.

His moan mixed with the symphony. Rafe and I, we were creating a masterpiece.

Rafe...Rafe...Rafe...

His name echoed though my head, a tick, a glimmer of truth, as if that single thought was trying to tell me something.

"Love my cock."

Rainbows of color swirled behind my eyes. In the darkness, I found freedom. Found the most unbelievable ecstasy possible. I parted my mouth, and when he pushed in, my pussy tingled, letting loose liquid fire between my thighs. I fastened my lips around his shaft, never tasting anything so sweet, and continued humming my notes, vibrating my masterpiece around the hardened silk filling my mouth.

What was that sound coming from him? Guttural, painful, sexy. I felt that low groaning in the flutter of my racing heart, the sweat on my back, deep in my belly where the ballerinas practiced pirouettes. My tongue lapped and lapped. I couldn't get enough of his taste, his texture.

This was madness. I'd never be able to stop. I sucked harder, pulled his tip into my throat, and gagged.

Holy hell. I drew him further down and gagged again.

"Shit, Lex!"

I choked on his cum, thrown off by the nickname, but it was so flavorful, like nothing I'd ever sampled before. I didn't want to miss a drop. He withdrew, and I whimpered, following with my tongue, still lapping. Lapping, lapping, lapping. Still tasting, still *needing*.

"Enough." He picked me up and tossed me onto the bed where my body sank into heaven. Fluidity surrounded me, enfolding my skin in cool satin. I fisted my hands in it, suddenly discovering their existence. Why had it taken me so long? Fingers curled, smooth texture clenched in palms —everything exquisite, especially the inflexible expanse of his chest brushing the tips of my breasts.

His breaths whispered across my face, rustling my hair like a summer-laced breeze. My jaw slackened, tongue relaxed against my teeth, and a finger pressed inside. I closed my lips and sucked the salt from his skin. "Mmm."

"God, I love you so much," he said.

Soaring at his declaration, my mouth pulled on his finger, drawing him deeper. Tasting. I never wanted to stop tasting.

"No, baby." He withdrew his finger. With a frown of displeasure, I chased it with my mouth. "Say what I want to hear."

"Mmm, you taste so good."

His laughter rumbled like a trombone. "I like you this way."

"What way?" I almost told him to stop talking and let me taste again, but his voice was a drug I couldn't resist.

"Higher than Mt. Fucking Everest."

The curve of my lips felt alluring. "That's pretty high."

"Tell me you love me," he demanded.

I loved everything about him. His taste, his touch, his voice. The way he made me feel, how he openly wore his vulnerability. The way he still loved me, protected me, even after all I'd done to him. Somewhere in the darkest corner of my mind, a siren sounded. A warning. Feeling this way was wrong...but I couldn't recall why.

"I love you." My chest squeezed as I uttered the words, and I imagined not only the love in Rafe's green eyes, but the promise of forgiveness.

The promise of forever.

He smothered my grin with his mouth, and I was pretty sure Mt. Fucking Everest was a speck of dust in my brilliant world.

SIX

RAFE

"I was sixteen the last time I set foot in this cabin." The door shut behind me with a soft thud of finality, and I turned and faced the stranger who, apparently, knew me better than my own brother. After the things he'd told me about the elusive years my psyche refused to acknowledge, I was beginning to think he just might.

"As far as your memory goes, yeah, but before the shooting, you were living here."

"Right," I said with a sigh, dragging a hand through my unruly hair. A sling trapped my left arm, rendering it useless. I wandered into the living room, cursing the huge gaping hole in my life, and studied my dad's cabin with new perspective. In so many ways it appeared unchanged. Same sturdy furniture, crafted by my grandfather's hands and worn from many summers of use.

Standing in this place was akin to setting one foot in the present while the other planted firmly in the past. So much remained as I remembered, yet the subtle changes—the uncluttered space, free of Dad's disorganized, spread-out existence—made my head swim with the evidence of what Jax had told me.

I'd been in prison.

My dad died while I was in there.

And I had no chance at ever fighting again—not in the way I'd dreamed of since I was old enough to throw a punch. Irritatingly, both Jax and Adam remained tight-lipped about *why* I'd been locked up, but Adam had made that last point abundantly clear; I'd left the world of fighting and had joined him in the family business. I was still trying to wrap my head around that piece of information.

"After your dad passed," Jax said, halting beside me, "you offered me a place to stay. I've been doing the upkeep since."

"Yeah, I can see that. Things look...different but the same. It's strange." I swerved my head toward him and he shrugged.

I moved toward the kitchen and sensed him following my slow steps. The room where Dad, Adam, and I had shared dirty jokes as we ate the day's catch appeared the same too, though impeccably clean compared to what I remembered. The disorderly array of tackle boxes, fishing poles, and Dad's overflowing ashtrays and beer bottles were absent. So was the musky scent of smoke. The paddle hanging by the back door was the only notable evidence of him.

An eerie chill drifted over my skin, almost as if someone had opened the door to the dead cold of winter, though the weather was mild for early June. I studied the kitchen table, drawn to it like a magnet, and the feeling I should recall something hit me with such significance, I froze, my feet stuck in place.

Drops of water pooling on the table, tangled hair, wet and wild, rioting down creamy skin. A perfectly round ass, reddened from the slap of wood. I blinked but the weird vision tingled down my spine in an odd way, making my dick stir.

I glanced out the windows and almost expected to see rain pummeling the ground, but the morning was just as clear and bright as it'd been when they released me from the hospital an hour ago. With a shake of my head, I lowered into a chair, being careful not to knock my sling into the table, and smoothed my palm across the course red oak surface, hoping to bring back that niggle of... something.

Jax pulled two beers from the fridge, popped the caps off both, and slid one over to me.

"Isn't it a little early for that?" I asked, gesturing toward the dark ale. It was barely 10 a.m.

"For this conversation?" He raised a brow. "Doubt it."

He turned the chair around and straddled it, and again I willed my mind to reach out and catch a memory.

"Did something happen here?" I gestured to the table spanning the distance between us.

"Lots of stuff happened here." His mouth quirked into a half smile, half smirk as he tipped the bottle back and took a swig. He set the beer back on the table with a loud clunk. "Look, I said we'd talk once you got out. I know you have questions, so let's get to it. What do you wanna know?"

That was a fucking loaded question. "Let's start with why I was locked up."

"The sheriff didn't tell you?"

I shook my head, remembering how he'd questioned me in the hospital, as if I were guilty of shooting myself or something. Lyle Lewis hadn't changed a bit, from what I could tell. His contemptuous attitude really dug under my skin. Fucking ridiculous that the town bully would become sheriff. "He didn't tell me shit, and he didn't give a rat's ass about finding the fucker who shot me either."

"I'm not surprised. Nikki told me about the uproar he's stirred in town. He's the reason half of Dante's Pass hates your guts, man." Jax winced. "Sorry, probably too brutal. Never been good with tact."

"When did you talk to Nik? Do you guys know each other?"

He took a long drink of his beer before answering. "We talked at the hospital."

The idea of Jax getting close to her bothered me, but I couldn't say why. Maybe because I still thought of her as mine, even though Lyle the-fucking-sheriff Lewis had made it a point to tell me they were engaged to be married in a few weeks.

"What'd you talk about?"

"You, mostly. She was pissed you wouldn't see her."

Shame fissured me. I hadn't wanted her to see me like that. I still didn't, but too much history existed between us to avoid seeing her forever, and refusing her visit had been a low, cowardly move.

Jax cleared his throat, the sound shattering more than just the unspoken *stuff* between us; it obliterated the facade. The sheriff, Nikki, and even Jax's involvement with her—none of it mattered as much as filling in the blanks of the last eight years.

"So we met in prison?" I asked, finally tiptoeing toward the core of the matter.

He nodded. "We were cellmates. We've had each other's back since the day you saved my life."

My eyes widened. "What happened?"

Jax wouldn't look at me. "Prison was tough on both of us. I think we should leave it in the past. What's done is done. All that matters is I owe you my life."

I wanted to push for an explanation, details of my time in there, but I left it for now. "How long was I in for? *What* was I in for?"

Jax lifted his brown eyes to mine, and his stare never

wavered. "You sure you're ready to hear this? I'm thinking your brother might be right. Losing your memory is heavy shit."

"I didn't take advice from Adam back then and I'm sure as hell not gonna start now. Tell me what happened."

He drew in a breath, let it out. "You were in eight years for rape."

What the...?

His words lingered, an echo that wouldn't stop bouncing between my ears. "There's...no. I couldn't have done it. That's just..."

"You didn't do it."

He sounded so matter-of-fact. I narrowed my brows, gripping the table to keep from springing to my feet. "How do you know? You said we met in there. Everyone in prison says they're innocent."

"Trust me. I know. You don't have an iota of rapist gene in you. Well, you didn't until she had you locked up for it. Her accusation tore your life apart. Dude, I'm being straight with you about this. You've done some fucked up shit, but you didn't do that."

"Who accused me?"

He took another draw from his beer, and the ensuing silence made me want to scream at him to spit it out.

"I'm not sure we should get into that shitstorm yet. Maybe you should give it some time. Wait for the memories to resurface on their own."

"Who was it, Jax?"

He lowered his head with a sigh, as if he regretted the words before he said them. "Alex De Luca."

I pushed back from the table so suddenly, the chair toppled over in my haste to get away. But there was no getting away from this. I might not remember the last eight years, but I remembered her. I recalled the delicate features of her face—high cheekbones, a kissable mouth I still ached to taste, and the sensual tones of her voice. Her image burned in my brain, as if I'd seen her just yesterday, and in a way, I had. My last memory of Alex wasn't from eight years ago; it was from a few weeks ago.

Turning my back to Jax, I propped my good arm against the counter and hung my head. Closed my eyes. Focused so intently, I gave myself a headache that rivaled the throb in my shoulder.

Nothing.

Just an empty vault where eight years of memories should reside. No matter what Jax said, I doubted my innocence. I couldn't believe I'd force myself on her, but she was...she'd been underage, and I wanted her with an uncontrollable urge so sharp, it sliced me up every time I got within ten feet of her.

I held that secret close. No one knew, except for maybe Alex herself. I gave a slight jerk of my head. I still hadn't reconciled the shift in time. Then. Now. It confused the heck out of me.

"You okay?" Jax asked.

I clenched my jaw. "Yeah."

She had to have known how I felt, especially considering the way we'd gravitated toward each other, orbiting with a forbidden vibe. How we'd pounced on every chance to banter and tease. Those intense glances she'd sent my way were too familiar. They'd imparted the same need I'd kept hidden since the day I noticed her as more than a child...more than the kid sister of my best friend.

No. Impossible. I wouldn't have done that, no matter how much I'd wanted to.

"You don't seem okay."

Was I okay? I had no fucking clue. I turned around. "What kind of 'fucked up shit' did I do?"

Jax hesitated, only for a moment, but it was long enough to make me squirm. "Maybe you should take a peek in the cellar."

"What the fuck does that have to do with any of this?"

He rose, scooting the chair back in a grating manner, and chugged the rest of his beer. He glanced at mine, still untouched on the table, and lifted a brow. But he didn't say anything about my aversion to drinking the day away. "Come see for yourself."

It felt odd to follow someone else in Dad's cabin, but I didn't complain as he led the way to the cellar door. He pulled it open and switched on the light. We descended the stairs, and upon first sight of a cage that closely resembled a prison cell, my mouth dropped open.

"What the hell is that?"

"That's where you kept Alex after we kidnapped her."

"We *what*?"

"Dude, she ruined your career and your reputation. One little lie from a De Luca and your life went up in smoke. Losing your dad was the final hit. I don't blame you for wanting revenge."

He continued speaking, but I couldn't hear the words through the blaring noise in my ears, the throbbing pain at my temples. My attention cut to the cage again. Had I built it? It was sturdy, the sort of prison that wouldn't be easy to escape from, and I didn't miss the hook in the ceiling or the cuffs dangling from it. What the fuck had I done? *Who* had I become?

A feeling I couldn't pin down fell upon my chest, making it difficult to breathe, and the fantasies I'd ignored since early adolescence surfaced. Those cuffs, the ability to lock away another human being...a sexy, vulnerable *woman*...I squeezed my free hand into a fist as my dick hardened. Fuck me and my deviant thoughts.

Just fantasies.

They didn't mean anything, and they sure as fuck didn't mean I'd lost my damn mind by acting on them. I stumbled back, gripped my head, and told myself to breathe. "I wouldn't have done this." My voice sounded far away, as if filtering through the hollow of a tunnel. Someone else's voice. Someone else's life.

Someone else did this.

"I'm sorry, man. This was what I was afraid of. I shouldn't have brought you down here."

With morbid curiosity, my eyes veered to the cage again, and one glaring detail finally punched me in the face. A locked up prison cell, but no prisoner cowering inside. If I'd kidnapped her...then where the fuck was she?

SEVEN

ALEX

The fall from euphoria was like hurtling through the air without a parachute. Hitting bottom hurt worse than anything. I remembered everything. How deliriously I'd wanted him, how strong our connection was during those hours when only an infinite amount of pleasure existed. Sorrow, grief, guilt...none of it had burdened me.

I didn't have to open my eyes to know the warm body against mine, clutching me possessively, was Zach's and not Rafe's. His hangover stench attacked my sense of smell. With a deep groan, I leaned over the side of the bed and vomited every last memory onto the hardwood, purged it all from my system. But my system refused to stop spiraling into the depths of horror.

I'd sucked his cock. Willingly, wantonly. Like the whore he always accused me of being. Somehow, in the confusion of my fucked up mind, I'd thought he was Rafe. How was that even possible?

"What did you give me?" I asked, my voice raspy from deep sleep. After we'd fucked half the night away and the restless energy in my veins subsided, I'd conked out like the dead.

"Just a little ecstasy."

I shook my head, untangling from his hold. "I've tried E before. That was...something else."

"That was the purest shit you'll ever come across." He rolled me until we lay face to face. "Plus I gave it to you anally. I knew it would open you up." He slid a hand down my hip, around my upper leg, and burrowed between my clenched thighs.

I shrank from his touch, and his eyes darkened. His hand inched higher while he tangled his other in my hair, yanking until my eyes watered.

"Let me go."

His hairy leg slid between mine, giving him enough room to shove his fingers in me. "You're gonna get wet for me, Lex."

I closed my eyes, clicked my teeth together, and tried to tune out his heavy breathing, but I couldn't ignore his touch. He spread me wide, thrust deep, pulled out, brushed my clit, and repeated the process over and over at an unyielding pace. A subtle pressure built in my core, increasing with the slide of his fingers. I drew blood from my lip to keep from rocking my hips.

Oh God. Why? Where had my armor of apathy gone?

He leaned forward, his lips expelling rapid breaths into my ear, and whispered, "Welcome back." Withdrawing his hand from my pussy, he forced his fingers into my mouth. "Taste that. That's want. That's *need*."

I chomped down hard. As he jerked away, trying to save himself from another vicious bite, I scrambled in the opposite direction and crashed to the floor. "I hate you!"

"Last night, you said you loved me."

"You drugged me!"

"No, I freed your mind and worked past all the shit you carry around with you. You think it's wrong for us to be together?" He propped himself up on his elbows and glared down at me from the edge of the mattress. "Last night, you didn't feel that way." He reached out and ran his thumb across my trembling lips. "And you weren't thinking of him, were you?"

Rafe. It was Rafe. I wouldn't have done that with Zach. Only Rafe. I blinked rapidly and pushed away, ass sliding across the floor in desperation. My spine hit a wall. The corner beckoned me, offering the illusion of safety, of escape. I huddled there, arms snaking around my knees as memories from the night before hit me with full force.

For a few hours, Rafe had been alive. In my arms, in my hands, in my mouth. Alive. Warm. Mine. I pulled in a breath, tried to force it deep into my lungs, and panicked when I couldn't. Tears blurred my vision, grief choked my throat, and the glaring truth flooded my senses. It had all been a drug-induced illusion my psyche had used to trick me. A pitiful sound escaped, part sniffle, part sob.

Zach climbed to his feet, the tangled sheets and bedding coming with him to hang over the side, taunting me with the evidence of our wild night of sex, one in which I'd been a full participant. The observation almost made me retch again, but I swallowed the sour taste of disgust burning my throat.

"Get up," he demanded, his tone leaving no room for argument. Once I stood on jittery legs, he herded me into the bathroom and switched on the shower. I clenched my hands into fists, eyes firmly shut as water flowed over me. The sobs wouldn't subside. They drummed out in soft shudders I couldn't control. If I didn't open my eyes, if I blocked out his touch, maybe I wouldn't totally lose it.

No, I was losing it. Pain was not a new entity, but this type of crushing anguish—the kind that made it nearly impossible to breathe, to think, too see beyond the next second, minute, hour—would make the strongest person crumble. And I wasn't strong. Not in this moment. My thoughts jumbled, zipping through my mind so fast I couldn't grasp any of them.

Save for one. Rafe was dead. Last night I'd lived a dream, so vivid I could still feel him against me. But I'd never feel him again. Never hear his voice, his laughter. Never breathe in the musk of his skin, feel the sweat of his brow at my breasts. Never again lose my breath to the vise of his hands around my throat. I'd give anything to get that back, even if giving up control terrified me.

Zach ran a blade up my leg, startling me. "Dry it up, Lex. You're pissing me off."

"I-I c-can't." A hiccup echoed in the stall, followed by another.

He took his time shaving my legs, and I let him. And he let me cry it out. Every atom of my body was fightless. Worthless. Eventually, he finished grooming me and tugged on my hand, urging me from the shower with a gentleness that penetrated the crazy state of my head. A towel landed around my shoulders, pulled tight in front, and he wrapped another around his waist before threading our fingers together. A hint of tenderness softened his expression as he led me into the bedroom.

"I know it feels like the end of the world," he said, leaving me standing at the side of the bed, "but it isn't. Things will get better. You'll adjust." He strolled to the dresser and withdrew clothing from the paper bags he'd brought in last night. "Get dressed." He tossed a sundress at me.

I held up the garment by a spaghetti strap, not only taking note of the short hem, but how oddly similar it was to a dress I'd owned as a teenager. That particular dress had disappeared after some random guy had complimented my legs while wearing it. "It's too short."

"That's the point. Put it on." His mouth curved into a wicked line. "No panties. You won't need them."

Something about his demanding tone, along with the fact he was choosing my clothes for me, made my back straighten. "You wear it," I said, throwing it at him, "since you like it so much." The towel didn't cover enough, so I grabbed the sheet from where it cascaded down the side of the mattress and tucked it around my body.

He crossed the room and stood before me, but I kept my gaze trained on my bare feet, refusing to raise my eyes to his. Anger radiated off him in palpable waves, and in my periphery, I saw his hands clench before unfurling. He yanked the sheet and pulled, rolling me with it until I fell onto the bed with my back facing him. The dress landed by my head. "Get dressed before I beat your ass."

"I'm not your fucking puppet, Zach."

Feet stomped across the room, and I heard a drawer open and slam shut. The ominous sound cringed through me like fingernails on a chalkboard. I curled into a protective ball, preparing for the strike of whatever he'd removed from the dresser. A belt? I stiffened as his strong hands pulled me toward him, rear end first. He inserted a finger in my ass, and I cried out, squirming to dislodge it, panicked at the thought of repeating last night. His body pressed me into the mattress as his finger flamed in my rectum.

"Hold still. Soon, you'll fly for me." He swept my hair back, and his mouth opened over the sensitive skin underneath my ear, hot tongue searing flesh. "You always taste so good."

Oh God...no...

The soaring feeling from the night before trickled in, and my body felt weightless.

Oh shit...yes...

"Grmmddd..." *Fuuuuck...*

What was I trying to say?

"I'll take care of you," his deep voice said, each word pronounced in slow motion. "I can make you happy, Lex." He withdrew his finger, and I heard the unmistakable sound of him spitting before he dipped it in again, making my insides clench in a blissful ache. "No one loves you like I do. I just wish it didn't take this to lower your guard."

Somewhere in my hazy brain, I knew I should feel shame at the moan that poured from me—long and continuous as his finger fucked my asshole. His palm kneaded my butt cheeks, and his other hand spread my legs, fingers reaching for my clit.

I fisted the messy bedding and groaned, my teeth clamping down on the twisted sheets. My hips bucked and tension coiled low in my belly as I impaled myself on his fingers. Again. Again. Shit...harder.

So close. Ooooh...good God. I didn't want this. It was wrong. So horribly detestable. A deep burn ignited in my chest, threatening to turn to me to ash. Rafe's face pulled at the edges of my mind, compelling me to follow, to free-fall into the memory of him.

I squeezed my eyes shut and allowed the fantasy to take over. Rafe's hands, his skin on mine, his breath in my ear. His fingers pulling at my hair. "More," I groaned. "I need to come."

He pulled away, and I cried out in protest, begging him not to stop. Every part of my body tensed, readying for release, needing it, and the longer he delayed, the more the ache intensified.

"Put the dress on." He tickled my back with what felt like silk before dropping the garment on the mattress. "Then I'll make you come." His steps retreated, gently padding away. The creak of a door sounded. I crawled to my hands and knees, turned my head, but he was gone. How could he leave me like this? I needed him, but needing him hurt too much.

My heart pounded at an alarming rate, and the burn still simmered in my chest, a moment away from incinerating. I doused the dark thoughts and clutched the dress, slid from bed, and my body poured like fluid onto the floor. With a sigh, I lifted the silky material and pushed my head through, wondering why I'd put up such a fight. Pure sin encased my flushed body, and I rubbed the silk between thumb and forefinger, over and over again, entranced by the texture, certain I could never stop touching it. Slowly, tension ebbed from my bones, my limbs, my hands. The fire in my chest was but an ember.

The door opened, and I blinked, the silk forgotten. I gazed at him in the doorway, and his crooked smile hit me in the chest. It was so open and free. So fucking sexy. In that moment, he resembled someone else, someone who struck a cord of comfort in me. I peered through the warped glass and tried to figure out the puzzle of the man standing on the other side.

"Come here," he demanded, holding out a hand. I moved with effortless grace, my feet gliding across the floor, and slid my palm into his. He lifted a cup to my lips, and the water that poured down my throat extinguished the fire.

"Your feelings for me are real." His fingers wiped my brow. "What I gave you doesn't make you feel things that aren't there. It frees your mind." He pulled me against him. "It's making you mine again."

EIGHT

RAFE

Ever since Jax showed me the horrors hidden in my cellar, I'd spent every waking moment digging into the past my brain refused to remember. I'd spent hours on the Internet reading about the rape trial, watching it unfold from the seat of a spectator, though I was the main star. I'd watched the police haul me from a training session, hands cuffed at my back. What I found most disturbing about that piece of footage was the guilty look on my own damn face.

As if reading about the trial wasn't torturous enough, I dug into Jax's background too, which I found nothing on. I wasn't sure he'd understand my need to know more about him, so I didn't tell him I was looking into his life, but I couldn't swallow the idea of a stranger living on my father's island.

What bothered me most, however, was Alex's disappearance. The media had yet to report on her miraculous return from the dead. Going by the news reports of her "death," authorities had found her car in the Columbia River two and a half weeks ago. Jax said we'd pushed her Volvo in after taking her from Portland. He also said I'd decided to let her go hours before I got shot.

So where the fuck was she?

I could think of only two possibilities. Either she was terrified by what I'd done and had gone into hiding...or something unimaginable had happened to her. While I agonized over her whereabouts, my partner in crime was too busy working or disappearing to care about what had happened. Jax's only concern was staying out of jail. As long as Alex didn't surface, we were safe from being charged for kidnapping. He also suspected she'd had something to do with the shooting, which didn't make him her biggest fan.

My amnesia ensured I didn't remember shit, and it was frustrating as hell.

There was only one person in this new reality I trusted. Certainly not the stranger at my side, or my own brother. No matter what Adam said about reconciled differences or how he thought I should come back and work at Mason Vineyards—familiar routines and all of that—I couldn't talk to him.

But fuck, I needed to get out of my own head or I was going to go crazy.

I took a deep breath and climbed the steep staircase

that led to the front door of Nikki Malone's house. It had taken some needling of old friends, but I eventually got her address out of a girl who'd had a crush on me in high school. Nikki's place was up the mountain, nestled between clusters of Douglas firs. The Columbia River peeked through the branches, and I wondered if she had a view of the island from the porch wrapping around her home. The place was huge, built more recently if the modern angles and vinyl siding accented with stone was any indication. She'd done well for herself.

I hesitated, feet planted on the welcome mat, my fist poised to knock. She was engaged to the enemy. Jax would probably rip me a new one for trusting her, but I'd known her too many years not to. I rapped on the door and waited. A white BMW sat in the driveway, and I assumed it belonged to her. She had to be home.

I lifted my hand again, knuckles nearing the wood, and halted at the unmistakable thud of steps.

She pulled the door open, and her eyes widened, her mouth gaping. Same golden hair, same seductive brown eyes, but something fundamental had changed in them. Like most things these days, I couldn't put my finger on it. Nikki was not the same Nikki I'd known before my mind decided to check out on me.

"Rafe," she said with a smile that lacked the warmth I remembered. She ran a thumb along the edge of the door.

"I should've let you visit me at the hospital," I said,

figuring her less-than-enthusiastic welcome stemmed from my turning her away. "I'm an ass."

"It's okay. I can't imagine what it must be like to lose so much of your memory. Confusing?"

"Something like that." I gestured toward the door she held close to her body. "Can I come in? I really need to talk to someone, and you're the only one I trust."

"What about Jax?"

I tilted my head. "How much do you know about him?"

She shrugged. "We talked at the hospital. But he goes on about you like you're his brother or something. Guess you guys are close."

"Were close, maybe. I don't remember him at all."

She glanced over her shoulder, and something oddly familiar slid down my spine. Like I was the one who should have been watching my back...hiding something from her? I shook the idea from my mind. It happened often—a seemingly inconsequential phrase, gesture, or object, such as the table in my own damn kitchen. There was history on that slab of wood, and I wasn't talking about the many years I'd spent there with my dad and brother. Something about it bothered me, yet excited me all the same.

"I could use some air," she said. "Want to walk?"

Why did this seem so familiar? I nodded, shaking off the weird feeling.

As she slipped into a pair of sandals, I saw into her home. Open, airy, with vaulted ceilings, a stone fireplace, and wide windows that overlooked the river. The sun cast a beam of light into her great room. She stepped outside and pulled the door shut, then wrapped her arms around me.

"I'm so glad you're okay." Her lips brushed my cheek as she backed away. "Do you remember anything at all about that night?"

"Afraid not."

We reached the stairs at the same time. I indicated for her to go first, but she halted, lifting a hand toward my face. "Wait, you've got a little..." She brushed her thumb on my cheek. "Wouldn't want people talking about how you were wearing my lipstick."

"People here talk," I said, thinking of the icy reception I'd received from the townsfolk—some who'd known me since I was a kid. "Regardless of lipstick malfunctions."

"No need to give them more fodder." Nikki withdrew her hand. "I think you're decent now."

The corner of my mouth curled up. "You and I both know I'm far from decent. The last memory I have of you proves that."

"And what's that?"

"Seattle." I raised my brows.

She ducked her head, an unmistakable flush coloring her cheeks. "I remember Seattle."

"What happened between us while I was locked up?"

"Let's not get into all of that." She descended the steps,

and apparently that thread of conversation was off the table.

I followed, close on her heels. "How about we start with you and the sheriff then? Lyle Lewis, Nikki?"

"We already had this conversation."

"Except I don't remember that conversation."

"Your brother and Jax say you're pushing too hard. They're worried you're going to make the amnesia worse."

Once we reached the bottom, I grabbed her hand and pulled her around. "You've been talking to them about me?"

"I've been doing the bookkeeping at the vineyard. Your condition came up."

"It's not a fucking condition, Nik. It's not like I'm crazy. I'm still me."

"Language and all," she muttered, disentangling from my grip. She strode ahead several paces and gravel crunched under our feet until we reached the paved shoulder of the road.

"Are you and Jax friends?"

"I barely know him, but I guess you could say that."

"Like you and I are friends?" I shook my head. "*Were* friends."

She stopped and turned, hands on her hips. "We still are, Rafe. There's too much history between us." Her defensive stance eased. "I can't imagine ever just walking away."

I reached out and tugged on her arm, bringing her

against my chest. Her hands rested on my shoulders, and I stiffened under her touch. Though I no longer needed the sling, my shoulder still ached.

"Nikki..." I licked my lips, tantalized by the thought of losing myself in her, and I almost forgot she was eight years older from the last time I saw her. The last time I fucked her. I tilted my head, closing the distance between us, and moved in for a taste of something I hoped would bring back a spark of sanity to my life.

She gripped my shirt. "What are you—?"

"Shut up and fucking kiss me."

Nikki stared at me for a few seconds that beat in my head like a gavel. She deliberated, indecision warring on her face—in the squint of her brown eyes, the downturn of her lips. All at once, she met me halfway, open-mouthed and as far from shy as I remembered. Her tongue thrashed with mine, trying to get the upper hand until she gave in. She always gave in. I gripped her hips, pulled her into the hard ridge of my jeans, and the whimper that escaped her throat told me all I needed to know.

I could conquer her right now, in broad daylight as the occasional car rolled past, and she'd let me. I lowered my zipper, pushed up the flirty skirt that hugged her ass too tightly, and wound her strong legs around my waist. We swayed for a moment, both hanging on until we regained balance. I was a moment away from tugging her panties to the side and thrusting into her, except something about this didn't feel right—beside the fact it was an insane, irresponsible public display of indecency. In my gut, it felt like a betrayal to someone else.

Our mouths disconnected, and her legs slid down my jeans slowly. My chest rose and fell in rapid succession, matching the movement of hers. I wiped the sweat from my brow and returned her perplexed gaze.

"I'm sorry." I gestured to the ring on her finger. "You're engaged, and I'm..." I paused long enough to yank up my zipper. "Really fucked up in the head."

She smoothed her hair, patted down her skirt, and stood up straighter. "You're not the only one. I kissed you back."

"I guess we have unresolved issues," I said, waving a hand between us.

"Our issues were forgotten a long time ago."

"Nothing seemed forgotten when I had your legs wrapped around me. Except for the last eight fucking years of my life, that is. What *happened* to us?"

"You went to prison!" She stumbled back, still fidgeting with her clothing. "That's what happened. Doing this again, it's too painful."

"Doing what?"

Angling her head downward, she tried to hide her sorrow. "I'm glad you don't remember, Rafe. That place did something to you."

"I can't stand the blankness." I pointed to my head. "There's nothing here and it's driving me insane. I'm imagining all sorts of things. How could I have gone away for *that*?" I swallowed hard. "Do you believe I did it? *Did* I do it? Please, just tell me."

She covered her trembling mouth with a hand and shook her head.

"You do, don't you? You believe I raped her."

"No!" She closed her eyes. "I've never doubted your innocence. I just...can't. You shut me out eight years ago and I refuse to open myself up to that again."

"Nikki—"

"No, you need to hear me. When you got out and came back home, I wasn't sure I'd survive it. But then we talked, and I put up the biggest front of my life. You didn't even blink. It was obvious you'd moved on from us, and you *definitely* didn't kiss me. I tried to let you go, Rafe. But seeing you now, it's like seeing the man you were before those bars closed on you. What happens when you remember?"

"I don't know, Nik, but being with you is the only thing that feels...normal."

She shook her head. "I won't be your crutch. You're just turning to me because you're scared."

"Who says I'm scared?"

"Please. I know fear when I see it." She jumped into motion and stalked past me in the direction of her house. As she climbed the stairs, I stood on the side of the road feeling like an idiot who couldn't break an old habit.

Fuck it. I went after her, feet pounding the ground as I covered the distance. I bolted up the staircase and shot out a foot to keep the door from closing at the last second.

"We're not done."

"Move your foot."

"No!" I shoved the door until it gave. Feeling like a Neanderthal, I forced my way into her foyer. She could run from me in public, but not here in her own home. "All I'm asking for is—"

She wasn't alone.

Jax stood in the middle of her living room, barefoot, his mural of tats disappearing from view as he pulled a shirt over his chest. His jeans hung open in the front. It wasn't his state of undress that bothered me as much as the guilty expression on his face.

NINE

ALEX

Zach's psychological warfare took a toll on my entire being. I often lost hours while he forced my body and spirit into an uncontrollable pleasure zone. Maybe I'd retain a small amount of sanity if my memory would only disappear into that dark hole.

But it didn't. I always recalled the total mind-fuck he put me through daily. Time soared past, as if it had wings, and while on the ecstasy, I not only believed I had wings, but I used them to fly. It was ironic, really. Zach drugged me because he thought doing so would bring me back to him, but when I was high, I fell into an alternate reality where Rafe was still alive for a few precious hours.

The crash back to Earth never failed to gut me. I stared at the waterfall in horror, unable to stop shuddering. Thick foliage protected us from discovery, but that rush of water, toppling over rocks and crashing below, threatened to pull me into its depths. The thought was irrational, yet every bone in my body believed the lie—the facade my phobia enforced.

It wasn't that long ago that Zach had laid me near the ledge, lifting the skirt of my dress up past my breasts. I'd been so high on his reality-altering cocktail, I'd opened my mouth to catch the spray misting down on us, unmindful of the threat that existed only a few feet away as he'd hunched between my spread thighs and feasted.

Again, some sick and twisted part of my psyche had believed it was Rafe. Maybe it was my subconscious tricking me in order to cope. All that remained was shame. Sadness. Sorrow that ran so deep, my muscles ached with it. I tried to hide my pathetic state from Zach, knowing how my tears pissed him off. He expected the old me—the girl who clenched her jaw and took his cock like a trooper —not this blubbering, serotonin-depleted shell of myself who pretended he was another man to keep from wanting to slit my wrists.

But the pain in my soul wouldn't stop overflowing from my eyes, and incurring his wrath was an inevitability.

"Time to snap the fuck out of it!" He lifted me from behind, arms winding around my waist, and carried me down the steep path to the water's edge. I kicked and screamed, nearly causing him to lose his balance on the way.

"No!" I shrieked. "You can't do this! Stop!" My shouting came out as sputters once he dumped me in the shallow part. I clawed my way to the rocky shore, hands and knees sinking into slimy dirt. My heart beat so fast, it caused a physical ache in my chest. Little by little, I scrambled away from the water, as if it called to the dark place in my mind that tempted me to sink into the depths and die.

For an instant, I considered it.

As I sprawled onto the rocks, Zach grabbed my wet hair, bringing me back from the perilous idea of death. He yanked my neck back until I gazed at him instead of the waterhole. "The moping is gonna stop. I gave you ecstasy so we could get beyond the bullshit, not so you could turn into a depressed zombie while straight. I've had to force you out of bed for the last three days. Enough is enough, Lex." He let me go and threw his hands in the air. "I don't know what to do. You're fucking sexy as hell when high, but you want nothing to do with me otherwise."

"What do you expect? You're drugging me all the time. I can't cope like this." I shoved my hair out of my burning eyes and hoped the water dripping down my face hid the tears.

"I just want you back."

"You never had me!"

"I did." He clenched his teeth, and tension spiraled off him in currents. "I had you. You can lie to me and to yourself, but you loved me."

"You killed Rafe! I could never love you. *Never*."

"Your precious boy toy isn't dead." Zach scoffed, rolling his eyes. "I had to know if he lived or not, so I went to

Dante's Pass yesterday." He crouched in front of me, tilting his head. "You know what I found, Lex? I saw him strolling through town without a care in the world. Didn't take him long to wind up on the doorstep of Nikki Malone. Remember her? I guess old habits die hard."

I shook my head, refusing to let hope rush in.

"It's true, so you can let go of the guilt and blame game because he survived." Zach stood again and gestured to the vast wilderness that enclosed us in hell. "But where is he now, huh?"

My heart leapt, despite knowing better. "Don't mess with my head like that. You're lying."

"It's the truth. He's not coming for you. Why would he? He has Nikki to keep his dick occupied. For fuck's sake, you sent him to prison. Do you honestly think he'd love you after you had him locked up?"

My sobs escaped in gasping, pathetic hiccups. I struggled to my knees and gripped my midsection, unable to catch my breath as the echo of his words struck me in the gut with sharp-edged truth.

Zach knelt down and held my face in his hands. "*I love you. No matter what. No matter how much you say you hate me or try to push me away, I love you. Always.*"

"You hurt me."

"You used to like pain."

With tears streaming down my face, I saw Zach in a warped light, blurred from the product of my sorrow. He believed every word he'd said. An image surfaced, a blip in time in which I saw him as my brother, the boy I remembered from what seemed like a different lifetime. The brother who would do anything to make me feel better. But that boy was gone. Not a facet of his innocence remained. A chill spread over me, and goose bumps broke out on every inch of flesh.

"Just because my body is fucked up, that doesn't mean I love you."

His hands slipped from my face. He stood, brows narrowed as he glared down at me. "He will never love you like I do. *Never*."

"You're right. He won't. But I'll never love you like I do him."

TEN
RAFE

It took four of them to hold me down, my cheek pressed to the gritty cement. The biggest and meanest straddled my thighs, his rough hands spreading my ass cheeks as he worked his cock between them. I tried to buck him off. His laughter gave him away; he was enjoying the struggle. More laughter sounded, deeper, gruffer, but it didn't come from the assholes doing this. No, it came from the assholes allowing this to happen. The scent of tobacco blanketed the shower room, wafting in the air so thickly, I nearly choked.

No choking. No sound. I'd fight, but they wouldn't drag a plea from me. I gritted my teeth, pulled against the vise grip of the other three pricks restraining me, and closed my eyes as a scorching burn ignited in my rectum...

I shot up in bed, my hands fisting the sweat-drenched

sheets. With a shudder, I let a breath out and fell against the headboard. The same nightmare had plagued me for the last four nights, but I didn't want to analyze it. I wanted to forget every fucking detail. I pulled deep breaths into my lungs and waited for the pounding thud of my heart-beat to slow, to stop hammering at my throat. Flinging the damp, gnarled sheet to the side, I slipped from bed and padded across the loft bedroom to the stairs that lowered to the first floor.

Two things beckoned me: a bottle of vodka I'd found stashed away in the back of a cupboard, and the smoking gun in the cellar—the cage. Landing on the bottom step, I glanced around the empty living room.

Jax hadn't been back since I'd caught him with Nikki, and I hadn't stuck around to hear their explanations.

Absently, I grabbed the stashed vodka, unscrewed the lid, and took a drink straight from the bottle. Darkness blanketed the cabin, as not a single bulb highlighted the shadows. I didn't feel inclined to turn on a lamp. The dark-ness called to me, the unassuming companionship it offered. Quiet solitude didn't pester me about my state of mind like my brother's phone calls did. It didn't ask if I remembered anything. But it also didn't tell me shit. That damn cage in the cellar might, if I could only force my brain to cooperate.

I swayed for an instant and did a double take at the bottle. Who knew vodka could go down so well. As I stumbled a path to the cellar door, I kicked myself for turning to alcohol. Booze only numbed the problem temporarily, and it turned smart people into fucked up stupid people. I pulled the door open and took an unsteady jaunt down the stairs, then came to a stop in front of the evidence I wanted so badly to deny.

Maybe you should take a peek in the cellar.

Jax's words from last week echoed through the space between my ears. I stared at the cage, my mind trapped inside, a prisoner to the unknown as I willed it to impart the things my brain refused to remember.

When Jax told me about my eight-year prison sentence, I'd had a difficult time believing him. When he'd told me about Alex's accusation, that had been even harder to accept. But the bigger part of myself, the part that was still stuck in the past by eight years, was horrified by what he claimed I'd done. To Alex.

I still remembered her as this too-tempting not-so-innocent girl that liked to play with my head. Alex and her jade come-hither gaze that never failed to burrow beneath my skin like a first degree burn. Constantly flirting, teasing, driving me fucked up crazy.

It might have been nothing more than a schoolgirl's crush, but underneath the flirting, I sensed she'd cared about me. I had no idea why. I was a ticking time bomb with too much pent up anger. Fighting was the only thing that gave me relief. If I psychoanalyzed myself long

enough, I'd probably find an insecure little boy with abandonment issues. Just another statistic who's mommy left
when he was too young. And the deviant sexual appetite...
well fuck, I was shot to hell once I added that into the mix.
If I was this fucked up now...back then...shit this was
confusing, then how badly had eight years of prison
messed me up?

I glared at the cage, but it continued to engage me in a
silent standoff. I lifted the vodka and took another swig.
Maybe the alcohol would facilitate my traitorous psyche.
Those bars would tell me the secrets they held, tell me
how I could have turned into the kind of man who would
kidnap a woman and lock her inside.

Not just any woman. Alex...who still hadn't emerged. If
I'd let her go, as Jax speculated, then where was she? Had I
tortured her so badly that she'd put a bullet in me and left
me for dead? Was she hiding somewhere, terrified I'd find
her and bring her back to the island?

And finally, it clicked. The island, water...fuck. I really
had tormented her.

"Tell me why I did it," I said, raising a hand menac-
ingly, finger pointing in accusation at the prison. I tipped
the bottle back and chugged. Jax said I'd wanted revenge. I
didn't buy it. If I'd truly wanted retribution or comeuppance, there were other ways. I could have dug until I
proved my innocence. I could have unleashed public
humiliation on her.

Or maybe I'd been guilty all along.

I might not remember taking and locking her inside that homemade prison, but deep down I knew why I'd done it. I'd taken her because I'd wanted to. My hand fell, no longer accusing metal and concrete of unspoken sins, and drifted to the front of my tented boxers.

Closing my eyes, I imagined her helpless behind those bars, her arms pulled above her head tightly, painfully, feet arching as she tried to balance on her toes. Creamy, round breasts, perfect nipples erect, waiting to be punished. Her mouth spread wide with a gag, and my belt secure around her throat. Tight and inescapable.

Her body, her will, her freedom, trapped to my every whim.

I'd force her legs apart, rub my cock between them, taunting, taking power and leaving her with none, all the while pulling her head back by the strap of leather imprisoning her delicate neck.

With a groan, I freed my dick and slid a palm over the wet tip before closing frantic fingers around the base. I tightened my hold, pretended her fingers stroked me. More pre-cum escaped, and I swiped my thumb over the soft head, envisioning Alex on her knees, lips surrendering to my cock, her tongue lapping while her small hands encased my shaft in warm ecstasy as she sucked and bobbed. Shit, what I wouldn't give to yank at her curls right now.

"Fuuuuck...Alex..."

I shot my load all over the ground, wishing like hell my dick was shoved down her throat for real. After my breathing settled and I'd adjusted my boxers, I returned to the bottle of vodka. A few long swigs later, I eyed the mind-numbing liquid with narrowed eyes. I didn't know what prompted me to launch it across the room. Maybe the crushing shame of my fantasy and the equally shameful desire of wishing it was real.

The vodka collided with several wine bottles on the rack, and the shattering glass echoed in my ears with a haunting omen. For a split second, I saw an older version of Alex, naked, body shaking as she aimed the jagged edge of a broken bottleneck at me. The flash left just as suddenly, and I wished I had something else to throw. I fell into the wall, eyes squeezed shut as my fist pounded concrete. Why couldn't I remember? Some part of me was desperate to remember, as if my life depended on it.

"Remember anything?"

I jumped at the sound of his voice. Squinting through my drunkenness and the shadowed space, I saw Jax leaning against the wall near the stairs, stocky figure hidden in darkness.

I let my hands fall to my sides. "How long have you been standing there?"

He pulled a cigarette from behind his ear and stuck it between his lips. A second later, a lighter sparked. "Long enough," he mumbled around the butt. He took a drag then exhaled with the ease of a practiced smoker.

"Thought I'd come back for some stuff, but I heard a noise down here."

"I didn't know you smoked."

"I quit months ago. Guess I'm taking up the habit again." He lifted a finger toward me. "Guess you are too."

"Whaddya mean?" I glanced toward the broken glass. The heavy scent of tobacco mingled with the vodka tainting my floor. "Did I hit the bottle a lot? *Do* I drink a lot?" I found that hard to believe. I never drank, as alcohol interfered with training. Except I wasn't training anymore and I'd just finished off a good portion like it was nothing.

"No, beyond the occasional beer or two, you're not a drinker." His lips curled. "I was referring to your private moment with the ole Alex De Luca fantasy."

I rubbed both hands down my face. "What am I doing?"

"Hopefully remembering something."

"Not even close." My attention swerved to the broken glass again. "Except..."

He stood up straighter. "What is it?"

"A flash of something...no. Never mind. It's nothing."

"Spit it out, Mason."

"It doesn't make any sense. I saw Alex threatening me with a wine bottle, and she was"—I summoned the image, and my fucking cock came to life again—"naked."

Jax laughed, an unexpected reaction. "I'd say that's a memory. You didn't let that piece of ass wear a thing up until the day you decided to let her go."

"Did I fuck her?" As soon as the words tumbled from my mouth, I wanted to yank them back.

Jax lifted an incredulous brow, and the wicked grin that spread across his face sent a gob of dread to my gut. "Damn right you fucked her." He pointed upward. "You fucked her right on the kitchen table while I watched. That was after you paddled her ass for trying to escape."

I gaped at him, shaking my head. "I can't believe I did that." I lowered to the floor and parked my ass on the cold cement.

"You did that and a lot more." He wandered to where I sat and took the space next to me. "Are we gonna talk about Nikki?"

"You mean are you gonna tell me why you're sneaking around with her?"

He took one last drag of his smoke before grounding it into the concrete. "It just happened."

"I didn't figure you for the cliché type."

"Look," he said with a sigh, "I know she used to be your girl, but not long ago, Alex was your girl."

"No, Alex was my prisoner." My attention stalled on the cage, eyes narrowed. "You and Nik...that just doesn't make sense. You can't stand to be touched, for one."

"What'd you say?"

"It doesn't make sense."

"No, the last part."

I turned back to him, head tilted. "You can't stand to be touched?" The words hung between us, but Jax didn't say anything. I opened my mouth, my mind struggling to comprehend what I'd just said. "How do I know that?"

"You tell me."

"I don't know, I just...do."

"Anything else you suddenly just know?"

I reached inward, poking at the blank spots in my past, and came up empty. "I guess not."

"It'll come back. Maybe you're trying too hard."

"Maybe." I dangled my hands between my bent knees. "Do you care about her?"

Slowly, he nodded. "Yeah, I do. She's the first person since..."

"Since what?" I asked, not about to let him toss out that tidbit of information just to pull it back.

"Since I had to let go of someone else."

"What happened?" I probably already knew the details, somewhere in the locked area of my brain.

Jax returned my gaze, and something about the intense longing there made me shiver. I missed the warmth of my buzz. The booze still corrupted my veins, but the shield of not-giving-a-fuck was long gone.

"Wasn't meant to be," he said. "I've accepted it."

"And you think sneaking around with Nikki is smart? She's engaged." Fucking hypocrite. Hadn't I stuck my tongue down her throat a few days ago? If not for the unnerving sense that being with her was wrong, I would have done a lot more than that.

Jax's mouth formed an angry line. "Lyle Lewis is scum.

All the shit-talk he's done about you. He had half the town believing you were involved in Alex's death."

"From what you told me, I *was* involved in her 'death.'" I added air quotes on the last word.

Jax waved off my logic. "Yeah, but he didn't know shit, Rafe. We covered our tracks. He wasn't pointing the finger at you because he thought you were guilty. He used what happened to tear what little reputation you had left to shreds. He was trying to run you out of town."

"Why would he do that? It's not like I'm causing him any problems living here on the island."

"You're a threat to him."

"Because of *Nikki*?"

Jax raised a brow.

I shook my head, laughing. "Yet you're the one seeing her. How fucking ironic is that?"

Jax wasn't laughing. "Does it bother you?" He shifted, hunching over his knees, and tilted his head. "Because if it does, I won't see her again."

"But you're in to her."

He smiled, the first genuine, care-free grin I'd seen him wear. "I still can't handle her touch, but yeah. I like her. Fucking crazy that she seems to feel the same way." The smile bled from his face, and he pierced me with his deep stare. "But I'm not burying my head in the sand. She'll run if you snap your fingers. I know it, and Lyle knows it."

"His ring is on her fucking finger, so maybe he should get over it."

Jax sighed. "I have no idea why she's wearing that asshole's ring. I doubt we know the whole story. She talks about the jerk like she's scared of him."

That made me sit up straighter. "You think he's hurting her?"

"I don't know." He shook his head, gaze on the ground between his feet. "How did everything go to hell so fast?"

"Fuck if I know," I said, glancing at the broken glass on my floor. "But I can't sit around and do nothing." Missing so many years was dangerous. Even though we sat in a cellar full of incriminating evidence, talking about women and the screwed up shit we'd done together, Jax still felt like a stranger to me.

And Alex...

Her disappearance wasn't going away on its own. "I have to find out what happened to her, Jax. Maybe I should talk to Abbott."

"Are you insane? You were convicted of raping his daughter. You can't just knock on his door and say, 'Hey, how's it going? By the way, have you seen your dead daughter lately?'"

"No shit." With a sigh, I sank both hands into my hair and pulled. "But I've gotta do something. I'm responsible for her."

"No," Jax said. "I'll do something. I've already been looking into it. You stay away from this."

I studied his profile. Shaggy blond hair brushed his brows, and the scruff on his face, combined with a crooked nose, gave him an unkempt look. He managed to pull it off. How could I have shared a cell with this guy and not remember him? "You'd do that for me?"

He swept his hair back from his eyes. "I'd be dead if it weren't for you. I'll always have your back."

ELEVEN

ALEX

Under the influence of pure ignorant bliss, I'd slipped up and called him Rafe. The silence that blasted from Zach was so loud, I cowered in the corner with my hands over my ears.

Time was an elusive concept while high. I had no idea how long I'd been sitting like this. I vaguely recalled dragging myself across the floor, far, far away from the rage surging through the veins cording his arms. I peeked through the messy curls obscuring my sight and found him hunched on the bed, his head clutched in his hands. I swiped the damp strands from my face.

"Zach—"

He jumped to his feet, and I shrank against the wall, pressing so tightly I felt as if I could melt through to the other side.

He grabbed a bottle of water from the nightstand and

came toward me, the floor quaking with every stomp of his feet.

"Drink this. As soon as you crash, I'll deal with you." When he stalked across the room and slammed the door, the vibration rattled through my bones.

I was already crashing. Crying out one man's name while another fucked me had a dousing effect on the high. Unscrewing the cap, I sat up straighter and brought the mouth of the bottle to my lips. God. So fucking thirsty. Unable to sit still any longer, especially since he'd left me alone, I stood and wandered toward the bed as I emptied the bottle.

The familiar weight of desolation landed on my chest, making it difficult to breathe. I climbed onto the mattress, drew up my knees, and stifled my wailing into a pillow. Every thought and feeling raced through my being, muddying my sense of reality. I tried to latch on to something tangible, something I could form, if only mentally, but I couldn't snatch anything in the chaotic processes of my mind.

Time continued its useless ticking. Zach returned and found me curled into a ball, eyes staring unblinkingly ahead, though I saw nothing. This room, my whole existence, blurred until only shapes and shadows emerged.

My life had shape-shifted into something distorted and sick.

So had Zach. He'd been morphing all along, I just hadn't realized to what extent until it was too late.

He didn't say a word as he rolled me to my back. He positioned me on the bed so my thighs draped open and the bottom of my ass nearly hung off the mattress. I tried to sit up, but he shoved me down with such little effort, I didn't try moving again. A rip sounded and the unyielding stickiness of duct tape attached to my skin. He rendered my limbs useless by restraining me, wrist to ankle on either side.

He leaned over, fists depressing the mattress by my head, and a hint of fear scattered through me. He reeked of the whiskey he loved so much. Rage and alcohol didn't mesh well in people, and that was especially true for Zach.

"I'm going to fuck your brains out. No drugs to numb your agony, baby girl. Just my cock ripping through you." One hand clutched my hair as he unzipped his jeans and let them fall down his muscular thighs. He fisted his erection. I tried moving my face to the side, but his grip tightened in my hair. "Don't you fucking take your eyes off of me."

He pushed in with a fierce plunge, and I grunted from the grating burn. My foggy state dissolved, whisked away by the harshness of his thrusts.

"Feel that, Lex?" He ground out as he pumped, his gaze commanding mine, challenging me to break the contact. I didn't dare. "That's my cock in you. Not his. *Mine.*"

Tears leaked from my eyes as he plowed into me mercilessly. The salty drops trailed down the sides of my face and pooled at my ears.

"Apologize for being a whore, and maybe I won't choke you with my dick."

"I'm sorry," I said, despising the whining plea of my tone. I wasn't sorry at all—I was only sorry I'd let Rafe's name slip from my lips. He plowed against my cervix, and I shrieked.

"What the fuck is my name?"

"Zach."

He withdrew, removed the belt from his loops as he shuffled back, and brought the strap down on my pussy. I squealed like a pig, the pain so searing, he might as well have used an electric prod.

"Say it again."

"Zach!"

"Scream it!"

"Zach!" I sobbed. "This isn't you. Please, remember us. *Please.* You used to make me feel safe."

"And you never appreciated it." He tossed the belt on the floor then rammed me so hard, my ass slid up the mattress a few inches. My cries echoed, hoarse from screaming for him to stop. I don't think he even heard me.

He'd snapped, and I couldn't reach the human part of him. The part that was my brother. This untamed creature was unrecognizable, blind with bloodlust and rage. He'd waited until I crashed from the ecstasy to unleash the beast, mouth snarling and teeth gnashing, knowing how I'd be incapable of becoming aroused after coming off the drug. Every thrust of his cock bruised, burned, and rubbed me raw. Whatever tenderness he'd shown in the past couple of weeks had vanished. He was wasted and pissed, and no one was coming to save me.

"Zach...stop..." My voice failed me, coming out as nothing more than a whimper. "*Stop.*"

"You don't fuckin' tell me what to do." The rip of tape screeched through my ears, and he secured a strip over my mouth. "Go on, Lex. Say his name now. I dare you to try." His laughter tingled down my spine. He withdrew his knife from the pocket of his jeans. "I'll make sure you never forget who's fucking you again."

The cool edge of his blade pressed into my stomach. On the inside, I screamed in agony, but only a pathetic whine escaped my sealed lips. My heart pounded in my chest, panic rising as I struggled, digging my feet into the mattress and pushing up the bed a couple of inches. His forceful hands grabbed my thighs and yanked me back in place, and his cock plunged in again.

"Hold the fuck still." His knife sliced into my skin, deeper this time. I kept my attention on his face, terrified of seeing the damage he was doing, but also giving one last attempt at reaching him with my eyes.

"Fucking gorgeous." He swiveled his hips and moaned. "Fuck...your cunt never felt this good." He continued carving, saying more, but the words were indiscernible beyond my smothered cries. I feared he would kill me, dig the blade in too deeply, slash an organ. With that last thought came the disturbing discovery that maybe he'd finally give me a way out. No more pain. No more guilt or shame. No more surviving.

I'd been surviving for ten years, and I was tired. Second by second, my body grew limp, hands and feet losing strength, limbs going listless. The broken organ in my chest was ready to give up. I didn't have any fight left. Only acceptance. I'd never get out of this hell. The days would continue, erasing any remnant of my brother, only to be permanently replaced by this brutal impostor driven by alcohol, obsession, and the most dangerous of all—jealousy. The will to fight abandoned me.

As he slashed and fucked, his thrusts slow and erratic, I closed my eyes and gave up.

"Mmm, this is gonna be my favorite way to fuck you. You're so sexy, vulnerable, with my name carved in your skin." He bent down, and the wet slide of his tongue lapped at where he'd sliced. "You're mine to brand. Shit, baby. I should've taken you years ago. No one's standing in our way now." Sliding up my body, his stomach smeared the blood I knew tainted my belly, and he pushed his cock deeper.

I gave in to the blank place in my mind where I didn't exist. The small cubbyhole where I could hibernate for the rest of my life. But something wouldn't let me go. Hope licked the edges of my consciousness, demanding more.

I don't have anything left to give.

Fight, dammit! Find a way to escape.

Can't.

Rafe is still alive.

My heart skipped. *He doesn't want me.*

Zach lied to you. Of course he wants you. He would never turn his back.

I hurt him too much. He couldn't forgive me.

You need to forgive yourself first. After you get the hell out of here.

I tried! Zach will never let me go.

Try harder.

Shut up, shut up, shut up! I mentally screamed as laughter rumbled in my chest. God, I was losing my mind. But I didn't need the crazy phantom in my head giving me false hope. Rafe wasn't coming. I wasn't worth it.

You don't know that.

Shut up!

I was on my own, and I couldn't even blame Rafe. He'd had to deal with eight years of imprisonment. Just because his incarceration had been at the hands of the system didn't make it any less horrific than what I suffered now. He'd been raped, just like me.

Zach grunted, pulling me from the turmoil of my mind, and his cock stilled in my bruised cunt. He let out a frustrated growl. The alcohol flooding his system messed with his libido, making it difficult for him to come. I preferred when he stuck it in and got it over with. But he'd wanted to unleash his anger, and I was his favorite plaything. His hands moved to my burning wrists.

"Every time you say his fucking name, I'll carve mine

into your body." His knife, tainted with my blood, cut through the tape and freed me. He ripped the strip from my mouth, tugged on my arms, and forced me into a kneeling position on the bed. His large hand fisted my hair and brought my mouth to his glistening cock.

"Need you to suck me off." He pushed between my lips and shoved to the back of my throat. Gagging, I slapped at his hard abs, hands uselessly pressing against his stomach, but he used both fists to hold me flush with his abdomen, smothering my airway as he choked me with his girth.

I flailed, panicking as my lungs burned, as vomit rose in my throat. He yanked out only to thrust in again. In that moment, I no longer existed. I was just a shell, a thing made up of skin and bones, my sole purpose to submit while he pummeled my holes.

Fight, Alex! Find a way out before he completely destroys you.

Stop! Stop! Stop! Stop! I covered my ears, my frantic scream gurgling in my throat. His erection gagged me again, and I was certain I'd drown in my own vomit.

"Oh fuuuuck, Lex..." His cum shot down my throat, but I couldn't stop screaming. He pulled out, and I spewed cum and what little I'd eaten that day onto the floor. He wrenched my hands free from my ears, and I realized I was still wailing. Hysteria didn't touch the state I was in.

"Knock it off!" He brought his face within inches of mine. "What is wrong with you?"

What was wrong with *me*?

Everything. Every decision I'd made, every mistake, spawned from cowardice, led to this moment. I was too stupid to live. My gaze flickered to the bed where he'd dropped the knife between cutting me and making me choke on his cum.

Find a way out.

I sucked air into my lungs, catching my breath, and tramped down the need to throw up again. "Water," I blurted, holding my throbbing head. "I'm too hot. I'm gonna get sick again."

He glanced down at the vomit at his feet, his mouth twisting with disgust. "It was just a fucking blow job, Lex. Does my dick repulse you that much?"

I shook my head quickly. "No, it-it's the drugs. I need water." I hated the meek sound of my voice, despised it. Why couldn't I be stronger? Why couldn't I jump to my feet and pound my fist into his face?

Don't enrage the beast further. There's only one way out, and you know it.

That was not the same voice of hope from a few minutes ago. That was the real me, the voice of despair who gave cold, hard truth.

Zach stood and his expression softened, as if a hint of my brother had returned. Or maybe he was sobering up, now that the frenzy had passed. Now that he'd emptied his cum and his rage into me. I tried not to glance at the knife again, and prayed he'd leave it behind.

"Be right back." He grabbed it and left the room, taking

my hope with him. My heartbeat thudded as his quiet steps receded down the hall. Desperation corrupted my soul, and the overwhelming need to end this possessed me.

Do it now. Before he comes back.

I sprinted to the bathroom, shut and locked the door, then searched the cabinets and drawers for a razor. Empty. Empty, empty, empty! He'd shaved my legs days ago. Where were the razors? I found nothing, save for a lone Q-tip. I flung it to the floor in disgust then scoured the tiny space for something to break the mirror with, my whole body shaking. Finding nothing, I settled for pounding my fist on the glass, wincing against the pain, though it didn't compare to what Zach had put me through.

What he'll put you through if you don't succeed.

A piece broke free, and I clutched it in my bloodied hand. I birthed an unknown creature inside me, one who thirsted for my death. That creature whispered in my ear and told me to turn on the faucet in the tub. Told me to ignore the panic squeezing my chest as the water splashed into the bottom. I stepped over the side, placing one trembling foot inside, before lifting the other over the rim.

Zach banged on the door, words I couldn't make out screeching through the wood. I couldn't hear him above the roar in my head—the scream that told me to sink into the depths of my phobia and let it dispose of me. My back slammed against the cold porcelain, and as the door shook under his weight, I took the piece of mirror and gouged it into my left arm, dragging the sharp edge up my forearm to my wrist.

Just like Mom.

I wept, chest heaving uncontrollably, and a tremor of remorse went through me, but it was fleeting. I took the glass, held awkwardly in my left hand, and tore into the opposite wrist. Blood bathed my skin, hiding the faint scars from years of silently screaming.

Free. Finally free.

The glass fell from my fingers. I slumped into the tub, arms plopping into rising water, and closed my eyes as my head dropped against the rim. I wondered if Mom had felt this way. Had she experienced this same clarifying sense of relief? The certainty that the suffering would end soon. I couldn't wait to see her. I ached to feel her arms around me, craved the sweet scent I still remembered, even to this day. Jasmine. God, I could already smell it.

A crash sounded, and Zach's scream tore me from my serenity. "Lex!"

He lifted me from the water and held my body to his quaking chest. "Why?" Gut wrenching remorse coated that single word. I cracked my lids open, and through the haze I found his cheeks wet with grief.

I blinked several times until he came into sharper focus. "Can't do this anymore." The room narrowed, shadows deepening around the edges. "Zach," I said, my voice growing weaker. "I'm scared."

"No"—a sob burst from his mouth—"hang on, baby!"

I felt weightless in his arms, jostled like a rag doll, as he strode from the bathroom. I clung to the protective shell of numbness enclosing my heart, chasing the fear away. I was safe, as light as a feather and floating toward the promise of infinite peace. He laid my drenched body on the bed, where I crashed back to Earth before he disappeared from sight.

What had I done? I lifted my arms, rotated them so the bloody gashes in my skin faced me, and shivered. Cold. Why was I so cold? Why was I still awake? Still alive? Had I done it wrong?

No! I couldn't even kill myself right. I should have dug deeper.

You did the best you could. Now use this to get out of here.

Why was the voice back? I cried out, horrified by the desperation choking me.

Zach returned, a phone wedged between his shoulder and ear. He held my wrists to the mattress and applied pressure. "Oh God, hurry!" His shoulders shook as tears careened down his face, and the phone toppled to the floor.

"Don't leave me. Please...I'm sorry. Don't go. Please don't go. Lex?" His hands banded around my wrists with incredible strength, as if he could hold the life inside me. "Help's coming." He dropped his head onto my stomach, his cheek smearing the bloody product of his madness, and bawled.

Help's coming.

Those two words echoed like a blessed chant. His lips moved against my skin, but I didn't hear what he said. All I heard was his promise.

I was getting out of here.

TWELVE
ALEX

Voices surrounded me, some asking questions, some giving indistinguishable orders. I tried to open my eyes, but my lids were so heavy, as heavy as the weight of my thudding heartbeat.

"Zach?"

What was happening? My body jostled on a thinly padded surface, and a siren blared in my ears. I swayed, and my stomach dropped. Felt like I was being transported. I spaced in and out of consciousness, and the crisp scent of pine and nature disappeared, replaced by a hint of fresh water and fish. It reminded me of being on Rafe's island.

Was I near a river? Where was he taking me this time?

"Zach?" Why wasn't he answering me?

"Hang on," an unfamiliar voice said. His tone was deep, reassuring. "We're almost there."

I must have blacked out again, though I vaguely recalled the shout of voices, commands, and haste motion.

"Alexandra."

That voice I recognized, and it drifted to me faintly. I tried to lift my lids, but they stuck to my eyeballs. "Dad." I moaned, turning my head and finally forcing my eyes open.

The fuzzy bulk of his form sat to my left. He leaned to one side and brought a hand to his chin, stroking the graying stubble there. The gesture reminded me of Zach and caused a chill to go down my spine. He leaned forward and settled his much larger hand over mine. "I can't believe you're here. I thought I lost you."

"What happened?" My gaze darted around the nondescript room. The blinds were cracked slightly to allow the sunlight in. I angled my head back and noticed the medical equipment above the bed.

"You don't remember?" he asked.

Coming fully alert, images went off like flashes in my mind. Rafe, the island, Zach...my last desperate attempt to free myself from him forever. A horrified cry tumbled from my mouth, and I lifted my arms. White bandages covered both to a few inches below my elbows, wrapping in mummy-like fashion.

"The doctor said you were lucky you didn't damage any tendons." He cleared his throat. "Thank God it appeared worse than it was."

"How..." I met Dad's gaze. "How did I get here?" Memories surfaced as soon as the words left my mouth. Zach sobbing his grief and remorse onto my stomach as he used his hands to stem the flow of blood, how he'd pleaded with me not to leave him. The same hands that inflicted so much pain had banded around my wounds to save me. Even now his actions seemed counterproductive, considering all he'd done.

But he had saved me. In his own sick and twisted way, he'd loved me enough to let me go, if letting me go meant I wouldn't die.

"A ranger found you. You were in a cabin near Mt. Hood. An anonymous caller reported your suicide attempt, but you were alone when they found you. Do you have any memory of how you got there, or how your car ended up in the Columbia River?"

Rafe...he'd freed me from a life I'd wanted to escape, then Zach had imprisoned me with the shackles of his obsession. I nodded slowly, looking at the last few weeks from all angles. "I remember, but it's not what you think."

He gave a pointed look at my arms. "Talk to me."

"It was Zach. He wouldn't let me go. Dad"—I lowered my head, facing away in shame—"he took me. It was all him. He's been r-rap—"

"Alexandra." His tone made me gulp, and I felt like I was twelve again. "Your brother has been busy at our new MMA training camp in Seattle for the past month. We announced it formally this morning."

His words hit me with the force of a sledgehammer. He

was doing it again. Protecting Zach. No doubt paying people to say what needed to be said. Fabricating photos and controlling what the media reported. I didn't have to see the evidence—he'd done it so many times already, hiding Zach's downward spiral into alcoholism, his erratic behavior during training sessions and events, but I never thought he'd throw me under the bus.

His own daughter.

You're not his daughter though. Not by blood.

I trembled at the voice in my head, and I hated how my eyes burned from hurt. Struggling to sit up, I hefted my legs over the side of the bed and stood. On wobbly limbs, I turned to confront him. "I can prove Zach did it. His fucking sperm is still inside me."

I lifted my gown to just below my breasts and put Zach's carving on display. Glancing down almost made me retch, but I swallowed the rancid taste in my mouth. Zach hadn't exaggerated; he'd carved his name into my skin so clearly, a first grader would be able to read it. "I suppose I did this to myself too, right? Or maybe it was another man name Zach who took me, raped me, and drugged me out of my mind."

Dad wouldn't even look at me, and that pissed me off more than anything. "He can't get away with this. I can't keep living this way."

"My poor girl." He shook his head. "I'll get you the help you need."

"It was Zach!" I screamed, losing my balance and stumbling into the side of the bed. Propping myself up with both hands, I tried to ignore the bandages, but they sat between us, as if to perpetuate the deception. I hadn't wanted to die. I'd just wanted...free.

He rose from the chair and stepped to my side. "Get back in bed before you fall down."

I yanked away from his touch and climbed beneath the blanket under my own steam. "This isn't my fault. I didn't do this."

"It's okay to admit you need help," he said, his voice unusually soft. "Your mother fought it too, but you don't have to make the same mistake. And you don't have to fight this battle alone. You have your family. You have Lucas. He still wants to marry you."

"That's not happening. I don't want to see him again." The wedding was off the moment I removed his ring from my finger, before Rafe had shown up on my doorstep.

Dad placed a palm on my shoulder, and his fingers curled, gouging bone as I tried to inch away. "I had hoped marrying Lucas would help you move past your unhealthy fixation with your brother."

My mouth hung open. "*My* fixation with him? Are you crazy?"

He was twisting everything around, making me look like I was the one with the problem. Just the crazy daughter who'd come too close to repeating the same suicide attempt as her loony mother. He would always protect Zach. Always. Even if it meant I got trampled in the process. I bit my lip to hold back tears and finally let go of the hope he'd someday love me like he did Zach.

I clenched my hands. "You can lie to society," I said, proud at the strength in my tone. "Even make the media do your bidding, but you can't lie to me. Zach kidnapped me, he *raped* me, and he faked my death. I've been his prisoner for weeks." At his unchanging expression, the familiar pang of rejection tore through me. "And I'm going to do everything in my power to make sure he rots in jail for it. I was only thirteen when it started." I'd wanted to tell him for so long and now that the words were out there, dirtying the air with their horror, I felt the weight lift from my chest.

I had someone else to cover for. Someone who deserved it. Rafe deserved a full exoneration, and if stepping so close to death had brought anything to light, it was him. He might have done some *very* sick and questionable things to me, but he'd had eight years of his own hell haunting him, driving him to seek what he'd believed was due retribution. In some sane crevice of my mind I understood I was justifying what he'd done, making excuses because I loved him. If I had an unhealthy fixation on anyone, it was Rafe Mason.

My father leaned forward and pierced me with the same hazel-eyed stare as Zach, though his held a shrewdness his son's lacked. "Since we're being so candid, let me make something perfectly clear, Alexandra. I love you. I've always loved you like a daughter. But you and I both know Zach didn't sink your car into the river."

I opened my mouth, but words failed me.

"Rafe did." He straightened to his full height and folded his arms over his chest. The ink in his corded muscles appeared harsher than usual under the lighting. "If my son goes down for this, so does Rafe." He reached into his back pocket and pulled out a bundle of envelopes I'd never planned for anyone to find, least of all my father. He tossed them next to me on the mattress. "Judging by your own words, he matters a great deal to you."

I shook my head back and forth in disbelief, in denial, like a pathetic Bobblehead. "I don't know what you're talking about."

"You know exactly what I'm talking about." Dad grabbed my hand and squeezed so hard, his knuckles whitened. "You had a mental breakdown, understand me? I don't care what you come up with, but *you* did this. If you want to keep Rafe out of prison, you'll do the same for your brother." His calculating stare knocked the breath from my lungs, and his grip tightened further. "That sperm you talked about? Rafe's name will be the one attached to it."

My eyes widened, and I gaped at him, barely breathing. "How?"

"Wouldn't be the first time, Alexandra. How do you think he was so easily convicted? Because of your word?" He thrust his face close. "Your word means *nothing*. I control you. I've always controlled you. Your bout with anorexia? That was my doing, and you fell for it like the naive little girl you are."

"But I wasn't eating..." Why did my tone come out so uncertain? "I was anorexic."

"No, dear daughter. You'd lost your appetite after the abortion and trial. It wasn't hard to fill your impressionable head with the idea that you had a problem."

I blinked, feeling sick to my stomach. "Why would you do that?"

"For Zach, of course. While you were locked away in that treatment center, he finally yanked the stick from his ass and took the Chandler Vs. De Luca fight seriously. For a few weeks, he wasn't thinking with his dick."

Footsteps sounded outside the door to my room. A doctor stepped inside, and Dad let go of my hand. The coldness in his features instantly melted. I shouldn't have been surprised at how quickly he shifted personas, but I was. The threatening, ice-hearted bastard I'd yearned to love me since I was six was absent, replaced by the caring and doting father I'd allowed myself to believe in all these years.

The father who'd known about Zach raping me all along. The father who'd somehow known about Rafe kidnapping me. He'd left me on that island to be tortured.

I sank into the pillows and closed my eyes, too exhausted and disheartened to analyze the implications, though one thing I knew for certain.

Abbott De Luca hadn't just fooled the world; he'd fooled his own daughter.

THIRTEEN
RAFE

"Are you sure you wanna do this?" Jax stalled outside the entrance of the hospital, one brow lifted in a dubious arch.

"I'm not sure of anything, but I can't not see her." Gritting my teeth, I stared through narrowed eyes at the building. News of Alex's resurrection from the dead hit the media that morning. I was hoping she'd give me answers, but mostly, I had to know she was okay.

"Have you stopped to consider this stunt might land us both in jail?"

"Yeah, I have. Look, you don't need to go in there. I won't blame you for taking off." We'd cleared the air the other night, but things were far from settled between us. He still hadn't moved back into the cabin, and the subject of Nikki seemed to have moved into taboo territory.

Jax slumped his shoulders, and his sigh ruffled his hair. "Dude, this is a bad idea."

"Undoubtedly." I stepped past him, and the sliding doors opened. Jax hurried after, his steps thumping quietly on the polished floors. I didn't know what had happened to Alex, how or where she'd been found. According to the media, she was in stable condition, but that was all I'd found out.

After a quick stop at the information desk to ask which floor she was on, my heart pounded as Jax and I waited for the elevator. He shuffled his feet, looking like he wanted to be anywhere but here. The arrow lit up, and the doors opened with a ding. A group of people exited, each giving us weird glances, their eyes roving over our bare arms and the ink on our skin.

Never failed to get a reaction from some people.

"I'm telling you, this is a mistake," Jax said once the heavy doors slid shut and we were the only two that remained.

"I don't care. After everything I put her through, I owe her this much."

"Bullshit," he muttered. "What *you* put *her* through?" He leaned against the wall, arms crossed. "She screwed you over, man. She had it coming."

"No one deserves that."

"Her spoiled ass did."

"A couple of days ago you cared enough about her 'spoiled ass' to look into her whereabouts."

Jax sighed. "I did it for you. Not like it did any good though. She must've been hiding on the moon."

We arrived on the fourth floor, and I stepped out before Jax could further needle me. His footfalls landed with more attitude than usual. I couldn't put my finger on it, but something about the situation rubbed him the wrong way—besides the whole we-could-go-to-jail aspect. Something about *Alex* rubbed him the wrong way.

We turned the corner and headed down another hall. Up ahead, a circular reception desk took up the middle. A woman sat on the other side of the counter, eyeing me behind feminine pink glasses, when a bulky form stepped in the way.

"You've got balls to show up here."

I met the hard-as-nails gaze of Abbott De Luca, a man I'd once admired. The calendar told me a lot of time had passed since then, but it seemed like only yesterday his opinion of me mattered. The man I remembered had given me his utmost respect. Time and accusations sure had a way of changing things. Now he stared me down as if I were a cockroach that needed exterminated.

"I've always had balls. You know that." He'd been impressed with the way I handled myself during fights. Determined with a ruthless edge, was what he used to say about me. Though Zach never admitted it, I knew my relationship with his father had bothered him.

"What are you doing here, Mason?"

"I came to see Alex." I cleared my throat, wondering if she'd told him about the kidnapping. "Is she okay?"

His gaze darted left then right. "Let's go into the lounge." His attention glanced off Jax, and I introduced them as we moved into the vacant room. Abbott closed the door before turning to me with a glare capable of icing the bowels of Lucifer.

"You've got one minute to explain yourself before I have you removed by force."

I held up my hands. "I'm not here to cause trouble. I don't remember shit about the last eight years. Doctor calls it dissociative amnesia."

"How convenient."

"Just tell me, is she all right?"

"She's fine. She'll recover."

His tone hit me in the chest hard. It was so...unfeeling. "I want to see her." I had to see her. Something wasn't right about all of this.

He lifted a brow. "Do you honestly think I'd let my daughter's convicted rapist anywhere near her? You're lucky I don't call the cops." He stepped forward, bringing his chest inches from mine. I held my ground, refusing to back down.

I opened my mouth, ready to defend myself, to say how I was innocent...except I didn't know for sure. How could I know what I was guilty of if I couldn't remember?

He poked a finger at my chest. "I want you out of Alexandra's life."

I tilted my head. "I'm not in her life."

He thrust his face into mine. "I know you kidnapped her. I don't give a shit if you remember or not, but if you come anywhere near her again, I'll do far worse than have you arrested."

Jax slumped into a chair. "Told you this was a bad idea."

I returned Abbott's hard stare. "She told you?"

"Please," he scoffed. "She didn't have to."

"Why aren't you pressing charges?"

"Alexandra has been through enough. The last thing she needs right now is another trial. She needs treatment. Because of you, she almost killed herself, just like her mother."

His words punched me in the gut. I turned away, unable to return his disgusted gaze. Or maybe the disgust I saw in his eyes was a reflection of my own. Jax hadn't given me details on what I'd put her through after we'd taken her, but for her to feel the need to end her life...

"Please, just let me see her once. I need to know she's okay." I needed to fucking tell her how sorry I was. I faced him again, but my plea didn't soften his stance.

"You want her to be 'okay'? Then give her a clean break. She has some sort of misplaced infatuation with you because of the kidnapping. If I let you in to see her, make it clear whatever this *thing* is between the two of you is over. Can you do that?"

I nodded.

"She's in room 427."

I traded a glance with Jax before exiting the lounge, which was really just a space where families waited in agony to hear news on their loved ones. Other than a middle-aged couple speaking to the woman at the reception desk, the area was empty. She pushed her glasses up on her nose and eyed me. I gave her my I'm-a-nice-guy smile, but I wasn't sure she bought it. Spanning the hall in seconds, I slowed as the numbers climbed. 423, 424, 425, 426...

Once I reached her closed door, my feet refused to move. Something told me to turn around and run. Never look back. Did I really want to open that door and look inside? I lifted a hand, curled my fingers around the handle, and prepared for the worst.

She'd scream at me, say I was the reason she was in the hospital. She probably hated me.

I pushed the heavy door open and was unprepared for the sight of the frail girl swallowed up by the bed. Her eyes were closed, long lashes fanning over pale cheeks. Her curly hair lacked the vibrancy I remembered. Even the flash of her I'd seen in the cellar didn't compare to the brokenness of the girl...woman lying in that bed.

Moving slowly so I wouldn't startle her, I pushed the door shut until it made the slightest click, then I stepped to her side. Her chest rose and fell in perfect rhythm. My gaze landed on her delicate collarbone and an intense vision of choking her hit me. To my horror, my dick hardened, straining against the zipper of my jeans. I clenched my hands at my sides. The mental picture was so vivid it could have been straight from my fantasies.

I knew it wasn't. It was a memory. I retreated several steps, my heartbeat pulsing in my ears. Alex was laid up in the hospital, and my fucking cock wanted out to play. What the fuck was wrong with me?

"Rafe?"

My gaze shot to her wide, green eyes. God, those eyes... I remembered them well. Still full of mystery and shining with innate strength. I wanted to delve in and unearth all her secrets.

Her mouth parted slightly, as if she wanted to say something, or maybe, like me, she was having trouble drawing in a deep breath. She lifted an arm, covered in white bandages from wrist to just below her elbow. An identical bandage wrapped her other arm. My heart dropped to my stomach, landing somewhere in the dregs of my gut.

"What happened to you?" The words were out of my mouth before I could stop them, my feet across the floor and at her bedside before the second hand on the clock above the door could move two spots. I took her arm in my hands, my fingers sliding along the bandages.

And I forgot that I didn't remember, that I was supposed to tell her to move on with her life and forget about me. Getting into the subject of my amnesia wasn't part of the clean break Abbott insisted on.

"Alex?" My gaze landed on her face. Hurt and something else pooled in her eyes. It could have been so many things, a plethora of emotion all vying for residence in that stare.

Which told me shit, except that my presence made her cry.

She grabbed my hand in hers and squeezed hard, as if she feared I'd slip away. A tear slipped down her colorless cheek. "I thought you were dead. When he told me you weren't, I wanted to believe it, but I was scared."

"What happened?" How the fuck had she ended up in the hospital with bandages that suggested she'd slit her wrists? Why was she not furious or terrified of me? "Where have you been?"

"Doesn't matter. Oh God...you're real, right? I'm not dreaming?"

Something about the desperation in her tone fucked with my head. I pulled my hand away and stepped back. "I just came to make sure you were okay."

She blinked, her expression blanking for a few seconds before confusion took hold of her features. "What are you saying?"

I dropped my gaze to my feet. "You're better off without me. What I did, what you did, whatever we did together, we need to move on."

"No," she said with a resolved shake of her head. "Before Zach showed up, things were finally settling between us. I wanted to be with you. I still want that, more than anything."

I almost asked what Zach had to do with any of this. Maybe he was responsible for shooting me. He'd always been protective of her. I bit my tongue, holding back those questions and more. I didn't want to say anything that could give away my memory loss. She'd been through enough. I didn't know much else, but I knew I wanted to stay out of jail, and I wanted her to be whole again. Somehow, I got the feeling those two things contradicted each other.

"My father knows you were involved in my disappearance."

Inevitability was a bitch. I knew this was coming. I wanted to ask her if I'd raped her all those years ago, but I didn't want to burden her with my issues. She'd been through hell, and I'd put her there. I didn't know the details of how or why, but she was in that hospital bed because of me.

She'd tried to kill herself because of me.

"I'll turn myself in, if that's what you want."

Her startled gaze punched me in the gut. "No! Why would you think I'd want that?"

"After what I did to you, how can you not want me locked up?"

"You know how I feel about you. I want to be with you so badly, it hurts." She reached a hand out and curled her tiny fingers around my larger ones. "I thought you were dead, then Zach said you weren't. He said you couldn't forgive me, and I fell for it, Rafe. He had me so far out of my mind that I believed you didn't care enough to come after me."

I didn't know what she was talking about, so I treaded carefully. "Alex, what do you need me to do?"

"Forgive me. Take me away from here." She started sobbing, and the sound clashed in my chest, two warring emotions. Part of me glorified in those tears, a feeling that disturbed me on such a deep level, I thought I might vomit. The other part wanted to wrestle away her demons and pound them to dust.

"Alex." Her name escaped the vise strangling my throat. "I don't wanna hurt you."

She rolled to her side, her back facing me, and curled into a tight, protective ball. "You can't forgive me. I understand."

I clenched my teeth, wanting to ask what she wanted forgiveness for. I wanted to ask her about the night I was shot. Had she shot me? Had Zach? I needed those answers, but faced with the situation, with how much I'd fucked up when it came to her, the only thing left to do was say goodbye and end this. Let her move on and heal without the memory of me hanging over her shoulder.

Leaning over, I brushed my lips beneath her ear, inhaled a scent that sparked a memory my stubborn mind believed took place just a few months ago, when I'd held her as she cried over her mother's death. Even grief smelled good on her.

She twisted her head and pressed her mouth to mine. Breath stalled in my lungs, and the need to pin her to the bed nearly outweighed my sense of decency. Whatever my head didn't remember, being this close to her, our mouths moving together in hunger, the taste of her rioting through me, revived something primal inside my being.

A snarling beast that wanted to claim.

I tore my lips from hers. "I can't do this. I'm sorry." I stumbled across the room and wrenched the door open, and a heavy weight pressed on my chest, urging me to get the fuck out of there while I still could.

Her gut-splitting wails haunted me down the hall, long after I shut the door.

FOURTEEN

ALEX

"How are you sleeping, Alexandra?" the shrink asked as I sat in one corner of her couch, feet curled under me.

Feigning indifference, I shrugged. "Same." I'd left the hospital eleven days ago. The first few had been pure hell while my mind and body adjusted to going without a daily dose of ecstasy. I'd barely left my bed, despite feeling restless and unable to sleep much. Every part of me hurt, from the pieces of my fractured heart to the deep ache in my muscles.

"Still having nightmares?"

"Uh-huh."

Sandra crossed her legs. "Do you want to talk about them?"

I shook my head. I still had a difficult time addressing her by her first name, but she'd insisted. This was my second visit and I didn't want to be there, but my father made it clear I didn't have a choice. The hospital discharged me under his care, especially after I fed his bullshit to the police. My years of lying had worked in my favor; they'd bought the story.

Alexandra De Luca had suffered an episodic break, just like her mother. With shame, I remembered how I'd confessed to pushing my car into the river before hiding out at a cabin I'd heard my brother talk about. I'd even confessed to carving Zach's name into my stomach.

There were holes in my story, of course. Like how I'd arrived at the cabin, or how someone just happened to find me in time to call 9-1-1. They accused me of withholding information, of protecting an accomplice in my disappearance. But ultimately, they believed what my father wanted them to, and because of my warped version of the truth that didn't point the finger at anyone other than myself, Zach was safe from prosecution. So was Rafe.

So long as I cooperated and did everything my father asked, which included weekly appointments with the stranger sitting across from me. Anything to perpetuate the facade of a mental breakdown. At least I'd gotten to choose the shrink studying me, trying to read me with her analytical stare.

"How are you doing on the anti-depressants?"

I shrugged again. "Okay, I guess." I was starting to feel like me again, so that was probably a good thing, though being me wasn't much better than the version of myself who'd hit rock bottom while Zach held me captive.

"I'm here to help you," Sandra said, as if I needed to be reminded. "Part of you must want my help, or you wouldn't have sought treatment."

"I don't want to be here."

"Then why are you here?"

"It's complicated. My father thought I should come."

She wrote something down on the annoying notepad propped on her knee. A long black and white skirt flowed down her legs, the hem brushing her sandaled heels. From the decor in her office to the hip clothing she wore, she displayed a chic and competent style.

"Are you close to your father?"

A bitter laugh escaped. "Definitely not."

"But you'd like to be."

"Why would you think that?"

"Coming to see me on your father's wish indicates a need to please him. It sounds like you're seeking his attention and approval." She leaned forward, chin propped in one hand, and an auburn curl fell across her forehead. "But what do you want, Alexandra?"

"I want to turn back time."

"What would you change?"

"Everything."

"How about we start with the one thing you'd want to change most?"

I eyed her, some part of me yearning to spill. It would

be a relief to tell my story and have someone listen, believe me, maybe even reassure me it was okay to cry, okay to scream in the middle of the night after another nightmare in which I still lived trapped inside Zach's madness. Most of all, I wanted her to tell me it was okay to forgive myself for nearly taking the easy way out, the way my mom had.

"I wish..."

Our eyes met, and in hers I found quiet patience. She waited, giving me room to forge ahead when I was ready. Rafe's rejection edged to the forefront of my mind. The ache in my chest became unbearable, only this time I couldn't push it aside.

I sucked in a breath then cleared my throat. "I wish I could undo the hurt I caused someone."

"If that person was here right now, willing to listen, what would you say?"

Cursing the tremble in my lips, I hid behind a fist and closed my eyes, taking deep breaths through my nose until the burn of tears subsided. "I'd beg his forgiveness."

"Have you asked him for it?"

I nodded.

"What did he say?"

"Which time?"

She raised a brow. "So you've asked more than once?"

I thought back to the island, but all I remembered was the raging need he'd ignited inside me. I remembered his hands on me, his mouth, his body sheltering mine. The breathless quality of his words as he'd slid inside my soul, where even now, he still resided. I couldn't bear to relive those fleeting minutes in the hospital when his kiss had breathed life into me.

"I don't remember." I didn't know this woman, and I wasn't about to tell her my most intimate moments.

Her pen scraped across the page, stroke after stroke, nicking my sanity. I imagined jumping from the couch and ripping that pen from her hands. Tearing the paper to shreds.

"Alexandra—"

"It's Alex." I clenched my hands. "My dad is the only one who calls me that."

The lines around her mouth softened. "Alex, why don't you tell me about what happened at the cabin?"

I tugged at my sleeves, making sure they still covered my arms and the hideous destruction marring my skin. "I told you last week I wasn't talking about that."

She lifted a hand in my direction. "Yet here you are again."

"I don't have a choice."

"You always have a choice. You're not court ordered to be here. I believe I can help you, but I can't do it alone. You have to put some effort in too." She tilted her head. "Okay?"

I nodded, but my throat swelled, preventing me from saying anything.

"Why did you try to kill yourself?"

"You won't believe me."

"You won't know until you try."

I pulled a hand through my curls, yanking my fingers through the tangles. "I didn't do it because I wanted to end my life. I just wanted him to stop."

She sat up straighter. "Someone was hurting you?"

Chewing on my lip, I nodded. "I can't say who."

"Whatever you tell me is confidential, Alex."

"I can't say."

Scribble, scribble, scribble.

"Do you have to write everything down?" Regretting the bite of my tone, I winced.

"This bothers you?" She lifted the notepad.

"Haven't you switched to an iPad or something by now?" I crossed my arms. "You know, something password protected?"

Her tiny mouth curved up. "I find the simple task of writing soothing. Maybe you should try it. Jotting down your thoughts and feelings can be very therapeutic."

I thought of the letters I'd written to Rafe while he was in prison, the ones Dad found after I disappeared. Those words, written with the intent that they never be read, had given him ammunition. He'd discovered how Rafe was my biggest weakness. It was a reminder that nothing was private. Anything and everything could be used against you. My fingers brushed the purse beside me, where the letters were now safely tucked inside.

I pointed at the notepad. "I don't want you writing down the stuff I say. Can't we just talk?"

"Sure." She set the pad and pen aside. "You don't have to tell me anything you're not comfortable disclosing. And you don't have to give names either."

I let out a breath and stood. Strolling to the window, left partially open to allow a warm breeze in, I tried to ignore the tingles going down my spine, but her scrutiny blasted my back like a physical blow. Only once I stopped at the window, mindlessly gazing at the tree-lined street below, did I speak.

"He did things to me, bad, shameful things, and part of me liked it." I folded my arms around myself, cold despite the nice weather. "He made me do things that ruined another man's life." I shook my head as tears pooled in my eyes. "No, that's not entirely true. He made me, but I could have stopped it. I was too weak."

"You don't strike me as being weak."

"I was a coward. Label it however you want. When I think about saying the words out loud, my throat tightens" —I swallowed hard—"and I can't say shit. My silence enabled him for years."

"Speaking out and standing up for yourself is hard. It's brave. Is he still hurting you, Alex?"

"No." The single word came out strangled. I hadn't seen or heard from Zach since the night he carved his name into my stomach. Dad assured me he was far away receiving treatment for his alcoholism. Just because he wasn't physically hurting me any longer didn't mean my wounds had stopped bleeding. They still existed, as tangible as the wind—felt but not seen.

"I think you're a survivor," she said. "Your self-worth has taken a hit, but I believe you have what it takes to heal. The first step is asking for help, and you've done that. You're here."

I turned around, her words causing a spark of empowerment inside me. "You think so?"

"Most definitely." She shifted, crossing her legs on the other side. "You have a right to feel safe in your own skin. If the abuse starts again—"

"It won't." Not because Zach would never come back, not because my father would keep him away. *I* was done. Done being his silent victim. Done being a fucking coward. Now that the fog was clearing from my head, I had a lot to think about.

My father's actions.

Zach's actions.

My actions.

"But if it does, you can tell me, okay?"

"Okay."

Her eyes veered to the clock on the wall, a circular piece of art crafted with gold numbers. "We're out of time for now," she said, rising to stand, "but I'd like to see you again next week. I hope you'll come, and not because your father wants you to."

"I'll think about it." I shuffled my feet, itching to escape the confines of this room and the eerie way she had of pulling information from me, of making me look at myself differently. I followed her to the door. She pulled it open but hovered.

"This other man you talked about? Consider giving him another chance to forgive you. Maybe then you can forgive yourself."

FIFTEEN
ALEX

"I 'm so glad you called." My friend smiled at me from across the table, her gentle tone coaxing me to return the upward curve of her lips.

Instead, I pushed the lettuce around on my plate until I found another cherry tomato. "It's been ages," I said. After my appointment with my therapist, I hadn't been ready to go home to my father, so I'd called Evelyn. The last time I remembered seeing her was...

I couldn't remember the last time. Not in specific detail, anyway. We were never really close. Not like friends should be, but we'd spent occasional afternoons together having coffee or lunch. She'd talk my ear off about her latest boyfriends, and I'd quietly listen. That was the interesting thing about people who liked to talk a lot—they never expected me to contribute much because they were too busy going on about their own lives.

Their men.

Their new jobs.

Their gossip.

Their life-altering moments.

They, they, they. Most people would probably get tired of it, and Evelyn was especially self-focused. But I wouldn't call her selfish. Out of the few friends I'd managed to keep over the years, she was the first one willing to listen whenever I did get the inkling to unload something.

I had that inkling now, but the words lodged in my throat and refused to be spoken, so I continued to sit in silence and let her catch me up on her life.

She was going on about her latest boyfriend's prowess in bed, in particular, the size of his cock and some superpowered move he did with it, when she paused midsentence and gave me a funny look. "Are you going to chase that tomato around your plate all day, or are you going to eat it?"

I stabbed it with a fork, and a piece of lettuce fell victim to its spilled guts. Gutted. That's how I felt. Unloading on Sandra had been a dangerous thing. An addictive thing, because I wanted to do it again, only I didn't want to stick to vague answers this time. I wanted to tell someone all the shit life had thrown at me.

Besides Rafe, Evelyn was the closest thing I had to a real friend. Weren't friends supposed to tell each other their secrets? I wouldn't know. My secret had been too huge, too horrific, to share with anyone for years.

Until Rafe had tortured it out of me.

"Okay, something's on your mind. It was weird enough that you called out of the blue, but you're never *this* quiet, and that's saying a lot." She sipped her iced tea and settled back in the chair. "I heard about what happened in the papers. I wanted to call you. Truth is, I didn't know what to say. We'd drifted apart, and I just..."

"It's okay," I whispered.

"No," she said, her mouth set in a firm line as she shook her head. "It's not okay. My friend had a mental breakdown of epic proportions and I couldn't even bring myself to pick up the goddamn phone. I'm sorry, Alex. I'm here now."

"I didn't have a mental breakdown."

Her brows crinkled in confusion. "What happened then? Everyone thought you were dead."

A sheen of sweat broke out on my skin, and I felt a trickle sliding down my temple. I opened my mouth, commanded my tongue to work right and spill the words *my brother kidnapped and raped me*, but I couldn't. I had many reasons to keep it bottled inside, mainly, the threat my father held over my head. Over Rafe's head.

I'd been protecting him in some way or another for a nearly a decade, but he wanted nothing to do with me. Hurt infiltrated my chest and choked the life from my heart. How could he walk away so easily after what we'd shared? After what he'd done? Wasn't he afraid I'd turn him in?

Don't be stupid. He knows he has you wrapped.

"Alex?"

I jumped, only then noticing the mangled napkin in my hands. I'd managed to shred it while wrestling with my thoughts. Evelyn still waited. Choosing to take the familiar coward's way out, I was about to make up a story when my cell beeped.

"I should get this. I'll be right back." I scooted back from the table with a sigh of relief. My phone continued to chirp as I walked through the busy restaurant, out the front doors, and into the summer heat. The instant I answered the call and heard his breathing, I couldn't move.

"Don't hang up."

Hang up? I could barely function. My gaze darted around, studying the bystanders and taking a modicum of comfort in their presence. I tightened my fingers around the phone, willed my hand to pull it away from my ear and hit the end button, but somewhere between thought and action, the signal in my brain got its wires crossed.

"I miss you," he said, making my fingers freeze. "And I'm so, so *sorry*." His voice cracked on the last word. He sniffled, and I was pretty certain the bastard was crying.

"Dad said you'd leave me alone." I cleared my throat and infused my tone with a dauntless edge I didn't feel. "You can't hurt me anymore. Too many people are watching."

"Especially the guy to your right. The one in the

Beaver's hat and dark sunglasses? He's practically got his tongue hanging out."

Standing in ninety-degree weather, I shivered as if snow blanketed the ground. I'd meant the public in general, even the police, since they suspected I'd left out parts of the story. Slowly, I turned and found a man matching Zach's description watching me. He looked away the instant he realized I'd caught him staring. But he wasn't the real threat.

The real threat lingered somewhere nearby, preying on my fear. I scoured both sides of the street but found nothing. Just normal people going about their business. Numerous shops, cafes, and businesses lined the row, and Zach could be in any one of them right now, ogling me with the eyes of a wolf.

"I know what you're thinking," he said. "But I'm not here to hurt you. I just had to see you. I had to know you were okay."

"Why?" I fisted my left hand. "You didn't care if I was 'okay' when you beat me, when you raped me, when you sliced me up with your fucking knife."

"I fucked up, Lex. I know I went too far."

"You went too far ten years ago. What you did in that cabin was a hundred levels past deranged."

I heard him suck in a breath. "It wasn't always bad between us. After Rafe went away, you wanted me."

"I *never* wanted that. Get that through your head." My gaze veered left and right, cheeks flaming at having this conversation in public, but there was no way in hell I'd do this in an isolated area. "I despise myself for what we did, for what I did to him. I couldn't even control my own damn body, Zach."

"Please, Lex. I'm dying without you. It'll be different this time. Dad's making sure I'm getting treatment. I haven't had a drink since that night. Please—"

"Stop!" I began pacing, though I never stopped searching my surroundings. A group of college-aged kids came out of the restaurant and bumped into me. Instead of becoming irritated, I welcomed their proximity.

Stupid, Alex. Go back inside and tell Evelyn. Get help.

"You can't just say 'I'm sorry' after everything. It doesn't work like that." I should know—sorry hadn't worked on Rafe.

"I know." He sighed. "But I love you. I want you back. Can we just sit down somewhere and talk?"

"Even if I didn't think of you like my brother"—I lowered my voice—"I could never be with someone who did what you did." The hypocrisy of my words pinged through my head. Rafe had done acts deemed unforgiv able too, but I didn't feel the same way toward him. My heart wanted what it wanted, despite logic or reason, despite right or wrong. I supposed in that aspect, I could relate to Zach.

My chest tightened, squeezing the air from my lungs. I also understood why Rafe couldn't forgive me.

"I'll do anything," he said, his plea high-pitched and

awash with regret. "Please, forgive me. You're the only thing in this world I care about."

Unable to speak, I ended the call with a press of a button then walked inside the restaurant, passing by people that blurred around me. They didn't seem real. *I* didn't seem real.

"Everything okay?" Evelyn asked.

I shook my head. "My dad..." I cleared the fear constricting my throat. "My dad needs me home. He's got the flu or something." I let out an awkward laugh. "He's a big baby." For perfecting the art of lying, I sure sucked at it now.

She tilted her head. "Are you sure you're okay?"

"Yeah." I forced my lips into a smile. "Just family stuff. Can I get a rain check?"

"Sure, but I'm holding you to it." She pulled me into a hug. "You can call me anytime."

"I know."

We parted ways out front, and as soon as she got in her SUV and pulled away, I scurried back inside the restaurant and reclaimed my seat at the table, body shaking as I deliberated on what to do. I was scared to walk to my own car. I gazed out the window at the new Volvo parked by the curb on the side of the restaurant. Dad bought it last week to replace the one destroyed by the river, once I agreed to the appointments with the shrink.

Someone slid into the chair Evelyn had vacated, making me jump. Zach's hazel eyes stared back.

"Don't freak out and make a scene," he said. "I just want to talk to you." He must have taken my stunned silence as permission to continue. And to touch me. His hand crept across the table and clamped around mine, like a snake constricting the life from my fingers. "I never meant for things to go so far."

I opened my mouth but nothing came out. A voice screeched in my head, demanding that I do something. Knock my barely touched salad on the floor, tip over a glass of water. Shout for help. For the love of God, at least remove my hand from his grip.

Instead, I sat like a statue, barely breathing.

He leaned forward, closing some of the distance between us, and lowered his voice. "I've never been so scared as when I saw what you'd done. Lex..." He let out a breath. "I know you think of me as your brother and that's why you fight this so much. But your body doesn't lie. I know there's room in your heart for me." He lifted his head, gaze searching mine. "I hate that you love him, but I can accept it because I know you love me too. Please come back to me. I won't force you. I won't do anything you don't want me to. I just need you in my life. Please, Lex. *Please.*"

I jerked my hand from his and edged away. "I almost killed myself over you."

"Fuck, Lex..." He dropped his face into his hands.

Clutching my purse, I shot a glance through the window where the sun beat down on my car, and wished

I'd parked out front. I calculated how long it would take to cover the distance if I ran, but Zach looked up.

"I know I can't take it back, but you need to come with me. Please."

"I'm not going anywhere with you."

"I don't want you around him," he said.

"Leave Rafe out of it!" I stood. "He wants nothing to do with me, so you have no reason to go off the deep end again over him."

Zach also rose, his body rigid, mouth tight in a straight line. "I wasn't talking about Rafe. I'm talking about Dad. Get the fuck out of that house, Lex. He's the last person you should trust."

"If you're talking about his threat to have me committed, I already know about it." He'd made that abundantly clear when I'd fought him about seeing the therapist.

Zach grabbed my bicep. "I'm talking about something much worse. You need to come with me." He began yanking on my arm.

"Help!" I screamed, gaze zigzagging around the restaurant before landing on a beefy guy who looked like he could take my brother. He rose, expression startled, and Zach let go of my arm. I backed away as the guy neared. Zach came after me again until my rescuer detained him.

I whirled, the front door appearing so far away. Someone shouted, and I heard a ruckus indicating a fight had begun. People stood, mouths gaping as I flew past. I didn't remember leaving the restaurant, didn't remember rounding the building and getting into my car, or thrusting the key into the ignition. I stomped on the gas and shot into traffic.

SIXTEEN

ALEX

I spent thirty mindless minutes driving east along the Columbia River. Every couple of miles, I gazed into my rearview, but as far as I could tell, Zach's car wasn't part of the mid-day traffic. I pulled off at a rest stop, hands shaking too much to drive further, and tried three times to punch in the correct code on my cell. Finally, I unlocked my phone and dialed Dad's number.

As soon as he answered, all the adrenaline pumping through me crashed and burned, and I started crying, my whole body trembling.

"Dad! Zach was there." A black Beemer pulled into the spot next to me, and I almost jumped out of my skin, fearing it was my brother. But a young redhead exited the vehicle, pushing huge sunglasses on top of her head as she walked to the restrooms, hips swaying. "Dad...I'm really scared right now." I held my breath, waiting for him to say something.

Please, for once, let him give a shit about me.

"What happened?" he finally asked.

"After my appointment, I met up with Evelyn. We were having lunch when he called—"

"Alexandra," he interrupted. "I'll talk to your brother. It was just a phone call, but he knows better. I'll make sure it doesn't happen again."

"No, he was *there*. He caused a scene after Evelyn left. He won't stop. Please, Dad, I need to tell the truth about what happened. It's eating me up—"

"Come home and we'll talk about it."

I shook my head, though I knew he couldn't see me. My father's gigantic estate was the last place I'd feel safe. I could only think of one place I equated with safety, which was really ironic, considering I'd have to cross a river to get to it. My subconscious knew exactly what it was doing—I'd already driven halfway to Dante's Pass.

"Alexandra!" His voice rose, irritation more than apparent in the bite of his tone. Abbott De Luca wasn't someone used to being ignored. "You need to come home now."

"Okay," I said, the word coming out a whisper. "I'll be there soon." I hung up before he figured out I was lying. I made one more phone call to arrange for a boat rental, then drove onto the highway again. By the time my father realized

I wasn't coming home, I'd already be on Rafe's island. Of course, that depended on my ability to go near the river and set foot in a boat without having a full-blown panic attack.

My heart fluttered the whole way to Dante's Pass and turned into an unbearable pounding as I braked in the parking lot next to the boat ramp. I shut off the ignition, and my anxiety thundered in my ears for several minutes. I kept my head straight, focusing on the restroom and the woman that came out holding a little girl's hand. Sweat coated my palms, and my grip slipped from the steering wheel. To my left, I knew what waited for me.

How was I supposed to get into a boat when I couldn't even bring myself to look at the river?

Sucking in a noisy breath, I swiveled my head before I chickened out. It was only water, and I wouldn't even be alone, as the man I'd called on the way to take me to the island waited on the dock. Normally, his company only rented out boats, but I'd offered to pay extra if he'd take me.

If only I could get out of the stupid car and walk to the dock.

Quit being such a pussy.

The need to get to Rafe was more powerful than my phobia. I pulled on the handle then pushed open the door. One shaky leg lifted into the breeze. Another maneuver, a scoot of my butt, and both feet touched solid ground. I armed the alarm and crept down the slope toward the dock next to the ramp.

Images of suffocating, of dense blackness, assaulted me with each step, making me cringe, and I chanted *stop it, stop it, stop it* to wipe the stubborn thoughts from my mind, but they stuck to my brain with the strength of crazy glue. The only way to push past the terror was to chant until I heard nothing else. If I appeared on the verge of a total meltdown, the guy wouldn't take me to Rafe.

I stepped onto the dock, keeping my eyes trained on the man waiting for me, and purposefully ignored the gentle lapping of water on either side. It wasn't going to jump out and drown me.

Stop it, stop it, stop it.

"You the one wanting a lift to Mason Island?"

Unable to find my voice just yet, I nodded.

He frowned. "You sure that's wise? You know the guy who lives on that island is a sex offender, right?"

"I know what everyone thinks he is. They're wrong."

He gave me a perplexed look. "He know you're coming?"

"Yes." Not a chance in hell. I could barely believe I was about to willingly get into a boat. No one else would believe it.

"You sure?"

"Y-yes. He's expecting me." I clasped my hands together to hide the tremors in them. "I haven't been in a boat in a while. I'm just nervous."

"Nothing to it." He held out his hand and helped me inside. As soon as the boat wobbled under my weight, I slid my fingers under my sleeve and dug my nails in so hard, I came away with skin underneath them.

He narrowed his eyes. "I'm thinking you should rethink this, lady."

With a quick shake of my head, I plopped into one of the four seats. "I'm fine. Can we please go?" I fastened my gaze on the vinyl flooring—the only thing separating me from the murky depths of nothingness—and failed to see his expression.

Stop it, stop it, stop it...

"Do you know how to swim?"

I gave a quick nod, still refusing to look at him, and heard him sigh. He placed a life jacket in the seat next to mine before starting the motor, and we were off. I squeezed my eyes shut and clung to the armrests. Wind whipped my hair around, and my stomach lurched as the boat sped over choppy waters.

When he pulled alongside the dock on Rafe's island, my entire body quaked, and I was certain I wouldn't be able to find my voice. I stood on wobbly legs, thinking how that had been the longest two minutes of my life, and handed him the cash I owed him with shaking fingers.

"Th-thanks."

He stood from the driver's seat, grabbing my arm to steady me, and helped me find solid footing on the dock. "Call if you need me." His tone suggested more than just a ride back. I looked into his eyes and found concern in them. God, these people really believed Rafe was a monster, and it was all my fault. I had to make this right.

"I'm okay. Rafe Mason isn't the man you think he is."

"If you say so, lady. I'm friends with the sheriff. Call if you need anything."

I nodded but didn't answer. The motor fired up, and I heard him pull away. My feet wouldn't move at first. As I stood on the dock, memories assaulted me. The night I'd fallen in, the night Rafe put me into a boat and sent me off, thinking his actions would protect me.

But he hadn't come after me. Why? I thought of his rejection in the hospital and how odd that whole visit was. Now that my head was clearing, things were starting to prick at my mind. Questions arose.

The whole time I'd been under my father's thumb, recuperating from the kidnapping and my own attempt to end it, everything in my world had scrambled like a Rubik's Cube. Nothing had lined up the way it should.

Coming back to this island felt like coming home.

I started on the trail and hiked up the slight incline past a massive willow. The top of his A-frame cabin came into view, and I took a moment to really see it for the first time. Painted a dark brown-red with a huge front porch, trees towered around it, as if standing sentinel. I thought back to the night we'd left through the front door, but I couldn't recall leaving the cabin. I'd been too preoccupied with fear, too worried about Rafe and what he'd do. Too paralyzed by the thought of going near the water.

As I climbed the steps, I withdrew the letters from my purse. Taking a deep breath, I halted at his door, and I gave myself a moment to hope.

Hope that he still wanted me.

Hope that he'd love me even.

Hope that he'd help me end this, once and for all.

Zach was still out there, and everyone around me was nuts. Rafe had done horrible things to me, but he was the crazy I knew, the crazy I loved, the crazy I trusted with my heart *and* my life.

Looking at him was like looking into a mirror. We'd done so much to hurt each other, but we were the only ones who could fix each other. I believed that with every bone in my body. It'd just taken me a while to see beyond my father's manipulations, his threats, and I refused to be a puppet any longer. Not unless it was the man on the other side of the door pulling the strings.

Swallowing the lump in my throat, I lifted a fist and knocked.

SEVENTEEN
RAFE

"Y ou can tell my brother to shove it. Shit, Jax, I don't even remember working at the winery. Seems pointless to go back now." I paced in the kitchen, cell to my ear, and not-so-patiently listened while he tried to convince me that Adam was right. Hiding out alone on the island wasn't going to fix anything. I needed to move on with my life, memory or not. Move on from Alex.

So why wasn't I? Even I didn't know why I was stuck in purgatory, neither remembering the past nor moving toward the future. I was frozen in this lonely existence where Alex's wails haunted my dreams each night. Other stuff haunted me too. Men and their brutal hands taking every last thread of power from me. I shook the images from my head, as I always did when those nightmares sparked. They pierced me to my bones every time, but I took them as a sign that on some subconscious level, I craved the control I'd lost. Made sense, considering my life had become a huge clusterfuck.

"If you're not ready to talk to Adam," Jax said, "at least come meet up with me tonight. You've been cooped up on that island too long. We'll scope out a date for you."

I let out a bitter laugh. "Dating is the furthest thing from my mind, but I appreciate the thought." Tiring of pacing, I returned to the living room and lowered onto the couch with my laptop. Keeping tabs on the local fighting scene had become an obsession. I ached to step into the cage again, to experience the thrilling high that only came from choking out an opponent. But no legitimate organization would take on a guy convicted of raping a 15-year-old girl.

"Forget about women then," Jax said. "Just come meet me tonight. Say about nine?"

"I'll think about it." I scrolled through the latest fights and their outcomes. Some of the fighters I remembered, but a lot of the contenders were new names making a splash on the scene. "So how's Nikki?"

"Nikki is..." His sigh filtered over the line. "I'm trying to get her to postpone this fucking wedding."

"You're in over your head," I said, closing the laptop.

"You're one to talk."

"What's that supposed to mean?"

"Alex De Luca. She's the reason you're holed up in isolation on that damn piece of land."

I hated how he knew me so well. "I shouldn't have left her the way I did, Jax. She was a mess—"

"Let it go," he said, tone firm. "You don't even remember her."

"Oh, I remember her."

"I'm not talking about the girl. I'm talking about the woman. You lose your fucking memory, but somehow, you're still just as obsessed as ever."

I had no ground to argue on, so I didn't even try. A knock sounded, and I welcomed the distraction of an unexpected visitor. "Someone's here." I strode to the door, pulled it open, and found Alex standing on the other side, suddenly just there, as if my guilt had summoned her. "I'll have to call you back," I told Jax before hanging up on him. I pocketed my cell then stared at her with my mouth hanging open.

Fucking A. I was at a loss for words.

"I know you don't want to see me," she said, her gaze lowering to her sneakers. She expelled a breath that ruffled her hair before bringing her eyes to mine. Beautiful eyes full of pain and confusion and...something I couldn't put a name to but whatever it was it pulled at me in a way I couldn't resist. God, she was gorgeous. I'd noticed the differences in her at the hospital, despite her frail state, but seeing her on my doorstep, the sun shining on the crown of her curls, how her teenage body had morphed into that of a woman's...I had to take a deep breath to keep from reaching out and touching her.

My gaze darted behind her to the trees where thick branches and the incline of the terrain hid the water. "You crossed the river?"

She bit her lip and nodded. "I have nowhere else to go, Rafe. No one else to trust."

I was speechless. Birds chirped, a hawk squawked overhead, and the howl of a train roared in the distance. But me? I was fucking speechless.

"Say something, please." She gripped her arm, fingers curling into the long sleeve of a green shirt. The weather was too warm to cover up so much skin, but I knew why she did it. And she looked fucking scared.

Of me? But that didn't quite add up. What would cause her to set foot on this island, facing her worst fear and the man who'd kidnapped and raped her?

"After what I put you through," I said, keeping my tone gentle so I wouldn't run her off, "I don't deserve your trust."

She held out a stack of envelopes. "I wrote these while you were in prison. I want you to read them, but..." She backed away, her gaze roaming in every direction but mine. "I want you to read them alone. I'll wait out here."

I stepped onto the porch and took the letters, and our fingers brushed together. A shiver went through me as I thought of the answers I might find inside the envelopes, but there was no way in hell I'd leave her out here alone when she seemed ready to jump out of her skin.

"I'm not leaving you out here by yourself. You can go inside and wait. I'll read them on the porch."

She still wouldn't meet my gaze. "Is Jax home?" she asked.

"No. It's just me." Did being alone with me make her feel more threatened? "I'm not going to hurt you, Alex."

She looked up, her expression so openly startled, I felt it to the bottoms of my feet. "I already know that." Without another word, she moved past, her shoulder grazing my arm, and entered the cabin. The screen door swung shut behind her. I didn't move at first, still too stunned and barely grasping the fact that Alex had really shown up at my door.

Finally lowering to the first step, I eyed the bundle of envelopes. The one at the top of the pile had a date on it— just a few months after I'd gone to prison. Removing the rubber band that held them together, I noted how they were all dated. I opened the first one and pulled out a sheet of paper.

Rafe,

It's been three months, four days, thirteen hours, and some odd minutes since I felt your eyes on me in the courtroom. I'm a horrible person for so many reasons. I took your freedom, and I'm not dumb. I know I wrecked your career too.

But I can't come forward about your innocence. I've tried. You don't know how many times I've fingered my cell, even looked up the number for the detective who handled my case. I went to my father's car once, keys in hand, and got behind the wheel. I'm not even old enough to drive by myself yet, but I wanted to go to the police and tell them...things.

You're still in that place, so obviously, I didn't.

It's taken me this long just to put pen to paper and write you a letter I have no intention of sending. If I'm smart, I'll destroy this after I'm done.

But I won't.

I need someone to talk to, and you're the only person I want to talk to. Besides, the thought of ripping this up is too painful, as if these words were never real. As if my feelings for you don't exist.

I'm selfish like that. Keeping my mouth shut is something I have to do, for your sake, for mine. But I need to lean on you right now. I still remember the day of my mother's funeral. It was the first and only time you put your arms around me. You're the only person who's ever told me the words I always needed to hear:

Everything will be okay.

I love you even more for that. And God, I miss you. Your laughter made the pain in my life a little more bearable. Your presence was the only thing that had the power to make me smile, and I've always loved the jittery feelings you stirred in my stomach.

I have a few friends at school, no one that close. Definitely no one I can confide in, but sometimes they talk to me. They complain about those flutters, say they lose their tongue and can't talk to guys.

It's never been that way with you.

That jittery feeling always made me feel alive and connected to you. And we talked all the time, about your dreams of making it to the UFC, about your family. About mine. I envy the closeness you have with your dad. And I know you don't get along with your brother, but at least he isn't—

Never mind. Family is a sore subject for me. I used to pretend that you were there for me and not my brother, that you needed to be around me as much as I needed to be near you. I know I'm lying to myself with that one.

I'm just a kid. No one important. Someone who isn't worthy of you. I never was, and now, after what I've done, I never will be.

I don't have the courage to put into words why I did what I did. Maybe someday I will. Maybe someday I'll pour it all out into a letter and actually send it. Actually do the right thing.

But I can't, because I'm just as trapped as you are.

I need you to know this, Rafe. I'm sorry. I'm so sorry, and it's taken over my heart and each beat hurts, especially because I know you'll never forgive me.

But please try.

Yours always,
Alex

. . .

Intense relief settled in, and I wiped the sweat from my brow. I hadn't raped her all those years ago. Her own words proved it.

I tore into the stack of her secrets like a starved man, needing more. Most of them were similar to the first, yet the tone shifted with each envelope as time moved forward. A prominent note of desperation and self-hate tainted the ink of her words. Then I came across a letter that branded my insides like a hot iron.

Rafe,

I don't know what to do! I'm so scared. He's out of control. He put my science partner in the hospital today, all because the guy asked me out on a date. I wish you were here. I know it's irrational to wish that. I'm the reason you are where you are. It's all my fault. My existence has caused so much pain for others.

You're the only one I can talk to you about any of this, yet I'm still not being honest. I'm still holding stuff back. I'm afraid if I write it out, something really bad will happen. I know I'm being paranoid. Spelling out the words won't bring the ceiling down, yet I can't make myself do it.

I wish I were stronger. My mom was strong. I see that now.

She let go of this painful Earth because she felt she had no other choice. I hate that she left me, but I understand it now.

I wish I were as brave.

Yours always,
Alex

My hands shook as I pulled out another folded piece of paper. Her words became darker the more I read, and I was close to going inside the cabin and forcing her tell me what she hadn't said in the letters, but I couldn't tear myself away.

Rafe,

I got drunk tonight. Graduation is supposed to be cause for celebration, so I partook in the craziness. I shouldn't have because I was off my game when I came home. He was waiting for me in the shadows, enraged because he thought I'd fucked someone else.

He just left my room, and now...now I'm disgusted with myself and stone cold sober. I don't fight him anymore. Truth is,

I stopped fighting him after they took you away. I fucking hate myself, Rafe. Probably more than you hate me.

He made me come tonight. It's happened a few times before, but tonight was different. Tonight, he hit me, pinched my nipples so hard he had to smother my cries with a pillow. They weren't cries of pain, and that's why I'm so sick right now.

What is wrong with me?

Crazy thing is, as I write this and remember, I'm still turned on. But it's you I'm thinking of and not him. After I'm done writing this, I'm going to climb into bed and touch myself. I'll regret thinking of you in the morning because it's not fair to gain pleasure when you're where you are.

But I can't help myself right now. I need to wash away his touch and replace it with something else. When my fingers are sliding between my thighs, I'll pretend they're yours, pretend your tongue is down there too. He hasn't done that yet. I'm probably the only seventeen-year-old girl who hasn't had her pussy eaten out.

Tonight, in my heart, in my dreams, it'll be you.

Yours always,
Alex

Ah, holy hell. I dropped my head into my hand, her letter still clutched in the other. Reading between the lines filled me with rage. Someone had raped her for years, yet she hadn't named him. The logical conclusion, since she'd mention he'd been waiting for her when she came home, was that it was someone in her household, or someone who spent a lot time there. An associate of her father's? A random person hired on as help?

A boyfriend?

I wanted to hunt down whoever it was and castrate the fucker.

Her next letter called to me, and I couldn't resist the allure of her words. Words meant for me. Words written *to* me. The stack had thinned considerably, yet there was so much left untold.

Rafe,

Oh. My. God. I'm so sorry. I'm so close to destroying my last letter, but I promised myself I wouldn't. But that was TMI.

Yours always,
Alex

I shook my head, mouth turning up slightly, and like an addict, I pulled out another, and another. Her need to spill strengthened with each word, each tear that splotched the pages as she poured her heart out. I hurt for her. I hurt for me too, because the way she wrote it, she'd sent me to hell. A hell she hadn't fully grasped, though she'd sensed it. As I continued to read, a lump formed in my throat.

My nightmares came back to haunt me again, and I did what I hadn't been able to do before. I accepted them as memories. I'd been violated in prison. Something in that place made me snap, made me embrace the dark side of myself I'd fought for so long. I'd become the type of man who hadn't settled for fantasies. In Alex, I'd found the perfect excuse to justify an act that was and always would be unforgivable.

I carefully unfolded her last letter, hoping she'd finally tell me what I needed to know.

Rafe,

Today I graduated college. I should be over the moon, right? I'm not. I stopped to look back at my life these past seven years and that's when it truly hit me. I've left you to rot in that place all this time.

One more year, and you'll be out.

But what will I say to you? I want to see you so badly I

ache with it. The need is a beast inside me, tearing my chest open and spilling my heart onto the floor. My crush has turned into a full-fledged obsession.

Dad wants me to take over the position of managing accountant for the business. I've got the degree for it, but the MMA world is the last place I want to be. That's where HE is. I'm shaking as I write this because I want so badly to write his name, but I just can't.

At the very least, you deserve to know why I sent you to prison, and I need to get it out of me once and for all because I need to move on. Dad set me up with a business partner. He's much older, but he's nice. Best of all, he's not...him.

Maybe I'm clinging to the first opportunity to break free, though it feels like I'm trading one prison for another. I don't love this guy. I barely know him, but I can tell he's serious about me. He's already asked me to go with him to Paris for Christmas.

I'm stalling. I know I'm stalling. I've written you so many letters, but I've never explained. So here goes, from the beginning.

It started right after I met you. At first, I fought him. Over time, it was easier to give in. Then...I became a whore. I don't fight him anymore because he gets me off. It's sick and disgraceful. I know this. I've tried to get him to leave me alone, have even done some extreme things to break free for a while, but he always pulls me back.

When I was fifteen, he got me pregnant. I got an abortion, and when Dad found out, he went through the roof. I don't *know why he told Dad you raped me...no, that's not true. He did it because he was jealous of you. He's always been jealous of you.*

You're probably wondering why I went along with the lie. I ask myself the same thing all the time. But I've seen his rage, seen firsthand what he's capable of, and he threatened to kill you if I didn't back him up. Hindsight's 20/20, they say. I know now that I should have stood up to him. You're a big boy and could've taken care of yourself. At the time, though, the threat choked me.

Now it's too late. You'll be out in a year...less, actually. I need to let you go. I need you to get past this and be happy. I want your forgiveness more than you could know, but that's an impossible dream. I wouldn't forgive me. I can't forgive myself.

Rafe, this is the last time I'll write, and you'll be safe because you'll never read these letters. You'll live your life hating me, and I'll have to find a way to live with that. If I could say one thing to you right now, it would be how sorry I am. He did it because I love you.

Yours always,
Alex

I dropped the page, watched it flutter to the ground, and stared at it for what seemed like forever. She waited inside, and I found it ironic that she was scared to face me. That she wanted *my* forgiveness. I'd kidnapped and done unforgivable acts—things I couldn't even recall—to a victim of rape. Maybe I'd feel differently if I remembered the last eight years, but I didn't.

So that begged the question...what the fuck was I supposed to say to her?

Gathering her letters, I rose to my feet and pulled the screen door open. She'd left the front door cracked. Slowly, I stepped inside and the sound of running water brought me into the kitchen where I found her loading my fucking dishwasher like it was an everyday chore she did.

She must have sensed my presence because she shut off the faucet, though she didn't move or turn around. "You read them?"

"Every word." I wanted to ask her so many things. Why didn't she send the letters? Why was she giving them to me now? Most of all, I wanted to know the name of the scumbag who'd raped her. I had my suspicions, but I couldn't bring myself to believe it yet. I placed the envelopes on the table and fisted my hands. With all the pent-up rage rushing through my veins, I was surprised at how level my words came out. "Why are you doing my dishes?"

She shrugged. "To stay busy."

"Can you turn around and talk to me?"

"I'm scared, Rafe."

"I already told you"—willing the anger to leave my

voice and body, I unfurled my fists and relaxed my stance —"I'm not gonna hurt you."

"That's not what I meant." She propped against the counter, fingers clutching the edge. "I'm scared of what you're thinking. We've been through so much together, but letting you read those letters was like giving you free access to my journal."

"Why'd you do it then?"

She dropped her head. "I let everyone around me dictate my life. I've basically been a doormat. What I did, sending you away like that when you hadn't even touched me...if I could change one thing, it would be that." She inhaled then let the breath out in a whoosh. "I want to make this right," she said, voice fracturing, "but I don't know if I can do it alone."

"You're not alone. I'm here, and I won't let anyone hurt you like that again." It felt like a dick thing to say, considering how the words came from a hypocrite's mouth, but it was the truth. I wanted to tear into the person who'd done this to her. By the time I was through, no one would recognize his disgusting face. "Who raped you?"

She paused, back straightening before she whirled around to face me. "What?" Her large green eyes rounded in shock.

Shit. Fucking amnesia. The eight-year blank she knew nothing about.

"There's something you need to know." I gestured

toward the half-filled dishwasher. "Those can wait." I pulled out a chair and gave her a pointed look.

Rather than cross the few feet between us, she wiped her palms on her jeans. "Why are you acting like this?" Her voice rose, on the level of screeching, and the confusion on her face splintered through me. "Don't treat me like I'm breakable. I want you back! I *need* you back." She blinked rapidly, sucked in several breaths, and to my horror, tears leaked down her cheeks. "*Make* me sit in that chair."

I gaped at her, at a complete loss. "Alex...come sit down. We need to talk."

"I don't want to talk! I want you to turn back time and come after me." She doubled over, her shoulders quaking with sobs. "I want you to take back control! Stop acting like nothing happened between us." She wiped the hair from her eyes and slid to the floor, the fight bleeding from her body, then covered her face with her hands.

Carefully, I closed the distance and a sense of Deja vu came over me. I crouched in front of her, pulling her hands to the sides of her damp cheeks. "I don't remember."

"What are you talking about?"

"The last eight years, Alex." Of their own volition, our fingers entwined. "I don't remember any of it."

EIGHTEEN

ALEX

He didn't remember? I searched his eyes, looking for a hint of recognition as I attempted to process what he'd told me.

He didn't remember *anything*?

I tried to imagine what it would be like to wipe away that much pain and betrayal. Poof, gone. No more hurt, no more baggage, just a chance at a clean slate. Hadn't I tried to do the same, albeit a more permanent method born from desperation in a bathroom in the middle of nowhere?

His fingers tightened around mine, instantly grounding me. "Now you're the one who needs to say something."

"I..." What if he'd forgotten for a reason? What if deep down, he didn't want to know? "I don't know what to say."

He stood, pulling me with him, and led me to the chair. Though his hand pressed on my shoulder with a gentleness that surprised me, he made me lower into the seat. Some sick part of myself rejoiced in that. His odd behavior had unsettled me to my toes, his lack of imposing do-as-I-say presence. I wanted to wrap myself in it because it felt natural and familiar, and I needed that from him.

He tilted my chin up, and his mouth formed a hard line. "*Who* raped you?" Regardless of whether his psyche wanted to remain in the dark, some part of him still sought the truth, or he wouldn't push for it.

"It was Zach." I wasn't about to repeat the same mistake. Whatever he wanted to know, I'd tell him.

His touch fell from my face, and I missed the contact instantly. "Did I know that? Before I lost my memory?"

"Yes."

He let out a breath. "This is a lot for me to take in, Alex. I woke up in the hospital thinking I was twenty-one. The fight against Zach in Seattle is the last memory I have." He clenched his jaw. "What happened the night I was shot?"

Suddenly, it dawned on me. He hadn't come after me... not because he hadn't cared but because he'd lost his memory. "Zach showed up. You guys fought, then you made me get into a boat." I swallowed hard, but the memory of their last fight—the blast of the gun that still ricocheted in my head, even now—burned in my eyes and nose. "You tried to protect me, but he...he..."

"He shot me?"

I nodded, too choked up to speak.

He crouched in front of me, took my right arm in his

hands, and ran his fingertips down the material hiding the ugly scars that had scabbed over. All I wanted was to throw myself at him and beg him to hold me, to never let go. I wanted to hide in his embrace forever. What an impossible, dangerous idea. Zach wouldn't stop until he got what he wanted...me.

"Is he in jail?"

I shook my head.

"Why the hell not?"

"Dad's covering for him again." I tucked my lip between my teeth. "He said Zach would leave me alone, but he cornered me in a restaurant today."

Rafe pushed up my sleeve and caressed the wound I'd inflicted on myself. "Why did you come here? Why didn't you go to the cops?"

"You make me feel safe." I trembled under the warmth of his touch. "I don't trust anyone else. Don't make me leave."

"I fucking kidnapped you, Alex. I might not remember the details, but I know that much. Jax filled me in, and I saw the prison in the cellar. How can you feel safe around me?"

"Because I'm as twisted as you are."

"I think that's the first sensible thing you've said." His thumb rubbed over my scar. "Tell me what happened here."

I shook my head, my brain refusing to go back to that

cabin, even though I'd promised myself I'd tell him anything. "I can't talk about it. Please don't make me."

"*Make* you?" He looked at me in confusion. "You keep using that word."

"You've obviously forgotten the power you have over me."

"Then tell me. I need to know what happened. All of it."

"I can't."

"You can." He tangled his fingers with mine. "Because we're going to the police and they'll need to hear it."

I shook my head. "My father will have me committed. He's got everyone thinking I'm crazy, that I tried to kill myself."

"Did you?" His attention landed on my arms.

I studied our joined hands. "It's not what you think. I tried to get away from Zach, but he kept me high on ecstasy half the time." I blinked rapidly. "I convinced myself he was you, and..."

He squeezed my hand. "I'm listening."

Turning my head, I gazed out the window at the cloudless sky, too ashamed to face him. "He snapped after I cried out your name." I untangled our hands and slowly lifted my shirt.

Rafe stood, bringing my attention back to him. His jaw twitched and his green eyes went so dark, I was glad his anger wasn't directed at me. "*He* did that to you?" Fury drenched his words, flooded the space between us with an oath of retribution.

Closing my eyes, I nodded. "Afterward, I...I lost my mind and locked myself in the bathroom, broke the mirror and...I just wanted him to stop."

Without warning, he pulled me from the chair and into the shelter of his arms. One hand tangled in my hair as the other held me to his shaking body. "He'll never hurt you again."

Standing on tiptoes, I clutched his shirt and burrowed into the crook of his shoulder. "I wasn't the only one he hurt. He wrecked your life, Rafe. We both did, and I am so, so sorry. I know I need to turn him in but—"

"Stop." He pulled back and framed my face in his hands. "If it's forgiveness you're asking for, you've got it. Fuck, Alex, I'll never forget the sight of you in that hospital bed. If I'd known, there's no way in hell I would have left you there." He drew in a deep breath. "But none of it matters as much as you being able to heal from all of this. You were only fifteen, way too fucking young to be held accountable for a decision your rapist coerced you into making."

Hot tears slipped from my eyes, dripping down my face in relief. In the deepest and darkest crevices of my being, I'd never believed he'd be able to forgive me. A lump of anxiety formed in my throat, and I swallowed, but it only crashed into the pit of my stomach. His forgiveness wouldn't keep me safe from Zach's madness...wouldn't keep *him* safe.

"He'll come after us both. He's insane and jealous—"

"You need to turn him in, Alex." His hands fell from my face. "Zach belongs in jail. Fuck, *I* belong in jail. We're gonna do something about it, regardless of what your piece-of-shit father has to say."

My gaze darted through the window where trees obscured the bane of my existence. Those plans were terrifying—they involved getting into a boat again. They involved coming forward. I wasn't sure which I dreaded more. "I won't tell them what you did. If you want me to talk to the police, then you staying out of jail is my stipulation."

"I won't argue with that. I'd rather be here protecting you than sitting in a jail cell, so I guess we'd better get our stories straight."

NINETEEN
RAFE

I glanced at her in the passenger seat. The pallor of her skin worried me. So did the way she wrung her hands in her lap. She'd barely said two words since we'd left the island, except to insist on going to the sheriff's department here in Dante's Pass instead of filing the report in Portland. The boat ride had thoroughly rattled her, and I dreaded the trip back to the cabin. By the end of the day, I feared she'd hate my guts for making her go.

"The sheriff isn't my biggest fan, Alex. He's got everyone around here believing I'm a threat. I doubt he'll hear you out."

"Then I *want* to talk to him. This isn't just about turning Zach in. I want to clear your name too."

Overturning a prison sentence wasn't going to happen by filing a police report, but I didn't want to disappoint her. "I'm not even sure which law enforcement agency holds jurisdiction. Zach kidnapped you from the island, crossed county lines, and you ended up in a hospital near Mt. Hood."

"The police don't know he took me from your island, Rafe. I told them I pushed my car into the river before going to that cabin on my own."

"He held you in a cabin?"

"An isolated place in the middle of nowhere. I wouldn't even know how to get there. He said it belonged to a friend."

I cursed under my breath. "So what are we going to say then?"

Her brows furrowed in thought. "The truth with a few alterations. I'll tell them Zach kidnapped me. You drugged me, so I have no memory of you and Jax pushing my car into the river. I'll blame that on him too."

"I drugged you?"

"When you took me," she said quietly.

"And here you are sitting next to me in a fucking car." I shook my head, unable to grasp how she could use the word "safe" and my name in the same sentence. "What will you tell them when they ask why you're spending time with your convicted rapist?"

"The truth. You're innocent. I lied eight years ago, under the threat of Zach, and I came to you because I'm scared and want to make this right." She bit her lip and gazed out the window at the small-town businesses lining the main drag. I didn't agree with her about the innocence part, not in relation to the past few weeks, but I let it go for now. No good would come from arguing the point to death. Neither of us said a word until I pulled into the parking lot of the sheriff's department.

"You ready?" I asked.

With a nod, she pulled on the passenger door handle. I got out, rounded the car, and without thinking I placed my hand on the small of her back. We entered the brick building and found it deserted, save for the deputy manning the front window. I didn't recognize him, so I assumed he'd come to Dante's Pass after I left. I'd blown out of town before my graduation cap had time to hit the ground.

"I need to report a crime," she told the guy on the other side of the glass. I hung back, marveling at her strength as she told the deputy about the nature of the crime she wanted to report. He took her information before rising to get the sheriff.

Minutes later, a side door opened and Lyle appeared, the deputy on his heels. His gaze blasted me, and the scowl twisting his features made me want to yank Alex out of there immediately. But his expression softened when he asked if she was comfortable giving her statement to him.

She told him she was okay with that, then turned to give me a tiny reassuring smile. "I'll be back."

I wanted to go with her. I wanted to grab her and never let go, but I understood her need to do this on her own. They disappeared behind the door, and the deputy resumed his spot behind the window, his attention captured by a crossword puzzle.

I knocked on the glass. "I need to make a call. If she comes back before I do, let her know I'm right outside, okay?"

He waved me off without raising his head. What a prick. I withdrew my cell as I exited, and a strong breeze carrying the familiar scent of fresh water and a hint of fish rustled my hair. Scrolling to Jax's name in my contact list, I pushed the call button and waited for him to answer, all the while searching the area. This wasn't a conversation I wanted overheard, but I needed something fast and my instincts told me he could get it for me.

"What's up?" he answered.

I darted my gaze around the parking lot once more, satisfied that I was completely alone. "Can you do me a favor?"

"Depends."

"I need a gun."

"Come again?"

"You heard me. Can you get one?"

"Well, yeah, but why? What's going on?"

"It's Alex. She showed up on the island today. I don't wanna go into details, but she's scared. I need a weapon."

"Whoa...you need to back up there. What the fuck is going on?"

I sighed in exasperation. "Her brother is psychotic. He's the one who shot me, Jax. Can you get me a gun or not?"

"Are you gonna use it to protect yourself or her?"

I narrowed my eyes. "What does it matter?"

"You're doing it for her then."

Not a question. "So what if I am?" I shot back, tiring of his inquisition. "If you don't wanna do it, just say so. I'll find someone else." Though Jax was the only one I trusted even marginally with this. I was a felon. If I went down for getting my hands on a gun, well that would be tragically ironic.

And dangerous because Alex would be left on her own.

"You sure she's worth it?"

"Why do you hate her?" I asked, the disdain in his voice bothering me.

"I don't hate her." He lowered his confrontational tone by a few degrees. "You did, for the three years we shared a cell."

"There's a reason she did what she did." I kicked a rock and watched it ricochet off a bright blue curb. "She's trying to make it right, and she's fucking terrified, Jax. I won't stand by and do nothing."

He sighed. "You wouldn't be *you* if you did. Saving people is your MO."

I glance around again, tapping my foot. "So you'll get it for me?"

He didn't say anything at first, and I thought I heard him let loose a curse. "Yeah, I'll get you what you need. Tell me what you're looking for, and I'll get it to you tonight."

TWENTY
ALEX

The boat ride back to the island broke the final straw of my sanity. I collapsed onto the couch, tightened into a ball in the corner, and clung to the false shield of numbness protecting me. What a ridiculous illusion, the idea of safety.

Maybe my father was right in threatening to have me committed, because I sank into the term "crazy" with a vengeance, especially after Jax showed up and gave Rafe a gun.

Three days had passed since that night, and I still didn't remember breaking down with much clarity. I had vague recollections of wailing and clawing at Rafe and Jax when they tried to calm me, but I couldn't remember what had gone through my head, though something had triggered the episode. At first, I thought it was Jax's presence, but later that evening, when Rafe tucked the gun underneath his pillow on the couch, it hit me.

The image of Zach shooting Rafe wouldn't leave me alone. I saw it when I stared into nothingness, when I showered, when I slept.

Reporting Zach's crimes hadn't helped. The sheriff had patiently listened while I told him the changed version of my story, but I wasn't sure he believed me. And whatever he'd said to Rafe afterward had sparked his fury. He'd pulled me from the station, a shaky mass of anger, and had threatened to go to the media if they didn't do something about Zach.

We probably should have gone to Portland, but Portland was where my brother was...unless he was here in Dante's Pass, stalking me. I pictured him camped out somewhere near the island where he could watch the cabin with his relentless hazel gaze, noting when the lights shut off every night.

I cranked my head and peeked through the windows in the living room with single-minded focus, wondering if he was ogling me now through a pair of binoculars.

Fucking paranoid, Alex.

Zach would have to be high up in the hills on the other side of the river to even spot the cabin, much less see inside it.

"What's on your mind?" Rafe spooned me, one hand smoothing over my stomach underneath the T-shirt I wore, as if he could wipe away Zach's carving with his touch. The TV cast a dim glow in the room, though the volume had been turned so low, I strained to catch the real life horrors broadcasting through the screen. We'd been cuddling like this on the couch for the past hour after dinner.

Rafe wouldn't kiss me, and he never touched me like he used to—with demanding hands that didn't seek permission, with fiery passion that scorched me. I craved that side of him like a starved junkie, but I didn't know how to tell him, and he didn't remember the days we'd spent together, so I settled for what I could get. Stolen hours with him on the sofa each night before we went our separate ways to sleep. He cooked for me, worried about me, but always kept a distance that seemed insurmountable.

"You keep looking out the windows," he said at my continued silence. "Wanna talk about it?"

"I'm worried he's watching."

"He can't see in here, Alex."

"Logically, I know that." I untangled from his arms and walked right up to the glass. Peering into the blackness, I willed my heartbeat to slow. He *wasn't* out there. If I kept telling myself that, maybe I'd believe it. "You think the police are looking for him?" I asked.

"Yeah. I called the detective in Portland today." His footsteps vibrated the hardwood beneath my bare feet, and his body warmed my back. "They're on it, Alex. Lyle might be an ass wipe, but he did his job."

"Do you think Zach got spooked? Maybe that's why he hasn't shown up." I was scared to hope for it.

"Or maybe he knows better. I won't let him hurt you again."

I turned around. "Have you remembered anything yet?"

"No." He settled his hands on my shoulders, dipped his head, and his lips lingered near mine. "Nothing's coming back."

"You're so different this way," I whispered. He was more like...the guy I remembered from eight years ago.

"Am I really?" He pulled away. "Because when I think of you down in that cellar, I'm ashamed of myself."

The memory of that place called, like a siren's seductive song. Did he feel it too? The allure of the cellar had been silently summoning me since I'd first arrived on the island. So far, I'd been too much of a wuss to go down there, to soak up the place where Rafe first showed me his darkness...the place where he helped me embrace mine. Our twisted romance began down there.

A shiver went through me. On one hand, I'd been through hell in that dank, cold space, but on the other, experiencing his touch for the first time as a woman had been intoxicating.

"You've thought of me down there?"

"I've tried to remember," he said, though he avoided my eyes.

The uncertainty in his mannerisms unnerved me. He

seemed so lost, as if a huge part of him had gone missing, and in a way it had. "Do you want to remember?"

"Of course I want to remember." He rubbed a hand down his face, but he didn't wipe the fear from his expression. His mask had cracked, leaving behind a fissure where the broken man peeked through.

I tugged on his hand, impulse driving me. "Come down there with me."

His feet didn't budge. "Absolutely not."

God, he looked terrified. We both had demons to face in that cellar. Slowly, I slid my fingers from his. "Fine. I'll go down by myself, and I'll wait for you as long as it takes."

"Alex—"

The loud thud of my steps on hardwood drowned out the rest of his words. I yanked the door open, entered the dark space, and jumped when it slammed shut behind me. I felt along the concrete, heart pounding, and searched for the light switch in the blackness. My palm brushed it, and a moment later dim light flooded the room. With a sigh of relief, I descended the stairs. The cold penetrated first, then the scent of dirt, musty dampness, and concrete—a combination my mind equated with captivity. Instinct alone made me wander to the cage.

Everything crashed back with the strength of a tsunami. Naked, cowering in the corner, trembling from the cold, terrified because I hadn't known what Rafe was capable of. I folded my arms around myself, as if to ward off the memories and the chill in the air.

But I was safe. On the most fundamental level, my body knew that. It also responded in a way that used to make me loathe myself.

Not anymore. Not when it came to Rafe.

My gaze zeroed in on the cuffs dangling from the ceiling and warmth flooded between my thighs. He'd left the door to the prison open. I entered, this time of my own free will, and stripped the clothes from my body. Goose bumps broke out on my flesh, and my nipples tightened into aching buds. I lifted my head and eyed the cuffs again, noting how he'd left them unlocked. They spoke to me, whispering to slip my wrists inside and close the metal on my free will.

He'd probably think I was insane, and maybe I was, but something told me this would bring him back to me. I stood on tiptoes and worked one wrist into the circular restraint. The lock clicked in place, making my pulse speed up. After some maneuvering, I managed to secure my other wrist too.

There was no going back. I'd effectively trapped myself, leaving the decision of freeing me up to him. Suddenly, my stomach dropped. What if he didn't remember where he kept the key? I didn't have time to agonize over that too-late realization. The door creaked open and his footfalls announced his arrival. The instant he saw me, he froze.

I hung before him, naked, exposed, wrists bound as effectively as my heart was to him.

"Please tell me you know where the key is?"

"If I had to guess," he said, taking a step closer, "it's on my keyring." He gestured toward me. "Why are you doing this?"

"You know all my secrets, all my shame." I glanced at the cement floor, remembering how I'd awakened, naked and cold, with my hands restrained to the bars. "This is where you first brought me. You wanted to make me suffer the way you did. But we shared something, Rafe, and I want that back so badly." I shut my eyes, disturbed by the utter shock in his.

"I don't remember." I heard him come closer.

"I have faith you will." A tear slipped from beneath my closed lids, and the brush of his thumb caught it. I sucked in a breath. "I crave your touch so much. Please...make his disappear."

He grazed his fingers across my breasts. "He hurt you." His words came out strangled. He inched lower, hands drifting over the evidence of my brother's brutality, and smoothed a palm along my stomach, where Zach had branded me with his name. "And though I don't remember it, *I* hurt you too."

"Rafe—"

"Look at me," he interrupted.

I opened my eyes, and my insides melted from the heat in his. His palms cradled my cheeks with a tenderness that masked his need to conquer. He might not recognize the hunger in himself, but I did. That need colored the command in his tone, was evident in the wide stance of his feet and the bulge behind his zipper.

My heartbeat rocketed. What if he remembered and went back to hating me? "Please don't hate—"

He silenced me with his mouth, his unyielding hands holding my head in place as his lips forced mine open, tongue thrusting in gentle possession that claimed, commanded, owned. My lids shuttered, and I lost myself to his taste. His kiss infused me with a raging, burning need. An explosion went off at my core, spreading from my belly down to my thighs, all the way to the soles of my feet. I spread them and gained better traction on the ground. Cool air drifted between my legs, where I ached for him— for his touch, for his hot mouth kissing so intimately, for the girth of his cock.

He inched away, breaths puffing across my swollen lips. "Open your eyes, sweetheart."

My heart jumped at the endearment, and my lashes fluttered open. "You remember," I whispered, both fear and hope warring in my soul.

"No." His thumbs caressed my damp cheeks. "I don't need to remember to know that I want you." His brows narrowed, and he frowned. "It's the way I want you that worries me."

"Tell me."

He hesitated. "I've had fantasies for a long time." His gaze lifted to my restrained hands. "Dark fantasies I never thought I'd act on. I don't know what I did to you, or what that place did to me, but it scares the fuck out of me."

"You don't have to be afraid."

He stepped back and took in my nakedness with a single glance. "We've always orbited each other," he said, pausing with a shake of his head, "but I never imagined it would lead to...this."

"Never imagined we'd be so right for each other? Rafe, you already know how I feel about you."

"You had a crush on me."

"Is that how you saw me back then? Just an annoying kid?"

"At first, maybe." His green eyes flickered to my face again. "I felt it too. I won't deny it, but I've got eight years of memory missing, and you've been...so fucking scarred by Zach and me, I don't understand how you're standing on two feet right now."

"Technically, I'm on my toes."

The corner of his mouth turned up. "You surprise me. Your strength inspires me, Alex."

"Don't mistake me for being strong." Nighttime always hit hard, when the dark wee hours of morning choked me with loneliness. The scars on my body didn't compare to the ones no one could see, though I felt them each night, pressing on my chest until I couldn't breathe. "I'm here in shackles because I'm *not* strong."

"I don't understand."

"I need you. I'm sick with needing you." I cursed my

trembling lips. "No matter what you do, no matter what you remember or don't, I'm yours."

He groaned. "Even if I keep you strung up like that?"

"You've done it before, for hours in the dark. Naked, just like I am now."

"Why did I do that?" he asked, rubbing the back of his neck.

"Punishment."

"What the hell did you do to deserve that?"

Hurt pinged through me at the thought of him making me eat off the floor. But that happened before he'd known the truth. I regretted not telling him sooner. "I threw a tantrum." More like a plate of food.

"A tantrum?"

"Yes." I shifted my weight to the other foot and pulled at the restraints, though I knew I'd find no escape from the burn in my shoulders or the ache in my feet.

My restless movements caught his attention, and he adjusted his jeans. "Shit, seeing you like this...you have no idea what it's doing to me. I might not remember, but my body does. I want to hoist those legs up and fuck you raw. My cock is insisting you're mine."

"Your cock is right. You should listen to it."

He cursed under his breath. "Not tonight." Pulling a bundle of keys from his pocket, he tried two before the lock on my left wrist unlatched.

"You don't want me?"

"Of course I fucking want you." He freed my other

hand, and my arms dropped to my sides. He bent to gather my clothing before thrusting it all into my arms. "But not like this. Get dressed," he said, turning his back to me.

My hands shook as I pulled the shirt over my head. Hurt welled in my throat, making my voice wobble when I spoke. "Then why are you pushing me away?"

"Are you dressed yet?"

Tugging on my pants, I shot daggers at his back. "You've seen it all, so why the illusion of decency now?"

He whirled around. "Because I'm not the same person from a month ago." He grabbed the back of my head and pulled me close. "I don't even remember that person."

I licked my lips. A couple more inches and they'd connect with his. "He's still inside you."

"You want the guy who paddled your ass, is that it?"

My heartbeat skipped. "You know about that?"

"Jax told me."

A shudder of hot desire tore through me. "Did he tell you how it turns me on?"

"Holy fuck, Alex." He let go of me abruptly. "He failed to mention that part."

"I'm guessing he failed to mention a lot of things." I maneuvered around him and headed for the staircase.

"What are you doing?"

I lifted a foot onto the bottom step and glanced over my shoulder. "I'm going to bed. Don't worry about me, I know how to use my fingers." A thrilling sense of power stormed through me. I wasn't used to being so bold. Part of me wanted him to reclaim his dominance, to pull me over his knee and spank the attitude from me. But I kind of liked this side of him too—a mixture of the man he used to be with the dark guy hiding just beneath the surface. "If you need help with your hard-on, you know where to find me."

TWENTY-ONE

RAFE

I knew I was dreaming again, but like every other time it seemed vividly real. The gritty floor under my cheek. The rage firing through my veins at not being able to defend myself. Their hands banding around my wrists and ankles, keeping me immobile while their leader shoved his cock up my ass.

Nothing had ever hurt so much.

Nothing had ever made me feel so helpless, dirty, or ashamed.

As usual, I never saw their faces. I squeezed my eyes shut, and it took everything I had not to cry out, to contain the sting behind my lids so my shame didn't liquefy. All I could do was ball my hands and wait until he finished. But that wasn't the end. Not even close. They took turns, and at one point, they forced me to my knees and assaulted my mouth too. I bit the first one who shoved his filthy dick in and received a blow to the head for it.

The nightmare suddenly shifted and my hands fell free. Now I was the one on top, holding someone else down.

"Rafe, wake up."

Dream...it was a dream, so why couldn't I wake up?

"Rafe!"

Her voice finally penetrated, and I opened my eyes to find Alex's shadowed face inches from mine. She was sprawled beneath me on the couch where I'd gone to sleep alone, though now our bodies were pressed together, chest to chest, thigh to thigh. I restrained her hands above her head with one hand and propped myself up with the other so I wouldn't crush her.

"I'm awake," I said, struggling to catch my breath. "Did I hurt you?"

"Um...no."

Her uncertain tone made me grind my teeth. "Don't lie to me. If I hurt you, tell me."

"You didn't hurt me."

"Then what is it?" Sweat broke out on my temples and slid down my spine.

"You feel good, okay?" She inhaled then let the breath out in a whoosh. "You were having a bad dream, but when I tried waking you, you grabbed me and...I'm sorry."

"Why are you apologizing?"

"For wanting to jump your bones when you're still trembling from a nightmare. It's not okay. *I'm* not okay."

I shifted my weight to the side, pressed her into the back of the couch, and wound an arm underneath her body. "You feel pretty fucking okay right now." I grabbed her thigh and pulled her leg over mine, and my erection nestled between us. "Does that feel like I mind this?"

She groaned.

Or maybe I did. Suddenly, all the logic in the world didn't matter. I wanted her, she wanted me. The rest of the world could go to hell. Tomorrow, I'd flagellate myself over poor choices and my stubborn memories. I filled my hand with her ass, pulled her even closer, and thrust my cock against the hot center obscured by her panties. Fucking hell. Two thin layers of material was all that separated us. And her damn tank top. Her ridiculously tiny tank top.

"Rafe."

She breathed my name against my neck, and I shuddered. A good kind of shuddering, the kind that made me want to melt into her until we became one. I buried my nose in her hair and inhaled, feeling as if I would never get enough.

"This is insane," I said.

"What is?"

"Wanting you so fucking much." It was like she wore a pheromone with my name on it. "We can't do this, Alex. There are a million and one reasons why this is a bad idea."

Her breaths puffed against my skin in rapid succession. "Name one."

"The shit you've been through."

"You're doing a good job of distracting me." She nuzzled my jaw, and her fingers fisted in my hair.

"Fuck," I said with another tantalizing shudder. "This isn't the way to deal with it." But my hand shared Alex's agenda. It wedged between our bodies and freed my cock from my boxers. "Tell me to stop."

"Never." Her teeth lightly scraped along my scruffy face until she reached just underneath my ear, where her moan vibrated through me.

"You're killing me." I tugged her panties to the side and dipped a finger inside her wetness. "I don't have any condoms." Or if I did have some, I didn't remember where they were. She moved against my hand, moaning, and I added another finger.

"You fucked me before without them," she said with a gasp.

I halted. "This is more than fucking."

She arched her spine, a silent plea for me to keep going. "God, Rafe, it's never *just* been fucking between us. Not for me."

I clutched the back of her head, and we stared at each other, mouths parted, the air warming between us. I hooked my fingers inside her, eyes trained on her face to watch her reaction.

"Rafe!" Her nails dug into my damp shoulders, and she

trembled all over. "I need you inside me."

Her desperation slammed me back to Earth. "No, sweetheart, you need to face what's happened." Reluctantly, I withdrew my hand from her tempting pussy. "Whatever this is between us, we have time to figure it out." Letting her go, I rolled off the couch and took a spot on the floor, where I folded my arms around my knees. She propped up on one elbow, curls falling into her eyes, and glared at me. I understood her frustration, but fucking her wasn't going to fix anything right now. My cock throbbed, pissed with my decision. I was sure Alex and my wayward dick had forged an alliance against me.

She flopped onto her back with a groan.

"You know I'm right," I said. "I can't remember shit, and your psycho brother is still out there somewhere."

"I know," she said with quiet acceptance. "But I still remember, Rafe. I'll never forget what it was like with you. You made me feel things I didn't think were possible."

"Was that before or after I tortured you?" I still didn't know the details, but I must have done something horrendous for her to threaten me with a broken bottle. The flash of her terrified face would forever haunt me.

"What do you remember?" she asked, rolling to the edge of the couch.

"I told you. I don't remember anything."

"I don't believe you."

I dragged a hand through my hair. "Okay. They're just

flashes, but I'm pretty sure I choked you. What else did I do?"

"It doesn't matter what you did. I forgave you for it."

"How can you let it go like that?"

She scowled at me. "Have you not figured it out yet?"

"Why don't you fill me in?"

"I'm in love with you." She bit her lip. "I've been in love with you for years. I thought you understood that from my letters."

"You don't love me, Alex. For God's sake, you were only fifteen."

"Don't tell me how I feel!"

"It's fucking common sense. You might want to fuck me, but love? You don't even know me. Fuck, *I* don't even know me anymore."

"I know how I feel. I know we had a connection."

I shook my head. "We had sex—sex I don't even remember." Tears pooled in her eyes, and I wanted to kick myself for being such an insensitive ass. "Alex, I'm sorry."

"I *hate* that you don't remember us." She swiped at her eyes with jerky, angry movements. "But what we shared went beyond the physical. You were the only person who gave a shit about me."

Unable to stop myself, I slid a palm along her cheek, and my thumb caught a tear. My attention lingered on that salty drop, as if it called to me in some way. My gaze swerved to hers, and I licked my lips, imagining the unmistakable taste of sorrow.

"I still give a shit about you." I furrowed my brows, running that statement in my head a few more times. I *did* care about her, more than I should. More than I had a right to, which was why I'd do everything in my power to protect her, even from myself. I pushed to my feet and thrust a hand out for her to grab. "Go back to bed."

She let me pull her up from the couch. "Come with me."

"Alex," I warned.

"I don't mean to do anything. I just want you to hold me, like you do on the couch."

"I won't be able to stop at that. Not this time."

"Why hold back then?"

"Because I refuse to hurt you more than I already have." The dark urges pricked at me, growing with intensity the more I thought of thrusting into her. I didn't know if I could keep from flirting with disaster when it came to her gorgeous neck that tempted the strength in my hands.

"You won't hurt me," she said, tugging on my hand. "Come to bed."

"No." I disentangled from her grip.

With a growl of frustration, she stomped off in the direction of the loft, where hopefully she'd stay. I knew I wouldn't be able to say no again if she pressed her tight, seductive body against mine. Letting out a shuddering sigh, I reclaimed my place on the sofa and checked under the pillow to make sure the gun was still there, but falling back to sleep didn't come easily. My cock throbbed with the need for release. I'd already jacked off once tonight in the shower, before I'd called it an early night after Alex had stripped and shackled herself in my damn cellar.

I glanced at the clock on the wall. Just past midnight.

Fuck.

This was going to be a long night because jacking off wasn't going to cut it. I flopped to my side, facing the back of the sofa, and willed my dick to settle the fuck down. Eventually, sleep pulled at me, welcoming me into the embrace of oblivious relief. If not for the unexpected noise, I would have been out for good.

Footsteps.

Damn. Alex was going to be my downfall. I'd known it eight years ago but had ignored it. "Go back to bed," I mumbled.

Something sharp pricked the back of my neck. I shot up, twisted around, and barely made out a large shadow as I slumped against the couch, hand reaching for the pillow.

Then everything went black.

TWENTY-TWO

RAFE

Voices drew me from the black pit I'd fallen into, except I wasn't on the soft cushions of my couch. My cheek pressed against the hard floor where every footfall vibrated through my jaw with the force of a jackhammer.

"Hurry up," someone muttered. Liquid sloshed and chugged, and the formidable odor of gasoline burned my nostrils. "Watch it! Don't spill any on him."

More footsteps thumped, more words drifted in the harsh air. I guessed there were two, possibly three of them surrounding me. I thought of Alex alone upstairs, and panic tore through my veins. I tried to push off the floor, intending to lunge for my gun, but my limbs were heavy and useless.

"I doused every part of the island." Thud-thud-thud. Each step poked at the throb in my temples. "Is it done?"

"Yep. She's across the river. I gave her enough to knock her out cold for a long time."

"Good," a deep voice said. "Finish with the inside. We need to get outta here."

"What about him? Thought you wanted him to watch." A shoe nudged my body. "He ain't waking up."

A sinister laugh chilled my blood. "Sure he is. See his hands? He's itching to rearrange your face, dude. Hurry the fuck up."

Feet shuffled across the floor. "Get over here and help me with him."

Two pairs of arms dragged me to my knees. I tried to speak but only managed a groan. Forcing my gritty eyes open, I lifted my head, which felt as heavy as a bowling ball. Shadows surrounded me, and I couldn't make out their faces, couldn't tell for sure how many were in my house. Nausea rose, and my head pounded so hard, every word they spoke lanced through my brain like a spear. I dropped my head, chin to chest.

One of them yanked my neck back and a blow glanced across my cheek. "Time to wake up, buddy. You ain't gonna want to miss the show."

"Alex?" Her name was the only word I could force past my sandpaper tongue.

"She's safe, and she'll stay that way as long as you do what you're told. Understand?"

No. I didn't understand anything, except that I'd been

drugged. Another fist connected with my face, and I didn't have the energy to fight them.

"I asked you a question. Her life depends on your cooperation. Do you understand?"

I nodded, though my head drooped more than bobbed. "Yeah." Little by little, consciousness settled into my bones, though I still felt weighed down, as if ten wet blankets covered me. "What'd you give me?"

"You don't ask questions. You shut your mouth and follow orders, got it?"

When I didn't answer, two hands banded around my neck, fingers pressing hard on my carotid arteries. Spots danced in my vision, and I lifted my sluggish arms to ward off the assault, but the drugs had rendered my body useless.

He pulled away before I lost consciousness. "Take him outside."

Two men hefted me into a slumped-standing position, and we slowly stumbled to the front door. "Don't do this." Another blow to the face shut me up. My chest squeezed as they pushed me down the stairs of the porch. I plummeted to the ground, rolled, and tried to brand my mind with every detail of the place where I'd spent so many summers growing up. The fuckers were going to burn it down. My father's cabin. The island. All I had left of him.

"Why are you doing this?"

A boot shot out and struck me in the kidney. I grunted, back arching, and held my breath.

"Shut the fuck up!" one of them shouted, adding another kick to my side. "Stubborn asshole."

I peered up, trying to make out a face, but a baseball cap and sunglasses obscured his features. The other guy stood off to the left, remaining out of sight. Neither of their voices seemed familiar, though that didn't mean shit. Everything around me hit my ears in an odd way. Crickets sounded, normally a melodic chirp, but their call blared in my ears like a screeching alarm.

Footsteps thundered down the stairs. "Let's go. Get him to the dock." His buddies hauled me to my feet and forced me toward the path, and the guy at my back laughed. "Little early for the Fourth of July, but what a show, huh?"

I clenched my hands, tested my strength. Whatever they'd given me was beginning to wear off, though not enough that I could overpower three men. Maybe more. And Alex...

I swallowed hard. They had her somewhere. If I fought them, they'd hurt her...or worse.

What if they've already hurt her?

The idea sickened me, made me want to lash out and pound into them. My mind was fully alert now, demanding I *do* something, but my sluggish body wouldn't...couldn't fight. I'd never felt so weak as when I climbed the small hill that led to the dock. Sweat slicked down my bare back, though I trembled from the chill of the late night breeze. I fell to the ground twice on the way down, and their laughter hollowed through me each time, like a demon that taunted.

Evil. Whoever these men were, they were pure evil.

When we reached the dock, they pushed me to my knees, facing the island. I couldn't see the cabin from this vantage point, but the trees surrounding it towered, nothing more than shadows against the backdrop of mountains.

One of the men lit a torch and passed it off. "You get the honors. Make it quick. We need to get out of here."

I blinked, horrified by the sting in my eyes. I'd survived a lot and had never cried, but the thought of watching my father's island go up in smoke gutted me. "Don't do this. I can get you money." I risked looking up and met the dark gaze of someone who struck a cord of recognition in me, though I couldn't place where I'd seen him before. "What do you want?" I asked.

"I want you to suffer."

I opened my mouth, about to ask him what he wanted with me, when his fist slammed into my nose. I cupped my face and doubled over, crashing into the planks of the dock. Two hands wrenched me up. "Watch it fucking burn."

A billow of smoke surged upward, tinted an eerie orange-red from the glow of flames. A guy sprinted toward the dock. "Get him in the boat! Let's go!"

I shot out a fist at the first fucker who tried dragging me to my feet. He snickered. I didn't pose a threat to them

—I was so weak a kitten could probably beat the shit out of me. They lifted me and dumped my boneless body into a dinghy.

"He's heavier than he looks. Think our weight will sink this thing?"

"Shut the fuck up and get in." They piled inside, and someone started the motor.

The island grew smaller as we sped off. I gazed at my home, now nothing more than a raging inferno, some of the last memories I had left up in flames. Who were these men, but more importantly, why?

Why Dad's island?

Why had they taken Alex?

What did they want with me?

The ride ended a few short minutes later, and they hauled me from the boat and up the ramp. I didn't walk as much as shuffle toward the sedan parked a few yards away. A guy exited through the passenger side door and popped the trunk, revealing Alex's bound and gagged form inside. She wasn't squirming, wasn't even moving.

My heart raced as I weighed my options. I could try to fight them off, but I didn't know for certain how many men surrounded me. Three, four, five? I glanced over my shoulder and met the barrel of the gun Jax had given me. "Don't over think it, Mason. Get in the trunk."

A startling blast sounded. I jumped, adrenaline flooding my system, and stared at the fire engulfing the island. Not a gun shot. The propane tank outside the cabin must have ignited.

"We don't have time for this bullshit." Sirens blared, distant, but it wouldn't take long for the area to flood with emergency vehicles. Maybe I *could* fight them, stall long enough for help to arrive. "Get in the fucking trunk," he said, cocking the gun and swerving it toward Alex, "or I'll shoot your girl."

I could fight them. I might even hold them off for a few minutes, but what if they shot her? What if they killed me and took off with her?

I did the only thing I could. I crawled into the trunk.

BOOK THREE

FERVENT

HELLO DARKNESS

Darkness isn't chased away by light
It's merely oppressed
Hidden by the unconfessed
With shadows spilling through the cracks of hope
But the strong withstand
The brave cope
Triumph is an illusion
A trick of sadist's magician
Even the willful stumble
Crash headfirst into submission
Rebirth by death is the only way to survive
The sting of pain is the only way one feels alive

ONE

ALEX

I was swaying. Or maybe I was flying. I couldn't be certain, but the quiet thrum of an engine hinted at some sort of motion. That annoying rumble pricked at the edge of consciousness, threatening to take me somewhere I didn't want to go.

Zach.

His name stormed through my blood, turning it to ice. I was trapped. He'd trapped me, locked me away from the world and from myself, reducing me to something unimportant. Meaningless.

A voice tunneled through my ears and landed somewhere in the muck of my mind. I clung to the blackness, every part of me revolting at the thought of forcing my eyes open. I was safe in this place, in this nothingness where I could just *be*.

But the voice was persistent. Someone curled their

fingers around my bicep and shook me. Slowly, I came back to a reality I didn't want to face, to an existence that was unavoidable, inevitable even. Cloth stuffed the cavity of my mouth, and I choked on a muffled cry. The gentle sway of movement reminded me of a trunk, bringing about panic. Swift and debilitating—it held me in its unmerciful grasp.

That voice washed over me again as cold fingers pulled the gag from my dry lips. I let out a scream that was little more than a hoarse plea for survival.

"Shhh, you're okay," he said, slapping a palm over my mouth until the scream died in my throat. His voice resonated in the deepest part of my soul, even at the level of a breathy whisper, and my heart tripped over in its haste to beat.

"Rafe?" I blinked against the pitch-black, eyes burning with the threat of relieved tears. In that foggy state of *here and there*, I'd feared I was back in Zach's trunk, alone with the weight of Rafe's death pressing on me. I squirmed, trying to maneuver so I could turn over and face him, inhale his scent, hold on and never let go...except I couldn't move my hands.

As if he knew what I needed, he tugged at the bindings with deft fingers. I scooted forward and bit my lip, impatient to be in his arms.

"Hold on, baby." His tone was rife with the same impatience. Several long seconds passed in each thud of my heartbeat, and the rope loosened in tiny degrees before dropping free. "C'mere."

I wiggled to my back and bumped into his warm, naked chest.

"Just a little more," he said, inching back to give me more room. I flopped over, and he crushed me in his embrace.

"What happened?" I asked, burying my face in the crook of his shoulder. But it was a stupid question. This wasn't my first ride in the back of a trunk—as the dread in my belly and the fear souring my taste buds reminded me.

"You're okay. I've got you." Though his words came out calm, his pulse, sprinting to the fervent pace of mine, gave him away. We were far from okay. His nose nudged my temple, and I lifted my face in the darkness, shivering under the warm press of his lips on my skin. He brushed a kiss over each eyelid then dipped to my mouth, barely touching, and leaned his forehead against mine.

For a few moments, we just breathed.

No words.

No talk of what was coming next.

Nothing but comfort traded on the breath of our lips.

It didn't last. The moment was too perilous, and falling into its trap would only foster a false sense of calm.

"How did we get here?" I searched my memory for a clue but couldn't find one.

"They took us. Four or five of them, maybe more."

"Oh my God." A throb began at my temples and spread

to the rest of my skull. With a groan, I tucked my head under his chin, unable to think beyond the pain.

"Are you hurt?"

"My head's pounding."

"Probably from the drugs," he said. "Do you remember anything?"

"No." My breath shuddered against his neck, and a niggle of a memory flourished in my mind; the hint of soft footsteps, a drift of air as the sheet lifted, the hope that rose in me when the mattress dipped at the edge. "Wait... someone got in bed with me. I thought it was you. Next thing I know, I'm waking up here."

"They drugged me too."

Whoever had taken us, and for whatever reasons, I was glad we'd landed in this trunk together. At least we were still together.

"Do you think Zach had something to do with it?" I asked, though the number of men involved in taking us implied otherwise. My brother had always been a loner.

"I don't know." He fell quiet, and the length of that pause carried special weight, an air of significance. "They set the island on fire."

"They *what*?" Of course, Zach was my first suspect, but something seemed off, especially since Rafe was still alive, trapped in the trunk with me this time, and I couldn't think of a single reason why my brother would take the time to burn the island. "Who else could've done this?"

"Your father, maybe? And I'm not ruling out Zach."

"But you said there were four or five of them?"

"Yeah." He tried to hide a groan, and I imagined him biting his lip to silence the sound.

"What is it?" I asked, wishing I could see his face.

"The drugs are still in my fucking system. I'm useless, Alex. They broke in, and I didn't even realize it. I shouldn't have let this happen." He grabbed the base of my neck and tilted my head upwards, and his worried sigh breezed across my lips. "If they hurt you..."

I couldn't dwell on what they wanted, on how they outnumbered us. I clutched his hair and held him to me, finding sanctuary in his presence even if we were trapped in a trunk together, half dressed, drugged, and possibly facing death.

"At least I'm here with you."

"I don't want you here with me. I want you somewhere safe." He abruptly let go and rolled to his back. "If I can find an escape latch, or maybe break a taillight..." He kicked several times, each *thwack* of his foot escalating in effort. "Fuck!"

I pushed up on my elbows. "Something's glowing over there. See it? By your feet," I said, realizing he couldn't see where I was pointing in the blackness.

"Yeah. Looks like the escape latch." A loud thunk sounded, as if he'd bumped his head. "Damn it! I can't reach it."

"I might be able to." I leaned over him and inched my way down his stomach and thighs. Stretching for all I was worth, I curled my fingers around the glowing handle and yanked, but nothing happened. "It's not working!"

"Shit. They probably fucked with it." He shifted underneath me, and I planted a palm on the fabric lining of the trunk to steady myself. I gripped his leg with my other hand.

"Check down there for anything we can use as a weapon." He scooted again, causing me to plop between his legs, and we became a tangle of twisted limbs as we maneuvered.

I reached out but only found empty space. "There's nothing here, Rafe."

"There's gotta be a spare tire under here. Maybe I can find a lug wrench. Hold on." He rolled, taking me with him, and my backside pressed against the back of the trunk as he lifted the flimsy floor beneath us. "I feel the tire."

"Is there a wrench?"

A few seconds of unbearable silence passed before he answered. "No. Can't find shit. Can't see shit either." We rolled again, and his fingers clamped around my bare thigh. "Give me your hand."

I complied, and he yanked me up his body and back into his arms. "Alex...we don't know what's coming. When I tell you to run, promise you'll do it and never look back. Promise me."

"I'm not leaving you."

He grabbed my chin, as if to force my gaze even though

we couldn't see each other. "When we get out of here, you're gonna run for your life. Do you understand me?"

I tried shaking my head, but he wouldn't allow it. "I mean it, Alex."

"They could kill you."

"I can't defend us both against a gang of men. You running gives me my best chance."

He was feeding me a line of bullshit.

"Don't choose now to be stubborn," he said, as if he'd heard my internal protest. "Just do as I say."

The next few moments held me in a death grip, and a shiver went through me. This could be it. "Kiss me," I choked out.

"Alex..." he said, a touch of warning in his tone.

I angled my face, sensing the heat of his mouth. "Kiss me." The demand whispered from my lips, and I cursed the fear and grief stinging my eyes. He wanted me to fight, to believe we'd survive, but I wasn't sure I had it in me. Too much had happened and I didn't have any fight left.

But I needed his kiss. No matter what came next, I wanted the taste of him with me, on my tongue, branded in my memory. Maybe I could survive if I had that to hold on to.

He expelled a breath an instant before he pressed his mouth to mine. Parting my lips, he thrust his tongue inside and dueled me into surrender. One hand fisted my hair, yanking my head back, allowing him a deeper possession of my mouth. We both moaned, a sorrowful sound of desperation laced with need, maybe even hope.

Except hope was a sword that would slice us into pieces if we let it.

The frantic slide of his tongue speared through me with a delirious ache, and I whimpered. Everything fell away; the scars on my body, the coffin-like space that held us prisoner, the loss of his memory—it all vanished in the fray of our need for each other. Eventually, we severed the connection but hovered inches apart, our choppy breaths blending with the sound of the road beneath us.

Then the car slowed and the brake lights cast his face in eerie red. My pulse, already galloping from his kiss, took off in a sprint. "I love you, Rafe."

"Don't you dare say goodbye to me yet." His brows furrowed, and I couldn't resist running my thumb over one.

The car turned and we swayed with the motion. I held my breath, only letting it out after the vehicle regained speed. We clutched each other, awaiting the inevitable confrontation that would come when the tires stopped spinning. Time was lost to the lull of the road, distorted in every brake and turn. The wheels slowed to a crawl on rough ground, bouncing over potholes and ridges.

We lurched, hitting a particularly bad spot, and I cried out his name then pressed my lips to his again, wishing I could freeze this moment. I could live my life in this trunk with him, our bodies entwined, mouths fused, and find peace.

But that was impossible. We rolled to a stop and the rumble of the engine fell silent. Blackness and fear coiled around us as our fate hung on a thread. Heavy steps rounded the side of the car, and someone jingled a set of keys.

"I want you to run, Alex. When I tell you to go, don't even hesitate."

With a nod, I swallowed and managed to squeak my agreement, but deep down, I knew.

I'd die before leaving him to face this alone.

TWO
RAFE

Whatever they'd given me still blazed in my veins, stealing control of my body and fucking with my ability to protect her. The situation pressed on me like a thick slab of steel. My head felt woozy from whatever concoction they'd pumped into me, and my limbs were as useless as the tentacles of a jellyfish. I knew the odds weren't in our favor. We were about to face off a group of men intending to...fuck, I didn't know what they wanted, but I doubted they'd taken us to shoot the breeze.

The explosion on my father's island was a continuous echo in my ears, but thinking about the flames that ate away at my childhood memories, turning them to ash, would get us nowhere. I couldn't control what had happened. I could only control now, this moment and the next to come, and I'd be damned if I let Alex suffer without putting up the fight from hell.

The trunk popped open, and Alex clung to me with desperate hands, her face buried in my shoulder as she breathed, "Oh God," against my skin. Her terror raged through me, her tiny frame shaking in my arms.

Yet I knew she was stronger than me.

She had to be, to have survived so much and still have a heartbeat. I cursed God, fate, the universe—even the ball of dirt gravity glued us to—for dropping her into another horrifying situation. Had she not been through enough?

"Promise me," I whispered again, the plea lost in her hair, though I knew she heard because she held on tighter.

And that's when I knew. She wasn't going to run.

Because she was strong. Stubborn. Loyal.

Because she loved me.

The lid of the trunk creaked and cool air hit my back an instant before the barrel of what I assumed was a gun pressed into my spine.

"Get out slow and no one will get hurt."

The guy at the other end of the weapon backed off, and someone snorted, barely covering their muttered, "*yet.*"

Reluctantly, I freed Alex from the cage of my arms and turned in the confined space. Trees obscured the moon, and shadows hid the men's features, though their hatred poisoned the atmosphere and spiraled around me like a tangible entity. Only one held a gun, and he had it locked on me with relentless force.

Had I miscalculated the number of men on the island?

"Don't have all night, Mason. Get out."

I grasped the edge of the opening and hefted myself up, biceps flexing under the strain, and crawled from the trunk. One foot then the other touched the ground, and rough earth gouged the soles of my feet. A chilly breeze whispered through the trees. Even July brought cold nights with it.

"Hands up."

Raising my arms, I took stock of the situation. Three men, one gun, and the isolation blared its silence, save for the tumultuous chirp of crickets. I glanced at the sky, expecting to see the same galaxy of stars visible from the island, but the sky was faded, as if the glare from the city had snuffed out the brightness.

Considering the amount of time we'd spent in the trunk, I guessed they'd taken us close to Portland.

"Don't get any ideas," the guy with the gun said. He wore a dark hoodie, and his stance was aggressive, as wide as his broad shoulders. "I don't have to kill you to keep you from running. Your kneecaps will do." He lowered the weapon to make his point.

I clenched my teeth and stood up straighter, though weakness still lingered in my limbs. My arms trembled from the effort of holding them up. If I could overtake the guy, then Alex might have a shot at getting away.

But could she outrun the other two? And what if there

were more? I hadn't miscalculated. There'd been more than three men on the island, and one of them had worn a baseball cap and sunglasses, but he wasn't here now.

"Where are the rest of your buddies?" I asked, hoping to get a better idea of how many assholes we were up against.

Approaching headlights beamed from behind me, and Hoodie tilted his head so the light hit him at just the right angle to keep his face hidden in shadow. The car rolled to a stop, and doors creaked open and slammed shut. "Does that answer your question?" he asked.

Not even close.

From the corner of my eye, I spied motion. More weapons cocked, and I didn't have to look to know they were all aimed in my direction.

"What do you want with us?" I asked Hoodie.

He shook his head, and the hood of his jacket fell back just enough to reveal a face manic with the promise of pain. "Don't try anything stupid. If you fuck with us, she's the one taking the heat for it, got it?"

Suddenly, his form swayed in front of me. No, I was the one swaying. The trees behind him morphed in my vision, as if they danced lazily on the other side of a funhouse window.

I blinked several times until my sight cleared. Holy fuck. When would the drugs stop messing with me? Alex couldn't run. Not with all the guns and muscle surrounding us. I needed time. Time for the drugs to dissipate. Time to come up with a plan that wouldn't get her hurt, or worse, killed. Then I'd have a chance at taking them on. I didn't care what happened to me, so long as she got out of this alive.

Hoodie gestured toward her with his gun. "Get out slow like your boyfriend." She gave no indication of moving, and as he took a step forward, I backed toward the trunk.

"She's scared. Pointing a gun at her isn't gonna help." I cranked my head and glanced at her pale face from over my shoulder. "It's okay."

But it wasn't okay. I swallowed hard and willed my voice to remain steady. "Get out of the trunk." Every part of me rebelled at the thought of her crawling from that space and facing these assholes.

As she pushed to her elbows, the other men inched closer. What the fuck did they think we were going to do? Make a run for it in the dark with a bunch of assholes on our tails, guns firing? I was fucking useless, pathetically helpless, and I didn't like it one bit.

I'd let her down. She'd stood in my living room hours ago, gazing out the fucking window because something had bothered her. She'd sensed this coming, and I'd sent her to my bedroom alone, unprotected. I prayed to God they hadn't done more than just take her from my bed. A small hand slid into mine, bringing me back from the pit of self-flagellation I'd dived into.

"Good," Hoodie said. "Now that we're all here, let's take this underground."

"Where are you taking us?" I asked, not entirely sure I wanted to know what he meant by "underground."

"Shut the fuck up and move." Two men came from the sidelines, guns at the ready, and gestured for us to start walking. The guy I recognized from earlier, with the cap and sunglasses, shoved me forward, and my grasp on Alex's small fingers slipped. Without thinking, I swung around and slammed my fist into his face. He drew back then lunged for me with a powerful blow that pummeled me to the ground like I was nothing. I struggled to my feet, ignoring the sway of the scenery and the gun he pointed at my head, ready to deliver another punch, consequences be damned.

A cold, hard voice froze me to the spot. "Touch my brother again and I'll put a bullet in her head."

A skinny guy who looked to have more prep than hired goon in him held a gun to Alex's skull. I traded a glance with her, struck in the gut by the firm set of her jaw. She'd been conditioned to silently accept hell, even with the barrel of a gun pressed to her temple, and that pissed me the fuck off. She shouldn't have to accept this shit as normal, shouldn't have to harden herself against the next fight.

"Chill out, Vinnie," Hoodie warned his man. "He's got no power here." Even though he'd ordered the guy to stand down, Hoodie's dark eyes threatened retribution for the punch I'd unleashed on his buddy.

I dropped my arm just as Hoodie nodded to one of his men. Something sharp pricked the back of my neck and the world wavered. I slumped toward the ground, the enclosing wall of trees sliding horizontal, and Alex's scream echoed through what was left of my sanity.

THREE

ALEX

My piercing cries for help obliterated the air, but Rafe lay unresponsive on the ground, his crumpled body unmoving no matter how much I begged him to wake up. The two brothers of the group had me by the arms, their fingers banding around my biceps in bruising grips. They dragged me away from him, and I dug my toes into the ground.

"Rafe!"

"Screaming isn't gonna do anything. In case you hadn't noticed, there isn't a whole lot around these parts."

My gaze shifted through the darkness. Trees surrounded us in all directions, some tall and skinny, some with trunks wider than these two men put together. Ferns and other brush interspersed the isolated landscape. They pushed me further away from Rafe, from the road we'd come in on that was little more than a wide trail.

The guy Rafe had punched started down a steep path between two massive tree trunks covered in moss, while his brother—Vinnie, they'd called him—took up the end of our trek into the middle of nowhere, the barrel of his gun pressed to my spine. The quiet babble of a creek teased from somewhere nearby. Most would equate that sound with ambience, but I found it unsettling, a reminder of suffocation and terror.

"Where are we going?" I asked, hating how my voice wobbled. "Why are you doing this?"

"So many questions," Vinnie's brother said as we reached the bottom of the incline.

I skidded to a stop, letting out a squeaky cry as they pulled me toward a creek. "Please, no!"

"The fuck? It's just a little water. What? You scared of getting your pretty toes wet?"

Oh God. I swallowed the hysteria about to choke me, determined to cross the creek without having a total melt-down. It was a ridiculous reaction, as the water would barely reach past my ankles. I swallowed hard, preparing myself. They couldn't find out about my phobia—it would only give them more ammunition against me.

Upon the first contact with the icy stream, my feet ached clear to my bones. I wore nothing but a tank top and panties, and water splashed my calves like pin-pricks as we trekked to the other side. A hill rose on my right, trapping me between the creek and hillside as they propelled me downward, deeper into the woods.

The hike seemed endless. My legs ached for rest, but when we slowed, I wished to keep moving because stopping would mean it was over. I stiffened, expecting a bullet to the head, figuring they'd dragged me out here to kill me and discard my body. A sob bubbled up but caught in my throat. I hadn't said goodbye to Rafe. We were going to die out here, and I hadn't even told him goodbye. There was so much I hadn't said to him, and now I'd never get the chance.

"Wh-why are you doing this?" I asked again, the words laced with high-pitched terror. If they planned to kill me, I wanted to know why.

"Hurry the fuck up," Vinnie complained to his brother, completely ignoring my question. "It's fuckin' cold out here."

"Chill out. I'm looking for the latch."

From the corner of my eye, I spied Vinnie's tall frame, bordering on lanky. His brother was the opposite. He intimidated with huge muscles and arms sleeved in tats. He pushed ferns and moss aside to reveal a door in the side of the hill.

What the hell? Who had an entrance in the middle of a forest?

Vinnie pushed me against the steel door, face first, and wrenched my arms behind me as Muscle Guy entered a code into the keypad near the handle. A beep sounded and the door opened. They shoved me inside and down a short flight of stairs made of stone. We halted under an arch, at the mouth of a hallway. I shook, teeth clinking together as chills wracked my half-naked body. A long row of lights illuminated a tunnel that seemed to go on indefinitely.

What is this place? I didn't dare voice the question. They flanked my sides and pulled me down the passage, my feet dragging and stirring up dust. Mustiness flared in my nostrils, making breathing difficult. It reminded me of Rafe's wine cellar, except these walls were made of deteriorating stone and brick.

We moved deeper into the tunnel and eventually passed several doors, all shut to prying eyes, though chilling noises filtered through some of them. Moans. Screeching cries. Masculine voices that iced my blood. The unmistakable *thwack-thwack* of instruments on flesh, not unlike the sound of Rafe's paddle on my ass weeks ago.

My limbs trembled, threatening to give out completely. "Wh-where are you taking me?"

"For a little chit-chat with the boss."

"Who? What does he want with me? Where's Rafe?"

"Bitch has a lot of questions, huh?" Muscle Guy let out a harsh laugh. He flanked my right, baseball cap pulled low over his forehead, his eyes hidden behind dark shades, and dug the gun into my side. "Be quiet and keep moving."

That was the last any of us spoke.

But something about Muscle Guy—with his black and orange Beavers hat and intense stare I sensed behind the dark glasses—licked at a memory, and it came back with such startling clarity, I couldn't have spoken if I'd wanted to. He'd been on that busy street the day Zach called me from outside the restaurant. Even my brother had noticed him noticing me.

The shock still hadn't abated by the time we neared the end of the tunnel to face the last door. My feet ached from the long walk, and I shuffled them nervously.

"I'll take her in," Vinnie said, his fingers biting into my arm. "Wait out here."

"Yep." Muscle Guy slid the gun into his waistband and leaned against the wall, crossing his beefy arms.

Vinnie reached for the knob, and I squeezed my hands into fists. Whatever waited behind that door couldn't be worse than what I'd already been through. He shoved me into a room that was vastly different from the tunnel. The stone floor chilled the soles of my feet, but it was smooth and free of dirt. So were the neat brick walls that housed shelves of antiques. Another set of shelves held rope and other restraint devices, filming equipment, DVDs, and whips and paddles. My gaze veered to the fine art displayed on the walls. I'd bet a safe hid behind one of the paintings.

I forced my attention on the rest of the room. A large area rug covered the center where an oversized oak desk sat next to an odd piece of furniture that looked like a tall ottoman, though it had a restraint system and four wooden legs.

The air thickened with a musky vibe that could only be described as sexually deviant, especially considering the row of black and white photos hanging on the wall behind the desk. They were large, the size of posters, and all of them featured the same blonde in various poses of humiliation. I swallowed past the lump of dread in my throat, fixated on the signs of distress and fear on her stunning face. The grimace of pain, the open-mouthed cries that resembled screams of agony rather than ecstasy.

"What is this place?" I whispered, my throat too tight to manage anything else.

Vinnie shoved me into a chair facing the desk and stood nearby, his gun pressed to my head. From the corner of my eye, I saw him dig out a cell and punch in a number.

"The package is here, boss."

And that was that. Five little words, and I was merely a possession. Not long after, a door to the left opened, and a man I thought I'd never see again stepped into this crazy room that didn't make any sense.

Or maybe it made perfect sense and I just didn't want to admit it.

I raised my eyes, opened my mouth to say something, but could hardly form a coherent thought, let alone a sentence. This must be a crazy dream.

Lucas Perrone didn't smile, didn't seem smug. In fact, he seemed bored, and that expression struck me hard in the chest because he'd often worn that look while we dated. Even the night he'd asked me to marry him, he'd lacked excitement. I'd always assumed it was because my dad had set us up. Now, gaping at him in utter shock, everything I thought I'd known about Lucas was a lie, nothing more than dust on the ground.

He gestured to the guy standing sentinel at my back. "Leave us. She won't be a problem."

The pressure of the weapon disappeared from my skull, and I sensed Lucas' henchman moving away. I let out a breath at the absence of his gun. A few seconds later, the door clicked shut. But reality crashed in, and I wrestled beyond my state of shock to say something.

"Did my dad put you up to this?" My heart thundering behind my breastbone, I drew in a deep breath through my nose, determined not to give in to a full-blown panic attack.

Five in, hold, five out.

The twitch of his mouth interrupted the repeat part of my breathing ritual. He rubbed his chin, thumb whisking over the patch of hair sprinkled with gray, and folded into the leather seat on the other side of the desk. "Why would your father have you and Mason kidnapped?" Raising a brow, he ran a palm across the gleaming brown surface that matched the color of his eyes.

I glanced around the room, but my focus strayed to those unsettling photos displayed behind him. "If he didn't do this, then why am I here? Why did you take us?"

"The two of you took something from me."

"I-I don't understand. I barely know you. The only reason I know you at all is because of my dad, and Rafe..." I glanced at my lap, only then realizing how I twisted my fingers in a display of unease. "He's been in prison for the last eight years."

"Exactly."

"I'm not following."

His brow furrowed, the one with the scar severing the perfect arch. "There was a time when I wanted you." He rose and slowly rounded the desk. I kept my attention forward, but in my periphery I spied the strong build of his thighs at my side, hidden underneath the perfect fit of his slacks. He grasped my hair and tilted my head back until I returned his gaze.

"Rafe Mason is going to pay for what he did. You will too, for your part in this, but that doesn't stop me from wanting you still."

"I don't know what you're talking about," I said through gritted teeth. My mind raced in trying to decipher what Rafe and I could have done to earn his thirst for vengeance, but none of this made any sense. Unless my dad was involved somehow...that's the only thing that clicked.

"What would you be willing to do to save Mason's life?"

"What?" I jerked back, fighting against his hold.

"You heard me. What would you"—he let my hair slide through his fingers, and his hand descended to my lap—

"be willing to do to save the man you love?" There was nothing to bar his access—just a flimsy scrap of underwear I'd worn to bed, thinking I was safe in Rafe's room. Lucas parted my thighs and swiped my panties to the side, then he plunged a finger between my folds. I bit my lip hard.

"You never let me touch you like this when we were dating." He bent and pressed his face to my temple, inhaling sharply. "I'll spare his life if you let me fuck you."

"Let him go."

"That's not going to happen."

"I'll do anything..." My gaze strayed to the photos of the woman, and I wondered who she was. How could I have spent so much time with him and never sense the darkness beneath the expensive suits and charming demeanor? When it came to noticing the depraved fibers in people, I was broken, my evil detector in pieces, probably rotting in the same place as my innocence.

"I'll be your...your...slave. Let him go and keep me."

His mouth lowered to my ear. "You're perfect, Alex. Young, pliable, and best of all, trained to take a man's cock like a pro." He added more fingers and jammed them deep inside, stretching my opening with an uncomfortable burn. It was all I could do not to tense upon the crude intrusion. "But you're under the misguided impression that you have a choice in the matter, that you have the ability to negotiate with me. You," he said, his breath blasting my ear with moist heat, "are powerless here."

He unbuttoned his slacks and lowered the zipper.

"We'll start slow, but I need a token of your respect. Show me why I should consider your wants in this situation. Show me why I shouldn't kill Mason."

I leaned toward him, each second bringing my mouth closer to the hard-on straining behind his boxer briefs, and reached for the band of cotton, pulling it down...down a little more. I glanced up and wished I could smack the gleam of triumph from his expression. He was toying with me, thinking he'd already won.

And he had. I'd do anything for Rafe.

"If I give you a blowjob, you'll let him go?"

"Wrap that slutty mouth around my cock, and I might let him live."

A few weeks ago, I would have succumbed, would have bent under his threats. But I knew better now, could better judge when someone was using my fears against me.

When someone was lying to me.

Giving in wouldn't save Rafe.

His cock sprang free, and he thrust his hips forward until the tip brushed my cheek. "That's right," he said, hissing in a breath. "You know what to do with that mouth, don't you, honey. Give me a reason not to let my guys break you."

Saliva collected on my tongue. I opened my mouth, as if I were about to slide my lips over his shaft. Instead, I spit on the tip. "Go fuck yourself."

I expected anger, even a blow to the face. What I didn't

expect was a resigned grin. "You're not ready yet, but you will be." He jerked me up by the hair and marched me to the door where his men undoubtedly waited on the other side. Flinging it open, he pushed me into their strong hands. "You know what to do, guys."

FOUR

RAFE

Cigarette smoke burned my nostrils, but it didn't compare to the fire in my muscles. My hands were locked above my head, wrists shackled together, and my feet were anchored to the concrete with chains.

"Hey, Cleft," someone's voice thundered through my pounding skull. "I think he's comin' to."

Bodies moved and the putrid air around me stirred. I could hardly lift my head, which felt like a bowling ball on my shoulders. "Where's Alex?" I mumbled.

Someone slapped my cheeks. "Time to wake up."

"Whaddya want," I slurred, forcing my chin up.

The guy in the hoodie stood in front of me, and the dim bulb hanging between the rafters cast his face in light. If not for the hard lines in his skin, I'd guess he was in his mid-twenties. He took a drag from a cigarette, and something flashed in my memory. I couldn't hold onto it, though the notable cleft in his chin seemed familiar.

"Alex," I said again, refusing to back down until I got an answer.

"Relax. She's fine, but whether or not she stays that way is up to you. You hold all the power here."

"Find that hard to believe," I said, breath rasping out as I glanced up at my restrained hands, "seeing as how you assholes have me strung up." I pulled on the chains, and the clank of metal grated. Fucking futile. I glanced beyond the guy they called Cleft. The room spanned deep in a rectangle shape, and a bed sat tucked against a crumbling brick wall on the far end. A display of paddles, whips, crops and other implements of pain hung on hooks. Lighting equipment and camcorders were scattered throughout the space.

A second set of chains and cuffs dangled a few feet in front of me, empty now, but I feared they wouldn't be for long. Those things made me nervous. It was too easy to imagine them restraining Alex there, where they'd force me to watch them do their worst, so close but unable to stop them.

Fuck. I couldn't let this happen.

Clenching my hands, I glared at Cleft, wishing I could rip into his smug grin. "What the fuck do you want?"

He took another drag, and a door creaked open. His gaze darted behind me.

"Rafe!"

I jerked my head and watched two men bring Alex in. "Let her go!" I struggled against the restraints, my eyes never leaving her ashen face. They hauled her to where the other set of shackles swayed.

Waiting.

Taunting.

"Strip her," Cleft ordered.

I lurched forward and the chains strained from the ceiling, metal cuffs gouging my wrists, but my feet wouldn't budge another inch. They'd fully anchored me to the ceiling and floor. "Don't you fucking touch her!"

Cleft grinned, and the guy I'd punched earlier snickered.

"This is Brock," Cleft said, slapping his buddy on the back. "He's got a real hunger for pain, dontcha, Brock?"

His nefarious gaze, no longer hidden behind dark glasses, roved over Alex's shaking body. He removed his hat and tossed it to the floor, revealing his closely-shaved head. She seemed so small next to his massive frame, so breakable under the strength of his muscles. They were going to rape her. The certainty of it gnawed in my gut like a parasite. I almost vomited at the mental picture.

"If you hurt her—"

"You'll do what?" Cleft interrupted as Brock and the other goon he'd come in with slid the tank top over her head. The other men in the room hung back, arms crossed in casual observation while Brock and his asshole accomplice tore her panties free. She squeezed her green eyes shut and pulled her bottom lip between her teeth. She didn't even try fighting them as they strung her up and locked her into the same position as me.

"Damn, girl," Brock said, swiping a palm over Zach's carving on her belly. "Someone marked you up good." Brock circled her then slapped her ass hard.

"You don't need her," I said. "You have me. Let her go."

Cleft dropped the cigarette butt and ground it out with his shoe before closing the distance between us. He dragged a finger down my chest, his eyes alight with something close to glee. "I have you *and* her."

"What the fuck do you want?"

"Didn't we go over this on your piece of shit island? I want you to *suffer*." He gestured to Brock. "Make the bitch scream."

"No!" I sprang forward again, mindless of the chains trapping me.

Brock pulled a rubber band from his wrist and lifted her hair, securing it in a messy bun. He grabbed her chin and turned her face so he could drag his tongue up her cheek. She inched away from him, her mouth twisted in revulsion.

"Why are you doing this?" I shouted.

But Brock ignored me. They all fucking ignored me.

He let her go and waltzed to the back of the room where he eyed the various implements. God, I couldn't watch them hurt her. It would kill me. They had everything they needed to tear me apart, all wrapped up in Alex

De Luca. He removed a cane from the rack and strolled toward Alex.

"Answer me!"

"We don't answer to you, Mason." Cleft's lip curled, and he folded his arms as Brock halted a few feet behind her.

I captured her gaze and held it in the safety of mine. Our connection was the only thing left to get us through what he was about to do.

"Baby," I said, my voice cracking along with the rest of me because I couldn't stop this. "It's gonna hurt."

She blinked rapidly, as if to hold back tears. "I know."

"Lesson number one," Cleft said to me. "You don't fight us, *ever*." He nodded, and Brock struck the back of her thighs with an ear-splitting *crack*. She jerked forward, sucking in a noisy breath. Brock narrowed his bushy brows and swung again, harder this time, and the impact of cane on flesh reverberated off the walls.

She bit back a cry, refusing to give voice to her pain, though her eyes watered from the agony.

"Stop!" I shouted.

Brock licked his lips, as if savoring the challenge in her silence, and struck again. A small cry escaped her. With the grin of the devil, Brock unleashed his sadistic pleasure onto her ass and thighs, again and again until her escalating screams lashed through me. She cried my name, screamed until the sound of her anguish overwhelmed the room. She rose to her toes, biceps straining against the chains, body trembling, then her legs finally buckled.

My breath caught in my lungs, refusing to expel. Grief and frustration burned behind my eyes.

"Please," I said, not above begging. Not when it came to Alex. "No more. Let her go. Your problem is with me." I didn't know why, but whatever they were after, it had nothing to do with her. "Take it out on *me*." I growled the last word, swerving my attention between Cleft and Brock.

Cleft stopped in front of me and thrust his face within inches of mine. I tried going for his throat, regardless of my chained hands, but could only stand there with his hot breath in my fucking face.

"Please what? I like hearing you beg."

Something about him was darkly familiar, but I still couldn't put my finger on it, even though some part of my subconscious recognized him, responded to his presence with a level of fear I didn't understand.

Though I was beginning to. These men, whoever they were, had proven of what they were capable. Intolerable pain delivered with menacing smiles and hooded glares.

"Please," I said again, hating myself for sounding so pathetic, but I'd do anything to get them away from Alex. "Let her go. She isn't part of this."

"I warned you not to try anything, but look at Brock's face. You just couldn't help yourself, could you?" He turned and traded a glance with Brock. "More."

The bastard wailed on her, and Alex's hoarse shrieks ripped me to pieces. "Stop! I'll do whatever you want!"

Cleft's hand folded around my chin. "That's us going

easy on your girl. If the boss hadn't given us orders not to fuck her, we'd all be having a go at her. But he's saving her pussy for himself, so I guess we'll settle for beating the bitch."

I wanted to stop breathing, wanted to shut my eyes and find a place where I wouldn't have to witness them destroying her. If we didn't die here in body, we would die here in spirit.

"Again," Cleft ordered.

Brock lifted his right arm and swung the cane with a grunt. I jumped at the crack that struck my ears with such force, it rattled through me. I didn't know how she was still in one piece. Something warm and wet fell from my eyes, and her image blurred. I would have given anything to take her place. *I'm sorry, I'm sorry, I'm sorry, I'm sorry...*

The apology bled from my soul, and maybe some part of her deep inside heard it. She slumped, eyes screwed shut as her screams diminished to hopeless mewls. Right then, I knew I'd kill every last one of them, and not in the I'm-fucking-irate-as-hell-and-talking-a-good-talk way. I would literally kill them, would do so with the most disturbing satisfaction imaginable, and no one would find the pieces of their corpses after I was through.

Another crack assaulted the tormented space between my ears. Her head dipped, chin to chest, body entirely limp as urine trickled down her quaking legs. She'd given up fighting. Her fucking brother had driven her to stop fighting the day she'd tried to kill herself.

"Let her down. She can't take anymore." *Don't break on me now.*

Cleft gestured with a wave of his hand, and the bastard with the cane brought it down on her again. After three more strikes, he pulled the rubber band from her hair, and her curls tumbled around her shoulders in a mess of tangles. He freed her from the shackles, the fucking bastard apparently satisfied he'd broken her.

But she wasn't broken. She couldn't be. I wouldn't let her fucking break. She'd come too far for these assholes to do her in.

Depleted of strength, she crumpled to the floor. Blood slickened her backside, and the sight of the deep red horizontal lines on her skin turned my stomach. Brock and another guy picked her up and carried her from the room.

"Where are you taking her?" I shouted, cranking my head around. She lifted her lids, just enough for me to see a spark of the woman I'd do anything for. In that moment, I knew it was true. Alex had me by the soul, her love winding around me like an unbreakable rope of which I couldn't escape.

I didn't want to escape her, but we *had* to find a way to escape this place.

Cleft stood in front of me and folded his arms with an air of nonchalance, as if we were old friends having a friendly chat. "That was your first lesson. If you so much as sneeze without my permission, she'll take the punishment. Do you understand?"

"What do you want from me?" I asked through clenched teeth.

"You destroyed my family."

"I don't know what you're talking about."

"Same old memory problems." He rolled his eyes. "You're pathetic, Mason, but your head issues won't save you. I'm here to collect a debt, and I'll take it all, pound for pound, from your girlfriend's flesh."

I couldn't hold it in anymore. The chains were the only things holding me up as I vomited on the gritty floor. "Kill me," I begged. "She's innocent."

He tilted his head. "Is she?" He stepped closer, his sneakered feet bypassing the mess I'd made. "She's the reason you were in that fucking prison in the first place. One lie that sent you away," he said, pausing long enough to snap his fingers, "and my life is fucked. She's as much to blame as you."

"She was only fifteen. Don't do this. Whatever I did... just fucking kill me for it and let her go."

"Believe me," he said, his breath rancid in my face with the stench of tobacco. "I will cherish that day when it comes."

I wheezed air between my lips, muscles bunched, aching to pound him to a bloody, unrecognizable mass of body parts.

Cleft's fingers fell to the button of his jeans. He nodded to the other two men in the room, who had quietly watched the horror unfold without a word. "Get him on his knees." He retreated a few steps. "In fact, make him kneel in his fucking puke." He grinned in such a chilling way, the smile crawled down my back like a spider.

"Do your girl a favor and open your mouth big." He unbuckled, and I stiffened, my teeth grinding as he lowered the zipper. The fucker had a huge-ass erection.

My nightmares came back, flooding my conscious mind with details I hadn't been able to grasp until now. Something had seemed so familiar about Cleft. His smell especially—the odor of sweat and tobacco combined with whatever musky cologne he favored.

Now I knew why. He'd raped me in prison. Though I didn't remember it with clarity, I knew it was true.

He folded his hand around his dick. "You've got two options. You can suck me off, or Brock can have some more fun with your girl. Your choice."

I couldn't breathe. Oh my fucking God. There was no choice. Not even a little.

His goons loosened the chains keeping me upright, and I collapsed to my knees, right in the middle of my vomit. Goon number one grabbed the back of my head and held me in place while the other forced my arms in the air again with a jerk of the chains.

The moment was surreal, like an echo from a nightmare that twisted my insides. I opened for him, focusing only on memories of Alex—on what it felt like to wrap my body around hers, how hot and wet she'd been when I dipped my fingers between her thighs. The whimpering sound she made in the back of her throat when I possessed her mouth.

Cleft pushed his cock against my tongue, and I gagged.

Memories flashed behind my eyes, crashing through the barrier like a dam busting. The rapes in prison, how deep his hatred for me ran, though my psyche refused to stir up the reason why. It was there, tickling the edges of my memories, but that sick feeling returned and scattered the path to recollection, and my heart thumped so fast, I thought I'd black out.

He pulled back, and his dick slipped free. "Fuck this. I wanna fuck." A quick nod to his men sent them into motion. They released my hands and shoved me to the floor. I struggled in my vomit, my limbs little more than deadweight. Someone grabbed my legs, but I kicked behind me and pushed to all fours.

Laughter. Footsteps.

I crawled to my feet, body swaying, and faced the three of them. With a roar, I launched at them, but the manacles around my ankles tripped me up and sent me crashing to the cement again. Pain shuddered through my injured shoulder, and I bit back a groan.

The four of us grappled on cold concrete, grunting under the fight to get the upper hand. One of them slammed my face into the ground, and stars swam in my vision for a few seconds. Strong hands wrenched my arms behind me and shackled my wrists together.

"I'm gonna enjoy this." Cleft tugged my sweats down

with a too-familiar laugh. He settled his bulky frame over me and straddled my thighs, just like in my nightmares, only this was real.

Happening all over again.

They held me down by the shoulders, pressed my ankles to the ground. Eager fingers slid between my ass cheeks, separating, seeking entrance. Cleft nudged his erection against my backside, a moment away from shoving it in, when the door burst open.

"Get the fuck off of him!"

I twisted my head, and my whole world shattered, everything logical lost to insanity. Jax stood in the doorway, the light from the hall casting him in silhouette, though I'd known it was him the instant he'd spoken.

"We're just having a little fun," Cleft said.

"Fun's over. Fucking him isn't part of the plan."

FIVE
ALEX

Muscle Guy watched while I showered. His brother, the tall and lanky one, had left us alone. I braced myself against the grimy tile, my body still weak from the beating. The pipes overhead whined under the pressure of spitting out water, and the tepid spray sluiced over my head, slid down my stinging skin, and turned pink by the time the rivulets hit the drain at my feet.

The weight of his stare pressed on me, and the metal collar he'd locked around my neck threatened to choke me. He'd attached a chain to the hook at the center of my throat, and he held the other end in his large fist.

Every few seconds, he pulled on it to taunt me.

The water wasn't warm enough to stop the chills from tickling my skin. His strikes ran through my head on constant replay, especially the part where he'd managed to break what I thought had already been broken. I'd lost control of my fucking bladder.

If I'd given in and sucked Lucas' cock, would they have spared me this? Would my rebellion cost Rafe his life? The thought of what they might be doing to him tormented me, and I held my breath, unwilling to allow air into my lungs.

"Time's up," he said, voice echoing off the tiles.

Startled, I shot out a hand toward the faucet and shut off the water on the first try. Palming my breasts, I turned around. The room was one big shower stall with several showerheads on each wall, but it was empty save for us. His gaze dipped to my stomach, and he raised a brow.

"Wonder what your man thinks of that carving. Should I add my name to the mix?" He came at me, each step a calculated move of predator stalking prey. He raised a hand, and I froze, resisting the urge to flinch. I thought he was going to strike me again, or worse, but the door to the shower room opened, offering a perfectly timed interruption. A man I didn't recognize dragged a girl inside by the same type of collar that circled my neck. She crawled on her hands and knees, and her wide eyes—a startling shade of blue that rivaled the sky in the dead of summer—zeroed in on me. Huge drops fell from her thick lashes, and a plea trembled from her lips.

"Please..."

"No talking!" The guy gave the chain a swift yank, and her blond head jerked forward. He yanked her up by the arm and pushed her to the wall, then switched on the spray. She sobbed, her arms wrapping around her naked body as the water drenched her hair.

"Got a new one, huh?" Muscle Guy said.

"Yep, but she isn't gonna be much fun. She's already half broken, and I haven't even touched her yet."

She shrank away from him with a strangled cry, as if his words alone were enough to cause her physical pain. Sickened by the terror on her face, I turned away, but she started screaming. I whirled, my heart in my throat, expecting to see the guy hurting her, but her stricken gaze remained locked on me.

"Wh-what happened to you?"

My backside flared in pain at the reminder of Muscle Guy's cane, and he smirked before I could say anything.

"I want a shot at her before you start training," he said. "She's exactly the type of pussy our base wants to see on film. She'll put up a real whiny fight."

"No can do. She's a virgin. Boss doesn't want her on film. She's going to auction."

Her huge eyes begged me, as if she thought I could save her from a fate worse than a fiery pit. I bit my lip, hating how helpless we both were. They were going to ruin her—an innocent girl who barely looked eighteen.

And Rafe and I...

Lucas had his own agenda when it came to us, that much was clear. But we'd also seen too much in this place. There was no way they'd let us out of here alive.

"Well that's a shame," Muscle Guy said as he pulled me toward the door by the chain. "I like blondes."

"You like 'em all, as long as they scream for you."

A shudder tore through me, and I vowed that I would never scream or cry for him again.

"On your hands and knees."

"What?" I blinked at him.

"Don't make me tell you twice," he said with a hard shove until I dropped to my knees. "Crawl like the slut you are." He herded me back into the tunnel, naked, wet, and shaking from the chilly air.

The door to Lucas' office was closed, and silence blasted from the other side. He yanked me in the opposite direction and paraded me down the passage like a dog, my knees scraping the dirt ground. After passing several doors, he stopped and pulled a ring of keys from his pocket before jamming one into a lock. "Be a good girl and wait on the bed."

He pointed toward the claustrophobic darkness, and my hesitation cost me a kick in the ass. Pain scorched my backside, eliciting a wounded cry as I crawled inside. He latched the other end of the chain to an anchor in the ground before slamming the door shut. My breath came in panicked gasps as I pushed to my feet and searched for the handle. There wasn't one. My trembling hands smoothed over a panel where a doorknob should have been.

Hysteria flooded me, vibrating through my legs until they buckled. I fell to the ground and slinked across the dark space, chain clanking through the rocky dirt. My head hit the metal frame of the bed, and I planted a fist on the thin mattress to hoist myself onto it. Finding a blanket bunched in the corner near the wall, I wrapped myself in the scratchy material, curling in a tight ball on the cot, and wished I could wither away to nothing. If I could only erase the last hour as easily as the blood had vanished from my skin, then maybe I could fucking breathe. But that blood lingered, if not physically, then mentally.

So did the image of Rafe. He'd cried, actually shed drops of horror from his beautiful eyes. The man who'd at one time left me naked and cold in a cage, who'd fucked me after paddling my ass, had cried at witnessing my pain.

Palpitations seized my heart. Were they beating him? Killing him?

I couldn't cry. I *wouldn't*. If I started, I wouldn't stop. I bit into my lip, hard enough to puncture, and licked away the metallic taste. I should have done what Lucas demanded. If Rafe died because I'd refused to suck a dick...I wouldn't be able to live with myself.

I wouldn't be able to live at all.

Why had I chosen that moment to take a stand? For years, Zach had made me cower and submit, yet the one time Rafe needed me to do it for his life, I hadn't been able to.

Why was this happening to us? We should have run away together when we had the chance, gotten far away from this place and this madness and this cruel fate that kept unleashing its sadism.

I clutched the blanket to my chest and squeezed my eyes shut. And I prayed. To whom, I wasn't sure. To anyone listening.

Please get us out of here alive.

Whereas I'd wanted to end the pain not long ago by taking my own life, now I ached for the opposite. I wanted to live in peace with Rafe, hungered to submit my body and soul. I wanted to grow old with him, wanted to heal him...and maybe find a way to heal myself.

I'd gladly exist as a vagrant beside him, belonging nowhere or to anyone except each other.

My lids grew heavy, and as images of a life I'd never have flickered in my mind's eye, I allowed a fitful sleep to claim me. I was back in the cabin with Zach, body trapped under his punishing knife and held prisoner by his thrusting cock.

Except it wasn't Zach. Rafe took his place, one hand around my throat while the other drew the sharp blade into my skin.

"Mine," he said. "You'll never escape the pain of being mine." He rammed into me with one last grunt and spilled his seed, head thrown back, green eyes hooded while he watched me watch him. A breath hissed between his teeth.

"I'm going to destroy you, sweetheart."

The sound of my screams startled me awake. I shot up, hands rising in front of my face to protect me. Overwhelming darkness closed in, and my breathing escalated. The screaming continued, but I wasn't the one screaming.

"Please! Stop! I wanna go home," a shrill voice sobbed. A spine-tingling crack sounded on the other side of the wall and another shriek rattled my bones.

I tumbled to the ground and crawled toward the sound with quaking knees. She let out another horrific scream. I jerked to my side, hands covering my ears, body folding into the fetal position. But it wasn't enough.

I couldn't breathe. Dust from the ground clogged my nose and throat. I removed my palms, and her screams ripped through my eardrums. Unbidden, I dug my fingernails into my forearm, scratching down the scar from my desperate attempt to break free of Zach. My fingers glided over the ridges circling my wrist from when the men had restrained me.

From when they'd beat me...just like they were doing to that girl.

They were stripping her of who she was, shattering everything she'd known to be true until this point, this irrevocable moment when her life would change forever. Each strike, each cry that left her lips was another step toward submitting to a fate she couldn't fight. To a fate that would make her wish for death.

I was glad Zach had destroyed me, and not some faceless stranger. At least he loved me in his own sick way.

God. Even that observation proved how twisted my head was. I wasn't normal. I'd become too immune to the evil that lurked in people. If I could trade places with the girl on the other side of the wall, I would.

It was too late to save myself, but she was innocent. She was fucking innocent and I couldn't do a thing to help her, couldn't even tell her she wasn't alone. Her screams continued, and I buried my face in my arms to drown out her pleas for help.

SIX

RAFE

"Not part of the plan, you say?" Cleft's dark laughter shivered up my spine. "If you ain't gonna fuck him, why shouldn't I?"

"Because I said so." Jax's tone brooked no argument.

Cleft pushed off me, and I let out a sigh of relief as his heavy boots thumped across the floor toward Jax. "Just because you weaseled your way back in, don't think you're calling the shots now." He jabbed a finger at his chest. "If you don't do him, I will. One way or another, his ass is getting fucked and filmed. He's fucking Rafe Mason. That shit will sell."

"That's exactly why you're not filming him. It's too risky. You know my old man will side with me." Jax glanced around the room. "Besides, you're full of it. I don't see you filming shit here."

"Just warming up." Cleft rolled his shoulders. "Uncle Luke won't have a problem with a little fun."

"You're not gonna touch him." Jax curled his lip. "So back the fuck off."

"This is bullshit."

"No," Jax said. "The mess in here is bullshit. Fucking clean it up." He pulled a hand through his blond hair and moved toward me, his feet pounding the ground in angry stomps. "Get him on his feet. Move!" he yelled when the guys holding me down didn't budge. They scrambled into motion and dragged me upright. Blood rushed to my head, making my vision fuzzy as one of the goons bent to release my ankles. The other stepped behind me and freed my hands.

"You don't have the balls to do him," Cleft said with a taunting edge to his tone. "Even though you want to."

"He's off-limits. That's all you need to know." Jax glared at the two holding me up, but he wouldn't meet my eyes. "Get those filthy sweats off. We need to get him to the showers."

One guy bent and tugged my pants further down my legs. "Lift your foot," he said.

I did so, my head in a fog, and blinked several times, but the whole room and everyone in it wobbled. This wasn't happening. This was another nightmare. After he pulled the sweats free from one leg, I raised my other foot and nearly lost my balance. He tossed the soiled clothing to the side and grabbed me by the arm.

Jax nodded toward the door. "Get moving. Cleft can clean this shit up."

Cleft grumbled his dissent as they ushered me out the door and down a long tunnel. We passed a guy hauling a frail blonde by a leash, her skin damp and pasty. As she crawled past, she lifted her tear-filled eyes—eyes that grew huge as she took in my presence. She didn't even look old enough to graduate high school. I could only imagine how terrified she must be, and seeing a guy my size, naked and barely able to walk under his own steam, must have sent a devastating blow to her hope for survival.

But I couldn't think about that girl. Not now. Not with all the chaos raging through my head.

Jax's familiar stride echoed behind us. The fact that it was familiar at all was shocking enough, but to wrap my fucking head around the rest of it—his presence here and the implication of his words back in that room—I couldn't do it.

Thoughts bounced around my head, but I couldn't catch a single one, couldn't even form the words to convey the total mind-fuck this situation was. Words refused to leave my tongue. They were stuck there in surreal silence as Jax and the others pushed me into a room full of showers.

"Get lost," he told the other two goons as he switched on the water.

I leaned against the tile, arms bent and forearms flat against the cold surface, and tried to gather my strength.

As soon as the door shut behind the men, I lunged for Jax, hands going for his throat. But the floor tilted under me, and instead of attacking him, I used his shoulders to hoist myself upright.

"How the fuck are you behind this?"

He shoved me against the wall. Water washed over us in a chilly stream, dripping from my hair and soaking his T-shirt.

"You're wasting your energy. They dosed you with the same shit you gave Alex when we took her."

"Get your fucking hands off of me," I said through clenched teeth. I pushed against his stocky frame, but he wouldn't budge. Fucking drugs. It was the only way they'd keep me down, and they knew it.

Jax had known it. The fucker had shared a cell with me for...I didn't know how long, but he'd been there, and he'd been in my damn house, living under the same roof.

He'd helped me take Alex.

He'd gotten me a fucking gun to protect her.

Why?

"None of this makes any sense."

"Remember when we talked in your cellar?" He lowered his voice, as if he didn't want to be overheard. "I said I'd always have your back."

"Like you have my back now? Don't do me any fucking favors."

He retreated with a sigh, and I went after him, my rage propelling me across the slick floor too fast. Slamming into him, we plummeted to the ground, and his skull hit the tile with a jolting thud. Veins pulsed at his temples as he fought me. He gained more ground each second, his muscles bulging under the exertion. With a roar, he shoved me off and rolled on top of me, straddling my thighs.

"Calm the fuck down before they come back in here," he said, face inches from mine. "You need to trust me."

"You're crazy. You're behind this whole thing. They fucking hurt Alex. They destroyed the island. You think I'm gonna trust you now?"

Jax closed his eyes, and his shoulders slumped. "I loved that land almost as much as you did."

"Why are you doing this? Fucking tell me that much, at least."

Voices filtered in from the hall. Jax rose to his knees and allowed me to push to my elbows. With a frown, he glanced toward the door, and we listened to the scuffle of movement on the other side. "You won't get out of here alive without me. I'm the only one on your side."

"If you're on our side, then get us the fuck out of here."

"Can't do that."

I studied him—the furrow of his brow, the defeat in his expression, and replayed the words he'd exchanged with Cleft. He'd referred to his old man...who apparently was the guy in charge around here. "You've got no real power, do you?"

"I haven't had any fucking power since the day I was born." He stood and pulled me to my feet.

The room spun, causing bile to rise in my throat. I swayed for several moments, sure I was going to spew what was left in my stomach onto the ground. Jax propped me up, one arm winding under my armpit, and we shuffled toward the spray of the shower.

I planted a hand against the tile to steady myself. He let go, retreating a few steps, and I closed my eyes as the water washed away the vomit and sweat from my skin. He stood nearby with silent patience, so I took my time, hoping it would be enough to regain some strength. I couldn't protect Alex like this—fuck, I couldn't even protect myself. This was bad.

"Where's Alex?" I tilted my head and sent him a glare through the water dripping down my face. "Is she okay?" The question ended on a shaky note. I was fucking terrified of hearing the answer. I couldn't stand to think of her as *not okay*.

Jax clenched his jaw, and his gaze lowered to his soaked sneakers. "How bad was it?"

"Bad. He used a cane on her."

"Finish up." He tapped his foot for a few seconds, his brows scrunched together, as if he were mulling over something. "I'll take you to her."

I switched off the water before taking a few cautious steps. The room swayed slightly, but at least I could walk on my own.

"You got this?" he asked.

"Yeah."

With a nod, he gestured at the exit.

"You're gonna make me walk out of here like this?" I raised my arms, indicating my naked state.

"Don't have any clothes for you. If Cleft had his way, he'd be fucking you right now, so I'd say beggars can't be choosers."

Getting to Alex was the only thing that mattered, so I stepped through the door, water trickling from my body, and let him lead me down the tunnel-like hall that never seemed to end. "Where the hell are we?"

He glanced up and down the tunnel before speaking in a low tone. "Underground."

"Underground where?"

He pointed behind us. "That end leads to the old man's office and connects to the basement. Some of the Shanghai tunnels ran to the house, but this portion was built during prohibition." He shook his head with a scowl. "Now it's used to traffic girls."

I raised my eyes toward the ceiling, where the pipes hung low. Some leaked in a few spots, creating small puddles of mud on the ground. "What about the other end? Where's it go?"

"Somewhere in Forest Park."

So we were in Portland, close to the bustle of people that could help us if they only knew this place existed. I wasn't sure why Jax was telling me this, and I didn't get a chance to question him further. A scream echoed from down the hall.

I staggered forward, every muscle bunching in preparation for a fight, adrenaline coursing through my veins.

"It's not Alex," Jax said.

He halted at a door, and another scream tore through my ears. He appeared stoically detached, as if the screech of pain was something he was used to hearing on a daily basis.

Maybe it was.

Maybe I hadn't known him at all, even before I'd lost my memory.

He pushed in a key. "She's in there." He wedged the door open and removed a penlight from his pocket. The beam bounced across an empty cot. Mouth flattening into a line, he shoved the door wider, and the tiny stream of light lit up a huddled form on the floor.

"There's no light in these rooms, but at least you got a bucket to shit in." He swerved the beam to the other end of the room.

I couldn't care less about the bucket or the lights or his casual, helpful tone. He sure as fuck wasn't a friend of mine. I gazed down the hall, toward the end that led to the middle of nowhere in Forest Park, and wondered how much time it would take to get Alex out, assuming I could knock Jax on his traitorous ass first. The drugs were definitely wearing off, but the edges of my vision were still

hazy, and I had shit for strength in my arms. She'd probably need to be carried out of here.

"Escaping isn't gonna happen."

My attention snapped to him. I was a moment away
from trying to knock him out anyway, but the two goons—
the ones who'd walked my pathetic ass into the showers—
appeared a few feet down the tunnel.

Jax shut off the penlight and leaned against the wall,
arms crossed. "We're both stuck here, whether we like it or
not."

"Don't play the victim, Jax. This is fucked up."

"Yeah, tell me about it." He shoved me into the room
and slammed the door. I turned, and my hands smoothed
over the surface, but he'd already clicked over the lock.

Suffocating blackness strangled me, blocking my air—
blocking out everything except the stream of memories
that flooded my head. I slid to the floor, my limbs shaking,
losing strength as the last bit of adrenaline left my system.

Another shriek came through the wall, knifing through
me, as pieces of my past resurfaced.

SEVEN

ALEX

I jumped when the door burst open. Light beamed into the blackness, but it was too quick to note anything other than Rafe's presence. He spoke to someone for a few moments, though I couldn't understand what he said. Then he stumbled inside and the clank of the lock echoed, leaving us in complete darkness. Silence thickened the air, broken into pieces by the screams of the girl next door. Between the wailing, I listened, waiting for him to say something, do something, make some noise that indicated he was there, because I knew he was.

So why wasn't he talking to me?

Gritting my teeth against the pain, I forced myself into a sitting position and slowly pushed to my knees. "Rafe?" I called, crawling in the direction of the door. The chain attached to my neck crept after me like a snake. At least, that's what I envisioned.

He remained eerily silent as I spanned the distance between us. Terror gripped my heart, and my breath came fast and noisy. "Talk to me," I said, but everything I was, all the shattered pieces of me, fell through the cracks. Fear iced my heart. Oh God. What had they done to him? My limbs shook violently as I lowered to my haunches next to him, and that's when I heard it.

A low groaning, interspersed with quick, shallow intakes of breath. As if he were trying not to breathe. As if he were trying to hold it in. I knew what that was like.

My eyes burned with grief. "Rafe..." I reached out to touch him, but he shifted away at the first brush of my fingers. Fear and rejection darted through me, leaving in its wake tiny holes where stubborn hope seeped. I had to believe we'd find a way out of this. Giving in to the alternative would surely get us killed.

"What...what happened?"

"I remember."

Letting out a breath, I reached for his hand, and my fingers wrapped around his on the first try, as if they knew exactly where they belonged. I held on tight, refusing to let him withdraw. "What did you remember?"

"The hole in prison. The guards let him in..."

"Let who in?"

"Cleft smells like him." He returned my grip painfully. "He fucked me in there. Cleft fucking *smells* like him."

"Who's Cleft?"

"The fucker in the hoodie."

I stiffened, still unable to get the hatred in that man's eyes out of my head. "He was in prison with you?"

"I think so. I can't remember...I couldn't see a thing in the hole."

And we couldn't see a thing in here. I ran my thumb over the back of his hand, blinking rapidly to hold back the simmering grief. I'd failed him eight years ago. I wouldn't do the same now. I'd be strong for him, a rock for him to lean on. "Did he d-do it again?"

I waited with bated breath, my heart pounding in my ears. Another *thwack* and scream came from the other side of the wall, and I jumped.

Rafe jumped too. "Jax stopped him." His voice sounded off, almost as if he'd rehearsed his void tone. I recognized the underlying shock because it matched the way I felt.

"In prison?"

"No, here. He's here."

"Jax is involved?"

"I don't know how or why. None of this makes any fucking sense. He wants me to trust him, but I don't even know him. How can I trust him when he won't even tell me what the fuck is going on? All I know is they're hurting you because of me."

"I-I'm okay."

"Don't lie to me."

"I will be okay. Just don't shut me out." I moved to straddle his lap, needing more than anything to wrap my arms around him, but he held me off.

"I'm naked, Alex."

I sucked in a breath, sickened by the implications of why they'd remove his clothing. But we only had each other, so I straddled him, despite his protests, and lifted my hands to his rough cheeks. "So am I."

He laughed. He actually laughed. But the pitch was off, like he was trying hard not to cry or scream or punch something. "I don't know why this is happening. They said I did something in prison, but I can't remember shit."

"I don't think this is just about you. After they drugged you in the woods, they brought me in to see Lucas."

"Who?"

"Lucas Perrone," I repeated, then faltered because he had no idea who I was talking about. How could he? He didn't remember any of it. "He was a business associate of my dad's. We dated for a while. He...he asked me to marry him the night you took me."

"Did you accept?"

That wasn't what I expected him to say, and I definitely hadn't expected the note of possessiveness that tinged his tone. I lowered my hands to his shoulders. "Yes."

"Why?"

"I thought it would protect me from Zach."

"So you didn't love him."

"There's only one man I've ever loved. You already know that."

"You have shitty taste, sweetheart."

"I have a taste for you." I lowered my head, and our

breaths mingled. Electricity zinged through the darkness, crackling over our naked skin. Everywhere we touched sparked with heat. I inched back because being so close sent vivid images through my twisted head. I wanted to forget about Lucas, Jax, the fact that we were both prisoners in a dank room, naked and sitting in the dirt.

I wanted to lose myself in him, except we couldn't just ignore reality. The threat wasn't going away on its own.

"Why do you think Jax would do this?" He wasn't the first person I'd trust, but Rafe had trusted him enough to share the cabin with him.

"Fuck, Alex. I don't know. I'm pretty sure they're all working for someone though. Jax mentioned his father." Silence ensued, and we both stilled as the implications settled in.

"But that would mean..."

"Perrone is Jax's father," Rafe said, the words hoarse and barely audible. "What did he want with you?"

I squirmed on his lap, hesitant to go into Lucas touching me or nearly forcing his cock into my mouth. "He wanted something I wasn't willing to give, not unless he agreed to let you go."

"Alex..." he warned. "Don't you dare try to bargain for my life."

"It didn't work anyway. He sent me into that room and..."

"And they beat you," he finished, his voice cracking. He burrowed his face into the crook of my shoulder and crushed me in his embrace, holding on as if letting go meant he'd splinter apart. "I'll kill them all," he whispered.

My ass was burning something fierce, but I clenched my teeth until the pain dulled. I was just starting to relax, calmed by the shelter of his embrace, when another screech bled through the wall. We both froze, suspended in quiet horror.

Her screams reached every part of me, and my skin erupted with goose bumps. I'd been through a lot. Some would say I'd been to hell and back. But they were baptizing that poor girl by fire, taking her from everything she knew and loved just so they could torture her into becoming nothing.

A thing with holes to fuck, like Zach had treated me in that cabin. I shuddered at the thought.

"I won't let them hurt you again," Rafe said.

I knew he meant every word, but he was only one man. "I know," I whispered. I wouldn't upset him by telling him that I had little faith left. We were trapped in a dark room underground somewhere, and no one would find us.

"I won't let them," he repeated. We settled into each other, bodies pressed together, mouths parting over warm skin, and breathed the other in as the monster next door elicited more screams from his victim.

EIGHT
RAFE

This confined, dark pit of hell was fucking with my head. Or maybe Alex's naked body sent me spiraling through the deviant holes of my mind. She lay next to me on her stomach, her warm thigh pressed over my dick, and I couldn't stop touching her. The cot was barely big enough for the two of us, which was fine by me because I wanted to keep her close anyway. But being so close tested my limits, and being trapped in this never-ending blindness had awakened a certain part of me. The part that enjoyed tracing a finger over the welts on her ass, following the angry lines branded in her flesh.

I'd traced her skin for hours, finding the act somehow soothing.

Blind captivity skewed reality to the point where time was meaningless, and it had a way of driving a person mad. It seemed like weeks had passed since Jax slammed the door, though it couldn't have been more than a few days. Sandwiches and bottles of water arrived every so often through a slot in the door, apparently on some schedule I couldn't track due to the pitch-blackness that made it impossible to measure time.

The longer we remained trapped in this dark cell, the closer I came to fissuring, and that pissed me off. I couldn't let whatever issues lurked in my screwed up head pull me under now.

Thank fuck the screams next door had silenced on the first day. I kept torturing myself with what that girl might be enduring, and I felt like a bastard because I was grateful Alex was in here with me, safe from the monsters outside this room.

But that only left me to question the nature of the monster inside this room with her. Her vulnerability sparked something ugly in me. Something shameful. Something that threatened to unlock what I'd forgotten.

I didn't want to remember what I'd done to her, but I was obsessed with finding out.

She whimpered in her sleep, indicating another night-mare was on the rise, and I gently shook her shoulder to wake her before the horrors of her mind trapped her in the past.

"Wake up, baby."

She awoke with a sharp intake of breath and pushed to all fours, barely missing my balls with her knee. The bastards had leashed her, and the chain slid along the ground anytime she moved. I brushed my fingers over the cool metal running down her back.

"They were...they..." She sucked in another quick breath.

"It was just a dream."

Letting out a shaky sigh, she settled against me again. "I'd rather have nightmares of the cabin. At least Zach was...someone I cared about. How messed up is that?"

"Everything about this is fucked up. I'm not surprised you're having nightmares. I've been having them for a while too."

"I remember," she said quietly.

Of course she did. I'd practically attacked her in my sleep our last night on the island. Figuring we could both use a distraction, I patted the mattress above my head and searched for the tube of cream someone had slipped through the slot in the door. If I had to guess at who had been feeding us and slipping first aid items inside, I'd put my money on Jax.

Still didn't make a shred of sense though. I kept replaying his words, trying to find the angle that clicked into something recognizable, but I only went in circles. Jax was the son of Perrone, who'd proposed to Alex. Perrone was behind all of this, but he also had ties to Abbott De Luca, who could easily be involved too.

How the fuck did Jax fit into the equation?

Maybe I couldn't figure it out because I couldn't

fucking see beyond the darkness trying to choke the monster in me.

Fisting the tube, I squirmed out from underneath her and maneuvered to my knees, depressing the mattress on each side of her legs. I unscrewed the cap and squirted what I hoped was the right amount into my hand, then I palmed her firm, round ass. "Was it this dark in the cellar?" I asked as I rubbed in the ointment.

"Mmm-hmm," she hummed, the pressure of my hands inducing a relaxed state. I finished applying the cream and glided my palms upwards. Brushing her hair to the side, I massaged her shoulders.

"God, that feels good."

Her words tingled down my spine, heating my blood to simmering. I was a pussy, fucking terrified of remembering, but I couldn't help but want to. I wanted to know what it felt like to own every part of her.

"Tell me more about the cellar."

"Why?"

"Because I need to know. I need to know everything." I pressed my fingers deep into her muscles and worked out the knots.

"You left me naked in the cage. I didn't have a blanket or any clothes. The thing I remember most is the cold. And the shame. You hated me, but I couldn't blame you for it."

"Me hating you...I find that hard to believe." I lifted my leg and rolled her out from under me, onto her side, then stretched beside her on my back. I draped her over my body, not thinking, only acting on instinct as I embraced her, my fingers moving in slow circles down her spine. She caged me between her knees, and my dick nestled at the opening of her sex, fully erect and begging for entrance.

"Rafe," she whispered, letting out a strangled moan.

Our captors could burst through that door at any moment, and I was sick for wanting to fuck her like this.

While being held captive.

While the remnants of Brock's cane still sent unbearable amounts of pain through her system.

She couldn't move without sucking air through her teeth. I only knew this because I heard her trying to hide it every time she shifted. I feared they'd do it again, that they were giving her time to heal so they could inflict more damage.

It's what I'd do...if I were a psychotic bastard.

Fuck. My cock grew even harder. I didn't want her to suffer...I *didn't*...but my body responded in a shameful, disgusting way at the thought of being the one on the other end of the cane. I'd never hurt her the way he had, but I wanted to make her cry. The urge intensified the longer we were locked in this dark hole together. Denying it was useless, but maybe if we poked and prodded at my memories, I'd understand it better.

Bury your head in the sand some more, Mason.

The dark tendencies had always been there, but something had made me snap, had propelled me to act on them. I wanted to remember what that something was.

She moaned again, face nudging the side of my neck. Rolling her hips, she slid her mound up and down my length in sensual madness.

"Fuck, Alex." I twisted my head and nipped her lips, nudged her chin until she turned and bared her ear. My breath wafted over the delicate skin beneath her earlobe, and I whirled my tongue, savoring the salt of her flesh. The urge to bite became overpowering. I couldn't help it, couldn't stop it. My mouth had a mind of its own, and I sank my teeth in with a groan.

She pulled at my hair with frantic fingers, and my traitorous hips jutted up to meet hers. "Don't stop talking. What happened next?"

"You left me in there for a few days. You fed me"—her wet center teased my tip, and she gasped—"gave me a bucket to piss in. That was a dick thing to do, by the way."

"What other *dick* things did I do?" I tried not to think of how close my dick was to pushing inside her.

"You cooked breakfast for me, let me take a shower. Made me eat off the floor."

"I fucking *what*?"

"I knocked my plate off the table, so you made me eat off the floor."

I'd been a mean sonofabitch, and I didn't know how she could relive that while grinding on me, her pussy slick over my shaft. Fucking teasing. She could easily impale herself on me, but instinctively, I knew what she was waiting for.

She wanted me to force her cunt onto my cock. I grasped her hips and almost pushed her downward. She'd fit me like a glove. I knew she would. I couldn't wrap my head around the fact that I'd already been inside her. How could I forget something like that?

"Later that night, you fucked me."

I groaned at the mental picture of her helpless beneath me, skin doused in sweat, her body shuddering. "Tell me when you were most scared."

"When you made me tell you about Zach...or maybe the night I almost drowned in the river. Both were pretty fucking terrifying, Rafe."

I stiffened all the way to my toes. "Talking about the past is a bad idea." I pushed against her, but she only held on tighter.

"You're scared you'll remember."

"I *want* to remember."

"Are you trying to convince yourself or me?"

I sighed. "Both, maybe. Going there will open something that can't be closed. Whether it's my memories or a lunatic who'll do worse damage—"

"You can never do worse," she interrupted.

"What was our first time like? Did I hurt you? Did I make you cry?"

"You're right. Let's not do this." Her voice wavered, telling me all I needed to know, yet I couldn't stop picking at the scab of our history together.

"I did, didn't I?"

"You were angry." But I heard the pain behind those words. Our first time still haunted her, ached somewhere so deep, she'd never forget it existed.

"You didn't deserve that. There's wrong, then there's wrong. I don't need to recall those missing years to know I crossed a line."

"Then uncross it," she whispered. "Fuck me like it's our first time."

I groaned, but before I could protest, she slid down my chest, her dainty palms warm on my skin, and the cool metal of her leash followed suit. Her hair brushed my abs, her breath a tempting blast of heat on the tip of my cock.

"Don't," I told her.

"Why not?"

"Not the time or place."

"We might not get another time or place. This might be it." She paused. "Or is there another reason you're holding back?"

Good fucking question.

I was kidding myself by not answering. She was too willing. Something about this room, about the suffocating blindness, drove me crazy. I tamped down the urge to force her onto her back, but my mind sprinted ahead. I imagined straddling her chest, my weight pressing her to the mattress, one hand fisting her tiny wrists as I shoved my cock deep into her mouth. Her eyes would pop open, her lips stretching as they wrapped tightly around my shaft.

Struggling to breathe, I bucked her off. That hadn't

been a fantasy, but a memory. I'd forced my cock between her lips in my room back on the island. The one that was undoubtedly turned to ashes now.

"What'd I do wrong?" The tremor in her voice sliced me deep, but it also sent a rush of blood straight to my cock. How could I hurt so much at the pain in her voice, yet want to force tears from her eyes all the same? I licked my lips, craving the salt of sorrow.

"It's not you."

"What is it, then?" She shifted on the bed, and her chain rattled through the darkness.

I became obsessed with that thing. It would be the perfect way to restrain her to my bed, the band of metal around her throat a constant reminder of my power over her.

Perfect...if I weren't also trapped inside this dungeon with her.

Fuck. What the hell was wrong with me? This room, the welts on her body, that chain...all of it poked at my own personal Pandora's box.

That chain...

Holy fuck. We had a weapon in here. Why hadn't I thought of this sooner? I scrambled off the bed and wrapped a loose fist around the chain, following it to the hook in the floor. Reaching out, I slid my fingers down the smooth surface of the door, roughly two feet away.

Those assholes would come back, and when they did, I'd tangle them up in their own leash before they had the chance to drug me again. I prayed to God I could get my hands around their throats and apply enough pressure to subdue them. I'd fucking kill them if I had to. It'd be risky, especially if they were packing heat, but if I could get ahold of a gun...

We were out of options. I'd searched every inch of this room by touch, had spent hours listening, hoping to find something that would give me a clue. We weren't getting out of this damn dirt hole unless we tried.

"What are you doing?" she asked, her voice small. Timid. Hurt.

Rejected.

"I want to fuck you, sweetheart. Believe me, I do. But I just had an idea."

"An idea?" Disbelief dripped from her tone.

I had a lot of ideas tumbling though my chaotic mind, most of them deranged and dirty and involving her at my mercy. None of them involved being in this place and at the mercy of others.

I tightened my fist around the chain. "Yeah. An idea."

NINE
ALEX

The persistent *thump thump thump* of my fists on the door blasted my ears. I was surprised everyone in the place wasn't screaming at me to quiet down. But having someone yell at me and possibly bark threats would be a step up from them outright ignoring me.

"Can anyone hear me?" I shouted again. I'd been wailing on that door for several minutes, though it felt closer to an hour. Faltering, I drew in a deep breath and listened carefully for the hint of footsteps, the jingle of keys. I couldn't see a thing, but I knew Rafe waited nearby, chain held tightly in his hands, ready to trip up whoever opened that door.

First, I had to lure them into the room.

"Please!" I cried again. "I need some help in here!"

Footsteps sounded on the other side. I bolted away, the

darkness whirling around me, and sat in what I hoped was the middle of the room so Rafe would have enough slack in the chain. The welts on my ass burned, but there was no time to change position. Someone pushed a key into the lock, and I held my breath, trying to calm my trembling limbs. This had to work. God, please, let this work.

The door burst open, and someone stood in the entrance, their tall build a silhouette against the bright backdrop of the tunnel. "Whaddya bitching for?" His beam tore through the blackness and lit me up like a spotlight.

"I'm bleeding," I said, leaning back on my elbows and spreading my thighs. "I need a tampon." I bit my lip, which probably came across as coy to him, but I was really trying to mask my fear. This plan was screwed if I couldn't get him into the room.

The guy took a step inside and shone the light between my legs. "Where's your boyfriend?"

I spread my legs further, hoping to keep his attention. "Can I get a tampon? Please?"

He took another step toward me, the beam of his flashlight casting over the bed, and I let out a sigh of relief.

"I asked you a question, bitch. Where's the guy?"

"On the shitter."

He swerved the light to the other end of the room, where the unoccupied bucket sat, and let out a curse under his breath.

Rafe's shadow moved from behind the door, and he

flung the chain over the guy's head, bringing him down with a bone-jarring thud. The flashlight dropped to the ground and went out. I fisted my hands as the pull of the chain on my neck tightened. A scuffle broke out, and grunts and groans ensued. A bundle of shadows wrestled.

"Rafe?" What would I do if he didn't answer? What would I do if this didn't work? What had we done? They could kill him. This was stupid. So stupid.

"Rafe!" I said in a loud whisper.

One of the shadows rose and yanked on the chain, propelling me across the ground. I grabbed at it with ineffectual hands, barely rising to my feet, and dug my toes into the dirt. Fear constricted my throat with each step forward. Strong hands grabbed my shoulders, and that's when I recognized the heavy breathing. Rafe's breathing.

I slumped against him, close to losing it, and his arms wound around me for a moment.

"Gotta get moving, baby." He let me go, and a few seconds later, the flashlight switched on. He aimed it at the prone form of the guy who'd opened the door. He didn't look like he was waking up any time soon.

"If he doesn't have a key for that thing..." Rafe said, shining the beam at the choker around my neck. "There's no way in hell I'm leaving you here." He bent and patted down the guy's body, paying special attention to his pockets, and withdrew a set of keys.

I shuffled my feet, my pulse skittering too fast, as Rafe started his way through the bundle. "Hurry."

"Just breathe," he said on his fourth or fifth try. "We're getting out of this fucking room, I promise." He pushed in another key and turned it, and this time, the chain fell free of the choker.

Rafe grabbed my hand. "Let's go."

"You didn't find a gun on him?"

"No."

Stepping into the hall was blinding. After spending days in total darkness, the light seared my eyes. I glanced up and down the tunnel, in disbelief that it was actually empty. Clinging to Rafe's hand, I followed him down the passage toward the office, acutely aware that we were naked, and that at any given moment someone could discover us and send our hope for survival crashing through the ground.

"Maybe we should go the other way," I whispered, a tremor taking my voice hostage.

"The office is this way. I'm hoping to find a gun in that room." His fingers flexed around mine.

We approached the last door just as another opened somewhere down the tunnel. I held my breath as Rafe tried the knob and turned it without resistance. We scurried inside, and the flashlight lit up the office in weak illumination. Rafe made a beeline for the interior steel door Lucas had come through on my first night here.

"There's a fucking keypad." He leaned his forehead against the steel with a loud sigh. "Fuck!" He turned, and I felt the weight of his stare through the darkness. "How well did you know Lucas? Any guesses at the code?"

Biting my lip, my gaze veered toward the ceiling, trying to remember anything of significance. "His birthday is October twenty-eighth."

"What about the year?" He turned back to the keypad and punched in some numbers. "I doubt he'd use his birthdate though."

"He was born in 1969."

"Of course the bastard was. Fuck, Alex. He's old enough to be your father."

"I was desperate and...stupid." Shaking my head, I rounded the desk and began pulling drawers open. "Shine that thing over here."

He joined me and aimed the light into the drawers, but they were mostly empty, only housing stray pens, paper, and sticky notes. The filing cabinets underneath the poster-sized photos of the blonde were locked with no key in sight. Even the desk's surface was free of clutter. No phone, no computer, not even a letter opener we could use as a weapon.

This room was a shell of an office. A sham, much like its owner. No wonder the door hadn't been locked. The paintings, the shelves with art and antiques, the humongous desk—they were all props to give off an intimidating vibe to whoever set foot in this room.

Rafe met my eyes, and even in the dim light, I detected the heart-wrenching defeat in them. It only lasted a moment, but it was enough to tell me that he was losing hope, giving in to the bleakness of our situation.

"Okay," he said, backing away from the desk. He turned around and aimed the light at the shelves. "The guy I took down will wake up soon, we can't call out for help, and there's Jack shit in here to use as a..."

He swerved the beam, stopping on the whips, paddles, and restraints. As he shot across the space, I headed in the direction of the heavy-looking vase on the other shelf.

It didn't weigh as much as I'd hoped, but it was better than nothing. Or was it? I eyed the bulky ceramic piece and wondered how much strength it would take to knock someone out with it.

Rafe pulled out a set of handcuffs with a sigh. "How long would you guess the tunnel is?"

"Long, at least thirty minutes to reach this end."

"Damn," he said with a sigh.

"There's nothing but forest out there, Rafe. We walked quite a ways before entering the tunnel."

"We'll worry about out there once we *get* out there."

But his tone wasn't one of hope. He didn't think our chances of reaching the other end were good, and if this door was anything to go by, we'd probably find another keypad at the other exit too.

"Can we fight our way out of here?" I asked. "What about the other hostages? Maybe we can free them and fight our way out as a group."

"We don't know how many there are, or the extent of

their injuries." He shook his head. "I don't want to leave anyone behind, but you're my only concern right now. I'm getting you out, then we can get help for the rest."

We both glanced toward the door. First, we needed to make it down that tunnel.

Rafe took the vase from my shaking hands and placed it on the shelf. "I can do more damage with the flashlight. Hold on to these though," he said, holding the cuffs out to me. "They might come in handy."

I nodded with a hard swallow, and we both sent a longing look at the door with the damn keypad blocking our escape.

"Stay close, baby."

"Always."

He reached for the knob, but the quiet thump of footsteps echoed from the tunnel, growing louder, closer, and Rafe switched off the flashlight. His fingers folded around mine, and he pushed me behind him as we moved to the side.

The door opened, and I held my breath, my pulse throbbing in my ears. A stream of light flooded the space between the door and the jamb, and a slim, shadowy figure filled the entrance. A hand reached out and flipped on the overhead light.

Rafe launched at the guy with the speed of a rattler, the flashlight cracking against the other man's skull in three swift strikes. He wrestled him into a choke hold, the muscles in his arm bulging as he applied pressure to the guy's throat. They slammed into the wall, and the flash-light dropped to the floor.

Jax stormed inside, his dark eyes swerving between Rafe and me, then he yanked me in front of him and pressed a gun to my head. The handcuffs slipped from my trembling fingers and clattered to the ground.

TEN
RAFE

"Dude, let him go." Jax pressed the barrel to Alex's temple with a steady hand, but the lines around his eyes hinted at his reluctance. "C'mon, man. Don't do anything stupid."

I tightened my hold on the guy who'd found us. He was a puny little thing, probably not even old enough to drink a fucking beer, and I wondered what the hell he was doing in a place like this. He flailed in my arms, but I refused to give an inch. Just a little more pressure and the guy would sink to the floor, out cold.

Jax wrenched Alex's head back and placed the barrel under her chin. "Don't make me do this. Let him go."

The longer I stared at Jax, at the gun he threatened Alex with, the more I wanted to squeeze the life out of this guy.

Alex returned my gaze from beneath hooded eyes. Her

lips parted, breaths escaping in shallow puffs. She clawed at her arms, nails digging into the jagged scars left behind from when she'd sliced herself up.

"Put the gun down," I said, keeping my voice even, much calmer than the boiling rage rioting through me.

"Let him go!"

Cursing under my breath, I removed my arm, and the guy slumped to the ground like deadweight.

Jax let out a breath. He took a step backward, pulling her with him, and kicked the door to the office shut. "I don't wanna do this. If you'd just stayed put...fuck, Rafe! What part of 'trust me' did you not get?"

I gestured toward his weapon. "Why don't you put the gun down so we can talk all about it?" I lifted both hands, a show of surrender, and hoped to keep him talking.

"We were like brothers." He removed the gun from her chin and dropped his arm. "I consider you family more than my own fucking blood."

"Then why are you going along with this?" I asked, watching him carefully. His gaze kept straying to the wall behind me. I cranked my neck and studied the photos on display. I hadn't paid them much attention before, as I'd been too focused on finding a way through the door that led to escape, but now the crude nature of the poses stormed through my veins.

"She was my mother," Jax said quietly, face pinching in remembered sorrow. "My sister looked just like her." He raised the gun toward the photos, hand trembling. "She was the old man's favorite."

Was.

Memory or not, I doubted I'd known any of this.

"Jax..." I drew in a deep, calming breath because despite the pain in his expression, what I really wanted to do was yank that fucking gun from his fingers and turn it on him. Talking was my only option though. "Why are we here?"

"It's complicated."

"Why don't you uncomplicate it for me?"

"Wish I could, man." He swerved the gun in my direction. "There's no way out of this, so why don't I take you guys back before someone a lot meaner than me finds out you're gone?"

"How about you punch in that code and let us go?" I raised an eyebrow.

"Can't do that. If you escape, they'll know it was me, and I can't afford to get kicked out now." Jax pressed his fingers into Alex's arm and shuffled toward the door leading to the tunnel.

"Someone got something on you? Is that why you're going along with this?"

"Something like that. Let's go." He gestured toward the guy at my feet. "I still have to deal with him, not to mention the stupid idiot that let you out in the first place." He pressed the barrel of the gun to Alex's head again. "So get the door. I'm right behind you."

Alex and I traded an ominous glance. I wanted to wrap her in my arms and hide her from all of this, but we both knew she'd end up paying the price for our botched escape attempt.

I kept failing her. I'd dropped the ball when I'd left her in that damn hospital after she'd broken free of her brother, and I'd ignored the fact that we'd been sitting ducks on that island. We'd thought Zach was our biggest threat, but an evil more potent than her brother had lurked from the shore, just waiting for the perfect unguarded moment to strike. Jax had known they were going to attack. Was that why he'd gotten me the gun?

But they'd unarmed me too easily...as if they'd known exactly how to rip apart any defense system I might have in place. They'd drugged me, taken my own fucking weapon, and had used it against me.

Yet here was Jax, acting like he fucking gave a shit about what happened to us.

I reached for the handle, my hand shaking, and turned the knob. The door creaked open, and the breath I'd been holding exhaled in a resigned sigh. Cleft stood on the other side, mouth curved in a wide smirk, body blocking the exit. Before I could make a move, he sprang forward and jabbed a needle into my neck.

The ground rushed up to meet me, but my blurry gaze never left his face. He bent over my useless heap of bones, his features pinched in rage.

"She didn't...didn't..." I licked my lips, blinked, and

tried to force the words out. "*My* fault. Don't..." Fuck, my tongue was little more than a dead slug in my mouth. I couldn't even plead on her behalf.

Cleft narrowed his dark eyes, and the intent in them made me want to scream. "Everything you do goes back to her." His words hollowed through my ears, then a black void sucked me in and swallowed me whole.

ELEVEN

RAFE

"This is a bad idea," a disjointed voice muttered from what sounded like a far-off tunnel. "We're gonna get our fuckin' asses chewed over this shit. I'm tellin' ya."

"If Cleft says get the guy, we get the guy."

"Yeah, but Jax will be pissed if—"

"Will you chill out, bro?"

"He's the boss's kid. I'm just sayin'."

A bright light seared my eyelids, but I didn't know where I was, couldn't immediately recall what had happened—I only knew that I felt like roadkill, and at least two men were standing over me.

Rough hands yanked me upright from the thin mattress. "Time to wake up and play." They held me up by the arms, and I forced my eyes open as they herded me out the room. It was the same rancid shithole they'd held us prisoner in. Like a pipe bursting, memories flooded me—using the chain to take down the guy Alex had lured inside, and the subsequent confrontation with Jax. Then the fuckers had drugged me again.

"Fuckin' cowards," I slurred. "Need to drug me 'cause you're all pussies."

A weak blow glanced off my jaw. "I'll lick your girl's pussy. Bitch would probably like it."

"Calm your ass down, Vinnie. Don't let him get to ya."

I squinted, but the lights in the tunnel made my vision spotty. "Where is she?" I swallowed hard, and my head lolled on my shoulders, jostled by the jaunt down the hall. Nausea rose and burned in my throat.

"She's waiting for you, lover boy." The one on my right snickered. I recognized that laughter and the cruel grip of his hands. Brock wasn't someone easily forgotten. "We're gonna make a fucking kick-ass film. You guys will be super stars."

We shuffled down the tunnel, stirring up dust, and they ushered me back into their torture room with the concrete floor. Alex hung by her wrists from the rafters, her skin darkened from dirt and bruises. She was entirely helpless with her head drooping toward her tits. The men shoved me to where those damn chains waited, so fucking close yet too far away to touch her. I slammed to my knees and swayed for a few precarious seconds, then I lifted my chin and peered up at her.

"Now that's a fine piece of ass."

Snickering.

Laughter.

Words blending together in a long string of threats and taunts I couldn't understand because everything from my sight to my hearing was garbled.

Except for Alex. Her presence came through achingly clear, and my apprehension choked me. I couldn't speak, couldn't plead. So long as they kept pumping my system full of drugs, I was fucking *nothing*.

How much pain would she suffer because I couldn't fight for her?

"Fuck me...just leave her alone." I tried rising to my feet, but the floor swerved, and I fell sideways. The contact bolted through my brain, throbbing with an incessant pound. Blood pooled on my tongue from where I'd bit down hard.

More laughter.

"I'm not into dudes, sorry." Brock bent and yanked my head up. Vinnie disappeared from view. "I'd rather watch the two of you get it on."

"Fuck you." I spit in his face. He snapped back and planted his fist into my jaw, and fuck, he had a better arm on him than his scrawny brother.

I glared at him, ignoring the deep ache that radiated to my teeth, and a sense of satisfaction spread through me as he wiped my saliva from his cheek. "*Fuck you*," I said. "Go ahead, hit me again."

Better me than her. The longer I kept the focus on me, the longer he'd leave her alone.

He pulled his arm back, preparing to strike, but a single demand from Cleft, who appeared in the doorway behind him, made him freeze.

"Save it for the camera." Cleft sauntered into the room. "Getting started without me, I see."

"Nope, just warming up." Brock retreated, and I pushed to my knees as the room spun around me for a few seconds.

Cleft assessed the situation with a nonchalant glance. "Let her down. But him..." He jabbed a finger in my direction. "I want him on his toes. Don't rely on dosing him. He's a mean sonofabitch. Gave me hell on the inside, even while I had my cock shoved up his ass."

A chill penetrated my bones, and I lowered my gaze as his boots came into view.

"What I wouldn't give to have a piece of your ass again, Mason."

"Fuck me all you want. Just leave her alone."

"That's a tempting proposition. I might take you up on it later."

Cleft released her, and she slumped to the floor with a whimper. He stepped down on her face, pressing her cheek to the rough cement, and threatened to add more pressure.

She cried out, her eyes popping open.

I struggled to my feet, but his words halted me. "Don't

make me hurt her," he said, withdrawing a gun from the waistband of his jeans. He cocked the weapon, making his point. "Give Brock your hands."

Seeing Alex's head sandwiched between his boot and the concrete, her parted lips sucking in air, green eyes huge and full of horror—the decision was a no-brainer. There were three of them and one drugged-up me.

I held my wrists out, allowing Brock to shackle them. The third goon pulled on the chains and hoisted me to my toes, arms straight above my head. I had enough trouble balancing, considering my doped-up state, and the position put me at a disadvantage. I couldn't even kick without losing balance.

Passing the gun to Vinnie, Cleft lifted his foot, then he forced Alex to her knees in front of me, his grip tight in her hair. Brock moved the cameras and lighting equipment to where we were grouped together, and the spotlight he flipped on blared in my eyes. I glanced down at the crown of her dark curls, blinking the spots from my sight. Brock switched on the camera.

"Sugar," Cleft said. "You've sucked off your boyfriend before, right? Good sluts know how to give great head."

She lifted her sad gaze, and somehow, I knew what she was thinking. She'd pleasured me with her mouth, maybe she'd even enjoyed it, but I didn't remember. These bastards were taking our second chance from us, under the glare of lights and rolling cameras.

Under the threat of violence.

She was right. We should have taken our chance while we had it. At least that was something they couldn't take away.

"Don't just look at him. Get his limp dick up." Cleft smirked in my direction. "Aren't you man enough to get hard for your girl?"

"You're a sick fuck."

"You're the one about to get sucked off, and something tells me you're gonna like it, so who's the sick fuck now?"

At the thought of her lips wrapping around me, my traitorous dick stirred.

He jolted her head violently. "C'mon, bitch. Get your man up."

"Okay," she cried. "I'll do it." She took my cock in her warm palm, and at the first touch of her hand to my shaft, my own fucking sickness rose, tearing through me with the devastation of a torpedo. I closed my eyes, drew deep breaths through my nose, but her dainty fingers pulled me under. It was the first time she'd touched me—that I could remember anyway—and my cock grew into a rock hard piston of shame.

"Eyes open, Mason. It's only respectful to watch your slut suck you off." Cleft wrenched her hands behind her. "Hand me a pair of cuffs, Vinnie."

Bulky leather restraints exchanged hands, and Cleft fastened her wrists at her back. "You wanna mouth-fuck him, right sugar?"

She didn't answer, and his expression darkened. He smacked her on the cheek. "Answer me!"

"Yes!"

"That's what I thought." He brushed a thumb over her trembling lips before wedging his fingers inside, stretching her wide open. He slid her mouth onto my dick, and fuck... it was like coming home. My cock nestled in her wet heat, and the suction of her mouth, the sensual whirl of her tongue, the wide-eyed way she gazed at me—each were lethal on their own, but the combination of sensory overload ignited a war in my veins.

I was scum. Worse than scum.

She'd been shoved to her knees, her mouth forced to fuck me, and I wanted nothing more than to explode down her throat, camera, assholes, and spotlights be damned.

"Sweetie, let's hear some moaning." Cleft pushed her further onto my dick. "Make it good for the audience."

Brock snickered. What I wouldn't give to send my fist into his face again. I yanked at the chains, and the clink of metal on metal echoed through the room.

Alex moaned, and my whole body twitched at the vibration of her tongue. Pressure built in my balls. I clenched my hands into fists. "Don't make her do this."

"Unless you want Brock to bloody her ass again, you'll keep your fucking swimmers inside your balls until I give you permission." Cleft's lips curved into a ruthless smile. He pressed against her skull and shoved her flush with my groin. Her throat had no choice but to suck down my cock.

She gagged, but her eyes...fuck, those eyes never wavered from mine for a moment. Smudges of dirt sullied her forehead and cheeks, and her curls surrounded her face in a riot of tangles, but she'd never looked so gorgeous.

Or tempting.

My legs quaked from the effort of keeping myself upright on my toes, and each pump of blood in my body rushed straight to my dick.

Cleft yanked her off then impaled her on my shaft again.

She moaned. I moaned.

We were both fucked, because in that moment, I knew she was getting something out of this too.

"Make him beg to blow his load." He tugged on her hair, and my cock sprang free, jutting straight out and leaking my shame all over her heaving tits. "If he ain't begging, you ain't doing it right. C'mon, slut. Give us a good show."

She sucked and bobbed, letting out tiny whimpers and slurping noises, and I bit back a groan. My balls tightened, and my hips had a mind of their own. I thrust deeper. Fuck. I couldn't get deep enough.

"Beg," Cleft ordered. He pulled her back slightly and folded his fingers around the base of my dick, pumping while Alex's lips slipped on and off my tip in quick, maddening slides.

Squeezing my eyes shut, I groaned. I wanted to turn it

off—the need tearing through me, leaving me in shattered pieces, all of them hurtling toward her amazing mouth.

"Grab the whip, Brock."

"No!" My eyes flew open, but Brock was already passing the camera off to Vinnie.

Cleft clamped her nose between thumb and forefinger, and he held her to me, her lips stretching wide around my base.

"Your man's not begging. Guess he's got balls of restraint. Tell me, sugar, can you take Brock's lashes without chomping off your boyfriend's junk?"

Alex fought his hold. "Never mind, don't answer that, seeing as how you can't talk or breathe right now." He allowed her a few seconds to suck in air through her nose before he plugged it again.

"Don't do this," I said, my gaze glued to Brock as he grabbed a coiled whip down from the rack.

"Ah, now we're gonna get to the begging part." Cleft shifted to the side as Brock approached Alex. He stood several feet behind her, clenching the handle of the whip in his eager fist.

"I'll give you one last breath." Cleft released her nose, and she drew in air, her eyes huge and pleading with me as her lungs filled. "Try not to take off your man's cock, okay?"

Something familiar tickled my mind, a flash of her hoarding air as if she were about to die, her naked body submerged in water between my legs. Before I could examine the memory further, the whip swooshed through the air and struck her backside. Screeching around my shaft, she clamped down hard with her teeth.

I hissed in a breath, my muscles taut, and lost balance. Extending to my toes again, I tried not to cry out like a pussy. She loosened her jaw, and the pain echoed through me, a warning of the damage she might do if she lost total control under the next sharp bite of the whip.

Cleft allowed her a moment to breathe as his dark gaze pinned me. "Beg to blow your load."

"Please," I said.

"That didn't sound convincing enough."

"Fuck you!" I winced, immediately regretting my loss of temper because Brock struck her again. Her teeth came close to ripping into my cock, which would hurt like fuck, but I was more furious at myself.

I couldn't stand her mouth around my dick, hot and tight and so fucking *perfect*, couldn't stand the way her throat opened for me, sucking down my length until she made continuous gagging noises. Most of all, I couldn't stand the spasm of pain that tightened her muscles, because while she was enduring the brutal lashings, I was getting off on it.

Her helplessness made me harder, desperate, and fuck, I wanted to explode down her throat, despite the scrape of her teeth.

Cleft grabbed my chin. "Fucking *beg*."

Shame flared, searing my flesh and heating several layers below. "Please let me come."

"Still not buying it. Hit the bitch again," he told Brock.

Another bite of leather on flesh, and Alex's muffled cries shuddered around my shaft, pulling at the beast in me. I groaned, heaving in air, my heart rate thundering in my chest. I had to stop this. If I came...

Fuck.

What would they do to her then?

"Make your stubborn piece of shit boyfriend beg like he means it!" Cleft shook her head, and she sucked harder.

"Don't hurt her!"

"Make me believe it, Mason. Last chance."

Alex and I exchanged a heavy glance, and she didn't need words to plead. The way her eyes pummeled me said it all. She wanted me to give in and find pleasure in her mouth. Wanted me to end this already.

Ah, fuck. "Please, I'm begging you."

"Begging me for *what*?" Cleft asked.

"Fucking let me come in her mouth!"

He bobbed her head in rapid thrusts, his fingers fisting her hair, and Brock returned to filming our humiliation. Her mouth gloved me in blessed hell, sucking my cock so deep, I thought she might swallow me whole.

"How bad do you want it?" Cleft asked.

Bad, more than I'd ever wanted it in my life. I gritted my teeth, lips pulled tight, and threw my head back with a long groan. I couldn't speak, couldn't breathe. A woman's mouth had never felt so fucking good.

"You don't have permission."

Too fucking late. God himself couldn't stop the eruption. I pumped my seed down her throat, letting out several hoarse cries, limbs rigid from the rush of release. Cleft let go of her hair, and she inched back, her tongue lapping at my tip to catch the final drops.

The ensuing silence was profound yet tenuous, and as Alex lowered to her haunches and hung her head, the disquiet spelled fucking doomsday.

TWELVE

ALEX

"**S**ugar, your boyfriend has a defiant streak." I ignored our tormentor's taunt and kept my head bowed, peeking at Rafe. The tribal tattoo covering the left side of his heaving chest drew my focus. Black lines danced over his abs as he tried to catch his breath from his eventual dive into ecstasy.

My heart wouldn't stop galloping, and a flush bathed my skin in sweat. I was hot and wet between my thighs. Rafe did that. *We* did that to each other. His release still echoed in my mind, an arousing whisper that infiltrated my system until I wanted to squirm.

I couldn't bring myself to look at his face. I knew I'd find only shame and self-hate. He hadn't been capable of holding back, and though that thrilled some sadistic part of me, it would douse him in guilt because Cleft and his men would punish me for it.

But wasn't that the point? They were doing this to fuck with his head, with both of our heads.

Someone grabbed my shoulders and hoisted me to my feet.

"Leave her alone!" Rafe shouted.

I didn't bother fighting. There was no point, but beyond that, I refused to give them the satisfaction. Firm fingers turned my head, and I met Brock's eyes. He leaned forward and dragged his tongue up my cheek.

"Stop tasting the bitch and chain her up," Cleft said.

Brock wrenched my arms behind me and forced my body into a bent over position. I spread my feet for traction and lifted my head, finally peering at Rafe through my thick, messy curls.

He pulled at the chains mercilessly, and panic strained his features. He looked ready to rip out of his skin to get to me.

The heavy thump of Brock's footsteps halted behind me. He took his time, prolonging the torture of waiting for that first strike.

It was going to hurt. I knew it before the whip sliced the air. The leather cut across my ass with scorching impact, and I locked my gaze on Rafe, pretending he'd ordered the lashing.

I'd been bad. Maybe I'd come before he'd given me permission, or I'd done something more serious, like piss him off with some sort of reckless behavior. I could see myself doing that. I was, after all, the girl who'd tried to kill herself in an attempt to escape a psychopath.

My scattered thoughts were on the brink of reality. Even acknowledging that didn't slow the wheels of my mind. We had no way out, no way of knowing how long either of us would live.

I wouldn't let them take this from us. Pain...pain between Rafe and I was supposed to be good, so with each *thwack* of that whip, I pretended it was from him. Squeezing my legs together, I hoped they wouldn't notice the evidence of my arousal.

I was sure Rafe knew though. He read me too easily, and my face was on fire as I returned his heated gaze. Neither of us said a word, as if we'd come to a mutual understanding. After several more lashings, Brock dropped the whip with a clatter and exchanged a glance with Cleft.

"She's hot from getting him off. Those fucking endorphins." Sighing, Cleft paced the area between Rafe and me. "Gotta say I'm disappointed. Mason got to blow his fucking load, and you," he said, stopping to grab my chin, "seem to be impervious to pain at the moment."

Letting go of my face, he ran a hand through his brown hair and halted to confront Rafe. "This is a bit unfair, dontcha think? If you get to come, I think I should too."

Rafe shook his head, his eyes spitting poison. "Not with her. You wanna fuck someone, do me."

"Rafe!" I jerked forward, pulling the muscles in my

shoulders, and nearly lost my balance. "No!" I'd rather Cleft fuck me. I could take it. But Rafe...he'd been raped in prison because of me. This was all my fault. I couldn't stand the thought of him enduring it again.

"Ignore her," Rafe said. "Fuck me. I know you want to."

"No!" I shouted. "You can do whatever you want to me. Leave him alone."

Cleft frowned. "Gag the bitch," he told Brock.

Brock disappeared then came back a few moments later with a large ball gag held tightly in his fist. I shook my head, squirming in my restraints. Tears threatened, an unbearable burn behind my eyes.

Brock shoved the gag against my mouth. I groaned, pressing my lips together, and shook my head back and forth. His mouth flattened into a mean line as he forced the gag in. My protests came out as whines, screeching higher, and Vinnie cocked a gun and pressed the barrel to my temple.

Cleft dragged a chair near Rafe, then released him from the chains. "You see that gun? If you fight me even a little bit, Vinnie will blow her brains all over the place."

I didn't recognize Rafe in that moment. His eyes were alight with something I couldn't name. He averted his gaze as he bent over the armchair, baring his ass to Cleft, who stood behind him, stance wide and cocky. He slowly unbuckled his jeans and pulled the zipper down. Cleft palmed his ass, fingers gouging skin, and Rafe's whole body twitched. He fisted his hands.

He was really going to do it—allow this bastard to rape him, all to protect me.

The burn of vomit lingered in my throat, and I closed my eyes, panicked at the thought of puking while gagged. Five in, hold, five out. There wasn't time for the repeat part.

Rafe hissed in a breath, and my eyes flew open.

Cleft worked the tip of his cock between Rafe's ass cheeks. I pleaded for him to stop, but no one paid attention to the smothered whines emanating from my throat.

Then the door banged open and Lucas stood in the doorway. "What the hell do you think you're doing?" he shouted, his face red with fury.

THIRTEEN

RAFE

Cleft backed off, and I let out a breath. This was the second time someone had stopped him from violating me. I didn't know how much more of this I could take. I glanced at Alex, feeling like shit, because she'd suffered far more than I had.

I stood, and the room whirled around me for a few unsteady seconds. I wanted more than anything to go to her, but Vinnie remained at her side, gun dangling at his thigh, and I'd probably fall on my ass if I tried. I reached for the back of the chair and propped myself up.

The guy who'd burst through the door jabbed a finger at Cleft. "This place is full of pussy, yet you're trying to ram your prick up *his* ass? I can't turn my back for a fucking second without this place going to hell."

Cleft opened his mouth, his gaze darting in my direction. "Uncle Luke...I didn't mean any disrespect."

So this was the fucking father figure Alex had almost married. A swift rush of possessiveness crashed over me, and I wanted to pound on him. I settled for squeezing the chair until my knuckles whitened.

"You never mean any disrespect, but you keep fucking up. You and Jax both. If you weren't my blood, you'd be dead by now." Perrone began pacing, one hand rubbing his chin, and his gaze ran over Alex's restrained body. Slowly, he made his way to her and ran a palm over her face, down the valley between her hanging tits.

I wanted to kill him for touching her.

Leaning closer, he sniffed her skin and scowled. "Which one of you idiots touched what's mine?"

I clenched my teeth, taking serious issue with that statement.

"We didn't touch her," Cleft said, exchanging a worried glance with Brock.

"Someone's cum is all over her. Who ejaculated on my property?"

"Um...we filmed her sucking off Mason."

Perrone whirled, his expression thunderous and pummeling Cleft from across the room. "Did I give you permission to use her like that? I thought I made myself clear. She belongs to *me*. I gave you explicit freedom to break her through corporal punishment. Mostly to goad him," he said, pointing at me. "*Nothing* more. Did you not understand those very simple instructions?"

"No, we just thought—"

"I don't care what you thought. I've heard enough." He turned back to Alex and unbuckled the strap keeping the gag between her lips. The rubber ball dropped to the floor. "Were you fucked?"

She hardened her jaw and turned her head, but he trapped her chin between his fingers. "I asked you a question."

"N-no."

"Did anyone in this room touch you, sexually, aside from the blowjob?"

She blinked, her gaze straying to me, and Perrone tightened his grip. "Eyes on me. Don't make me repeat myself."

"No."

"Good." He let go of her face and glared at Cleft. "Go get my son, and have Mick and Zander fetch the blonde."

"Which blonde?"

"The only fucking blonde in this place right now worth mentioning. Tell them to *bring her to me*."

"Yes, sir," Cleft said, scurrying to the door.

"You two," Perrone barked at Brock and Vinnie after the door slammed shut. "Why is Mason fucking standing around? We have restraints in this room for a reason."

Vinnie swallowed hard, and he and Brock stalked toward me. My attention shifted between Alex, Perrone, the goons, and the door. I stumbled back, but my fucking head swam. The damn door seemed miles away, and Alex even further.

Vinnie raised the gun. "Boss? He's not wanting to cooperate."

"For fuck's sake. I've hired idiots! Shoot him if he gives you any trouble."

I raised my arms and allowed them to shove me toward the chains before stringing me up again. Perrone cast an appreciative glance at Alex, his tongue darting out to wet his lips.

"So you're the guy in charge," I said, trying to draw his attention away from her. "Obviously, I did something to piss you off, so why don't you have your assholes take her back to the room, and the two of us can have it out?"

I wasn't stupid enough to think he'd let Alex go, but maybe I could talk him into shutting her away in that shithole, where at least she'd be safe for a while, tucked out of reach from this room. Whatever was about to go down, I didn't want her around for it.

Perrone arched a brow at me. "You've done far more than merely piss me off. And she's not going anywhere. She needs to see this as well." He rounded, his expression pinched with rage as he took in his two remaining men. "You all need a fucking lesson in respect! This is my place. *I'm* the boss. Nothing happens from here on out without my knowing about it."

He circled Alex, his lips curving upon seeing the damage to her ass. "Honey," he said, smacking her sore bottom. "Give me what I want, and I can make all of this go away."

"I'd rather have Brock whip me again."

The way she stood up to him made me proud, but at the same time, I wanted to slap my hand over her mouth. Because he was fucking stalking her, just waiting for her to step wrong.

He stalled in front of her and bent down, bringing his face close to hers. "From what I can tell, they went easy on you. Do you know what real pain feels like?"

She spit in his face, and I stiffened, terrified for her.

Perrone retreated, his fingers wiping off her spittle. "Did you spit out Mason's cum? Or did you show your respect by swallowing?"

She twisted her head, refusing to answer or meet his gaze.

"Answer the question," he said, his voice dangerously low. He could have screamed and it wouldn't have been more intimidating.

"I swallowed every last drop," she said, her gaze imparting wrath. "You don't deserve my spit."

He smacked her, and the slap of palm to cheek tightened my teeth. I clamped my jaw shut, because speaking now wouldn't help either of us.

The door flung open, and Cleft pushed Jax inside. Puffy, red skin surrounded his left eye, as if he'd been hit.

Perrone rounded on him. "Are you still denying it, boy?"

"It wasn't me," Jax said, his shoulders slumping, breathing labored.

I swerved my gaze between the two of them, trying to decode what was happening here, but I had no clue. Perrone seemed unpredictable, easily enraged. Why else would his men cower at his presence, including his own son?

"Do you think I'm stupid?" He advanced on Jax, his face reddening with each second that passed. "You opened your big mouth to your new girlfriend."

But the only woman Jax had been with recently, as far as I knew, was Nikki. A chill slid down my spine.

Perone's voice rose. "Mason disappeared, and your slut ran straight to the cops! So tell me," he said, jabbing the air with a finger. "If you kept your fucking mouth shut, like you claim, then how did they find their way to me?"

"I don't know," Jax said. He straightened his spine but never quite met his father's eyes.

"You are *lying* to me. I had to pay off my guy on the force to make this go away. I thought you were serious about proving yourself, but apparently, you need a reminder."

Jax shook his head. "I swear. I didn't say a word."

"Hmm." Perrone gestured to Cleft. "Bring her in."

I didn't want to watch what I feared was coming, but I couldn't tear my gaze from Cleft as he opened the door wide. Two guys shoved Nikki into the room, and he caught her before she tumbled to the cement. Cleft held her up under one arm, and her head lolled to the side. They'd obviously drugged her.

"She didn't do anything!" Jax yelled. He staggered forward, his face as white as his father's button-down shirt.

Perrone pointed toward a chair. "Sit the fuck down."

Jax did so without hesitation. He was terrified of his father, and I was terrified for Nikki.

My gaze shifted to Alex, whose wide eyes pummeled me. I couldn't protect either one of them. "Hey!" I shouted. "You want to hurt someone, you fucking bastard? Hurt *me!*"

Perrone narrowed his brows. "Someone gag him."

Brock picked up the gag from the floor and stalked toward me, his mouth curving up at the corners. He wrestled my lips open before shoving the rubber ball in.

I was useless, unable to plead for Nikki, and when Jax lowered his head into his hands, I yanked at the chains in a fit of panic. Jax was freaking out—I was fucking freaking out—and I couldn't do a thing about it.

I couldn't save Nikki.

Couldn't save Alex.

How the fuck had we gotten to this place?

"You guys should be ashamed of yourselves," Perrone said. "I've got prisoners waltzing into my office, unauthorized filming going on, and my own fucking son can't keep his big mouth shut!"

"Please," Jax begged, lifting his head. "She doesn't know anything."

"Bullshit. *She* went to the cops with too much info— info she wouldn't have known unless you told her. She's

Mason's ex-girlfriend, you idiot! Did you think she was going to sit on her hands when that island went up in smoke?"

Lifting her head, Nikki groaned. She squinted at the people surrounding her and began fighting their grasp on her arms. "I h-have a son. Please...please let me go. I don't belong here." She hung her head, and a sob escaped her lips.

She had a son, someone who needed her, who depended on her...holy fuck. I wanted to tell her how sorry I was, but I couldn't even speak.

Perrone lifted her chin. "Honey, if you want to live, prove your worth. My son has an unhealthy aversion to women—"

"Whose fault is that?" Jax jumped to his feet. "Maybe if you hadn't forced them on me..." He dragged his hands through his hair and took a deep breath. "Let her go. She didn't do anything wrong. Please...Dad."

That was the first time I'd heard him refer to his father in such a personal way, and saying that single word had cost him. Nikki was in real trouble.

Perrone pushed Jax back into the chair. "Bring the blonde. I want her on her knees for my boy."

Nikki pleaded, and Cleft smacked the whine from her as he dragged her across the floor, her heels digging in the whole way. He pushed Jax's knees wide open and shoved her to her haunches between them.

"Unzip so the slut can suck you off." Perrone began

pacing. "If she can get your confused cock to work, I might let her live."

Nikki sobbed as Jax unzipped with shaking hands. His erection jutted out, but the sight of his own arousal seemed to horrify him. His face crumbled as Cleft shoved Nikki's head into his lap, muffling her cries with the girth of his cock.

Chewing on his lip, Jax closed his eyes and fisted his hands until his knuckles turned white. Cleft bobbed her head, pushing her downward when she started gagging. She struggled for a few moments before he yanked her head up, and my insides twisted at witnessing her pain. Snot ran from her nose, blending with the tears drenching her face.

Jax lifted his lids with a quick intake of breath, and when he gazed at Nikki, moisture erupted from his eyes.

"Fuck this," Perrone said with a sneer. He shoved Cleft out of the way and wrenched Nikki to her feet. Holding her immobile against his chest, he pulled a knife from his pocket.

Time fucking screeched to a stop.

I yelled through the gag, blasting every bit of energy toward Nikki, praying someone would stop this. Her overflowing eyes met mine, and the truth in them nearly stopped my heart.

She knew it. I knew it.

Perrone switched open the blade, and Jax knew it too

because he charged his father, mouth open in a silent scream, hands reaching for Nikki.

But it was too late.

Perrone was already slashing a red horizontal line across her throat.

Blood.

Gurgling sounds.

So much blood.

Soaking through her clothing.

Silencing her sobs.

Her body crumbled to the ground, and Perrone tossed the knife to the side. He stepped back, out of reach of the blood pooling on the concrete, and that's when Alex started screaming.

FOURTEEN

ALEX

The room erupted in chaos. I blinked and it seemed as if a lifetime had passed in that mere second. The gurgling noise had stopped. So had my screams. But Jax bawled as he held the blonde's limp body, his devastation pouring from his eyes in streams of grief. Blood stained his clothing, but that didn't stop him from sheltering her in his embrace, rocking her as if she were merely sleeping.

Rafe's gaze swerved between her and me, his glassy eyes round with horror, shock, disbelief. The ball gag kept him quiet, though his rage burst free in his fisted hands, in the veins cording his bunched muscles. In the violent way he pulled at the chains.

He was a caged lion, bound by metal and madness, and this place was a zoo.

I glanced at Jax and the blonde again, and something inside me cracked, allowing memories to creep inside. As Brock freed my hands, I saw sunlight and white lace curtains. Murky water, dark with the kind of death that bled out my mother. I collapsed toward the floor, and Brock caught me in his arms as if I weighed nothing.

"Take her to the cell," Lucas said, voice booming off the walls. "I'll deal with her in a bit."

Brock and Vinnie herded me out of the room amidst Rafe's smothered protests. Hysteria rose in my chest, refused to release. I squeezed my eyes shut as they hauled me down the hall, toes dragging the ground.

"C'mon, use your feet," one of them said, hoisting me up. "Almost there."

I lifted my lids, and the tunnel spanned before me in a line of hazy crimson. Blood dripped from the pipes like a leaky faucet, forming puddles where the walls met the floor. That liquid death expanded, stalked in a furtive slither. I was going mad. That was the only explanation because logically, I knew the blood wasn't really there, but the deep red tore through my mind in a cacophony of whispers. I glanced at my forearms and gasped. Sticky red poured from the slashes as if the wounds had never healed.

"Make it stop!" My breath caught in my lungs, and I fought the grip of their fingers. "Get the blood off of me! It's not real! Not real...not real...not real..."

Lucas' minions shook me, propelling me forward. A

door creaked open, and the haze of red morphed to black as I hurtled to the dirt. I scratched at my wrists, as if I could remove the blood with my fingernails.

"What's wrong with her?"

"Fuck if I know. The bitch is going batshit crazy."

The light from the hall cast their figures in an otherworldly blur. My eyes burned with too many emotions that boiled, writhed, cut through me. I wanted to cry and sob and scream, but I couldn't.

I needed to *hurt*.

As Vinnie attached my leash to the hook in the floor, I dragged my nails down my arms hard, sucked in shallow breaths, and dug deeper.

"I think she was broken long before we got to her."

"Rafe..." Even saying his name incinerated me.

"Your boyfriend isn't comin'."

So much blood.

Pumping from Rafe's neck in thick spurts.

No! They hadn't killed him. My mind was only playing tricks on me, editing the continuous loop of knife to flesh slashing through my sense of reality.

Blond hair.

I grasped that piece of truth, because Rafe's hair was beautifully dark, just like his soul. My mother's face flickered in my mind, and I jerked my head back and forth, my thoughts overflowing with chaos, with bloody water and a bathtub full of dead mothers and lost hope.

Five in—

Can't breathe.

I screamed, though the wail didn't come from me. A wild animal thrashed inside my being, screeching its pain.

Someone hefted me up and sent a hard smack to my cheek. "Snap out of it!"

Gulping air, I returned Brock's wide-eyed stare.

"You're gonna sit on that bed and calm the fuck down. Do you understand me?"

I nodded, mouth trembling, and stumbled toward the bed. My legs gave out, and I plopped onto the cot's thin mattress, ass flaming from the welts. Rather than fight the burn, I embraced it, wrapped myself in its blessed relief.

Brock pivoted, running a hand over his shaved head, and he and Vinnie left. The door shut with a quiet click, as if it didn't want to ignite the screaming again.

I rocked back and forth on the bed, nails clawing my skin. I couldn't wash away the blood. I was bathing in it, reliving it. Those fucking tears needed to burst from my eyes and drench my face. I *needed* to cry, but I was a brimming cactus in the middle of a desert, and nothing could extract my despair.

Someone inserted a key into the lock, and I jumped. I could have lost minutes or hours—I had no way of knowing. Lucas stood in the doorway holding the handle of a lantern. He set it on the floor before picking up a bucket he'd left outside the entrance. The door slammed behind him, and a soft glow filled the space. So did the malevolent shadow of his form. He came toward me with purposeful steps.

"Now you know what I'm capable of," he said, bending to set the bucket on the floor. "I have no problem killing Mason. You have the power to keep him alive."

"You want to fuck me," I said, voice as dead as I felt on the inside.

"I can do that anytime I want. You're helpless here, Alex, and you can't stop me."

"What do you want then?" I lowered my gaze and imagined blood all over the shiny black surfaces of his shoes.

"I want you to *want* me to fuck you."

"That will never happen."

"Are you sure about that?" He placed a hand on my chest, between my breasts, and gently pushed until I flopped to my back. Grabbing my legs, he slid them onto the bed before bending and spreading my knees. I closed my eyes and found that place I hadn't ventured to in a while—the place where I'd sought refuge when Zach had pushed me beyond my breaking point in that cabin.

The scrape of the plastic bucket on rough ground pulled me from that mental sanctuary. I sensed him shifting, and the mattress squeaked under his weight. Water sloshed, eliciting a shudder, and warm drops dribbled over my breasts. Goose bumps broke out on my skin. My nipples tightened, begging to be touched, pinched...bitten.

I wanted Rafe. God, how I wanted him—to get me out of here, to make my body bend, to fucking love me.

Lucas' sleeve brushed my stomach, and I silently cursed my body for displaying any sort of reaction. He ran the sponge over my mouth and chin, wiping away the musk of Rafe, and continued to my breasts.

"My men fucked up. They should have separated you from Mason upon your arrival."

I scoffed at his tone. He made it sound like we were his guests. "Let us go." I swallowed hard. "If not me, at least let him go."

He let out a heavy sigh. The sponge dipped between my thighs, and his fingers followed. Unlike the brutal force of his touch the first time he'd thrust his fingers into me, now he dipped into my center with such teasing skill, something inside me twitched to life.

I hated myself for that twitch.

He caressed my clit, soft and light as a feather. I gritted my teeth. "Just fuck me and get it over with."

His low laugh rumbled through the room. "I'm not fucking you today. But you'll beg me to, believe me."

Over my dead, bloodied body.

"My personal slaves learn to serve me with pleasure, Alex. Some men like to forcefully take. I like to forcefully take what is given."

"I'm not giving you anything."

"You already have. You gave me a piece of yourself months ago. I saw your potential, your passion. And now," he said, pressing on my clit with firm pressure, "you're giving me your reluctant arousal." He burrowed his fingers deep.

"Do you think this will work?" I asked, disdain bleeding from my lips. "You're a sick, disgusting bastard who rapes women. You destroy them." I thought about the young girl one of his men had brought to screams for hours on the other side of the wall.

And I thought of the blonde whose throat Lucas had so carelessly slashed. He'd pulled that blade across her neck as if she were an animal, as if she meant nothing. She'd been someone's daughter, someone's sister...someone's mother.

She'd had history with Jax and Rafe. They'd both cared for her.

"Why are you doing this to us?"

"Some people believe in that old adage, 'an eye for an eye.' I'm underwhelmed with that saying. When someone wrongs me or mine, I don't stop at the eye."

He might as well have been speaking in Pig Latin. "Why are you telling me this?"

"Because you need to grasp the reality of your predicament. You're not getting out of here." He leaned over me, and his breath hit my face. "You feel my fingers inside you? I *will* have my cock there." He ran his tongue along my earlobe. I cringed, but a rough hand kept me from retreating. "Maybe I'll keep Mason alive long enough to hear you beg for it."

I spread my legs as wide as I could. "I have nothing left to give, so you're gonna have to take it." I was playing with fire by inserting that challenge into my tone, but I didn't care. Maybe I was still in shock. Numb. Seeing red.

It didn't matter. He was going to kill Rafe. If anything had the power to break my pieces, it was the certainty of his death busting through me like a wrecking ball. I'd rather die on our terms. *Our* time. I'd rather call Lucas' bluff and die now than continue to bend.

He removed his fingers and stood. The sponge splashed into the bucket, and he reached for the button of his pants. "I'm visiting him next." He paused, and my heart pounded out of control during those tense seconds. "You sent him to prison, Alex. Do you know what he did while he was in there?"

"No," I whispered, barely able to get that single word out.

"Mason killed my blood, so I'm going to kill him."

Now that he'd said the words, I wanted to bend.

Oh God.

"He's not a killer."

"Maybe you don't know Rafe Mason as well as you thought."

No, I knew Rafe. Lucas, on the other hand, I hadn't known at all.

"If you won't beg me to fuck you, maybe you'll beg for his life."

Fear seized me, choked me. I wanted to feel numb at

the thought of Rafe's death and my servitude living as Lucas' adoring pet, leash and all, but I wasn't strong enough. Pushing off the bed, I slid to my knees and begged in Lucas Perrone's language—I yanked down his zipper and wrapped my lips around his shaft.

FIFTEEN

RAFE

He'd killed her. I kept running those three words through my mind, thinking they'd penetrate, but I still couldn't believe it. That whole scene had been a nightmare because them dragging Nikki in didn't make any sense.

Perrone slaughtering her didn't make any fucking sense.

I must be delirious, drugged beyond what my body could handle. I'd hallucinated the whole thing. Tilting my head up, I pulled at the chains holding my wrists hostage. Assholes had strung me on my toes again, back in the pitch-dark room I'd shared with Alex. The echo of her name invaded my head to the bursting point.

The door opened, and I went on full alert even though I couldn't do shit to protect myself. Perrone filled the entrance, lantern hanging at his side. He set the flickering light on the floor and quietly shut the door before wandering to me, his stride casual, unhurried.

"Alex has an exquisite mouth," he said. "I'll give you that. She just demonstrated her exceptional skill on my cock."

I blinked him into focus, and he struck fast, pummeling my mid-section. I groaned and would have doubled over if my hands weren't chained to the ceiling.

He grabbed my jaw. "So I understand why you had trouble keeping your cum inside your prick."

I shook my head free, sucking air between my teeth. "I'll fucking kill—"

He sent a fist to my jaw, and the pain jolted through my teeth, burned behind my eyes.

"She's quite malleable. She got to her knees of her own free will and gave me the best damn head I've ever had."

She wouldn't have done that without being coerced. Unless...

Unless he'd threatened my life.

I wanted to scream at him, gouge his eyes out with a lethal jab of my fingers, rip his fucking cock off and mouth-fuck his goons with it, so I was shocked by the laughter that poured from me. Void of sanity or rationality, I laughed until my stomach cramped where he'd socked me.

I was manic, insane. Probably both. Maybe this was all a screwed up fantasy, and I was a mental patient living inside my own head.

"Why the fuck are you laughing?" Taking a step back, he folded his arms.

"She did it for me. She sucked your tiny dick because she loves me. She'll always love me." His eyes widened, and I laughed some more. "You can't break that. No matter what you do, you can't break what she feels for me."

He brought a knee up and rammed me in the stomach. "How about I just break you then, starting with every fucking bone in your body?"

The blow strangled me, but I was still laughing through the pain, and it was a sick mixture of agony and madness.

Perrone's mouth flattened into a line. He released my hands, grabbed my head, and slammed his knee into me, again and again until I couldn't laugh anymore.

Until I couldn't breathe. I slumped to the floor, wheezing air between tight lips.

"I was going to kill you, despite Alex's oral bribery tactics. But now I think I'll keep you around for a while, just long enough for you to hear the slut beg for my cock."

The air stirred as he retreated. I heard the door slam shut, and he must have taken the lantern with him because the never-ending darkness came back. I pushed to my hands and knees, limbs quaking under my weight, and struggled to the cot.

I sprawled on that bed for hours, maybe even days, months...a whole fucking lifetime, and as I drifted in and out of consciousness, images of Nikki's murder infiltrated my nightmares. So did Alex's broken pleas for me to save her. I also dreamed of Cleft's cock in my ass, the strong grip of fingers holding me down.

And the laughter. Always the fucking laughter.

Time passed in a jumbled mess of nightmares that never failed to spring me up from bed, drenched in sweat and shaking to my bones. I was pathetic. I couldn't even protect the woman I loved.

I loved Alex.

Fuck.

I'd never told her.

I'd also loved Nikki, maybe not in the same intense, out-of-my-fucking-mind way I did Alex, but I'd loved her.

Had I ever told her? Even once?

I'm pretty sure I hadn't. I was a fucking pussy incapable of telling anyone how much they meant to me. I didn't need a shrink to tell me I had abandonment issues. I could blame it all on my mom for leaving the way she had, but I was an adult, even if I'd grown into adulthood on the inside of four prison walls. Even if I didn't remember that transformation, I was twenty-nine fucking years old.

So where did that leave me?

Alone, fucked, and about to die without having ever said those important three little words to anyone.

To my own son.

I held my breath, heart thudding so hard, I thought I might save Perrone the trouble of killing me.

I had a kid.

Nikki.

Holy fuck.

I gripped my head and squeezed my eyes shut. I remembered nothing else, but I knew it was true. She'd had a son, and he was mine.

And now he was motherless, about to be fatherless. But he'd been fatherless all along. I wasn't fit to be a parent anyway. I wasn't fit to be loved by Alex either.

Fucking dying down here was for the best.

Eventually, that door opened again, but I didn't move or acknowledge whoever had ventured into this shithole. Part of me wished they'd just end this hell already.

"You here to kill me?" I asked, a challenge in my tone.

The door shut with a quiet click and a flashlight came on, the beam gliding over my prone figure on the bed. Footsteps sounded, and my pulse sped up in preparation for a fight, because even though I wanted them to get it over with already, I couldn't go down without one last battle. And I wanted a fair fucking fight. It'd been a while since they dosed me with drugs, and I wouldn't get a fair go at whichever asshole was in here if he pumped me full of them again.

A bundle of denim landed beside my head, followed by soft cotton. I sprang up and launched myself at whoever was here to drag me into another scene of torture.

"Rafe!" Jax said in a low whisper.

I let go of him and stumbled back.

He aimed the beam of light into my face. "I'm getting you outta here. Get dressed."

I didn't move at first, too stunned in trying to wrap my head around what was happening. Jax blinked several times, and the stress on his face, the defeat in his grievous eyes, sent a spear of dread through me.

"Is Alex...?" I swallowed hard, but I still couldn't get the words out. If she was gone, she was in a better place now, but I about hit the ground at the thought.

"Alex is fine." He hung his head. "Nikki's gone. What happened to her is on me." Taking a deep breath, Jax appeared to shake it off and gestured to the clothing he'd tossed on the mattress. "I have to end this. I'm getting you guys out of here, but we don't have much time. The old man will be back in a few hours."

I grabbed the jeans and pulled them on. "What's the plan?" I asked before yanking the T-shirt over my head. My pulse pounded, and I gritted my teeth. Trusting Jax wasn't easy, but what choice did I have?

"We need to get to the office. It's our best shot out of here. But getting down the tunnel is gonna be tricky. I need you to pass yourself off as Cleft."

"How the fuck am I supposed to do that?"

Jax shrugged out of his jacket. "He wears a hoodie just like this. Can you pull it off?" he asked. "Once we break Alex out, she'll have to crawl down the hall. It's the only way we're getting out of here."

"I'll do whatever it takes."

With a nod, Jax pushed the hoodie into my hands. I shoved my arms through the sleeves and flung the hood over my head, burrowing my face into the soft lining.

"Got a smoke?" I asked.

Jax aimed the flashlight at my face. "You've never smoked."

"No, but Cleft does."

"Quick thinking." Jax pulled a pack from his pocket and passed it to me. I pulled out a cigarette as he sparked a lighter to life.

Hopefully, the stench of tobacco, along with the hoodie and the leashed girl, would be enough to convince any passerby that the man at Jax's side was one of them. Since Cleft and I were about the same height, this might work.

I put the nasty butt in my mouth but didn't inhale. "What about you?" I asked. "Is anyone gonna question you roaming the tunnel?"

"I learned a long time ago how to put up a good front. The old man thinks he put me in my place." He turned his head away for a moment, his Adam's apple bobbing. "It's back to business as usual. He's a fucking heartless bastard."

"Why'd you go along with this then?"

"We'll get into all of that shit later. Let's just get the fuck out of here."

"It's about time," I muttered, stomping the cigarette with my bare heel. I prayed to fuck no one would notice how I wasn't wearing shoes. The jeans were on the long side and would hopefully hide the barefoot problem.

"Ever since your escape attempt, the guys have been on high alert, and today the clients are visiting the underground to sample the goods, so keep an eye out."

A sense of smothering fear overcame me. "What about Alex? Is she safe?"

Jax reached for the handle. "She's the old man's pet. No one's touching her but him."

That didn't make me feel any less sick. "She doesn't deserve this."

"You used to feel differently," he said.

"I'm not the same guy. Shit, I don't even remember that guy."

But I put too much effort into convincing myself it was true. Even now, with my memories gone and a drop of decency careening through my bloodstream, I'd wanted to own her in this dark cell, had thrilled at thrusting my cock down her throat in their torture room.

How long before I snapped and let the monster possess me?

Could she handle it if I did?

Could I?

Jax wrenched the door open, taking the lead. I walked at his side, vigilant of every sound, which left me with no time to question or war with myself. If we didn't get out of here, none of it would matter anyway. A man entered a room down the tunnel, and the faint pleas of a woman drifted to me. She wasn't a willing participant in whatever he was about to do to her. None of them were. If we got out of here, I vowed to take this place down and free these women.

Jax halted a few doorways down and inserted a key. The room was dark and nearly identical to the one they'd held me in. At the soft pads of our footsteps, Alex sat up, grasping the blanket to her chest. Jax's flashlight lit up her face.

God. She looked like hell. She'd been through too much, seen too much, had experienced too much.

For years. She'd been going through this shit for *years*.

I was about to hurtle the distance and crush her in my arms, but she shrank back at the sight of our towering forms, her eyes squinting against the light.

"It's me, baby."

"Rafe!" The blanket pooled around her, and she catapulted into my arms.

"We're getting out of here," I said, words muffled in her hair. "But I need you to act like I'm Cleft. Can you do that?"

She nodded, her hands roaming my cheeks, her gaze wondering over my face, lowering to my chest, as if checking to make sure I was in one piece. "I thought he was gonna kill you." She buried her head in the crook of my shoulder and inhaled. "God...I thought you were dead. It's been days."

I shared a look with Jax. Had it really been that long? Man, had I been out of it.

"Timing, man. It's now or never." He lifted his shirt, revealing the gun jammed in his waistband. "You have no idea what I had to do to get this thing. Old man took my damn weapon."

But one gun wouldn't do shit against a bunch of guys with guns and access to human shields. Alex shifted in my arms, and her chain grated my ears.

"Tell me you have a key for that?"

"Sure do." He bent and released the lock with a quick turn of a key. "But you're gonna have to crawl," he told her. "Keep your eyes on the floor, like a slave would, and we might make it out of here."

With not a tinge of hesitation, Alex dropped to her hands and knees and lowered her head.

"Let's do this." He wedged the door a crack, peeked into the hall, then opened it all the way. I followed, Alex behind me on all fours, and we hadn't taken more than a few steps when a man exited a room.

"What're you guys up to?" he asked.

Jax slowed, and I turned to Alex, yanking on her chain with a growl. "Sit," I ordered in a low voice, hoping to fuck the guy didn't realize I wasn't Cleft. Curling my toes inside the hem of the jeans, I kept my attention on her dark head and hoped it was enough to shield me from the guy's scrutiny.

"Boss is on his way in," Jax explained. "He wants her in the office."

"What about the boyfriend? Should we grab him?"

I watched from the corner of my eye and recognized the puny kid I'd taken down during our first escape attempt.

"Nope. I think she has a private date with the boss and his spanking horse."

"Lucky for him, huh?"

"Yep. Mason's out cold. He won't be a problem." Jax turned to me. "Ain't that right, Cleft?"

"Uh-huh."

The kid laughed. "Boss is making the two of you work together? Man, he must really be punishing you." He slapped Jax on the back before ambling down the hall.

Jax let out a breath. So did I.

"Fuck, that was close," he muttered.

We made frustratingly slow progress down the hall, as Alex could only move so fast on her hands and knees without drawing attention to ourselves. We passed by two more men, though they didn't stop to talk. Keeping my head low, I hoped it was enough to hide my face in shadow. Once we reached the door to the office, Jax glanced down the hall. A door opened and shut somewhere.

"If we don't make it out of here—"

"We will," I interrupted his quiet words.

"But if we don't, I just wanna say I'm sorry, man."

I peered over my shoulder. "Just open the damn door. You can kiss my ass all you want later."

He let out a shaky breath and rapped on the door.

Was someone else in on this? Was this a fucking trap?

But I didn't have time to process shit. Jax pulled the gun out and raised it. The damn thing shook in his hands, but the firm set of his mouth said he meant business.

"What are you—"

The door opened, Cleft's eyes widened, and Jax pulled the trigger.

No warning.

No hesitation.

The blast ricocheted down the tunnel, through my ears. Voices echoed, but Jax was already yanking Alex to her feet. I shoved him out of the way and tossed her over my shoulder, and we stepped over Cleft's body and into the office.

SIXTEEN

ALEX

"Why the fuck did you do that?" Rafe shouted at Jax. He nudged Cleft's body out of the way and slammed the door before turning the lock. He set me on my feet then grabbed a chair and wedged it underneath the knob.

I stood frozen in place, arms wrapped around myself. I couldn't rip my gaze from Cleft. He stared at me with unseeing eyes, his head at an odd angle, as if he'd fallen and broken his neck. Blood pooled from underneath his brown hair, and the edges of my vision started to go red again. The gunshot rang in my ears, a continuous *bang* that muffled all sound, even the thump of my heartbeat. I felt it at my throat, my temples, pounding through my chest.

"Alex." Rafe shook my shoulders, and my attention snapped to him. "That's it. Look at me." But his worried gaze swerved toward the back of the room.

I turned and found Jax fingering one of the oversized portraits of his mother. He lowered his arm, glanced at Cleft, and his face went pale.

"He deserved it." His jaw slackened, as if he couldn't believe he'd pulled the trigger.

"Jax!" Rafe shouted as footsteps thundered from the tunnel. "Punch in the fucking code!"

Blinking with a jolt, Jax dragged his gaze from Cleft and hurried to the door that stood between us and freedom. His fingers trembled as he entered a string of numbers, but nothing happened. "Fuck!" He rested his head against the door, closed his eyes for a few moments, then tried again.

Someone banged on the door leading to the hall. "What's going on in there? Cleft?"

Rafe and I exchanged a glance, and his fingers threaded through mine. The doorknob jiggled.

"Hurry," Rafe told Jax in a loud whisper.

More beeping. More cursing. More footsteps.

"Open up!" That sounded like Brock, and the consequent body-slam that shook the door supported my suspicion. I jumped, and Rafe and I backed toward Jax, who wrenched the heavy door open. We scrambled up the darkened staircase, but Jax stalled at the bottom to close and lock the entrance.

"Can they get through there?" Rafe asked.

"No. Door's made of steel and no one but me and Cleft knows the code...knew the code." He slumped toward the bottom step. "I killed him..."

"Get the fuck up," Rafe said, taking a step downward. "You can have a pity party later."

Jax's features hardened in determination, and he began climbing the stairs. He squeezed past us and opened another door. The three of us entered what must be the basement of the house. Decades worth of furniture and art cluttered the space between the slab walls.

Rafe slid the hood off his head and shrugged out of the jacket. "Can you get that fucking thing off her neck now?"

As I pulled the hoodie on, covering my breasts, Jax shuffled through several keys until he found the one he was looking for. I tilted my head back, baring my neck. The lock clicked over and the choker fell free, dropping to the floor where the chain pooled around the collar.

I drew in a deep breath, but it didn't quite fill my lungs. "Can we get out of here now?" I wouldn't be satisfied until this place was behind us. I didn't know if I could handle getting this far just to have Lucas toss us back into that tunnel. I thought about the women still trapped down there and shuddered.

"What about the others?" Rafe asked, as if he'd read my mind.

"We'll figure it out after we get the fuck outta here." Jax strode toward another door, and we climbed another flight of stairs. Entering the ground floor of the estate was like stepping into an alternate reality. The decaying brick and stone, the dusty rooms, the darkness—all of it was gone, replaced by open spaces that allowed the sunlight to stream through the windows. My bare feet glided across the smooth hardwood in the dining room.

I'd been here before, sitting at that very table with Lucas as he wined and dined me. A whole world of horrors had existed at my feet, several layers below the earth, while he'd attempted to work beyond my indifference with his charming smile and conversation.

Jax led us through a French door, but the alarm started its countdown. Cursing under his breath, he punched in a code, silencing the beeping with a sigh of relief. Sunlight hit my face, and I nearly gasped at the warmth, the blinding brightness. I lifted my chin toward the sun and closed my eyes for a few seconds. A slight breeze ruffled my hair. It was almost too much, after being confined in darkness for so long. Rafe tugged on my hand, and we padded over the grass, like silk underfoot.

"My van's parked over there," Jax said, pointing to a shaded spot between two trees just off the driveway. We changed direction and Rafe came to an abrupt stop, his attention locked on a gas generator standing a few feet from the house.

"Does that thing supply power to the tunnel?"

"Yeah, why?"

Rafe cranked his head, apparently searching for something, and his gaze landed on a shed. "I have an idea."

I swallowed hard, remembering what happened the

last time he had an idea. He pulled me along after him, and Jax scuttled to catch up.

"What're you doing, man? I just killed my cousin down there. The old man is gonna be on our asses soon. We need to get the fuck outta here."

Rafe tried the knob on the shed without success. "Stand back," he warned, letting go of my hand. I retreated, and he studied the door for a few seconds before sending a swift kick below the knob. After four more strikes, all impacting the same spot, the frame cracked at the latch, and Rafe pushed open the broken door.

"Dude, what the hell are you doing?" Jax followed him inside.

"Looking for something," he mumbled.

I pulled the jacket tighter around my body and cast a furtive glance toward the driveway that ended at the garage, expecting to find Lucas' black SUV pulling in. The next minute passed in an eternity, and I heard nothing but my rapid breaths mixing with the subtle chirp of birds and passing of vehicles.

They exited the shed, playing tug-of-war with a gas can.

"Don't be stupid!" Jax shouted. "If you blow the power, those girls will never be seen again. They'll just move the operation elsewhere, and the old man will lay low, protected by his fucking cop buddies until it blows over." He yanked the jug from Rafe, and fluid sloshed inside. "We need some time to figure this out."

Rafe swiped a hand through the air. "I'm not fucking kidding. Hand it over."

"No way!" Jax put the jug back in the shed. "What are you thinking?"

"He's gonna pay for this! That's what I'm thinking. He killed Nik...that bastard fucking hurt Alex."

"It's always about your lying whore, isn't it?"

The harsh words punched me in the gut, and Rafe pummeled Jax in the nose. They tumbled to the ground, Rafe wailing on his face, unleashing blow after blow as if he couldn't stop.

As if he *wouldn't*.

"Stop it!" I screamed.

Jax pushed against his shoulder and raised a knee. He squirmed from beneath Rafe by a few inches, and they rolled. But Rafe was too irate.

Out of control.

His face scrunched in exertion, blanketed with sweat. Rafe pinned him to the ground again, his hand reaching for the gun in Jax's waistband. He pulled it free and held the barrel to his head, then pressed an arm across his throat. *"You* did this."

"Rafe!" I grasped his back, but he applied steady force to Jax's neck, and he wasn't letting up. He was too far gone.

"You're killing him. Please, Rafe! He got us out!" Biting back a sob, I tried pulling on his shoulders, but they were like rocks under my hands. "Rafe!"

With a roar, Rafe sprang to his feet, breath coming fast and hard, his body trembling from the surge of adrenaline.

Jax gasped for breath, fingers clawing his throat, feet kicking the ground. He rolled to his side and spasmed with coughing fits.

"Her brother raped her!" Rafe waved the gun in the air. "Those fucking assholes in there violated her. *I* fucking violated her. Don't you *ever* call her a whore again, do you understand me?"

Jax pushed to his knees and stared up through his shaggy hair, the tips tinged with the blood dripping from his nose. "I got it," he said, pulling his T-shirt off. "She's not a whore." He bunched the shirt and pressed it to his nose.

"She's fucking mine, and I'll kill anyone who touches her again."

"I'm on your side. I got her out, didn't I?"

"Which is the only reason you're still alive."

Rafe's words seemed to pummel Jax more than his fists had. His shoulders drooped. "Won't happen again."

"You let this happen," Rafe said, jabbing a finger at Jax's defeated form. "You could have stopped it, but you didn't. You let them fucking beat the shit out of her."

"She lied to you," Jax said, wheezing air between his lips. "She made you go crazy in that prison. I was there, and that's all I knew. That's all I had to go on. I had to do it."

"You didn't have to do anything."

"This isn't the place to talk about this, man. We need to get the fuck outta here."

"I'm not leaving until Perrone comes back." Rafe jammed the gun into his waistband.

"You're not the only one who wants payback. Get into the damn van. We'll figure something out."

"And go where?

"We have a safe house, you and I. Money. No one else knows about it."

Rafe frowned. "You could've gone off on your own and no one would be the wiser. Why'd you get us out of there?"

"Because you're under my fucking skin the way she's under yours." Jax stomped past us and headed toward the van.

SEVENTEEN

RAFE

The sun kissed the horizon in fiery red-orange by the time Jax pulled into the place he called a "safe house." I wanted to scoff at the term. I'd yet to find a place that inspired a sense of safety. Even my own fucking island hadn't been safe. The engine fell silent, and I glanced over my shoulder at Alex's dozing form. She'd curled on the bench seat, one hand pillowing her cheek, yet her muscles hadn't given in to sleep yet. She was too rigid, too unrelaxed, and probably headed for another nightmare.

I sent a sideways glance at Jax. Dried blood lingered around his nose, and his right cheek was red from my fist. He had both hands locked on the steering wheel, eyes focused straight ahead. We hadn't said two words since we'd left Perrone's estate.

He claimed we were like brothers, and he *had* gotten us

out, even if it was several days too late. Fuck, he shouldn't have let them take us in the first place. I studied the profile of his face.

"You still don't trust me," he said.

"Kinda hard to."

"Cleft was my cousin, my fucking blood, and I shot him."

If he hadn't done what he'd done, Alex and I wouldn't be in this van with him. "Why'd you shoot him? I mean fuck. You didn't even hesitate."

He glanced at Alex in the rearview. "Let's go inside. Take care of her first and get some rest. We've got time to deal with shit."

"You're stalling."

"Maybe." He let out a breath, and it drifted through his hair. "But I think we could all use some rest. We won't have room for error when we go after my old man."

"You got a plan?"

"Possibly. Actually," he said, opening the driver's side door, "you gave me an idea back there, when you wanted to go all *Carrie* on the old man's estate."

He never referred to him as his father or dad. Always old man. Considering what Perrone was capable of, I guess I didn't blame him. I shoved my door open before sliding the back door to the side so I could reach Alex. She stirred but didn't wake.

Wedging my arms underneath her body, I lifted and cradled her against my chest. She wound her arms around my neck, mumbling something incoherent in her sleep. The fact that she felt safe enough to let her guard down blew my mind.

She trusted me with her life. But was she wise in trusting me with her heart?

Fuck, I hoped so.

Jax climbed the steps to the front porch of the small house nestled deep in the woods. The nearest highway was at least twenty miles away. We'd come in on a county road, then a long dirt driveway that seemed to go on forever. I wasn't sure I could find my way out of here, if I needed to, and that made me nervous. But at least it wouldn't be easy for others to find us...unless this was a trap.

Knock it off.

They'd had us right where they wanted us. If not for Jax busting us out, we'd still be locked in that dark underground hole, practically buried alive. Fuck, it sure had felt like it. I shivered at the thought, my pulse racing upon remembering the blackness, the dripping faucet...wait. There hadn't been a dripping faucet in that room. The pipes in the tunnel, yes, but not in that cell.

I hated this—the absence of memory. A piece of my identity was missing, hiding underneath the layers of my fucked up mind. Every now and again, a small nugget escaped and confused the heck out of me.

Jax handed me a key. "That's your copy. The place is already stocked, and the money's in the safe. Most of it is yours. I contributed what I could from working for your brother."

I shook my head as he jammed his key into the lock and turned the handle. "You've got a *lot* of explaining to do."

"I know."

Alex clutched my hair, and her warm breath breezed across my neck. "We here?" Her voice was heavy with sleep.

"Yeah, baby. We're here."

"I need a shower."

I wasn't surprised that was her first priority. She probably couldn't wait to wash off the memories of that place from her skin. Jax pointed down the hall. "There's two bedrooms, each has a bath. Yours is on the right."

I cast a glance around the place. The living room was tiny with a futon and matching chair. The kitchen seemed even dinkier on the other side of the bar that separated the space from the living area.

"Does any of this look familiar?" he asked.

None of it sparked a thing.

"No, sorry."

Why was I apologizing to him? He'd done so many fucked up things, yet at the very core of my being, I trusted him.

He headed toward the small kitchen, and I was tempted to follow, to demand he tell me what I wanted to know, but Alex needed me. She clung to my neck, as if loosening her grip would mean she'd crash to the floor and shatter.

I hesitated, indecision freezing my muscles. This was stupid. He'd busted us out. No one was coming to drag us back. We all just needed a little time to adjust.

Jax pulled a bottle of vodka down from a cupboard and parked his ass on a stool at the bar. He poured the clear liquid straight down his throat.

And that was that. He wanted to be alone with his bottle of misery.

Letting out a frustrated sigh, I ventured down the hallway, pushing the door on the right open with my foot. The bedroom was surprisingly spacious, considering the size of the rest of the house. A large king-sized bed, four posters and all, dominated the room. My gut clenched. Instinctively, I knew why that bed was important. No matter where we ended up, I'd always need a place to restrain her.

It was ingrained in me.

I set Alex on her feet, and her quick intake of breath told me she understood the significance too. She stepped forward and let the hoodie slide from her shoulders, forgotten on the hardwood floor. I spotted an ajar door to the left.

"Bathroom is that way." Placing a hand on the small of her bare back, I pushed her toward the one place she needed. The place where she could hide and let it all out, safe in the shower as the water washed away the last few days.

I searched the wall and switched on the soft light,
thankful it wasn't too bright. Our eyes had become accustomed to pitch-black. The sunlight today had been a
glaring ball of pain in my eyes.

The bathroom ran long and narrow, and a large tub sat
front and center. Alex backed into me, her breaths coming
in quick gasps.

I wound my arms around her midsection and nudged
her neck with my nose. "What is it?"

"I don't take baths."

"How come?"

She let out a half-laugh, half-snort. "I just don't."

I wanted to push for what she didn't say, because I was
sure she was keeping something to herself, but for now, I
let it slide. This whole day was surreal, especially this
moment as she stood naked in my arms, staring at a
bathtub as if it would jump out and drown her.

And that's when it hit me. Water.

I kept forgetting. I knew she couldn't swim, and I
remembered how fucking terrified she'd been when Zach
had pushed her into the pool when she was younger, but
I'd had no idea her fear extended to a simple tub of
water.

Then again, she'd found her mother dead in a bathtub.

Maybe I *had* known all of this. Maybe I'd even used it
against her. I'd definitely played on her fears by holding
her captive on the island.

"You're safe here. You don't have to use the tub. There's

a shower over there." I pointed around the corner, not sure how I knew, but I did.

We shuffled past the tub and turned, and sure enough, the nook opened into a shower stall. Alex crossed the threshold and turned on the water, but she didn't step into the spray.

"Do you wanna be alone?" I didn't want to leave her, but if she needed space, time on her own to process and let it out, I'd give it to her. Besides, I was itching to strangle answers from Jax. He needed to start talking, and people armed with booze tended to have loose lips.

"I don't want you to go." Her naked vulnerability gutted me.

Everyone coped with trauma in their own way—I knew that better than anyone. My psyche had chosen to block it from my mind. But shit, I wanted to be her rock, the one she clung to for support and safety. I wanted to puzzle over her pieces until I found where they fit.

Fuck, Jax could wait.

"Tell me what you need, baby."

"I just need you."

EIGHTEEN

ALEX

The spray of the shower sluiced over my skin. I closed my eyes, feeling his intense stare on my body, and let the water run over my head in hot rivulets, but nothing could wash away the blood. It clung to my mind, just like the musty scent of that tunnel burrowed several layers beneath my skin.

I slid to the tile, and my arms snaked around my knees. I couldn't bring myself to look at him. I wanted him to take the lead, to come inside and take me the way he should have in that fucking cell. I wanted him to take away the pain. I clawed my arms, chewed my lip, squeezed my eyes shut.

A zipper sounded, and clothing rustled. A soft thud landed by my feet before he slid to the floor behind me and dragged my ass to his groin. He engulfed me in the shelter of his arms and legs.

"Let it out, baby. Scream, cry, do whatever you need. Just let it out."

"I want to hurt myself."

He stiffened. "You're not fucking hurting yourself. I'm here. I've got you."

I grasped his arm and held on tightly. "I want you to fuck me."

"Alex," he warned.

"No!" I struggled against the cage of his body, but it was fruitless. He was too strong. Slumping against him, I sighed. "Stop holding back. You're scared, I get it. But I'm scared too. We're sitting in a shower naked, Rafe. You can't get any more intimate than this."

"Intimacy isn't what I'm worried about."

"We're gonna wake up tomorrow, or the day after, or whenever we can bear to crawl out of bed, but for right now, I just need you to *fuck me*."

"Why?" he whispered in my ear, his lips soft and warm and wet against my lobe.

"Only you can take it all away." Reaching behind me, I wedged a hand between us and rubbed his cock. Immediately, it sprang to life against my palm. He couldn't help but groan. I swirled my thumb over the head and spread the moisture collecting at the tip.

He pushed upright, bracing his back against the tile, and pulled me with him. He whirled me around, bringing us face to face, and shoved me against the opposite wall.

"I know you're hurting right now, probably in shock.

There's no easy way to get through what we've just escaped." He planted his hands on either side of my face, and his chest rose and fell quickly. "I want inside of you, but not tonight." He pushed away from the wall. "Tonight, I want you to crawl in bed and sleep as much as you need."

The burn of tears threatened, and panic bubbled up. I wasn't ready to let them out yet. Somehow, those hot, salty drops would make it all real. Cement it in history. I blinked, reaching out blindly, and planted my palms on his heaving chest, smoothing down his abs before lowering to my knees.

"Alex?"

The cold floor numbed my skin. "Let me do this," I whispered, my lips nearing his arousal. They'd forced us into this just days ago. Now, I needed to make a new memory. I slid my mouth over his tip, tongue laving the underside.

"Alex...fuck. I'm powerless here."

That was all the encouragement I needed. I impaled myself on his shaft then worked my way back down the length, my tongue circling the head before I pulled away with a *pop*. I clasped my hands at the small of my back and peered at him. "Take it back."

"Take what back, baby?" His fingers brushed my cheeks, slid into my hair, and pushed the soggy strands from my face.

"What they took. Take back control. It's yours, not theirs or Zach's. Only yours."

He tugged me toward him. "This is what you want?"

I wanted him to remember. I wanted him to unleash the beast inside him, the one that didn't give a shit about what I wanted. But I was also scared of him remembering. What if this soft side of him, the side I was falling even more in love with, completely disappeared? Was it too much to want the whole man?

"I want you. No, I *need* you. I don't care what's happened. That might sound heartless, but God...please, Rafe. Take it all away."

He let out a rough breath. "Then open your mouth."

"No."

"No?"

"Don't tell me what to do. *Make* me do it. You once told me that you had some fucked up fantasies. I want them. I want you to take what you need from me. I want you to strip me of everything so I can think of you and not that fucking dark place."

He tugged me by the hair, bringing my mouth to his cock, and nudged my lips. I pressed them together, wanting him to force his way in. He slid his tip along the seam of my lips before slapping my cheek in silent command, then he pushed against my tongue and made me hold still for several seconds. Warmth flooded the aching spot between my thighs, and my nipples hardened into tingling buds.

"Is this making you hot?" he asked in a breathless whisper.

My moan vibrated around his shaft, and he rammed all the way to my tonsils until I gagged uncontrollably. Pressing a hand on my throat, he massaged where his cock nestled.

The way his breathing filled the shower excited me, made me even wetter, and his raspy groans drove me up the wall in wanting him. He was so close to coming, just from having my mouth wrapped around him.

This was the part I craved, the reason I freely gave him the reins. In taking power, he was giving it back—in the way he dove over the edge at the touch of my mouth, the sensual slide of my tongue. In the way he took what he wanted, yet cherished the gift all the same.

He slipped out, then shoved in again. "I don't wanna come in your mouth," he said, words a hoarse plea colored by desperation. "I want inside you, your legs spread. I want you fucking begging for it." But his control snapped, and he pistoned his cock down my throat, each downward thrust bringing him closer to the point of no return. My gag reflex kicked in again, fueling his fire.

Rafe became an uncaged animal, his reservations tossed to the side, all sense of guilt forgotten. He fucked my mouth with abandon. My heart raced behind my breastbone, and I pulled air through my nose, willing my throat to relax under the onslaught of his cock.

"Oh fuck..." He pulled out and yanked me to my feet, and his mouth crashed onto mine, his tongue conquering, dividing my lips and demanding entrance.

I severed the connection, inching back as my rapid breaths fanned across his mouth, and wondered if he liked the taste of himself on my lips. "You didn't finish."

"Your mouth is fucking amazing, but it's not what I want." He lifted me, urged my legs around his waist, and water rained over us as he pushed me against the wall again.

Then he slammed into me, plunging so deep he reached the center of my soul. I clawed his shoulders, and the wantonness inside me unraveled as he stretched me, filled me.

With his body, his spirit, his whole being.

"God, Rafe," I said, lips teasing his earlobe. "You belong there. Don't ever leave me."

A moan caught in the back of his throat, and he fastened his mouth on mine again. He held me to the wall and sought control by seizing my wrists and raising them above my head. I tasted desperation on his tongue, and it zinged through my veins until I fought the band of his fingers.

I yanked my lips from his. "Let me touch you."

He freed my wrists and wrapped both hands around my neck. The action stunned him. I saw self-disgust in his eyes but also the overwhelming need to take my breath. This wasn't the gentle pressure of a few minutes ago, when he'd had his cock deep in my mouth. He wanted to choke me. I sensed it in the barely restrained energy emanating from his grip.

He hesitated, and I wondered which part of him would win the battle.

I fisted my hands and didn't move, even though I ached to run them through his soaked hair. Slowly, he moved inside me again, his thrusts the speed of a crawl as he flexed his fingers. Memory or not, the need to take my air was embedded in him.

"You can't break me," I whispered.

"But I want to." He leaned his forehead against mine and shuddered. "I want to make you beg for mercy, watch you shatter. Does that make me a monster, Alex? Does that make me no better than them? Than your brother?" He let up on my neck, and I placed my hands over his, urging him to squeeze harder.

"Get your hands back up there," he ordered.

The hard edge of his tone made me shiver. I extended my arms. "You *can't* break me. I need this from you. I need it because you need it."

"Sweetheart, once we open that can of worms, there's no going back." He gnawed on his lip, eyes narrowed, then dropped his head to my breasts—maybe to hide from me, or maybe because that's where he belonged.

Suddenly, I understood. His reluctance, his bullshit talk about right and wrong. It wasn't to protect me. It was to protect him.

"Fuck...you feel so good." He scraped my nipple with his teeth, darted his tongue out to tease, and I trembled from the hot, wet stroke of his mouth on my breast. "I could stay inside you forever. Just like this, Alex, with my hands around your neck, my cock buried deep in your cunt. Not moving *at all*."

I let out a restless whimper, my hips jutting forward uselessly. He had me pinned in place, unable to move. "Please..."

"Please what, baby?"

"Don't hold back." I swallowed under the firm weight of his grip.

"I'm not choking you," he said. His hands fell away, and he grabbed my ass before turning from the wall. We stumbled out of the shower, past the dreaded tub, and found our way to the bed with our mouths glued together. Water dripping all over the place, he pinned me to the mattress, and his cock owned me as he worked my body like it was made for him.

His thrusts were shallow, hitting the perfect spot at just the right rhythm, and he kept that pace up for what seemed like forever. I quaked underneath his powerful body as warmth pooled around his slippery cock. His name ripped free of my lips, but he forced his fingers into my mouth, pressed on my tongue, and stifled the sound as he plunged to the hilt. He buried his head in my shoulder and rumbled a groan along my skin.

I dug my feet into the mattress, widening for him, arching to meet his thrusts with muffled gasps. The fact that he'd gagged me with his fingers was a major turn-on.

The pressure built, turning me into a writhing animal, and holy fuck, the plummet stole my breath.

He removed his fingers and kissed me, his tongue battling mine, eating up my cries. I came undone, broke into pieces as my release poured from me, dampening the bedding on the last cresting wave.

He sank his teeth into my shoulder and smothered his own grunt of completion. By the time we both crashed, our limbs tangled in a sweaty mess, darkness had fallen over the room. He rolled to his back, taking me with him, and the moon filtering through the window illuminated our entwined bodies in the shadow of night. The lack of light didn't feel suffocating, and the walls weren't caving in like they had while locked in that cell. I placed my head on his chest and draped a leg over his, content to just be.

To doze.

To feel safe for the first time in forever.

"Why do you love me?" he asked, pulling me from the allure of sleep.

I opened my eyes and lazily traced a finger over his tattoo, following the dark tribal design toward his belly button. His muscles quivered under my touch, and one glance at his cock gave away his renewed desire. "What kind of question is that?"

"The kind of question I want an answer to."

I stalled my hand just below his belly button, and his sharp intake of breath thrilled me.

"I don't know why. Maybe it started out as a crush, like you said on the island." I lifted my head, and his fingers tunneled through my hair. "When I finally told you about Zach, you wanted to fight for me. You weren't disgusted or running away. You wanted to kill him for me. No one has ever cared that much. That's what I love about you. I love you for your strength, because I have none. I love you for the way you make me feel, because I feel nothing when I'm not with you."

"You're not weak. You're stronger than you give yourself credit for." He tugged me closer by the hair, his clutch a deep burn in my scalp, and brought my mouth to his.

"I love you," I whispered against his lips, "for wanting to make me hurt in the best ways possible."

"I've never said it, Alex."

"Said what?" My heart raced so fast, I thought my chest would rip in two.

"That I love you."

"You didn't have to."

"Because I wasn't sure that's what it was."

"But now you know?"

"Yeah," he said, his lips teasing mine for an instant before he pulled away enough to incinerate me with the heat in his eyes. "When you became more important to me than my own life, that's when I knew. And it makes no fucking sense because I have so few memories of the two of us together."

"Love doesn't have to make sense. It just is. Something

pulled us together. Maybe it was the darkness in each of us. Does it really matter?"

"No, sweetheart. It doesn't fucking matter. C'mere." He hoisted me on top of him and spread my thighs until I straddled his cock. "I'll never get enough of you. Ride me, baby. Fucking ride me."

NINETEEN

RAFE

"Did ya fuck her?" It was the first thing out of his mouth after I left Alex sleeping alone in the bedroom.

I stood on the threshold of the living room and folded my arms. Other than the light from the stove, darkness shrouded the space. Jax sat in the chair, shoulders hunched and the bottle of booze gripped in his hands, hanging between his knees. He'd blown through way too much of that shit already.

I stomped toward him, my bare feet vibrating the hardwood, and yanked the bottle from his hands. "You've had enough."

"Prob'ly so." He lifted an arm, dangled it like a zombie, and jabbed a finger in the air. "So did ya?"

"That's none of your business." Instead of dumping the

vodka down the drain, I plopped onto the futon and took a swig.

"You used to share shit with me," he said. "You used to be my friend."

I took another drink before setting the bottle on the floor with a loud thud. "Explain to me how a 'friend' sells you out to his psycho father to be killed?"

"I wasn't gonna let you die."

"Well that just makes it all better. Is this the part where we pretend you didn't let them torture Alex?"

Jax shrugged. "Girl's got kahunas. I knew she could handle it."

I squeezed my hands into fists, and it took everything in my power not to launch the few feet between us and throttle his pathetic neck. "She shouldn't have to handle anything. Aren't you at least a little sorry for what you did?"

"Yeah I'm fucking sorry." Jax bolted to his feet and veered sideways. He shot an arm out and steadied himself on the arm of the chair. "I didn't know she'd been abused. I didn't know shit because you didn't tell me any of it."

"I didn't remember any of it, until she told me." We were on a conversation merry-go-round.

"I'm talking about the island, before you lost your memory." He flopped back into the chair and ran his fingers through his hair. "She changed you, man." He raised his eyes and deep lines wrinkled his forehead. "You went from a fucking hard ass to a fucking pussy."

"Why are you mad at *me*? What am I missing, Jax?"

He let out a cold, bitter laugh. "You've gotten up close and personal with my family. Mom's dead, the old man will be dead if I can help it, my sister is—" His voice cracked. "You're all I got left."

Shit. Something about his tone tunneled beneath my anger. He didn't resemble a man. He looked like a lost little boy—the same boy who'd experienced a childhood of hell down in that tunnel.

"I'm listening. You got something to say, well say it. Tell me how all of this went down."

"Give me the bottle first." He reached across the coffee table, his leg knocking into the wood.

I almost fought him about the booze, but fuck, he was a grown man. If he wanted to get shit-faced, who was I to tell him he couldn't? Especially after all the shit we'd been through. I grasped the bottle by the neck and passed it to him. Besides, I needed to keep him talking.

He wrapped his mouth around the opening and tossed his head back, gulping down a long swig of the burning liquid. Wiping his lips with the back of a hand, he shoved the bottle between his legs and settled into the chair again.

"Me and Cleft got busted for sex trafficking. That's why I was serving time."

"Did I know this?"

He shook his head. "I didn't talk about my fucked up family. Nikki was the first person who pulled it out of me, and that's just because I got stupid drunk after you got shot." He blinked rapidly. "She didn't fucking believe me, so I thought, no harm, no foul." He dragged another drink from the bottle, liquid sloshing as he tipped it. "Guess she thought twice about it after the island went up in smoke. I got her killed. That's on me."

Nikki's death burned in my gut like an ember, threatening to flare into an inferno if I gave it the chance. I ground my teeth together, refusing to fall to pieces until after Perrone paid for what he'd done.

"That still doesn't tell me why your father took us, why he was out for my blood. They said I did something in prison. What happened? Just be straight with me. I can handle it."

"I was planning to take the whole organization down. Cleft's dad was already on the inside. He figured something was up, so he tried to kill me before I could talk. You stopped him."

"Wait a second...I beat the crap out of your uncle, so your family goes psycho on me for it? That doesn't make any sense."

He buried his head in his hands. "Can we not do this now? You really don't wanna hear this, trust me."

"Spit it out, Jax."

He raised his head. "You've had memory problems before. The infirmary docs thought it was from the concussions."

I sifted through my memories of my fighting days, but I couldn't recall more than two occasions where I'd had a concussion. I'd been cleared both times. "What concussions?"

"Guards were running a fight club. You were their favorite bet. Dude, it was brutal. You took some nasty beatings."

"I participated in unsanctioned fighting in there?" That didn't sound like me.

"Didn't have much choice." Jax rubbed his chin. "Guards used Cleft and his crew as enforcement. The rapes weren't stopping until you started fighting."

Holy fuck. No wonder I didn't want to remember any of this.

"That still doesn't explain why Perrone wanted me dead. C'mon, he's out for revenge because of a prison fight? What aren't you telling me?"

He sighed. "You thought it was a fight. Like I said— memory problems. Fuck, Rafe, you didn't want to remember."

"What are you saying?" But the implication dropped to the bottom of my stomach and formed a ball of dread. Some part of me, buried deep inside, already knew.

"You didn't beat the shit out of my uncle. You choked him to death."

I'd known what he was going to say, but those words banded around my chest anyway. I sucked in a breath, let it out in the space of five seconds. I'd had my hands around Alex's throat, tempted as fuck to steal her air while I fucked her.

What had I done?

"You had my back in there," Jax said. "You fucking saved my ass, man."

"But you sold me out."

"I did it for Tawny."

"Who's Tawny?" I asked, thinking back to our conversation in my cellar before all of this went down. "Is she the one that got away?

"Come again?"

"In my cellar, you said you had to let someone go."

"Tawny's my sister." He reached for the vodka again, and his gaze landed somewhere over my shoulder. "I was talking about you."

I blinked, fucking dumbfounded. Speechless.

"Yeah..." he said, letting out a breath that ruffled his hair. "You never did catch on about that. It's not that I'm averse to women—"

"Just their touch." That much, I remembered, and it still stunned me that I *knew* it, despite most everything else remaining a huge gaping blank.

"My old man tried *fixing* me when I was a teenager..."

I wasn't sure I wanted to hear more, but I remained quiet and waited for him to unload.

"He forced a few of the slaves on me. This one...shit, I'll never forget her. Sick bastard forced anal, and she was a fucking virgin." He shuddered. "I didn't actively partici-pate, just laid there like a pathetic wuss while they forced her onto my dick." He gritted his teeth, his whole face hardening in remembered horror. "It fucking hurt her like hell, but that didn't stop me from coming in her ass. I've never heard anyone scream the way she did. Sometimes, I swear I hear her still." He lifted the bottle to his lips again.

My gaze fell to his bare feet. The guy had been through some shit. "What happened to your sister?"

"My uncle wasn't the only one who knew something was up. Old man sold her after I went to prison. He suspected I was gonna turn state's evidence." Jax chewed on his lip. "He's dangled her location over my head ever since. Everything I've done...fuck man. It was you or my sister, and the only way he'd let me back into the underground was if I helped bring you in."

"Damn," I said, shaking my head. "What kind of bastard sells his own daughter? And why the fuck would you want back in?"

"I needed to find her. He keeps records of every girl he's sold. I had to believe he'd done the same with Tawny." A scowl darkened his face. "Cleft was her handler. He actually liked Tawny, protected her against the clients and their filthy wandering hands, but when it comes down to orders from the boss, they all scuttle."

"That why you killed him?"

"He had it coming."

I leaned forward, resting my elbows on my knees. "Did you find what you needed down there?" If he had, at least all of this wouldn't have been for nothing.

"No. I'm guessing he's keeping the info somewhere in

the mansion. Her file wasn't in the office with the others. That was my next step—finding a window of opportunity to search the estate—but after Nikki..." He dropped his head into his hands. "I couldn't do it anymore."

I wasn't about to tell him he was off the hook for Nikki's death. Some part of me still blamed him, would probably always blame him, but I could understand the spot he'd been in.

He lifted his head. "There's more, Rafe." He paused long enough to rub his palms down his face. "Nikki has... had a son."

"I know."

His eyes widened.

"After what happened in that room, it came back to me. I don't remember details, just that she had a son and he's mine. You don't think he'd hurt an innocent kid?" Even as the words left my mouth, I realized how ridiculous they sounded. Perrone had ruined his son and sold his daughter into sexual slavery. The man was the devil.

"He doesn't know he's yours," he said. "I checked on Will after Nikki—"

"Will?" I asked, my heart pounding an erratic rhythm in my chest.

"The kid's name."

"My middle name."

He nodded. "He's with Nikki's parents."

I rose and paced the length of the futon, both hands pulling at my hair. "Your bastard father is gonna pay for all of this. We've gotta bring him down." Perrone had ruined so many lives, including the lives of his children. But he'd fucked up by killing Nikki. He'd fucked up by bringing Alex into it.

He'd messed with the wrong motherfucker.

TWENTY

ALEX

As I pulled the rolls from the oven, I blatantly eavesdropped on the tense conversation coming from the living room. Rafe and Jax had turned the television on low, but their voices rose above the white noise of the news.

"This is seriously whacked," Jax said. "It's risky, might even get us killed...but it could work."

"Assuming he hasn't already cleared the tunnel."

"Doubtful. He thinks he's invincible." Jax scowled. "He's got so many guys in his pocket, I'm surprised he has room for anything else. But that does present a problem. We can't call in the cops to catch those assholes when they leave the tunnel."

Rafe jerked his hand out. "Give me your cell."

"What?"

"Your cell," he said. "I know you have one."

Jax dug into his pocket. "Who're you calling?"

"Lyle Fucking Lewis. You said Nik's body is out there somewhere in the woods, right?"

"They've got a dumping spot, but I don't know where it is."

"Lyle was going to marry Nikki. I don't trust him to spit right, but he's always had a weak spot for her. Hopefully he'll be good for something besides wasting space in the sheriff's station."

"You're twisted, man, calling in your enemy as the cavalry."

"I don't see what choice we have. There's no telling how many cops your father has on his payroll, but I doubt he's got the sheriff of Dante's Pass in his fucking pocket. And like I said, Lyle has a personal stake in this—he just doesn't know it yet."

Rafe dialed information before stepping outside to make the call.

Chili simmered on the stovetop. Cook dinner, he'd said. He had a monster to take down and slaves to free.

How was this our life?

My belly in knots, I knew I wouldn't be able to stomach the food, so I dished up two bowls and carried them to the table. "Food's ready."

Jax scraped a chair across the floor and sat down. He grabbed an apple from the fruit bowl and pulled out a pocketknife to slice it. My attention lingered on that knife, on the blade slicing through the proverbial forbidden fruit.

I envied that apple.

Rafe entered the room, startling me from my fixation on the knife, though the image stuck to my brain like crazy glue. He joined Jax at the table.

"You get him on the phone?"

Sliding the cell across the table, Rafe nodded.

"That must have been an interesting conversation."

"Kept it short and anonymous. I told him I had info on Nikki, and if he wanted to know more, he'd better wait for a call tomorrow and have some of his guys ready 'cause something's going down." Rafe absently pulled the bowl of chili closer. "Trust me. He'll be on his toes waiting."

I set the rolls on the table, and a chill traveled down my spine at the mention of Nikki. She'd been Rafe's girlfriend at one point, and now she was dead.

Because of my lie.

I went to move away, but Rafe grabbed my arm.

"Aren't you eating?" His gaze swerved between the food and me.

"I'm not hungry."

Shaking his head, Jax let out a low whistle. "She's anorexic, man."

"What?" Rafe bolted upright, and I shrank back, pulling from his grasp. His expression softened, and he reached out a hand. "C'mere. I'm not gonna hurt you. I was just caught off guard and..."

"Angry with me."

He grabbed me around the waist and sat back down,

planting my ass on his lap. "Why would you do that to yourself?"

"I didn't," I said, but Jax snorted. I shot him a glare. "You think you know all about me, but you don't."

He held his hands up. "If you say so."

I returned my attention to Rafe. "After what happened with Zach, my dad admitted he'd manipulated me into believing I had a problem with anorexia. Some people stress-eat. I do the opposite."

"Why would he do that?"

"To protect Zach, I guess. He made me think I was sick so he could shut me away in a treatment center."

Rafe pushed his bowl away. "I'm not eating until you do. How's that for manipulation?"

"I told you, I don't—"

"Your father is an ass. He probably did play you, but that doesn't change the fact that you need to eat. You're not starving yourself under my watch." He raised an eyebrow. "I've said that before, haven't I?"

"Sort of, yeah."

He closed his eyes for a moment. "That's why I made you eat off the floor."

My breath caught in my throat. His memories were slowly trickling in, and the idea of him regaining those missing years excited and scared me in equal amounts. I slid from his lap. "I'll fix myself a bowl."

"Good girl." He smacked my ass. Hard.

I peeked over my shoulder, expecting to find a teasing

grin curving his mouth. Instead I found the glint of dark temptation dilating his pupils. His green eyes were a deep jade. I recognized that look. I hadn't seen it in a while, but that right there was the guy who'd bent me backwards on the island. The man who'd promised pain, indefinite imprisonment, and a thirst for my tears.

Swallowing hard, I scooped some chili into a bowl as he and Jax returned to debating the best way to break into Lucas' estate without setting off the alarms.

On my way back to the table, the image of my father's face on TV froze me. The newscaster's lips moved, but I couldn't hear what she was saying. I moved across the room and flipped up the volume.

"...was arrested on charges of corporate conspiracy and embezzlement. Authorities say De Luca—"

"That's another example of the old man's power," Jax said, pointing toward the TV. "He learned De Luca paid off a judge in your trial, so he went after him too. He's been planning his downfall from the beginning."

I stared in shock at the image of my father's face. "That's why Lucas wormed his way into the business, got on my dad's good side...wanted to marry me? To ruin us?"

Jax didn't answer, but he didn't have to.

Rafe cursed under his breath. "Abbott's arrest is the only good thing that came out of this." He crossed the space between us and tilted my chin up, forcing me to meet his eyes. "Your father can't hurt you anymore, and once I find Zach, he won't be a threat either." His mouth formed a determined line.

"No." The idea of Rafe going after my brother terrified me. The moment Zach shot him replayed in my mind. Rafe had lost his memory because of what happened that night. We'd both lost so much. "Let's just get far away from here. I don't want you going after Zach."

I didn't want him going after Jax's father either, but I understood why they needed to do it. Those women were still prisoners, their whole lives spreading before them, just out of reach because sick and perverted men saw them as nothing more than possessions.

"Where's this coming from?" Rafe asked. "After everything that happened, you know as well as I do that Zach won't give up. Don't you want him to pay for what he did?" He narrowed his eyes. "Or is it something more? You feel something for him?"

"No!" I blinked, fighting tears. "He shot you. I just...I can't—"

The newscaster's voice interrupted, and we both focused our attention on the TV at the mention of Mason Vineyards.

"A devastating fire broke out at Mason Vineyards early this morning. It's not clear yet if the fire was accidental, according to Deputy Fire Chief Stanton, who says his department is still investigating. There were no reported deaths from the fire..."

The bowl of chili slipped from my fingers and cracked at my feet. Rafe sank into the chair and buried his head in his hands. Jax shut off the TV, and the silence that tore through the room disturbed me on such a deep level, I wanted to scream just to break it. I lowered to my haunches and placed my hands on his knees.

"I'm sorry."

He looked up, his eyes tired and defeated. "They already burned the island, and now the vineyard. Perrone is systematically destroying my family's legacy." My hands fell away as he stood.

He began pacing, but Jax gripped his shoulder. "And tomorrow, we're gonna destroy my legacy."

TWENTY-ONE

ALEX

Rafe's soft snores should have offered me comfort. They assured me he was beside me, alive. Breathing. Still with me. But it wasn't enough. Everything pressed on me too heavily—the destruction of Mason Vineyards, my dad's arrest, Rafe and Jax planning to go after Lucas.

The turmoil inside me was a beast, its teeth gnawing from the inside, claws scratching to get free. I'd conditioned myself to keep my eyes dry for years, even while Zach thrust his cock into every part of me. Especially then. I'd learned to deal with emotions another way.

It was unhealthy and abnormal, but causing pain was the only way I knew to dampen the clutch of the beast inside me that stole my breath and turned my chest into a pressure cooker. Pain brought a blessed sigh of relief as my skin tingled and burned. It was like a drug. I caught a whiff of my next fix now, except gouging flesh with the sharp edge of my fingernails wouldn't be enough this time.

I couldn't unglue my mind from Jax slicing into that apple with a blade.

Slipping from bed, I made my way quietly into the bathroom, shut the door, and switched on the light. The mirror above the sink whispered to me, and I stared at the damage Zach had done to my abdomen. I craved the sting, craved the sharp bite of a blade drawing a line of crimson. I wanted red to wipe away those carved letters, thirsted for the subsequent relief that would follow the cut.

I wanted the death of his fucking name.

Spurned on by the need raging in my blood, I switched off the light and left the bathroom, my bare feet padding across the hardwood toward the hall. I cracked open the door and waited a few seconds, listening.

Rafe's breathing continued, uninterrupted.

I crept toward the kitchen with soundless steps, navigating through the shadows of night, and prayed Jax wouldn't find me wandering the house naked. My blood begged to be spilled, cried from within my veins, an accomplice of the ever-thirsty beast that possessed me. I pulled a drawer open and grabbed the biggest butcher knife I could find, then I tiptoed back to the bathroom, praying I wouldn't wake Rafe.

I had to do this, *needed* it with a driving force I barely grasped, so how could I expect him to understand it? No doubt, he'd be furious, and this would probably hurt him as much as me, if not more, but that didn't stop me from shutting myself in the bathroom and slicing down my stomach, right through the *A* in Zach's name. I closed my eyes and sighed as the sting radiated from that spot, breathed easy for a few glorious moments when reality narrowed to the pain and overshadowed the hollow ache in my chest.

Yet the tears still wouldn't come. I needed more. *More, more, more.*

Teeth grinding, I slashed again, this time horizontally through every single letter. My fingers shook around the handle, knuckles whitening from holding it so tightly, and I used my free hand to smear the blood. Finally, hot and bitter drops fell from my eyes, one after the other in an endless stream that fed the beast.

Like a finger painting, the red obscured Zach's name, though it still weighed heavily on my skin, a constant reminder that he'd always be with me no matter how far I ran from his memory. No matter how much time passed and the rest of me healed.

Letting out a sob, I sliced again...again and again and again. God, it wasn't enough. I might be erasing Zach, but what about everything else? The days spent in the dark with Rafe, certain we were going to die? I couldn't breathe, but I didn't want to halt the ambush of sorrow flowing down my face in rivulets of shame either. My lids shuttered, and I embraced the release, cherished the thrill of power I got from that blade.

A fist clamped around my wrist, and my eyes flew open. Rafe squeezed hard until I involuntarily dropped the knife. Through the chaos barreling through my being, I had trouble registering his presence, or what the tick in his jaw meant.

His hooded gaze pinned mine by way of our reflections in the mirror until he spun me around to face him. He wrenched my arms behind me and held my wrists together. Something sparked alive in my veins, trilled deliciously in my ears.

"Don't move an inch."

With a quick nod, I swallowed hard. He slowly let go of my hands, framed my cheeks with warm palms, and kissed the tears from my face.

"Why are you in here unraveling on your own?" His tongue darted out and caught another drop.

"I don't know." I forced the words beyond the lump in my throat. "I need the pain. I need his name gone. I need it all gone."

Letting go of me, he opened the medicine cabinet. Neither of us spoke as he cleaned up the blood. I stood, my hands clasped behind me, while he applied antibiotic ointment and taped a bandage over the reddening slashes.

"At least you didn't slash too deep." He stood back, arms falling to his sides, and I burned under his fierce scrutiny. "You could've really hurt yourself. There are other ways to remove his name, Alex. Cosmetic surgery, ink. This isn't the way."

"I'm sorry." I bit my lip, my cheeks flaming. His disappointment stung.

"I won't let you self-destruct, so you've only got one option. You're gonna let it out right now. All of it."

I shook my head, eyes downcast.

He gripped my shoulder and pushed me from the bathroom. My heartbeat raced as the shadows reached from the corners of the room, threatening to choke me, but I wasn't afraid. Not while Rafe was with me, his body warm and steady at my back. The strength in his capable grip grounded me.

He pushed me toward the bed. "Bend over the end."

I tumbled onto the bed, palms bracing myself, and laid my cheek on the soft comforter.

His determined steps thumped across the floor. He didn't have to tell me not to move as he rifled through the dresser drawers, his back to me, body cast in silhouette. We both knew I wasn't going anywhere. He pulled out a belt and moved toward me, the thick strap of leather looped in his fist, ready to unleash punishment.

A drift of cool air blasted my backside as he stepped behind me, out of sight. I drew in a quick breath, preparing for the jolt of pain I knew was coming.

"If you need me to stop, tell me, okay?"

The pressure built in my chest again, and the sting in my eyes became unbearable, so I squeezed them shut. "Make it hurt."

"Why?" His voice cracked, his anguish and confusion

bleeding through that single word. "God, Alex. I've got a fucking hard-on from hell right now. The thought of hurting you shouldn't do this to me. I don't understand why you need it, why I do."

"Then don't question it."

His rapid breaths filled my ears. "Don't you ever cut yourself again." The strap of leather bit into my ass with a harsh *crack*.

I jerked upright with a cry, my legs quaking from the force of the strike. He shoved me back to the mattress with a firm hand, and another lash landed on my ass, as unforgiving as the first.

Panting, I cursed the heat igniting between my thighs and pressed them together, waiting for the next strike.

"Don't hide from me. Spread your legs."

I groaned but did as instructed, certain my arousal was on full display, despite the cloak of shadows from nighttime. He shifted, pushing a draft of cool air toward my core, and trailed the belt down my back, tickling my spine. Gooseflesh broke out on my skin, and shivers wracked my body as he dragged the leather between my ass cheeks.

"Do you want more?"

"Yes."

"I won't strike you again until you tell me what you're getting from this."

I opened my mouth but couldn't find an explanation. The silence, along with the loss of each second, coalesced into a standoff. "Please, Rafe."

"You can beg all you want." His finger slid through my wetness, dragging it to my clit, and I groaned. "I'm not giving you more until you tell me why pain does this to you."

"It's not just the pain. It's..." I clenched my teeth, despising myself for being so weak as I moved against his finger. "It's the loss of control. It's knowing you'll take care of me, even if it's all on your terms. The pain...is a painkiller."

Inserting a finger inside me, he brushed his lips at the small of my back, and his need for me puffed out in hot breaths that moistened my skin. He slipped another finger in, eliciting a moan, and increased the tempo. My hips bucked recklessly, my cries escalating with each forceful plunder. I arched my back, on the verge of convulsing around his fingers.

Abruptly, he stepped back, and the cruel bite of his belt stole my breath. I gasped, air suspended in my lungs, legs trembling. I closed my thighs again, and he blasted the leather even harder on my ass.

"Wide open, sweetheart."

The endearment hit the most vulnerable part of my being, and I cried out something unintelligible. Holy hell, I was burning.

"More?" he asked, his voice a low growl.

"More," I groaned.

Crack!

I wailed louder with each lashing, and something

inside me finally broke free. He hit me until my eyes willingly bled the pain from my soul, until I could breathe again without the pressure crushing my heart.

"That's it, baby. Just let it out."

He placed the belt on the bed then gathered my wrists in his huge hand. He caged me with his body, his chest rubbing my skin, the heat of his thighs irritating my stinging ass. He wound my hair around a fist and tilted my face toward his. And he just kissed me. Long and slow, with the kind of patience I didn't share because the throb between my legs was the most unbearable type of pain possible.

"I need you," I said.

He jerked my head back, pulling tight on my scalp. "Every time you self-destruct, I'm gonna make you ache here." He let go of my hair and slid his hand between my thighs to cup me. "I'll make damn sure you hurt here until you're out of your fucking mind."

"Please..."

"You will *never* pull the bullshit you just did again, do you understand me?"

All I could manage was a whimper.

"I expect an answer."

"Yes."

He kissed me again, his moan of desire lost on our tongues. "You have no idea how badly I want to fuck you right now." He let go of my wrists and stood back. "Turn over."

I flopped to my back, a pulse of excitement zapping straight to my core.

"Remember this, Alex. When you punish yourself, you punish me too. I want inside you so fucking much right now, but it's not happening." His words washed over me like a tidal wave of disappointment I should have seen coming.

"Why?"

His gaze fell to the bandage hiding the ugliness on my abdomen, and my skin blazed with renewed shame. "Spread your legs."

I parted my thighs, my breath catching, and sensed him reeling me in.

TWENTY-TWO

RAFE

er legs parted before my eyes like an unwrapped present. She was in the perfect position; round ass, still red from my belt, practically kissing the edge of the mattress, and her thighs unabashedly spread wide, pussy glistening in tempting beauty. She sprawled there—opening her heart, body, soul —with her hair fanning her face in a sea of dark curls. I dropped to my knees and lapped up her juices, sucked her swollen clit into my mouth, prepared to lick her until she moaned like a slut.

She panted, holding it in, but I wasn't about to let her. She was going to wail my name, writhe against my tongue, and beg until she couldn't beg anymore.

Fucking hell, I was lost.

I dipped my fingers inside her and flicked my tongue over her clit in a way I knew would drive her mad. She bucked, ass rising several inches off the bed, and I smiled against her cunt. She let out a shrieking plea, but I rose to my feet before she had the chance to tip over the edge. Leaning over her, I grabbed my belt, thighs pressing into the mattress, and the heat of her skin seared through me. I stared into her eyes—two green orbs that held so much trust—and my hands trembled.

"You know I'd never hurt you, right?"

She nodded.

I lifted her head, wound my belt around her neck, and jerked the leather strap, bringing the back of her skull flush with the mattress. Her mouth formed a surprised O. I couldn't resist claiming her lips. She jutted her face forward, trying to deepen the kiss, but I yanked the belt and held her down.

"No," I said, fists gouging the bed to hold me upright. "You're gonna lay here and take what I give you." I plunged my tongue into her mouth and battled hers into submission. "Touch yourself for me."

With a breathless cry, she reached between us and obeyed. My cock brushed the back of her frantic hand. She worked her fingers over her clit so fast, the motion rivaled a vibrator. Whimpers sounded in the back of her throat, and her breasts heaved, nipples pebbling against my chest.

"Alex," I whispered, my lips trailing across her cheekbone to her ear. "Do you want me inside you?"

"Mmm-hmm."

"You aren't getting my cock."

She let out an adorable growl, and her hand stilled. "Then why am I touching myself?"

"Because I told you to." I inched back, keeping a firm grasp on the belt. I wanted to wrap my hands around her neck, but I didn't trust myself with that responsibility yet, especially after the things Jax had told me.

"That's enough. Hands above your head." With a groan, she raised her arms again. I overpowered her with the sheer size of my body and settled between her legs, and she eyed my cock as if it were a prize, her tits heaving, tongue darting out to wet her lips. She'd gladly take me in her mouth, and holy hell how I wanted to sink inside that wet, hot place and lose myself. But not if it gave her any satisfaction. I had the job of protecting her, whether she liked it or not.

I folded my fist around the base of my dick and slowly ran up the length, watching her reaction. "Do *not* move your hands." I leaned toward her mound, as if I were about to sink inside her, but pumped my cock instead, the tip just inches from her drenched opening.

"Rafe?"

"Shut up and watch me."

She pressed her lips together, and I worked my shaft, overcome with the need to connect with her in a way other than intense eye contact. I wanted to shove my cock in every part of her—her mouth, cunt...her tight little ass.

I wanted to own her body, command her mind, and make her drunk off me. Shame flushed my skin, swift and hot. I shouldn't want any of that—she shouldn't want any of that. Maybe we were both beyond screwed up. Maybe I should just give in because we couldn't go back after all the shit we'd been through together. Maybe I should say to hell with it, sink inside her, and lose my fucking mind.

Or maybe I should just choke the fuck out of her.

A strangled cry escaped my mouth, and I closed my eyes. Thick cum coated my shaft. I was so close, driven by the need inside me, by the images hurtling through my head of her fighting me, nails digging into my skin, my name tearing from her lips in a silent scream as I took her air.

"Rafe, stop shutting me out. Look at me."

If I looked at her now, I'd be a goner. My lips tightened, spreading over my teeth, and I groaned—long, hard, guttural—as I spilled onto her mound. The release was so powerful it pulled me under for a few seconds, and my grasp on the belt slipped.

She veered up, pushing against my chest, and licked my shaft with a greedy tongue. My eyes shot open, and she returned my stare, her gaze huge and round and never fucking leaving my face. I thought I was punishing her by withholding, by making her watch me get off on my own, but I'd underestimated her conniving prowess. It was hard to punish someone whose only aim in life was to please.

I yanked her head back to the bed, gripping the leather strap tight, and pushed her dainty fingers between her legs again. "See what you did? You wear my cum like a fucking prize, Alex."

She pressed a finger over her clit and furrowed a brow. "You're still angry with me."

"Damn right I'm angry with you. You drive me fucking crazy." I slapped her thigh. "Tell me why you're being punished."

She moaned, her hand stalling on her clit, and thrashed her head back and forth. A wayward curl fell across her forehead. "I hurt myself."

"Not just yourself. It kills me to see you like that." Anger burned through my chest until I shook with it, but I wasn't really angry at her—I was angry that she felt the need to harm herself.

I was angry that I had to leave her tomorrow in order to keep her safe. She was going to be pissed when she realized I wasn't bringing her with me. Keeping her far away from Perrone was my top priority, but now she'd given me a new problem to face.

How could I leave her alone, even for a few hours, while Jax and I put our plan into motion? What if she went fucking slice happy on her skin again?

Shit. I'd have to restrain her.

"Alex..." With a sigh, I dropped my head between her tits and slid my hand over hers, into the mixture of our desire for each other. "The next time you feel like you're gonna break, come to me. I'll help you break, baby, then

I'll put you back together afterward." I lifted my head. "No more hiding."

Her lower lip trembled, and she pulled it between her teeth.

"Say it, Alex."

"No more hiding. I'll come to you. I promise."

TWENTY-THREE

RAFE

The stench of tobacco ruined the crispness of approaching dawn, though considering what Jax and I were about to do, I wasn't going to tell him to snuff out his cigarette.

"She cut herself last night." I rubbed my arms for warmth. Birds chirped an annoying morning song of delight, and I wished for a fucking pellet gun.

Jax took a drag from his cancer stick, and his lips rounded as he blew it out into the chilly morning air, creating rings. "Did you put a stop to it?"

"Fuck yeah, I shut it down." I frowned. "Probably went too soft on her."

"How'd you handle it?"

"Took my belt to her ass. Withheld orgasm."

He snickered around another drag. "From what I remember, that works on her."

I gave him a funny look. "How close were you to that fucked up situation on the island?"

"Not as close as you're thinking. I was busy juggling work and the old man's demands. But like I said, you and I used to talk. You told me things."

"Fuck, Jax, when I saw her slicing herself up...I can't fuck this up."

"You'll get there. You guys are still figuring shit out."

"Yeah, well this latest disaster is creating a new problem. I don't trust her to leave her alone. Not so soon after what happened."

"Sounds like a simple fix to me. You rigged that bedroom to restrain her. Check underneath the end of the bed."

I arched a brow. "Why'd we get this place?"

"In case shit went to hell on the island. I kinda pushed for it. You couldn't see past imprisoning her on that island. Talk about single-minded focus."

That seemed to be my problem when it came to her. Even back when she was fifteen, before I'd gone to prison, I couldn't go near the De Luca mansion without my head getting stuck on the seductively forbidden jailbait of Alex fucking De Luca.

How ironic I'd gone away for something I hadn't yet done. My pulse skyrocketed. Maybe I'd deserved that prison sentence. Eventually, I would have crossed the line.

Probably.

Definitely.

"Check under the bed, man. Do it before she wakes up. It'll make things easier." He reached for the doorknob. "We need to get going soon. Bastard never misses his morning jog. It's fucking clockwork."

"You don't think he allowed access to any of the other guys?"

"Not a chance." He chewed on his lip. "He allows very few people inside the estate, and now with Cleft gone..."

Now he had a chance to get inside, unobstructed, in hopes of finding his sister's whereabouts.

We entered the shadowed house, and I padded down the hall, hoping Alex hadn't awakened yet. Considering her late night date with a knife, and the subsequent lashing and sexual mind-fuck I'd put on her, I expected to find her out cold for at least another hour. The sun had barely crawled an inch above the horizon.

So I was caught off guard when I found her by the window, arms folded around her body as if she could ward off the next attack with sheer willpower alone. It would take a while before she believed no one was coming to hurt her. Perrone and the rest of his men would pay for what they'd done, and Jax and I would free those slaves today.

The real question though, was how far was I willing to go?

Gawking at Alex's nude form, cast in silhouette in front of the window, I knew I'd go to the blazing pits of Lucifer's den to ensure her safety, to give her peace of mind in knowing Lucas Perrone would never threaten her again.

I crossed to the bed and bent to search underneath, where I found a hook in the floor and a coiled chain attached. Despite my quiet presence, she didn't stir from her stance. I sank to the hardwood and reached behind me, curling my fingers around a shackle.

"Alex?" God, how I wanted to wrap her in my arms and never let go. I'd failed her. No one should have to go through what she'd been through, the horrors she'd experienced, beginning with her own brother at the age of thirteen. But knowing what had happened to her all those years ago was vastly different from witnessing those bastards trying to break her.

How the fuck was I supposed to deal with that? How was she?

Maybe that was the problem. Neither one of us knew how to get beyond this. She'd finally let it out last night, but at what cost? More scars on her skin.

"Alex," I said again.

She jumped, as if my voice was just now registering. "Sorry...I was thinking."

"C'mere." I patted the floor next to me. "What's on your mind?"

Her feet glided across the hardwood, and she lowered next to me. "You."

"What about me?"

"The way you made me feel last night. You helped me breathe, Rafe."

"I left you fucking aroused as hell."

"That part I'm not thrilled about, but the rest of it..."

"Sweetheart," I said, pulling her to me so our mouths hovered close together, "then don't piss me off again."

Her breath escaped in a moist whisper against my lips. "Why are we sitting on the floor?"

"Give me your ankle, baby."

"Why?"

"Don't question or argue. Just do it."

She scooted her butt and rested her foot in my lap. I pulled the shackle from underneath the bed, and she tried yanking away, but I held firm and locked the metal around her ankle.

"What's that for?" Her voice shook, and she glanced around us, eyes wide.

"To keep you safe." I jumped to my feet and headed toward the bathroom. The chain slid along the floor as she followed, and my fucking cock wanted out to play.

Damn. Chaining her up was a turn-on.

Before she could enter behind me, I slammed the door and locked it. Her fists pounded on the wood, her voice high-pitched with frantic questions. I ignored them, and for the moment, I ignored her.

Taking stock of the bathroom, I began by studying the mirror. If she broke it, she might try to slit her wrists like she had in that cabin, when Zach had taken her.

I shook my head, letting out a long breath. I didn't think she'd do it. She loved me, was happy here with me, but something had set her off last night. I didn't want to chance her doing something stupid while Jax and I were gone. I grabbed the plunger, turned it around, and used the handle to break the mirror. The pieces fell into the sink, and a few chunks dropped to the floor.

The pounding on the door grew in intensity.

Grabbing the wastebasket, I carefully picked up the glass and tossed the pieces into the trash. Next, I searched the medicine cabinet and drawers for anything she could use against herself. The razors went the way of the mirror. The tub was the only danger left, but I couldn't see her drowning herself. She was too terrified of water. Besides, I didn't think she was suicidal, just unpredictable when it came to coping.

Satisfied the bathroom was safe, I unlocked the door, yanked it open, and squeezed past her. She pitter-pattered after me, on my heels as I carried the trashcan toward the hall.

"Please don't go," she said. "I need you. Let's just run away and leave this place."

The chain stopped her from pursuing me, and she let out a curse. I entered the kitchen and dumped the glass and razors into the trash. Jax raised a brow, one corner of his mouth curving up in a smirk. A cup of coffee steamed between his hands. "I knew your badass self was still in there somewhere."

"Shut up," I said as I grabbed some granola bars and a few other food items to get her by for a few hours.

Jax's laugh carried into the hall, and I shut the door, silencing his know-it-all attitude. She sat on the bed, the picture of defeat, though her eyes spit fire at me. I set the food on the dresser, along with Jax's cell.

"I'm only leaving the phone in case of an emergency."

"You mean in case you don't come back."

"I *will* come back, Alex. But if it takes longer, or..."

"I get it. You want me to be safe. It's always about that, isn't it?" She lifted her foot. "Hence the fucking leash." She drew in a deep breath. "If I never see another chain again, it'll be too soon."

"I'm sorry, baby." I crawled onto the bed, but she turned her head away.

Grabbing her chin, I forced her mouth my way and captured her lips. She turned to liquid in my arms, her body sinking into the bed under me. I followed, my hands and knees depressing the mattress on either side of her. She brought a leg up and flung it over my back, and the chain clinked through the devious parts of my mind.

I nibbled her lips, lowered to her tits and caught a nipple between my teeth. She cried out, and her fingers gripped my shoulders, holding me to her.

"Stay with me. Please, Rafe. I have a bad feeling. Every time we think things are gonna get better, something bad happens."

"Not this time." I inched down her body, lowering

between her legs, and buried my face in her pussy. I fucking made her forget everything—what Jax and I were about to do, how I was going to leave her chained to my bed. I made her forget her own name because she was too busy crying out mine.

I glided my tongue between her folds, my fingers working her cunt, and she shuddered, muscles spasming as the orgasm claimed her. I sat up and licked my lips. "That was me saying I'm sorry." Before she could stop me, I slipped from bed and spanned the distance to the door.

"I'll never forgive you for this!" She threw a pillow at my head, but I easily dodged it and tossed it back.

"Yes you will. Our whole fucking existence is based on forgiveness. I love you," I said, pulling the door open. "See you soon."

TWENTY-FOUR

RAFE

Nothing bad would happen this time. I kept picturing Alex, her face bunched in fury at the way I'd manhandled her, though desolation had lurked underneath her ire.

I had to make it back to her. I *had* to.

"Having second thoughts, man?" Jax asked as he hammered on the padlock that blocked our way into the crawl space. To avoid tripping the alarm, we'd chosen to break into the estate by way of the passage Jax said led to the basement.

"Third and fourths too." I shook my head and sighed. "Let's just do this."

Any way we looked at it, getting those women out of there wouldn't be easy. Breaking into the tunnel would put them at risk, since Perrone's men outnumbered us, and calling the cops carried a whole other set of problems—mainly that we didn't know who Perrone had in his pocket.

"How much time do we have again?" I asked, shuffling my feet. Jax wanted to find info on his sister, and I wanted him to find what he needed.

"Maybe thirty minutes."

"That's shit for time."

"Tell me about it. Old man's runs are getting shorter." He hacked at the lock some more. "I was clocking his jogs before I busted you guys out, but getting past Cleft was a different matter." Jax finally broke the lock and lifted the door to the crawl space. A black square of nothingness faced us. Shit, I hated the thought of squeezing through that tight space.

Jax fell to all fours and disappeared inside. I followed suit, batting away cobwebs, and tried not to let the dark get to me.

"This seemed much bigger when I was eight." Jax slowed and aimed his flashlight above. A square hatch called from overhead, whispering for us to shove it open and escape this claustrophobic grave. "Here, shine this up there, would ya?" He handed the light to me.

I aimed the beam upward while he pushed against the hatch, his face straining.

"Shit," he said, slumping. "I'm positive this end wasn't locked."

Didn't mean Perrone hadn't secured it since we'd escaped.

Jax tried again, and the door finally creaked. Dust rained down and covered his face. He shook his head until his shaggy hair fell into his eyes. Brushing it aside, he threw his shoulder into the hatch and lifted, and it slammed to the floor of the basement with a vibrating thud. More dirt fell on us.

Jax disappeared into the opening, then he popped his head back through. "Bring in the cans, would ya?"

"Yeah, sure." I scooted backward through the passage and touched down on the hard earth behind the estate. We'd hauled in four cans of gasoline, and they sat untouched, lined up against the side of the mansion. I slid them forward through the space, scraping over rock and dirt.

Jax lifted them one by one into the basement, and I hefted my body through the opening and dropped to the cold cement. I didn't like that we were so fucking close to that tunnel. I eyed the door hiding the staircase, and for an insane moment I imagined someone bursting through and dragging me back.

Imagined Alex still down there, chained in their torture room, her flesh taking the brunt force of Brock's whip.

No. I had to keep my head in the game. Alex was safe, chained to my fucking bed like the temptress she was. The sooner we finished this, the sooner I could get back to her.

Jax headed toward the door leading upstairs, and I tailed him, following his lead as we made our way to the main floor. Early morning sunlight gleamed off the counters in the kitchen. I checked to make sure the gun was still jammed into the waistband of my jeans.

He shot me a worried look. "You sure you can handle this?"

Murdering Lucas Perrone in cold blood? Not really, but I wasn't about to back down. He'd destroyed too many lives, and I didn't hold out much hope that law enforcement would dole out justice. He probably had judges in his pocket, in addition to cops.

"You don't have to watch," Jax said. "I've been waiting for this day for a long time. The fucker deserves to burn."

A shiver went though me at his tone. He talked about killing his father as if it were a chore we were debating. And I got it, I did. I'd wanted to kill Perrone and his men too, but when faced with the actuality of taking someone's life...

"Maybe we should try the Feds, someone higher up."

"He'll never stop until we're dead. Even if we get lucky and they put him away, he's got too many connections. I would've run long ago, if I thought I could."

Standing in Perrone's kitchen, discussing his impending demise, made me twitchy. I didn't want his psycho father coming after Alex. In fact, I wouldn't be satisfied until he couldn't speak her name.

But killing the bastard...

That only reminded me that I *had* killed a man—I just didn't remember it. My mind had blocked it out, buried the memory long before I'd wiped out the whole fucking eight years.

We stepped down a few steps, crossed the humongous living room, and Jax halted at a door. He tried the handle, but it didn't budge. Stepping back, he kicked below the knob, just like I'd done with the shed, and repeated the blows until the door broke under the onslaught of his boot. He shoved it open and glanced at his watch.

"We have maybe fifteen minutes." Perrone worked from home, so his morning jog was the only time Jax knew he'd be gone with certainty. Jax strode over to the built-in bookshelves and began flinging open cupboards, rifling through files.

I checked out the rest of the room. The space was free of Perrone's nefarious nature—no signs of his thirst for sexual slavery. Deep mahogany paneling decorated the walls. The desk sat front and center, oversized and as masculine as the rest of the study, which reeked of prestige and money. I hated it on sight because it was so perfectly Perrone. Blatantly pretentious with an even larger collection of artwork and antiques than the wretched square box in the underground.

"Rafe, you're gonna wanna see this."

Keeping an ear out for his father's arrival, I moved to stand next to Jax. He extended a file to me. "He's got one on Alex."

Letting out a curse, I took the folder and turned away. The photos I found inside were all of Alex. Sleeping, picking at her food, staring off into space with that faraway look in her eyes—the look she wore when she was sad, worried, or scared. I shuffled through the pictures, and when I came to a few displaying the naked expanse of her skin, drops of water trailing between her breasts from showering, I wanted to punch something.

No. I wanted to fucking rearrange Perrone's face. He'd obviously been stalking her, putting her under surveillance, all while dating her.

The sick fuck.

I removed the photos and pocketed them before snapping the folder shut. "Anything on your sister?"

Jax slammed a drawer shut and opened another. "Nothing."

"I'm sorry, man." I handed him the empty file, but the chirping sound of an alarm froze us both. A series of beeps sounded, a door shut, and footsteps thumped over polished floors, drawing closer. I pulled the gun out and moved across the room with the stealth of a tiger in mid-hunt. The door shielded me from view, but Jax stood directly in front of the desk, arms crossed, preparing to confront his father.

Perrone stepped inside, still decked out in his drenched running shorts and T-shirt. I almost didn't recognize him without his trousers, shiny shoes, and air of superiority.

"How did you get in here? I know I changed the codes,

boy." He wiped his face with a towel, and I used the distraction to come out of my hiding place.

"Go take a seat," I said, jabbing the back of his sweaty head with the barrel.

"You've got some balls to break into my home. Into my office."

"You've got some balls to take photos of naked women." I propelled him forward, and the asshole laughed.

"Found the file, did you?" He meandered to the executive chair, his expression smug, casual, as if he didn't have anything to fear.

"Shut the fuck up." I shoved him to his ass and trained the gun on his temple. My gaze flickered to Jax.

"Where's Tawny?" Jax placed both hands flat on the desk and glared at his father. He grabbed the pen and notepad sitting to his right and thrust them toward Perrone. "Details, old man. Address, the men who bought her, how much she went for. I want all of it."

Perrone eased back in his seat, as if the barrel of my gun didn't bother him, and picked up the pen. He tapped it against the desk in a rhythmic beat that set me on edge.

"She went for a hundred grand. You should be proud of that. The buyer went by the last name of Perez. He took her to Mexico where the *whiny bitch died.*" Perrone smiled. "I heard she died just like Nikki Malone did. Perez didn't have the patience to train someone as strong-willed as Tawny."

Jax stumbled back, his face blanching in denial. "You're lying."

"'Fraid not, boy. Your sister's dead."

Tap, tap, tap with that fucking pen.

Perrone leaned forward, unfazed with how his words impacted his own blood.

"I don't believe you," Jax said, hands bunched at his sides.

I knocked him in the temple with the gun. Wincing, Perrone dropped the pen, and it slowly rolled toward him. He regarded me from the corner of his eye. "Did Alex tell you how she enjoyed sucking me off? I've got a big dick, and I rammed it so far down her throat, she cried."

The thought of Alex crying for anyone besides me filled my veins with too much energy—the dangerous kind that sparked and singed until I nearly blew.

"Bitch gagged on my cum."

Images of urine trickling down her legs, her screams as Brock's whip tore through her flesh, sent me into a tailspin.

I'd failed her.

This scum bucket had worn her down, made her give him something she'd resisted giving me—her fucking tears. He'd taken everything; the island, my family's vineyard, Alex's last shred of self-respect. The bastard had ruined his own children's lives.

As that pen drew closer, as Jax's shoulders drooped in defeat, I saw Nikki in my mind's eye. The mischievous spark in her gaze, the way her laughter used to fill me with contentment. She'd been the mother of my child.

And Perrone had taken her from our son in a bloody display of horror. One quick swipe of a knife, and she was gone, her life gurgling from her throat, hands wrapping around her neck as if she could contain her own life-force. Jax's grief as it slid down his cheeks...the way he'd held her, bawling like a broken man.

Everything hurtled through my head in a turbulent mural of rage.

I lurched forward, grabbed the pen, and stabbed Perrone in the neck, right where his veins pumped corrupted, evil blood to his brain. He jerked over the desk, fingers clawing at the pen, and pulled it out amidst a gush of blood.

Red...that's all I saw as I wrapped an arm around his neck and squeezed with every bit of strength I possessed. Letting the fucker bleed out wasn't enough. Jax shouted something, but I couldn't hear shit beyond the roar in my head.

Perrone struggled for a few intense seconds, a blip in the grand scheme of things, before he slumped over the smooth surface of the desk, gone to the world.

Dead.

Unable to hurt anyone else.

"You killed him." Jax grasped his blond hair and stared at me, mouth gaping.

I stepped back and lifted my blood-drenched hands.

The sticky red bathed my arms and shirt. Outwardly, I was the picture of calm, as if I'd taken a life without a second thought, but on the inside, I cowered in a corner and silently screamed.

Heartbeat racing way too fucking fast, I pulled out the throwaway phone we'd bought on the way to Portland. A tremor seized my fingers, and I had to punch in the sheriff's number twice before it went through.

He answered on the third ring with a barked, "Lewis."

"You'll find Nikki Malone's remains somewhere in Forrest Park. You'll need—"

"Who is this?" he shouted through the earpiece.

"Shut up and listen." The plan relied heavily on chance and Lyle Lewis actually acting on an anonymous tip. "You'll need several men, probably a few ATVs. There's an underground tunnel being used for sex trafficking." I relayed the general whereabouts of the entrance, though Jax and I had a hard time pinpointing the area on a map, which made explaining it over the phone next to impossible. If they didn't show, or if they did but couldn't find the right spot...

He began interrogating me, so I ended the call, and that's when the shaking started, the rush of heat flushing my skin. My stomach revolted, and my knees buckled.

Jax blinked, hands still clutching his hair as he stared in horror at his father. He blinked again, shook his head, and closed the distance between us. "C'mon. We gotta move."

He had to drag me down to that slab of a room, because I'd checked out. Whispers of the past taunted the edges of my sanity, and the mustiness of the basement incited flashes of my cellar on the island.

Alex. God, I could see her so clearly, her body shivering next to me, skin damp as I fisted her stringy hair in a tight grip. The clank of a lock. Her desperate pleas for me not to leave her in that cage.

Jax picked up a gas can and held it out to me.

We started in the basement, spilling gas into the crawl space since the other end was closest to the generator. Next, we hit the kitchen, the living room, dousing the furniture and curtains. The throw rugs.

But it was too much.

The putrid scent of gas reminded me of the night they'd taken us, and I relived that island going up in smoke. I dropped the last can, still half full. "Sorry, I need to get outta here."

"It's okay, man. Wait outside. I need to do this anyway."

"Don't blow yourself up."

Jax shot me a sad, crooked smile. "I'll try not to."

As soon as I opened the front door, the countdown for the alarm sounded, and Jax hurried to finish spreading the gasoline.

I stumbled down the steps and fell to my hands and knees in the driveway. The red on my hands struck me in the face. Groaning, I rolled to my back and stared up at the azure sky.

I'd killed a man.

My heart pounded a slow, laborious rhythm. An airplane crawled across the sky, and I wondered what it would be like to be on that plane, to be someone else who had a future.

Jax hurtled down the stairs, boots thumping. "Get up!" he yelled.

I struggled to my feet as he struck a match and tossed it toward the mansion. The gasoline ignited and fire spread rapidly, licking the beams propping up the balcony over the front stoop, flaring inside the entrance, eating the curtains in a violent blaze.

Something crackled, then a thunderous crash sounded. We backed away from the heat, but an explosion went off, the force powerful enough to knock us to the ground, and I realized the generator must have blown. Pain jolted my head, my limbs, straight to my bones. Garbled noise seized my ears, muffling Jax's shouts for me to get up.

Cops were on their way, he said.

I pushed to my knees and swayed.

And I remembered.

Everything.

As if the memories had always been with me.

I'd choked Jax's uncle in prison, my rage over Alex's betrayal a nasty entity that drove me in that moment. I'd squeezed his beefy neck, despite Jax trying to pull me off him, and hadn't stopped even when the vessels in his eyes burst.

I'd lost control and killed a man.

Devastation consumed me, making me dry-heave. It didn't matter if the guy had been on the verge of killing Jax. I'd taken the life of another human being, using nothing more than the strength in my own hands. Then I'd blocked it out, and Jax had let me exist in oblivion. But his uncle hadn't gone to the infirmary that day. He'd gone to the fucking morgue.

Then there were the rapes. God, the fucking rapes. I doubled over, holding my stomach, and the dry-heaves turned into full-fledged vomiting.

Alex.

This was hell.

I pulled at my hair, rose to my feet, and turned in circles as the urge to break something overcame me. The memories shredded what was left of my mind. I'd fucking tortured her. I'd forced her under water, had brutally fucked her. I'd left her cold, shivering, and freezing inside that cage, even after she'd nearly drowned. Holy fuck. I'd almost made her suck Jax's cock.

I'd treated her worse than a dog.

The truth was so much worse than what I'd feared. What kind of man does that?

The kind of man I'd become.

The kind of man who'd stabbed a guy in the neck,

choked him out like it was nothing, then burned down his fucking house.

Jax staggered to me, holding a hand to his bloodied head. "You okay?"

"Rafe Mason is dead."

"Dude, how bad did you hit your head? You're fine, but you won't be if we don't get the fuck outta here."

"I remember."

His eyes widened. "What? Seriously?" He wiped the bloody hair from his eyes. "What do you remember?"

"Everything."

Since I wasn't moving, he grabbed my arm and hauled me to the street. We walked the four blocks to his van, and thankfully any passerby was too worried about the billow of smoke pummeling the sky to pay us much attention.

Jax pointed to the passenger side of the van. "Get in."

Sirens blared as I slid into the seat. Jax started the engine and jerked away from the curb, tires spinning. He shot down the street, made a turn, then another, and the wail of sirens grew faint.

"I can't go back, Jax. I can't face her."

"You just got your memory back."

"I've taken enough from her. She's better off without me." I waved behind us, at the dark cloud of doom attacking the sky. "The threat is gone. She can move on, free from this, from her father, from me."

"She fucking loves you. Do you really think she'll just

get over it?" He braked hard on a yellow light, and I shot my hand out to keep from careening into the dash.

"It'll be hard at first, but I have to believe she'll find happiness, live a normal life. Fucking find some closure and heal. As long as I'm around, she'll never give me up."

"And her brother will never give her up," Jax pointed out.

I balled my fists. "I'll take care of him. He'll never hurt her again."

"I'll help you take care of him, but you need to get your ass back to her. You left her chained to your bed, man."

I railed against the idea of her restrained to my bed. I didn't think of freeing her. No, I thought of taking advantage, of choking her while simultaneously ramming my cock into her.

And she'd let me because she trusted me.

I didn't trust me.

"I can't do it, Jax." I shook my head, mouth forming a stubborn line. "Part of me wants to go back eight years and shake some fucking truth into her. None of this would have happened. She wouldn't have been so fucking broken. I wouldn't have gone through hell in prison." I paused, dragging my hands through my hair, and tamped down the strangling overflow of emotion. "I wouldn't have killed your uncle. None of this would—"

"And I'd be dead."

Jax's gaze held mine, and the utter quiet that settled over that moment was spine-tingling. The light turned green, and we rolled forward again. "I wouldn't be here if it weren't for you." He scrunched his brows. "Or her. Fuck, Rafe. I've hated her for all kinds of reasons, but I never stopped to think about it like that. If she'd told the truth, you wouldn't have been there to save my ass."

There was no easy way to look at the fucked up mess we'd created. Any way I contemplated it, someone ended up dead. But I couldn't help but wonder how things would have turned out if Alex had told the truth. Zach would've gone to jail, and I was positive my pull toward Alex would have brought us together. Could we have ended up happy? Normal? Me, living the dream in the UFC with a hot, kinky wife and a couple of kids at my side?

It sounded good, but it didn't sound like us.

We couldn't bury our history. It was a fucking zombie that would just keep coming, no matter how many times we thought we'd laid it to rest. Unlocking my memory had screwed us. The anger, the agony, the fucking pain of betrayal that squeezed my chest until I couldn't fucking breathe...

I wanted to choke her for it all.

I'd kidnapped her for a reason. I'd craved an outlet, and that gravitational pull that ensured Alex and I orbited each other wouldn't be denied. I'd needed her, only she'd needed a sane man who could put her back together again.

How could I fix her if I couldn't fix myself? How could I be the man she needed when all I wanted to do was bend her until she snapped?

"It's too late for us. What's done is done. Someday, she'll see it's for the best."

Jax sighed. "You think she's strong enough to stand on her own?"

"I know she is. She's stronger than me. I'm the one who needs her."

"Then fucking take what she wants to give. I don't see the problem here."

"The problem is me! I'm fucked. I've done too much."

"We've all done too much," he shouted, banging on the steering wheel. "Every one of us has done shit we'd take back if we could. You're just running away because you're scared." He jabbed his finger in my direction. "You're scared because you know she *can* handle what you want to dish out. Even more, she wants it. But you're scared of the responsibility."

"Fuck yeah, I'm scared! I'm terrified I'll hurt her. Every bone in my body wants to make her cry. I want her on her knees, chained to my damn bed not because I'm trying to keep her safe, but because that's where she fucking belongs. *That* isn't normal!"

"*You*," he said, "have never been normal."

I drew in a deep breath. "I can't do it." I gave Jax a pointed look. "I lost control with your uncle. I remember it all like it was yesterday. It was an accident, but what I did back there..." I gazed at the blood on my hands. The literal fucking blood. "I won't risk her life."

"You'd never hurt her."

"Not willingly."

"Okay then," he said.

"Okay?" I raised an incredulous brow.

"I ain't changing your mind about this, so why try?"

"Finally, something we agree on."

"I still think you're making a mistake. She's gonna come undone when you leave, man."

"You say you owe your life to me?"

Jax rubbed a hand down his face. "Yeah, I owe you."

"Then make sure she stays in one fucking piece. Until she's on her feet, watch her for me. Be there for her. You're not the one who wants to fuck and strangle her."

He glanced at me, slack-jawed.

"Jax, you're the only one I trust."

"What am I supposed to tell her?"

"The truth. The man she loves is dead."

THE SAGA CONTINUES

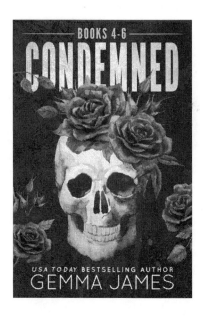

www.authorgemmajames.com/books

ABOUT THE AUTHOR

Gemma James is a *USA Today* bestselling author of sexy contemporary and dark romance. She loves to explore the darker side of human nature in her fiction, and she's morbidly curious about anything dark and edgy, from deviant seduction to fascinating villains. Readers have described her stories as being "not for the faint of heart."

She warns you to heed their words! Her playground isn't full of rainbows and kittens, though she loves both. She lives in Florida with her husband, children, and a gaggle of animals.

Visit Gemma's website for more info on her books:
www.authorgemmajames.com